THE DARFSTELLER AND OTHER STORIES

CORGI BOOKS

A DIVISION OF TRANSWORLD PUBLISHERS LTD

THE DARFSTELLER AND OTHER STORIES
CORGI BOOK 0 552 11950 4

First publication in Great Britain

PRINTING HISTORY
Corgi edition published 1982

"The Darfsteller" appeared in the January 1955 issue of *Astounding Science Fiction*, copyright 1954 by Walter M. Miller Jr.

"The Will" appeared in the January/February 1954 issue of *Fantastic*, copyright 1953 by Ziff Davis Publishing Co.

"Anybody Else Like Me?" originally appeared as "Command Performance" in the November 1952 issue of *Galaxy Science Fiction*, copyright 1952 by Walter M. Miller Jr.

"Crucifixus Etiam" appeared in the February 1953 issue of *Astonishing Science Fiction*, copyright 1953 by Walter M. Miller Jr.

"I, Dreamer" appeared in the June/July 1953 issue of *Amazing Stories*, copyright 1953 by Ziff Davis Publishing Co.

"The Lineman" appeared in the August 1957 issue of *Magazine of Fantasy and Science Fiction*, copyright © 1957 by Fantasy House Inc.

"Big Joe and the Nth Generation" originally appeared as "It Takes a Thief" in the May 1952 issue of *If*, copyright 1952 by Quinn Publishing Co. Inc.

"The Big Hunger" appeared in the October 1952 issue of *Astounding Science Fiction*, copyright 1952 by Walter M. Miller Jr.

This book is set in 9½ pt. Times Roman

Corgi Books are published by Transworld Publishers Ltd.,
Century House, 61–63 Uxbridge Road,
Ealing, London, W5 5SA

Made and printed in the United States of America by
Offset Paperbacks, Dallas, Pennsylvania

Now, together for the first time, a collection of gripping short stories from the master of science fiction who wrote the classic *A Canticle for Leibowitz* . . .

* *The Darfsteller*, in which an ageing actor rebels against a theatre controlled by robots.

* *The Will*, in which the determination of a dying boy enables him to overcome his fate . . . and time itself!

**The Lineman*, in which a lunar engineer is caught up in some deadly industrial power games.

Also by Walter M. Miller Jr.

A CANTICLE FOR LEIBOWITZ
CONDITIONALLY HUMAN AND OTHER STORIES

and published by Corgi Books

CONTENTS

THE DARFSTELLER

'Judas, Judas' was playing at the Universal on Fifth Street, and the cast was entirely human. Ryan Thornier had been saving up for it for several weeks, and now he could afford the price of a matinée ticket. It had been a race for time between his piggy bank and the wallets of several 'public-spirited' angels who kept the show alive, and the piggy bank had won. He could see the show before the wallets went flat and the show folded, as any such show was bound to do after a few limping weeks. A glow of anticipation suffused him. After watching the wretched mockery of dramaturgical art every day at the New Empire Theater where he worked as janitor, the chance to see real theater again would be like a breath of clean air.

He came to work an hour early on Wednesday morning and sped through his usual chores on overdrive. He finished his work before one o'clock, had a shower backstage, changed to street clothes, and went nervously upstairs to ask Imperio D'Uccia for the rest of the day off.

D'Uccia sat enthroned at a rickety desk before a wall plastered with photographs of lightly clad female stars of the old days. He heard the janitor's petition with a faint, almost oriental smile of apparent sympathy, then drew himself up to his full height of sixty-five inches, leaned on the desk with chubby hands to study Thornier with beady eyes.

'Off? So you wanna da day off? Mmmph—' He shook his head as if mystified by such an incomprehensible request.

The gangling janitor shifted his feet uneasily. 'Yes, sir. I've finished up, and Jigger'll come over to stand by in case you need anything special.' He paused. D'Uccia was studying his nails, frowning gravely. 'I haven't asked for a day off in two years, Mr. D'Uccia,' he added, 'and I was sure you wouldn't mind after all the overtime I've—'

'Jigger,' D'Uccia grunted. 'Whoosa t'is Jigger?'

'Works at the Paramount. It's closed for repairs, and he doesn't mind—'

The theater manager grunted abruptly and waved his hands. 'I don' pay no Jigger, I pay you. Whassa this all about? You swip the floor, you putsa things away, you all finish now, ah? You wanna day off. Thatsa whass wrong with the world, too mucha time loaf. Letsa machines work. More time to mek trouble.' The theater manager came out from behind his desk and waddled to the door. He thrust his fat neck outside and looked up and down the corridor, then waddled back to confront Thornier with a short fat finger aimed at the employee's long and majestic nose.

'Whensa lass time you waxa the upstairs floor, hah?'

Thornier's jaw sagged forlornly. 'Why, I—'

'Don't tell me no lie. Looka that hall. Sheeza feelth. *Look!* I want you to look.' He caught Thornier's arm, tugged him to the doorway, pointed excitedly at the worn and ancient oak flooring. 'Sheeza feelth ground in! See? When you wax, hah?'

A great shudder seemed to pass through the thin elderly man. He sighed resignedly and turned to look down at D'Uccia with weary gray eyes.

'Do I get the afternoon off, or don't I?' he asked hopelessly, knowing the answer in advance.

But D'Uccia was not content with a mere refusal. He began to pace. He was obviously deeply moved. He defended the system of free enterprise and the cherished traditions of the theater. He spoke eloquently of the golden virtues of industriousness and dedication to duty. He bounced about like a furious Pekingese yapping happily at a scarecrow. Thornier's neck reddened, his mouth went tight.

'Can I go now?'

'When you waxa da floor? Palisha da seats, fixa da lights? When you clean op the dressing room, hah?' He stared up at Thornier for a moment, then turned on his heel and charged to the window. He thrust his thumb into the black dirt of the window box, where several prize lilies were already beginning to bloom. '*Ha!*' he snorted. 'Dry like I thought! You think the bulbs a don't need a drink, hah?'

'But I watered them this morning. The sun—'

'Hah! You letsa little *fiori* wilt and die, hah? And you wanna the day off?'

It was hopeless. When D'Uccia drew his defensive mantle of calculated deafness or stupidity about himself, he became impenetrable to any request or honest explanation. Thornier sucked in a slow breath between his teeth, stared angrily at his employer for a moment, and seemed briefly ready to unleash an angry blast. Thinking better of it, he bit his lip, turned, and stalked wordlessly out of the office. D'Uccia followed him triumphantly to the door.

'Don' you go sneak off, now!' he called ominously, and stood smiling down the corridor until the janitor vanished at the head of the stairs. Then he sighed and went back to get his hat and coat. He was just preparing to leave when Thornier came back upstairs with a load of buckets, mops, and swabs.

The janitor stopped when he noticed the hat and coat, and his seamed face went curiously blank. 'Going home, Mr. D'Uccia?' he asked icily.

'Yeh! I'ma worka too hard, the doctor say. I'ma need the sunshine. More fresh air. I'ma go relax on the beach a while.'

Thornier leaned on the mop handle and smiled nastily. 'Sure,' he said. 'Letsa machines do da work.'

The comment was lost on D'Uccia. He waved airily, strode off toward the stairway, and called an airy *'A rivederci!'* over his shoulder.

'A rivederci, padrone,' Thornier muttered softly, his pale eyes glittering from their crow's-feet wrappings. For a moment his face seemed to change—and once again he was Chaubrec's Adolfo, at the exit of the Commandant, Act II, scene *iv,* from 'A Canticle for the Mars-man.'

Somewhere downstairs, a door slammed behind D'Uccia.

'Into death!' hissed Adolfo-Thornier, throwing back his head to laugh Adolfo's laugh. It rattled the walls. When its reverberations had died away, he felt a little better. He picked up his buckets and brooms and walked on down the corridor to the door of D'Uccia's office.

Unless 'Judas-Judas' hung on through the weekend, he wouldn't get to see it, since he could not afford a ticket to the evening performance, and there was no use asking D'Uccia for favors. While he waxed the hall, he burned. He waxed as far as D'Uccia's doorway, then stood staring into the office for several vacant minutes.

'I'm fed up,' he said at last.

The office remained silent. The window-box lilies bowed to the breeze.

'You little creep!' he growled. 'I'm through!'

The office was speechless. Thornier straightened and tapped his chest.

'I, Ryan Thornier, am walking out, you hear? The show is finished!'

When the office failed to respond, he turned on his heel and stalked downstairs. Minutes later, he came back with a small can of gold paint and a pair of artists' brushes from the storeroom. Again he paused in the doorway.

'Anything else I can do, Mr. D'Uccia?' he purred.

Traffic murmured in the street; the breeze rustled the lilies; the building creaked.

'Oh? You want me to wax in the wall-cracks, too? How could I have forgotten!'

He clucked his tongue and went over to the window. Such lovely lilies. He opened the paint can, set it on the window ledge, and then very carefully he gilded each of the prize lilies, petals, leaves, and stalks, until the flowers glistened like the work of Midas' hands in the sun-light. When he finished, he stepped back to smile at them in admiration for a moment, then went to finish waxing the hall.

He waxed it with particular care in front of D'Uccia's office. He waxed under the throw rug that covered the worn spot on the floor where D'Uccia had made a sharp left turn into his sanctum every morning for fifteen years, and then he turned the rug over and dusted dry wax powder into the pile. He replaced it carefully and pushed at it a few times with his foot to make certain the lubrication was adequate. The rug slid about as if it rode on a bed of bird-shot.

Thornier smiled and went downstairs. The world was suddenly different somehow. Even the air smelled different. He paused on the landing to glance at himself in the decorative mirror.

Ah! the old trouper again. No more of the stooped and haggard menial. None of the wistfulness and weariness of self-perpetuated slavery. Even with the gray at the temples and the lines in the face, here was something of the old Thornier—or one of the *many* old Thorniers of earlier days. Which one? Which one'll it be? Adolfo? Or Hamlet? Justin, or J.J. Jones, from 'The Electrocutioner'? Any of them, all of them; for he was Ryan Thornier, star, in the old days.

'Where've you been, baby?' he asked his image with a tight smile of approval, winked, and went on home for the evening. Tomorrow, he promised himself, a new life would begin.

'But you've been making that promise for years, Thorny,' said the man in the control booth, his voice edged with impatience. 'What do you mean, "you quit"? Did you tell D'Uccia you quit?'

Thornier smiled loftily while he dabbed with his broom at a bit of dust in the corner. 'Not exactly, Richard,' he said. 'But the *padrone* will find it out soon enough.'

The technician grunted disgust. 'I don't understand you, Thorny. Sure, if you *really* quit, that's swell—if you don't just turn around and get another job like this one.'

'Never!' the old actor proclaimed resonantly, and glanced up at the clock. Five till ten. Nearly time for D'Uccia to arrive for work. He smiled to himself.

'If you really quit, what are you doing here today?' Rick Thomas demanded, glancing up briefly from the Maestro. His arms were thrust deep into the electronic entrails of the machine, and he wore a pencil-sized screwdriver tucked behind one ear. 'Why don't you go home, if you quit?'

'Oh, don't worry, Richard. This time it's for real.'

'Pssss!' An amused hiss from the technician. 'Yeah, it was for real when you quit at the Bijou, too. Only then a week later you came to work here. So what now, Mercutio?'

'To the casting office, old friend. A bit part somewhere, perhaps.' Thornier smiled on him benignly. 'Don't concern yourself about me.'

'Thorny, can't you get it through your head that theater's *dead?* There isn't any theater! No movies, no television either —except for dead men and the Maestro here.' He slapped the metal housing of the machine.

'I *meant,*' Thorny explained patiently, ' "employment office," and "small job," you . . . you machine-age flintsmith. Figures of speech, solely.'

'Yah.'

'I thought you *wanted* me to resign my position, Richard.'

'Yes! If you'll do something worthwhile with yourself. Ryan Thornier, star of "Walkaway," playing martyr with a scrub-bucket! Aaaak! You give me the gripes. And you'll do it again. You can't stay away from the stage, even if all you can do about it is mop up the oil drippings.'

'You couldn't possibly understand,' Thornier said stiffly.

Rick straightened to look at him, took his arms out of the Maestro and leaned on top of the cabinet. 'I dunno, Thorny,' he said in a softer voice. 'Maybe I do. You're an actor, and you're always playing roles. Living them, even. You can't help it, I guess. But you *could* do a saner job of picking the parts you're going to play.'

'The world has cast me in the role I play,' Thornier announced with a funereal face.

Rick Thomas clapped a hand over his forehead and drew it slowly down across his face in exasperation. 'I give up!' he groaned. 'Look at you! Matinée idol, pushing a broom. Eight years ago, it made sense—*your* kind of sense, anyhow. Dramatic gesture. Leading actor defies autodrama offer, takes janitor's job. Loyal to tradition, and the guild—and all that. It made small headlines, maybe even helped the legit stage limp along a little longer. But the audiences stopped bleeding for you after a while, and then it stopped making even *your* kind of sense!'

Thornier stood wheezing slightly and glaring at him. 'What would *you* do,' he hissed, 'if they started making a little black box that could be attached to the wall up there'—he waved to a bare spot above the Maestro's bulky housing—'that could repair, maintain, operate, and adjust—do all the things you do to that . . . that contraption. Suppose nobody needed electronicians any more.'

Rick Thomas thought about it a few moments, then grinned. 'Well, I guess I'd get a job making the little black boxes, then.'

'You're not funny, Richard!'

'I didn't intend to be.'

'You're . . . you're not an artist.' Flushed with fury, Thornier swept viciously at the floor of the booth.

A door slammed somewhere downstairs, far below the above-stage booth. Thorny set his broom aside and moved to the window to watch. The *clop, clop, clop* of bustling footsteps came up the central aisle.

'Hizzoner, da Imperio,' muttered the technician, glancing up at the clock. 'Either that clock's two minutes fast, or else this was his morning to take a bath.'

Thornier smiled sourly toward the main aisle, his eyes traveling after the waddling figure of the theater manager. When D'Uccia disappeared beneath the rear balcony, he resumed his sweeping.

'I don't see why you don't get a sales job, Thorny,' Rick ventured, returning to his work. 'A good salesman is just an actor, minus the temperament. There's *lots* of demand for good actors, come to think of it. Politicians, top executives, even generals—some of them seem to make out on *nothing but* dramatic talent. History affirms it.'

'Bah! I'm no schauspieler.' He paused to watch Rick adjusting the Maestro, and slowly shook his head. 'Ease your conscience, Richard,' he said finally.

Startled, the technician dropped his screwdriver, looked up quizzically. '*My* conscience? What the devil is uneasy about my conscience?'

'Oh, don't pretend. That's why you're always so concerned about me. I know *you* can't help it that your . . . your trade has perverted a great art.'

Rick gaped at him in disbelief for a moment. '*You* think *I*—' He choked. He colored angrily. He stared at the old ham and began to curse softly under his breath.

Thornier suddenly lifted a finger to his mouth and went *shhhh!* His eyes roamed toward the back of the theater.

'That was only D'Uccia on the stairs,' Rick began. 'What—?'

'*Shhhh!*'

They listened. The janitor wore a rancid smile. Seconds later it came—first a faint yelp, then—

Bbbrroom*mmpb!*

It rattled the booth windows. Rick started up frowning.

'What the—?'

'*Shhhh!*'

The jolting jar was followed by a faint mutter of profanity.

'That's D'Uccia. What happened?'

The faint mutter suddenly became a roaring stream of curses from somewhere behind the balconies.

'Hey!' said Rick. 'He must have hurt himself.'

'Naah. He just found my resignation, that's all. See? I told you I'd quit.'

The profane bellowing grew louder to the accompaniment of an elephantine thumping on carpeted stairs.

'He's not *that* sorry to see you go,' Rick grunted, looking baffled.

D'Uccia burst into view at the head of the aisle. He stopped with his feet spread wide, clutching at the base of his spine with one hand and waving a golden lily aloft in the other.

'Lily gilder!' he screamed. 'Pansy painter! You fancy-pantsy bom! Come out, you fonny fonny boy!'

Thornier thrust his head calmly through the control-booth window, stared at the furious manager with arched brows. 'You calling me, Mr. D'Uccia?'

D'Uccia sucked in two or three gasping breaths before he found his bellow again.

'Thornya!'

'Yes, sir?'

'Itsa finish, you hear?'

'What's finished, boss?'

'Itsa finish. I'ma go see the servo man. I'ma go get me a swip-op machine. You gotta two wiks notice.'

'Tell him you don't want any notice,' Rick grunted softly from nearby. 'Walk out on him.'

'All right, Mr. D'Uccia,' Thornier called evenly.

D'Uccia stood there sputtering, threatening to charge, waving the lily helplessly. Finally he threw it down in the aisle with a curse and whirled to limp painfully out.

'Whew!' Rick breathed. 'What did you do?'

Thornier told him sourly. The technician shook his head.

'He won't fire you. He'll change his mind. It's too hard to hire anybody to do dirty-work these days.'

'You heard him. He can buy an autojan installation. "Swip-op" machine.'

'Baloney! Dooch is too stingy to put out that much dough. Besides, he can't get the satisfaction of screaming at a machine.'

Thornier glanced up wryly. 'Why *can't* he?'

'Well—' Rick paused. 'Ulp! . . . You're right. He can. He came up here and bawled out the Maestro once. Kicked it, yelled at it, shook it—like a guy trying to get his quarter back out of a telephone. Went away looking pleased with himself, too.'

'Why not?' Thorny muttered gloomily. 'People are machines to D'Uccia. And he's *fair* about it. He's willing to treat them all alike.'

'But you're not going to stick around two weeks, are you?'

'Why not? It'll give me time to put out some feelers for a job.'

Rick grunted doubtfully and turned his attention back to the machine. He removed the upper front panel and set it aside. He opened a metal canister on the floor and lifted out a foot-wide foot-thick roll of plastic tape. He mounted it on a spindle inside the Maestro, and began feeding the end of the tape through several sets of rollers and guides. The tape appeared wormeaten —covered with thousands of tiny punch-marks and wavy grooves. The janitor paused to watch the process with cold hostility.

'Is that the script-tape for the "Anarch"?' he asked stiffly.

The technician nodded. 'Brand new tape, too. Got to be

careful how I feed her in. It's still got fuzz on it from the recording cuts.' He stopped the feed mechanism briefly, plucked at a punchmark with his awl, blew on it, then started the feed motor again.

'What happens if the tape gets nicked or scratched?' Thorny grunted curiously. 'Actor collapse on stage?'

Rick shook his head. 'Naa, it happens all the time. A scratch or a nick'll make a player muff a line or maybe stumble, then the Maestro catches the goof, and compensates. Maestro gets feedback from the stage, continuously directs the show. It can do a lot of compensating, too.'

'I thought the whole show came from the tape.'

The technician smiled. 'It does, in a way. But it's more than a recorded mechanical puppet show, Thorny. The Maestro watches the stage . . . no, more than that . . . the Maestro *is* the stage, an electronic analogue of it.' He patted the metal housing. 'All the actors' personality patterns are packed in here. It's more than a remote controller, the way most people think of it. It's a creative directing machine. It's even got pickups out in the audience to gauge reactions to—'

He stopped suddenly, staring at the old actor's face. He swallowed nervously. 'Thorny *don't* look that way. I'm sorry. Here, have a cigarette.'

Thorny accepted it with trembling fingers. He stared down into the gleaming maze of circuitry with narrowed eyes, watched the script-belt climb slowly over the rollers and down into the bowels of the Maestro.

'Art!' he hissed. 'Theater! What'd they give you your degree in, Richard? Dramaturgical engineering?'

He shuddered and stalked out of the booth. Rick listened to the angry rattle of his heels on the iron stairs that led down to stage level. He shook his head sadly, shrugged, went back to inspecting the tape for rough cuts.

Thorny came back after a few minutes with a bucket and a mop. He looked reluctantly repentant. 'Sorry, lad,' he grunted. 'I know you're just trying to make a living, and—'

'Skip it,' Rick grunted curtly.

'It's just . . . well . . . this particular show. It gets me.'

'This—? "The Anarch," you mean? What about it, Thorny? You play in it once?'

'Uh-uh. It hasn't been on the stage since the Nineties, except —well, it was almost revived ten years ago. We rehearsed for weeks. Show folded before opening night. No dough.'

'You had a good part in it?'

'I was to play Andreyev,' Thornier told him with a faint smile.

Rick whistled between his teeth. 'The lead. That's too bad.' He hoisted his feet to let Thorny mop under them. 'Big disappointment, I guess.'

'It's not that. It's just . . . well . . . "The Anarch" rehearsals were the last time Mela and I were on stage together. That's all.'

'Mela?' The technician paused, frowning. 'Mela *Stone?*'

Thornier nodded.

Rick snatched up a copy of the uncoded script, waved it at him. 'But she's in *this* version, Thorny! Know that! She's playing Marka.'

Thornier's laugh was brief and brittle.

Rick reddened slightly. 'Well, I mean her mannequin's playing it.'

Thorny eyed the Maestro distastefully. 'Your mechanical Svengali's playing its airfoam zombies in *all* roles, you mean.'

'Oh, cut it out, Thorny. Be sore at the world if you want to, but don't blame me for what audiences want. And I didn't invent autodrama anyhow.'

'I don't blame anybody. I merely detest that . . . that—' He punched at the base of the Maestro with his wet mop.

'You and D'Uccia,' Rick grunted disgustedly. 'Except—D'Uccia loves it when it's working O.K. It's just a machine, Thorny. Why hate it?'

'Don't need a reason to hate it,' he said, snarly-petulant. 'I hate air-cabs, too. It's a matter of taste, that's all.'

'All right, but the public likes autodrama—whether it's by TV, stereo, or on stage. And they get what they want.'

'Why?'

Rick snickered. 'Well, it's their dough. Autodrama's portable, predictable, duplicatable. And flexible. You can run "Macbeth" tonight, the "Anarch" tomorrow night, and "King of the Moon" the next night—in the same house. No actor-temperament problems. No union problems. Rent the packaged props, dolls, and tapes from Smithfield. Packaged theater. Systematized, mass-produced. In Coon Creek, Georgia, yet.'

'Bah!'

Rick finished feeding in the script tape, closed the panel, and opened an adjacent one. He ripped the lid from a cardboard carton and dumped a heap of smaller tapespools on the table.

'Are *those* the souls they sold to Smithfield?' Thornier asked, smiling at them rather weirdly.

The technician's stool scraped back and he exploded: 'You know what they are!'

Thornier nodded, leaned closer to stare at them as if fascinated. He plucked one of them out of the pile, sighed down at it.

'If you say "Alas, poor Yorick," I'll heave you out of here!' Rick grated.

Thornier put it back with a sigh and wiped his hand on his coveralls. Packaged personalities. Actor's egos, analogized on tape. Real actors, once, whose dolls were now cast in the roles. The tapes contained complex psychophysiological data derived from months of psychic and somatic testing, after the original actors had signed their Smithfield contracts. Data for the Maestro's personality matrices. Abstractions from the human psyche, incarnate in glass, copper, chromium. The souls they rented to Smithfield on a royalty basis, along with their flesh and blood likenesses in the dolls.

Rick loaded a casting spool onto its spindle, started it feeding through the pickups.

'What happens if you leave out a vital ingredient? Such as Mela Stone's tape, for instance,' Thornier wanted to know.

'The doll'd run through its lines like a zombie, that's all.' Rick explained. 'No zip. No interpretation. Flat, deadpan, like a robot.'

'They are robots.'

'Not exactly. Remote marionettes for the Maestro, but interpreted. We did a run-through on "Hamlet" once, without any actor tapes. Everybody talked in flat monotones, no expressions. It was a scream.'

'Ha, ha,' Thornier said grimly.

Rick slipped another tape on the spindle, clicked a dial to a new setting, started the feed again. 'This one's Andreyev, Thornier—played by Peltier.' He cursed suddenly, stopped the feed, inspected the tape anxiously, flipped open the pickup mechanism, and inspected it with a magnifier.

'What's wrong?' asked the janitor.

'Take-off's about worn out. Hard to keep its spacing right. I'm nervous about it getting hung up and chewing up the tape.'

'No duplicate tapes?'

'Yeah. One set of extras. But the show opens tonight.' He cast another suspicious look at the pickup glideway, then closed it and switched the feed again. He was replacing the panel when the feed mechanism stalled. A ripping sound came from inside. He muttered fluent profanity, shut off the drive, jerked away the panel. He held up a shredded ribbon of tape for Thorny to see, then flung it angrily across the booth. 'Get out of here! You're a jinx!'

'Not till I finish mopping.'

'Thorny, get D'Uccia for me, will you? We'll have to get a new pickup flown in from Smithfield before this afternoon. This is a helluva mess.'

'Why not hire a human stand-in?' he asked nastily, then added: 'Forgive me. That would be a perversion of your art, wouldn't it? Shall I get D'Uccia?'

Rick threw the Peltier spool at him. He ducked out with a chuckle and went to find the theater manager. Halfway down the iron stairs, he paused to look at the wide stage that spread away just beyond the folded curtains. The footlights were burning, and the gray-green floor looked clean and shimmering, with its checkerboard pattern of imbedded copper strips. The strips were electrified during the performance, and they fed the mannequins' energy-storage packs. The dolls had metallic disks in their soles, and rectifiers in their insteps. When batteries drained low, the Maestro moved the actor's foot an inch or so to contact the floor electrodes for periodic recharging during the play, since a doll would grow wobbly and its voice indistinct after a dozen minutes on internal power alone.

Thorny stared at the broad expanse of stage where no humans walked on performance night. D'Uccia's Siamese tomcat sat licking itself in the center of the stage. It glanced up at him haughtily, seemed to sniff, began licking itself again. He watched it for a moment, then called back upstairs to Rick.

'Energize the floor a minute, will you, Rick?'

'Huh? Why?'—a busy grunt.

'Want to check something.'

'O.K., but then fetch D'Uccia.'

He heard the technician snap a switch. The cat's calm hauteur exploded. The cat screamed, scrambled, barrel-rolled, amid a faint sputter of sparks. The cat did an Immelmann turn over the footlights, landed in the pit with a clawing crash, then scampered up the aisle with fur erect toward its haven beneath Imperio's desk.

'Whatthehell?' Rick growled, and thrust his head out of the booth.

'Shut it off now,' said the janitor. 'D'Uccia'll be here in a minute.'

'With fangs showing!'

Thornier went to finish his routine clean-up. Gloom had begun to gather about him. He was leaving—leaving even this last humble role in connection with the stage. A fleeting realization of his own impotence came to him. Helpless. Helpless enough to seek petty revenges like vandalizing D'Uccia's window box and tormenting D'Uccia's cat, because there was not any real enemy at which he could strike out.

He put the realization down firmly, and stamped on it. *He* was Ryan Thornier, and never helpless, unless he willed it so. I'll make them know who I am just *once,* he thought, before I go. I'll make them remember, and they won't ever forget.

But that line of thought about playing one last great role, one last masterful interpretation, he knew was no good. 'Thorny, if you ever played a one-last-great,' Rick had said to him once, 'there wouldn't be a thing left to live for, would there?' Rick had said cynically, but it was true anyhow. And the pleasant fantasy was somehow alarming as well as pleasant.

The chic little woman in the white-plumed hat was explaining things carefully—with round vowels and precise enunciation—to the Playwright of the Moment, up-and-coming, with awed worshipfulness in his gaze as he listened to the pert little producer. 'Stark realism, you see, is the milieu of autodrama,' she said. 'Always remember, Bernie, that consideration for the actors is a thing of the past. Study the drama of Rome—ancient Rome. If a play had a crucifixion scene, they got a slave for the part and crucified him. On stage, but *really!*'

The Playwright of the Moment laughed dutifully around his long cigarette holder. 'So that's where they got the line: "It's superb, but it's hell on the actors." I must rewrite the murder scene in my "George's Wake." Do it with a hatchet, this time.'

'Oh, now, *Bernie!* Mannequins don't bleed.'

They both laughed heartily. 'And they *are* expensive. Not hell on the actors, but hell on the budget.'

'The Romans probably had the same problem. I'll bear it in mind.'

Thornier saw them—the producer and the Playwright of the Moment—standing there in the orchestra when he came from backstage and across toward the center aisle. They lounged on the arms of their seats, and a crowd of production personnel and technicians milled about them. The time for the first run-through was approaching.

The small woman waved demurely to Thorny when she saw him making his way slowly through the throng, then turned to the playwright again. 'Bernie, be a lamb and get me a drink, will you? I've got a butterfly.'

'Surely. Hard, or soft?'

'Oh, hard. Scotch mist in a paper cup, please. There's a bar next door.'

The playwright nodded a nod that was nearly a bow and shuffled away up the aisle. The woman caught at the janitor's sleeve as he passed.

'Going to snub me, Thorny?'

'Oh, hello, Miss Ferne,' he said politely.

She leaned close and muttered: 'Call me "Miss Ferne" again and I'll claw you.' The round vowels had vanished.

'O.K., Jade, but—' He glanced around nervously. Technicians milled about them. Ian Feria, the producer, watched them curiously from the wings.

'What's been doing with you, Thorny? Why haven't I seen you?' she complained.

He gestured with the broom handle, shrugged. Jade Ferne studied his face a moment and frowned. 'Why the agonized look, Thorny? Mad at me?'

He shook his head. 'This play, Jade—"The Anarch," well—' He glanced miserably toward the stage.

Memory struck her suddenly. She breathed a compassionate *ummm*. 'The attempted revival, ten years ago—you were to be Andreyev. Oh, Thorny, I'd forgotten.'

'It's all right.' He wore a carefully tailored martyr's smile.

She gave his arm a quick pat. 'I'll see you after the run-through, Thorny. We'll have a drink and talk old times.'

He glanced around again and shook his head. 'You've got new friends now, Jade. They wouldn't like it.'

'The crew? Nonsense! They're not snobs.'

'No, but they want your attention. Feria's trying to catch your eye right now. No use making them sore.'

'All right, but after the run-through I'll see you in the mannequin room. I'll just slip away.'

'If you want to.'

'I do, Thorny. It's been so long.'

The playwright returned with her Scotch mist and gave Thornier a hostilely curious glance.

'Bless your heart, Bernie,' she said, the round vowels returning, then to Thornier: 'Thorny, would you do me a favor? I've been trying to corner D'Uccia, but he's tied up with a servo salesman somewhere. Somebody's got to run and pick up a mannequin from the depot. The shipment was delivered, but the trucker missed a doll crate. We'll need it for the run-through. Could you—'

'Sure, Miss Ferne. Do I need a requisition order?'

'No, just sign the delivery ticket. And Thorny, see if the new part for the Maestro's been flown in yet. Oh, and one other thing —the Maestro chewed up the Peltier tape. We've got a duplicate, but we should have two, just to be safe.'

'I'll see if they have one in stock,' he murmured, and turned to go.

D'Uccia stood in the lobby with the salesman when he passed through. The theater manager saw him and smirked happily.

'. . . Certain special features, of course,' the salesman was saying. 'It's an old building, and it wasn't designed with autojanitor systems in mind, like buildings are now. But we'll tailor the installation to fit your place, Mr. D'Uccia. We want to do the job *right,* and a packaged unit wouldn't do it.'

'Yah, you gimme da price, hah?'

'We'll have an estimate for you by tomorrow. I'll have an engineer over this afternoon to make the survey, and he'll work up a layout tonight.'

'Whatsa 'bout the demonstration, uh? Whatsa 'bout you show how da swip-op machine go?'

The salesman hesitated, eying the janitor who waited nearby. 'Well, the floor-cleaning robot is only a small part of the complete service, but . . . I tell you what I'll do. I'll bring a packaged char-all over this afternoon, and let you have a look at it.'

'Fine. Datsa fine. You bring her, den we see.'

They shook hands. Thornier stood with his arms folded, haughtily inspecting a bug that crawled across the frond of a potted palm, and waiting for a chance to ask D'Uccia for the keys to the truck. He felt the theater manager's triumphant gaze, but gave no indication that he heard.

'We can do the job for you all right, Mr. D'Uccia. Cut your worries in half. And that'll cut your doctor bills in half, too, like you say. Yes, sir! A man in your position gets ground down with just plain human inefficiency—other people's inefficiency.

You'll never have to worry about that, once you get the building autojanitored, no sir!'

'T'ank you kindly.'

'Thank *you,* Mr. D'Uccia, and I'll see you later this afternoon.'

The salesman left.

'Well, bom?' D'Uccia grunted to the janitor.

'The keys to the truck. Miss Ferne wants a pickup from the depot.'

D'Uccia tossed them to him. 'You hear what the man say? Letsa machines do alla work, hah? Always you wantsa day off. O.K., you takka da day off, ever'day pretty soon. Nice for you, hah, ragazzo?'

Thornier turned away quickly to avoid displaying the surge of unwanted anger. 'Be back in an hour,' he grunted, and hurried away on his errand, his jaw working in sullen resentment. Why wait around for two humiliating weeks? Why not just walk out? Let D'Uccia do his own chores until the autojan was installed. He'd never be able to get another job around the theater anyhow, so D'Uccia's reaction wouldn't matter.

I'll walk out now, he thought—and immediately knew that he wouldn't. It was hard to explain to himself, but—when he thought of the final moment when he would be free to look for a decent job and a comfortable living—he felt a twinge of fear that was hard to understand.

The janitor's job had paid him only enough to keep him alive in a fourth floor room where he cooked his own meager meals and wrote memoirs of the old days, but it had kept him close to the lingering remnants of something he loved.

'Theater,' they called it. Not *the* theater—as it was to the scalper's victim, the matinée housewife, or the awestruck hick—but just 'theater.' It wasn't a place, wasn't a business, wasn't the name of an art. 'Theater' was a condition of the human heart and soul. Jade Ferne was theater. So was Ian Feria. So was Mela, poor kid, before her deal with Smithfield. Some had it, others didn't. In the old days, the ones that didn't have it soon got out. But the ones that had it, still had it, even after *the* theater was gobbled up by technological change. And they hung around. Some of them, like Jade and Ian and Mela, adapted to the change, profited by the prostitution of the stage, and developed ulcers and a guilty conscience. Still, they were theater, and because they were, he, Thornier, hung around, too, scrubbing the floors they walked on, and feeling somehow that he was still in theater. Now he was leaving. And now he felt the old bitterness boiling up inside again. The bitterness had been chronic and passive, and now it threatened to become active and acute.

If I could only give them one last performance! he thought. One last great role—

But *that* thought led to the fantasy-plan for revenge, the plan that came to him often as he wandered about the empty theater. Revenge was no good. And the plan was only a daydream. And yet—he wasn't going to get another chance.

He set his jaw grimly and drove on to the Smithfield depot.

The depot clerk had hauled the crated mannequin to the fore, and it was waiting for Thornier when he entered the stockroom. He rolled it out from the wall on a dolly, and the janitor helped him wrestle the coffin-sized packing case onto the counter.

'Don't take it to the truck yet,' the clerk grunted around the fat stub of a cigar. 'It ain't a new doll, and you gotta sign a release.'

'What kind of a release?'

'Liability for malfunction. If the doll breaks down during the show, you can't sue Smithfield. It's standard prack for used-doll rentals.'

'Why didn't they send a new one, then?'

'Discontinued production on this model. You want it, you take a used one, and sign the release.'

'Suppose I don't sign?'

'No siggy, no dolly.'

'Oh.' He thought for a moment. Obviously, the clerk had mistaken him for production personnel. His signature wouldn't mean anything—but it was getting late, and Jade was rushed. Since the release wouldn't be valid anyhow he reached for the form.

'Wait,' said the clerk. 'You better look at what you're signing for.' He reached for a wrecking claw and slipped it under a metal binding strap. The strap broke with a screechy snap. 'It's been overhauled,' the clerk continued. 'New solenoid fluid injected, new cosmetic job. Nothing really wrong. A few fatigue spots in the padding, and one toe missing. But you oughta have a look, anyhow.'

He finished breaking the lid-fastenings loose and turned to a wall-control board. 'We don't have a complete Maestro here,' he said as he closed a knife switch, 'but we got the control transmitters, and some taped sequences. It's enough to pre-flight a doll.'

Equipment hummed to life somewhere behind the panel. The clerk adjusted several dials while Thornier waited impatiently.

'Let's see—' muttered the clerk. 'Guess we'll start off with the Frankenstein sequence.' He flipped a switch.

A purring sound came faintly from within the coffin-like box. Thornier watched nervously. The lid stirred, began to rise. A woman's hands came into view, pushing the lid up from within. The purring increased. The lid clattered aside to hang by the metal straps.

The woman sat up and smiled at the janitor.

Thornier went white. 'Mela!' he hissed.

'Ain't that a chiller?' chuckled the clerk. 'Now for the hoochy-coochy sequence—'

'No—'

The clerk flipped another switch. The doll stood up slowly, chastely nude as a window-dummy. Still smiling at Thorny, the doll did a bump and a grind.

'Stop it!' he yelled hoarsely.

'Whassa matter, buddy?'

Thorny heard another switch snap. The doll stretched gracefully and yawned. It stretched out in its packing case again, closed its eyes and folded its hands over its bosom. The purring stopped.

'What's eating you?' the clerk grumbled, slapping the lid back over the case again. 'You sick or something?'

'I . . . I knew her,' Ryan Thornier wheezed. 'I used to work —' He shook himself angrily and seized the crate.

'Wait, I'll give you a hand.'

Fury awakened new muscles. He hauled the crate out on the loading dock without assistance and dumped it in the back of the truck, then came back to slash his name across the release forms.

'You sure get sore easy,' the clerk mumbled. 'You better take it easy. You sure better take it easy.'

Thorny was cursing softly as he nosed the truck out into the river of traffic. Maybe Jade thought it was funny, sending him after Mela's doll. Jade remembered how it had been between them—if she bothered to think about it. Thornier and Stone—a team that had gotten constant attention from the gossip columnists in the old days. Rumors of engagement, rumors of secret marriage, rumors of squabbles and reunions, break-ups and patch-ups, and some of the rumors were almost true. Maybe Jade thought it was a howl, sending him to fetch the mannequin.

But no—his anger faded as he drove along the boulevard—she hadn't thought about it. Probably she tried hard not to think of old times any more.

Gloom settled over him again, replacing rage. Still it haunted him—the horrified shock of seeing her sit up like an awakened corpse to smile at him. *Mela . . . Mela—*

They'd had it good together and bad together. Bit parts and beans in a cold-water flat. Starring roles and steaks at Sardi's. And—love? Was that what it was? He thought of it uneasily. Hypnotic absorption in each other, perhaps, and in the mutual intoxication of their success—but it wasn't necessarily love. Love was calm and even and lasting, and you paid for it with a dedicated lifetime, and Mela wouldn't pay. She'd walked out on them. She'd walked to Smithfield and bought security with sacrifice of principle. There'd been a name for what she'd done. 'Scab,' they used to say.

He shook himself. It was no good, thinking about those times. Times died with each passing minute. Now they paid $8.80 to watch Mela's figurine move in her stead, wearing Mela's face, moving with Mela's gestures, walking with the same lilting walk. And the doll was still young, while Mela had aged ten years, years of collecting quarterly royalties from her dolls and living comfortably.

Great Actors Immortalized—that was one of Smithfield's little slogans. But they had discontinued production on Mela Stone, the depot clerk had said. Overstocked.

The promise of relative immortality had been quite a bait. Actors' unions had resisted autodrama, for obviously the bit players and the lesser-knowns would not be in demand. By making dozens—even hundreds—of copies of the same leading star, top talent could be had for every role, and the same actor-mannequin could be playing simultaneously in dozens of shows all over the country. The unions had resisted—but only a few were wanted by Smithfield anyhow, and the lure was great. The promise of fantastic royalties was enticing enough, but in addition—immortality for the actor, through duplication of mannequins. Authors, artists, playwrights had always been able to outlive the centuries, but actors were remembered only by professionals, and their names briefly recorded in the annals of the stage. Shakespeare would live another thousand years, but who remembered Dick Burbage who trouped in the day of the bard's premiers? Flesh and bone, heart and brain, these were the trouper's media, and his art could not outlive them.

Thorny knew the yearnings after lastingness, and he could no longer hate the ones who had gone over. As for himself the autodrama industry had made him a tentative offer, and he had resisted—partly because he was reasonably certain that the offer would have been withdrawn during testing procedures. Some actors were not 'cybergenic'—could not be adequately sculptured into electronic-robotic analogues. These were the portrayers, whose art was inward, whose roles had to be lived rather than played. No polygraphic analogue could duplicate their talents, and Thornier knew he was one of them. It had been easy for him to resist.

At the corner of Eighth Street, he remembered the spare tape and the replacement pickup for the Maestro. But if he turned back now, he'd hold up the run-through, and Jade would be furious. Mentally he kicked himself, and drove on to the delivery entrance of the theater. There he left the crated mannequin with the stage crew, and headed back for the depot without seeing the producer.

'Hey, bud,' said the clerk, 'your boss was on the phone. Sounded pretty unhappy.'

'Who . . . D'Uccia?'

'No . . . well, yeah, D'Uccia, too. He wasn't unhappy, just having fits. I meant Miss Ferne.'

'Oh . . . where's your phone?'

'Over there. The lady was near hysterical.'

Thorny swallowed hard and headed for the booth. Jade Ferne was a good friend, and if his absent-mindedness had goofed up her production—

'I've got the pickup and the tape ready to go,' the clerk called after him. 'She told me about it on the phone. Boy, you're sure on the ball today, ain't ya—the greasy eight ball.'

Thorny reddened and dialed nervously.

'Thank God!' she groaned. 'Thorny, we did the run-through with Andreyev a walking zombie. The Maestro chewed up our duplicate Peltier tape, and we're running without an actor-analogue in the starring role. Baby, I could murder you!'

'Sorry, Jade. I slipped a cog, I guess.'

'Never mind! Just get the new pickup mechanism over here for Thomas. And the Peltier tape. And don't have a wreck. It's two o'clock, and tonight's opening, and we're still short our leading man. And there's no time to get anything else flown in from Smithfield.'

'In some ways, nothing's changed, has it, Jade?' he grunted, thinking of the eternal backstage hysteria that lasted until the lights were low and beauty and calm order somehow emerged miraculously out cf the prevailing chaos.

'Don't philosophize, just *get* here!' she snapped, and hung up.

The clerk had the cartons ready for him as he emerged. 'Look, chum, better take care of that Peltier tape,' the clerk advised. 'It's the last one in the place. I've got more on order, but they won't be here for a couple of days.'

Thornier stared at the smaller package thoughtfully. The last Peltier?

The plan, he remembered the plan. *This* would make it easy. Of course, the plan was only a fantasy, a vengeful dream. He couldn't go through with it. To wreck the show would be a stab at Jade—

He heard his own voice like a stranger's, saying; 'Miss Ferne also asked me to pick up a Wilson Granger tape, and a couple of three-inch splices.'

The clerk looked surprised. 'Granger? He's not in "The Anarch," is he?'

Thornier shook his head. 'No—guess she wants it for a trial casting. Next show, maybe.'

The clerk shrugged and went to get the tape and the splices. Thornier stood clenching and unclenching his fists. He wasn't going to go through with it, of course. Only a silly fantasy.

'I'll have to make a separate ticket on these,' said the clerk, returning.

He signed the delivery slips in a daze, then headed for the truck. He drove three blocks from the depot, then parked in a loading zone. He opened the tape cartons carefully with his penknife, peeling back the glued flaps so that they could be sealed again. He removed the two rolls of pattern perforated tape from their small metal canisters, carefully plucked off the masking-tape seals and stuck them temporarily to the dashboard. He unrolled the first half-yard of the Peltier tape; it was unperforated, and printed with identifying codes and manufacturer's data. Fortunately, it was not a brand-new tape; it had been used before, and he could see the wear-marks. A splice would not arouse suspicion.

He cut off the identifying tongue with his knife, laid it aside. Then he did the same to the Granger tape.

Granger was fat, jovial, fiftyish. His mannequin played comic supporting roles.

Peltier was young, gaunt, gloomy—the intellectual villain, the dedicated fanatic. A fair choice for the part of Andreyev.

Thornier's hands seemed to move of their own volition, playing reflexively in long-rehearsed roles. He cut the tapes. He took out one of the hot-splice packs and jerked the tab that started the chemical action. He clocked off fifteen seconds by his watch, then opened the pack and fitted into it the cut ends of the Granger tape and the Peltier identifying tongue, butted them carefully end to end, and closed the pack. When it stopped smoking, he opened it to inspect the splice. A neat patch, scarcely visible on the slick plastic tape. Granger's analogue, labeled as Peltier's. And the body of the mannequin was Peltier's. He resealed it in its canister.

He wadded the Peltier tape and the Granger label and the extra delivery receipt copy into the other box. Then he pulled the truck out of the loading zone and drove through the heavy traffic like a racing jockey, trusting the anticrash radar to see him safely through. As he crossed the bridge, he threw the Peltier tape out the window into the river. And then there was no retreat from what he had done.

Jade and Feria sat in the orchestra, watching the final act of the run-through with a dud Andreyev. When Thorny slipped in beside them, Jade wiped mock sweat from her brow.

'Thank God you're back!' she whispered as he displayed the delayed packages. 'Sneak backstage and run them up to Rick in the booth, will you? Thorny, I'm out of my mind!'

'Sorry, Miss Ferne.' Fearing that his guilty nervousness hung about him like a ragged cloak, he slipped quickly backstage and delivered the cartons to Thomas in the booth. The technician hovered over the Maestro as the play went on, and he gave Thornier only a quick nod and a wave.

Thorny retreated into misty old corridors and unused dressing rooms, now heaped with junk and remnants of other days. He had to get a grip on himself, had to quit quaking inside. He wandered alone in the deserted sections of the building, opening old doors to peer into dark cubicles where great stars had preened in other days, other nights. Now full of trunks and cracked mirrors and tarpaulins and junked mannequins. Faint odors lingered—nervous smells—perspiration, make-up, dim perfume that pervaded the walls. Mildew and dust—the aroma of time. His footsteps sounded hollowly through the unpeopled rooms, while muffled sounds from the play came faintly through the walls—the hysterical pleading of Marka, the harsh laughter of Piotr, the marching boots of the revolutionist guards, a burst of music toward the end of the scene.

He turned abruptly and started back toward the stage. It was no good hiding away like this. He must behave normally, must do what he usually did. The falsified Peltier tape would not wreak its havoc until after the first run-through, when Thomas fed it into the Maestro, reset the machine, and prepared to start the second trial run. Until then, he must remain casually himself, and afterwards—?

Afterwards, things would have to go as he had planned. Afterwards, Jade would have to come to him, as he believed she would. If she didn't, then he had bungled, he had clumsily wrecked, and to no avail.

He slipped through the power-room where converters hummed softly, supplying power to the stage. He stood close to the entrance, watching the beginnings of scene *iii*, of the third act. Andreyev—the Peltier doll—was on alone, pacing grimly in his apartment while the low grumble of a street mob and the distant rattle of machine-gun fire issued from the Maestro-managed sound effect system. After a moment's watching, he saw that Andreyev's movements were not 'grim' but merely methodical and lifeless. The tapeless mannequin, going through the required motions, robotlike, without interpretation of meaning. He heard a brief burst of laughter from someone in the production row, and after watching the zombie-like rendering of Andreyev in a suspenseful scene, he, too, found himself grinning faintly.

The pacing mannequin looked toward him suddenly with a dead-pan face. It raised both fists toward its face.

'Help,' it said in a conversational monotone. 'Ivan, where are you? Where? Surely they've come; they must come.' It spoke quietly, without inflection. It ground its fists casually against its temples, paced mechanically again.

A few feet away, two mannequins that had been standing frozen in the off-stage lineup, clicked suddenly to life. As ghostly calm as display window dummies, they galvanized suddenly at a signal pulse command from the Maestro. Muscles—plastic sacs filled with oil-suspended magnetic powder and wrapped with elastic coils of wire, like flexible solenoids—tightened and strained beneath the airfoam flesh, working spasmodically to the pulsing rhythms of the polychromatic u.h.f. commands of the Maestro. Expressions of fear and urgency leaped to their faces. They crouched, tensed, looked around, then burst on stage, panting wildly.

'Comrade, she's come, she's come!' one of them screamed. 'She's come with *him,* with Boris!'

'What? She has him prisoner?' came the casual reply.

'No, no, comrade. We've been betrayed. She's with him. She's a traitor, she's sold out to them.'

There was no feeling in the uninterpreted Andreyev's responses, even when he shot the bearer of bad tidings through the heart.

Thornier grew fascinated with watching as the scene progressed. The mannequins moved gracefully, their movements sinuous and more evenly flowing than human, they seemed boneless. The ratio of mass-to-muscle power of their members was carefully chosen to yield the flow of a dance with their every movement. Not clanking mechanical robots, not stumbling puppets, the dolls sustained patterns of movement and expression that would have quickly brought fatigue to a human actor, and the Maestro co-ordinated the events on stage in a way that would be impossible to a group of humans, each an individual and thinking independently.

It was as always. First, he looked with a shudder at the Machine moving in the stead of flesh and blood, at Mechanism sitting in the seat of artistry. But gradually his chill melted away, and the play caught him, and the actors were no longer machines. He lived in the role of Andreyev, and breathed the lines off-stage, and he knew the rest of them: Mela and Peltier, Sam Dion and Peter Repplewaite. He tensed with them, gritted his teeth in anticipation of difficult lines, cursed softly at the dud Andreyev, and forgot to listen for the faint crackle of sparks as the mannequins' feet stepped across the copper-studded floor, drinking energy in random bites to keep their storage packs near full charge.

Thus entranced, he scarcely noticed the purring and brushing and swishing sounds that came from behind him, and grew louder. He heard a quiet mutter of voices nearby, but only frowned at the distraction, kept his attention rooted to the stage.

Then a thin spray of water tickled his ankles. Something soggy and spongelike slapped against his foot. He whirled.

A gleaming metal spider, three feet high, came at him slowly on six legs, with two grasping claws extended. It clicked its way toward him across the floor, throwing out a thin spray of liquid which it promptly sucked up with the spongelike proboscis. With one grasping claw, it lifted a ten-gallon can near his leg, sprayed under it, swabbed, and set the can down again.

Thornier came unfrozen with a howl, leaped over the thing, hit the wet-soapy deck off balance. He skidded and sprawled. The spider scrubbed at the floor toward the edge of the stage, then reversed directions and came back toward him.

Groaning, he pulled himself together, on hands and knees. D'Uccia's cackling laughter spilled over him. He glanced up. The chubby manager and the servo salesman stood over him, the salesman grinning, D'Uccia chortling.

'Datsa ma boy, datsa ma boy! Always, he watcha the show, then he don't swip-op around, then he wantsa day off. Thatsa ma boy, for sure.' D'Uccia reached down to pat the metal spider's chassis. 'Hey, *ragazzo*,' he said again to Thornier, 'want you should meet my new *boy* here. This one, he don't watcha the show like you.'

He got to his feet, ghost-white and muttering. D'Uccia took closer note of his face, and his grin went sick. He inched back a step. Thornier glared at him briefly, then whirled to stalk away. He whirled into near collision with the Mela Stone mannequin, recovered, and started to pass in back of it.

Then he froze.

The Mela Stone mannequin was on stage, in the final scene. And this one looked older, and a little haggard. It wore an expression of shocked surprise as it looked him up and down. One hand darted to its mouth.

'Thorny—!' A frightened whisper.

'Mela!' Despite the play, he shouted it, opening his arms to her. 'Mela, how *wonderful!*'

And then, he noticed she winced away from his sodden coveralls. And she wasn't glad to see him at all.

'Thorny, how nice,' she managed to murmur, extending her hand gingerly. The hand flashed with jewelry.

He took it for an empty second, stared at her, then walked hurriedly away, knots twisting up inside him. Now he could play it through. Now he could go on with it, and even enjoy executing his plan against all of them.

Mela had come to watch opening night for her doll in 'The Anarch,' as if its performance were her own. *I'll arrange*, he thought, *for it not to be a dull show*.

'No, no, *nooo!*' came the monotone protest of the dud

Andreyev, in the next-to-the-last scene. The bark of Marka's gun, and the Peltier mannequin crumpled to the stage; and except for a brief triumphant denouement, the play was over.

At the sound of the gunshot, Thornier paused to smile tightly over his shoulder, eyes burning from his hawklike face. Then he vanished into the wings.

She got away from them as soon as she could, and she wandered around backstage until she found him in the storage room of the costuming section. Alone, he was sorting through the contents of an old locker and muttering nostalgically to himself. She smiled and closed the door with a thud. Startled, he dropped an old collapsible top-hat and a box of blank cartridges back into the trunk. His hand dived into his pocket as he straightened.

'Jade! I didn't expect—'

'Me to come?' She flopped on a dusty old chaise-longue with a weary sigh and fanned herself with a program, closing her eyes. She kicked off her shoes and muttered: 'Infuriating bunch. I hate 'em!'—made a retching face, and relaxed into little-girlhood. A little girl who had trouped with Thornier and the rest of them—the *actress* Jade Ferne, who had begged for bit parts and haunted the agencies and won the roles through endless rehearsals and shuddered with fright before opening curtain like the rest of them. Now she was a pert little woman with shrewd eyes; streaks of gray at the temples, and hard lines around her mouth. As she let the executive cloak slip away, the shrewdness and the hard lines melted into weariness.

'Fifteen minutes to get my sanity back, Thorny,' she muttered, glancing at her watch as if to time it.

He sat on the trunk and tried to relax. She hadn't seemed to notice his uneasiness, or else she was just too tired to attach any significance to it. If she found him out, she'd have him flayed and pitched out of the building on his ear, and maybe call the police. She came in a small package, but so did an incendiary grenade. *It won't hurt you, Jade, what I'm doing*, he told himself. *It'll cause a big splash, and you won't like it, but it won't hurt you, nor even wreck the show.*

He was doing it for show business, the old kind, the kind they'd both known and loved. And in that sense, he told himself further, he was doing it as much for her as he was for himself.

'How was the run-through, Jade?' he asked casually. 'Except for Andreyev, I mean.'

'Superb, simply superb,' she said mechanically.

'I mean *really*.'

She opened her eyes, made a sick mouth. 'Like always, Thorny, like always. Nauseating, overplayed, perfectly directed for a gum-chewing bag-rattling crowd. A crowd that wants it overplayed so that it won't have to think about what's going on. A crowd that doesn't want to reach *out* for a feeling or a meaning. It wants to be clubbed on the head with the meaning, so it doesn't have to reach. I'm sick of it.'

He looked briefly surprised. 'That figures,' he grunted wryly.

She hooked her bare heels on the edge of the lounge, hugged her shins, rested her chin on her knees, and blinked at him. 'Hate me for producing the stuff, Thorny?'

He thought about it for a moment, shook his head. 'I get sore at the setup sometimes, but I don't blame you for it.'

'That's good. Sometimes I'd trade places with you. Sometimes I'd rather be a charwoman and scrub D'Uccia's floors instead.'

'Not a chance,' he said sourly. 'The Maestro's relatives are taking *that* over, too.'

'I know. I heard. You're out of a job, thank God. Now you can get somewhere.'

He shook his head. 'I don't know where. I can't do anything but act.'

'Nonsense. I can get you a job tomorrow.'

'Where?'

'With Smithfield. Sales promotion. They're hiring a number of old actors in the department.'

'No.' He said it flat and cold.

'Not so fast. This is something new. The company's expanding.'

'Ha.'

'Autodrama for the home. A four-foot stage in every living room. Miniature mannequins, six inches high. Centralized Maestro service. Great plays piped to your home by concentric table. Just dial Smithfield, make your request. Sound good?'

He stared at her icily. 'Greatest thing in show business since Sarah Bernhardt,' he offered tonelessly.

'Thorny! Don't get nasty with me!'

'Sorry. But what's so new about having it in the home? Autodrama took over TV years ago.'

'I know, but this is different. Real miniature theater. Kids go wild for it. But it'll take good promotion to make it catch on.'

'Sorry, but you know me better than that.'

She shrugged, sighed wearily, closed her eyes again. 'Yes, I do. You've got portrayer's integrity. You're a darfsteller. A director's ulcer. You can't play a role without living it, and you won't live it unless you believe it. So go ahead and starve.' She spoke crossly, but he knew there was grudging admiration behind it.

'I'll be O.K.,' he grunted, adding to himself: *after tonight's performance*.

'Nothing I can do for you?'

'Sure. Cast me. I'll stand in for dud mannequins.'

She gave him a sharp glance, hesitated. 'You know, I believe you *would?'*

He shrugged. 'Why not?'

She stared thoughtfully at a row of packing cases, waggled her dark head. 'Hmmp! What a spectacle that'd be—a human actor, incognito, playing in an autodrama.'

'It's been done—in the sticks.'

'Yes, but the audience knew it was being done, and that always spoils the show. It creates contrasts that don't exist or wouldn't be noticed otherwise. Makes the dolls seem snaky, birdlike, too rubbery quick. With no humans on stage for contrast, the dolls just seem wistfully graceful, ethereal.'

'But if the audience didn't know—'

Jade was smiling faintly. 'I wonder,' she mused. 'I wonder if they'd guess. They'd notice a difference, of course—in one mannequin.'

'But they'd think it was just the Maestro's interpretation of the part.'

'Maybe—if the human actor were careful.'

He chuckled sourly. 'If it fooled the critics—'

'Some ass would call it "an abysmally unrealistic interpretation" or "too obviously mechanical." ' She glanced at her watch, shook herself, stretched wearily, and slipped into her shoes again. 'Anyway,' she added, 'there's no reason to do it, since the Maestro's *really* capable of rendering a better-than-human performance anyhow.'

The statement brought an agonized gasp from the janitor. She looked at him and giggled. 'Don't be shocked, Thorny. I said "*capable* of"—not "in the habit of." Autodrama entertains audiences on the level they *want* to be entertained on.'

'But—'

'Just,' she added firmly, 'as show business has always done.'

'But—'

'Oh, retract your eyeballs, Thorny. I didn't mean to blaspheme.' She preened, began slipping back into her producer's mold as she prepared to return to her crowd. 'The only thing wrong with autodrama is that it's scaled down to the moron-level —but show business always has been, and probably should be. Even if it gives us kids a pain.' She smiled and patted his cheek. 'Sorry I shocked you. Au 'voir, Thorny. And luck.'

When she was gone, he sat fingering the cartridges in his pocket and staring at nothing. Didn't any of them have any sensibilities? Jade too, a seller of principle. And he had always thought of her as having merely compromised with necessity, against her real wishes. The idea that she could really believe autodrama capable of rendering a better-than-human performance—

But she didn't. Of course she needed to rationalize, to excuse what she was doing—

He sighed and went to lock the door, then to recover the old 'Anarch' script from the trunk. His hands were trembling slightly. Had he planted enough of an idea in Jade's mind; would she remember it later? Or perhaps remember it too clearly, and suspect it?

He shook himself sternly. No apprehensions allowed. When Rick rang the bell for the second run-through, it would be his entrance-cue, and he must be in-character by then. Too bad he was no schauspieler, too bad he couldn't switch himself on-and-off the way Jade could do, but the necessity for much inward preparation was the burden of the darfsteller. He could not change into a role without first changing himself, and letting the revision seep surfaceward as it might, reflecting the inner state of the man.

Strains of Moussorgsky pervaded the walls. He closed his eyes to listen and feel. Music for empire. Music at once brutal and majestic. It was the time of upheaval, of vengeance, of overthrow. Two times, superimposed. It was the time of opening night, with Ryan Thornier—ten years ago—cast in the starring role.

He fell into a kind of trance as he listened and clocked the pulse of his psyche and remembered. He scarcely noticed when the music stopped, and the first few lines of the play came through the walls.

'Cut! Cut!' A worried shout. Feria's.

It had begun.

Thornier took a deep breath and seemed to come awake. When he opened his eyes and stood up, the janitor was gone. The janitor had been a nightmare role, nothing more.

And Ryan Thornier, star of 'Walkaway,' favored of the critics, confident of a bright future, walked out of the storage room with a strange lightness in his step. He carried a broom, he still wore the dirty coveralls, but now as if to a masquerade.

The Peltier mannequin lay sprawled on the stage in a grostesque heap. Ryan Thornier stared at it calmly from behind the set and listened intently to the babble of stage hands and technicians that milled about him:

'Don't know. Can't tell yet. It came out staggering and gibbering—like it was drunk. It reached for a table, then it fell on its face—'

'Acted like the trouble might be a mismatched tape, but Rick rechecked it. Really Peltier's tape—'

'Can't figure it out. Miss Ferne's having kittens.'

Thornier paused to size up his audience. Jade, Ian, and their staff milled about in the orchestra section. The stage was empty, except for the sprawled mannequin. Too much frantic conversation, all around. His entrance would go unnoticed. He walked slowly on-stage and stood over the fallen doll with his hands in his pockets and his face pulled down in a somber expression. After a moment, he nudged the doll with his toe, paused, nudged it again. A faint giggle came from the orchestra. The corner of his eye caught Jade's quick glance toward the stage. She paused in the middle of a sentence.

Assured that she watched, he played to an imaginary audience-friend standing just off stage. He glanced toward the friend, lifted his brows questioningly. The friend apparently gave him the nod. He looked around warily, then knelt over the fallen doll. He took its pulse, nodded eagerly to the offstage friend. Another giggle came from the orchestra. He lifted the doll's head, sniffed its breath, made a face. Then, gingerly, he rolled it.

He reached deep into the mannequin's pocket, having palmed his own pocket watch beforehand. His hand paused there, and he smiled to his offstage accomplice and nodded eagerly. He withdrew the watch and held it up by its chain for his accomplice's approval.

A light burst of laughter came from the production personnel.

The laughter frightened the thief. He shot an apprehensive glance around the stage, hastily returned the watch to the fallen dummy, felt its pulse again. He traded a swift glance with his confederate, whispered 'Aha!' and smiled mysteriously. Then he helped the doll to its feet and staggered away with it—a friend leading a drunk home to its family. In the doorway, he paused to frame his exit with a wary backward glance that said he was taking it to a dark alley where he could rob it in safety.

Jade was gaping at him.

Three technicians had been watching from just off the set, and they laughed heartily and clapped his shoulder as he passed, providing the offstage audience to which he had seemed to be playing.

Good-natured applause came from Jade's people out front, and as Thorny carried the doll away to storage, he was humming softly to himself.

At five minutes till six, Rick Thomas and a man from the Smithfield depot climbed down out of the booth, and Jade pressed forward through the crowd to question him with her eyes.

'The tape,' he said. 'Defective.'

'But it's too late to get another!' she squawked.

'Well, it's the tape, anyway.'

'How do you *know?*'

'Well—trouble's bound to be in one of three places. The doll, the tape, or the analogue tank where the tape-data gets stored. We cleared the tank and tried it with another actor. Worked O.K. And the doll works O.K. on an uninterpreted run. So, by elimination, the tape.'

She groaned and slumped into a seat, covering her face with her hands.

'No way at *all* to locate another tape?' Rick asked.

'We called every depot within five hundred miles. They'd have to cut one from a master. Take too long.'

'So we call off the show!' Ian Feria called out resignedly, throwing up his hands in disgust. 'Refund on tickets, open tomorrow.'

'Wait!' snapped the producer, looking up suddenly. 'Dooch—the house is sold out, isn't it?'

'Yah,' D'Uccia grunted irritably. 'She'sa filled op. Wassa matter with you pipple, you don' getsa Maestro fix? Wassa matter? We lose the money, hah?'

'Oh, shut up. Change curtain time to nine, offer refunds if they won't wait. Ian, keep at it. Get things set up for tonight.' She spoke with weary determination, glancing around at them. 'There may be a slim chance. Keep at it. I'm going to try something.' She turned and started away.

'Hey!' Feria called.

'Explain later,' she muttered over her shoulder.

She found Thornier replacing burned-out bulbs in the wall fixtures. He smiled down at her while he reset the clamps of an amber glass panel. 'Need me for something, Miss Ferne?' he called pleasantly from the step-ladder.

'I might,' she said tersely. 'Did you mean that offer about standing in for dud mannequins?'

A bulb exploded at her feet after it slipped from his hand. He came down slowly, gaping at her.

'You're not serious!'

'Think you could try a run-through as Andreyev?'

He shot a quick glance toward the stage, wet his lips, stared at her dumbly.

'Well—*can* you?'

'It's been ten years, Jade . . . I—'

'You can read over the script, and you can wear an earplug radio—so Rick can prompt you from the booth.'

She made the offer crisply and matter-of-factly, and it made Thorny smile inwardly. It was theater—calmly asking the outrageously impossible, gambling on it, and getting it.

'The customers—they're expecting Peltier.'

'Right now I'm only asking you to try a runthrough, Thorny. After that, we'll see. But remember it's our only chance of going on tonight.'

'Andreyev,' he breathed. 'The lead.'

'Please, Thorny, will you try?'

He looked around the theater, nodded slowly. 'I'll go study my lines,' he said quietly, inclining his head with what he hoped was just the proper expression of humble bravery.

I've got to make it good, I've got to make it great. The last chance, the last great role—

Glaring footlights, a faint whisper in his ear, and the cold panic of the first entrance. It came and passed quickly. Then the stage was a closed room, and the audience—of technicians and production personnel—was only the fourth wall, somewhere beyond the lights. He was Andreyev, commissioner of police, party whip, loyal servant of the regime, now tottering in the revolutionary storm of the Eighties. The last Bolshevik, no longer a rebel, no longer a radical, but now the loyalist, the conservatist, the defender of the status quo, champion of the Marxist ruling classes. No longer conscious of a self apart from that of the role, he lived the role. And the others, the people he lived it with, the people whose feet crackled faintly as they stepped across the floor, he acted and reacted with them and against them as if they, too, shared life, and while the play progressed he forgot their lifelessness for a little time.

Caught up by the magic, enfolded in the scheme of the inevitable, borne along by the tide of the drama, he felt once again the sense of belonging as a part in a whole, a known and predictable whole that moved as surely from scene *i* to the final curtain as man from womb to tomb, and there were no lost years, no lapse or sense of defeated purpose between the rehearsals of those many years ago and this the fulfillment of opening night. Only when at last he muffed a line, and Rick's correction whispered in his ear did the spell that was gathered about him briefly break—and he found himself unaccountably frightened, frightened by the sudden return of realization that all about him was Machine, and frightened, too, that he had forgotten. He had been conforming to the flighty mechanical grace of the others, reflexively imitating the characteristic lightness of the mannequins' movements, the dancelike qualities of their playing. To know suddenly, having forgotten it, that the mouth he had just kissed was not a woman's, but the rubber mouth of a doll, and that dancing patterns of high frequency waves from the Maestro had controlled the solenoid currents that turned her face lovingly up toward his, had lifted the cold soft hands to touch his face. The faint rubbery smell-taste hung about his mouth.

When his first exit came, he went off trembling. He saw Jade coming toward him, and for an instant, he felt a horrifying certainty that she would say, 'Thorny, you were almost as good as a mannequin!' Instead, she said nothing, but only held out her hand to him.

'Was it too bad, Jade?'

'Thorny, you're in! Keep it up, and you might have more than a one-night stand. Even Ian's convinced. He squealed at the idea, but now he's sold.'

'No kicks? How about the lines with Piotr.'

'Wonderful. Keep it up. Darling, you were marvelous.'

'It's settled, then?'

'Darling, it's *never* settled until the curtain comes up. You know that.' She giggled. 'We had one *kick* all right—or maybe I shouldn't tell you.'

He stiffened slightly. 'Oh? Who from?'

'Mela Stone. She saw you come on, turned white as a sheet, and walked out. I can't imagine!'

He sank slowly on a haggard looking couch and stared at her. 'The hell you can't,' he grated softly.

'She's here on a personal appearance contract, you know. To give an opening and an intermission commentary on the author and the play.' Jade smirked at him gleefully. 'Five minutes ago she called back, tried to cancel her appearance. Of course, she can't pull a stunt like that. Not while Smithfield owns her.'

Jade winked, patted his arm, tossed an uncoded copy of the script at him, then headed back toward the orchestra. Briefly he wondered what Jade had against Mela. Nothing serious, probably. Both had been actresses. Mela got a Smithfield contract; Jade didn't get one. It was enough.

By the time he had reread the scene to follow, his second cue was approaching, and he moved back toward the stage.

Things went smoothly. Only three times during the first act did he stumble over lines he had not rehearsed in ten years. Rick's prompting was in his ear, and the Maestro could compensate to some extent for his minor deviations from the script. This time he avoided losing himself so completely in the play; and this time the weird realization that he had become one with the machine-set pattern did not disturb him. This time he remembered, but when the first break came—

'Not quite so good, Thorny,' Ian Feria called. 'Whatever you were doing in the first scene, do it again. That was a little wooden. Go through that last bit again, and play it down. Andreyev's no mad bear from the Urals. It's Marka's moment, anyhow. Hold in.'

He nodded slowly and looked around at the frozen dolls. He had to forget the machinery. He had to lose himself in it and live it, even if it meant being a replacement link in the mechanism. It disturbed him somehow, even though he was accustomed to subordinating himself to the total gestalt of the scene as in other days. For no apparent reason, he found himself listening for laughter from the production people, but none came.

'All right,' Feria called. 'Bring 'em alive again.'

He went on with it, but the uneasy feeling nagged at him. There was self-mockery in it, and the expectation of ridicule from those who watched. He could not understand why, and yet—

There was an ancient movie—one of the classics—in which a man named Chaplin had been strapped into a seat on a production line where he performed a perfectly mechanical task in a perfectly mechanical fashion, a task that could obviously have been done by a few cams and a linkage or two, and it was one of the funniest comedies of all times—yet tragic. A task that made him a part in an over-all machine.

He sweated through the second and third acts in a state of compromise with himself—overplaying it for purposes of self-preparation, yet trying to convince Feria and Jade that he could handle it and handle it well. Overacting was necessary in spots, as a learning technique. Deliberately ham up the rehearsal to impress lines on memory, then underplay it for the real performance—it was an old trick of troupers who had to do a new show each night and had only a few hours in which to rehearse and learn lines. But would they know why he was doing it?

When it was finished, there was no time for another run-through, and scarcely time for a nap and a bite to eat before dressing for the show.

'It was terrible, Jade,' he groaned. 'I muffed it. I know I did.'

'Nonsense. You'll be in tune tonight, Thorny. I knew what you were doing, and I can see past it.'

'Thanks. I'll try to pull in.'

'About the final scene, the shooting—'

He shot her a wary glance. 'What about it?'

'The gun'll be loaded tonight, blanks, of course. And this time you'll have to fall.'

'So?'

'So be careful where you fall. Don't go down on the copper bus-lugs. A hundred and twenty volts mightn't kill you, but we don't want a dying Andreyev bouncing up and spitting blue sparks. The stagehands'll chalk out a safe section for you. And one other thing—'

'Yes?'

'Marka fires from close range. Don't get burned.'

'I'll watch it.'

She started away, then paused to frown back at him steadily for several seconds. 'Thorny, I've got a queer feeling about you. I can't place it exactly.'

He stared at her evenly, waiting.

'Thorny, are you going to wreck the show?'

His face showed nothing, but something twisted inside him. She looked beseeching, trusting, but worried. She was counting on him, placing faith in him—

'Why should I botch up the performance, Jade? Why should I do a thing like that?'

'I'm asking you.'

'O.K. I promise you—you'll get the best Andreyev I can give you.'

She nodded slowly. 'I believe you. I didn't doubt *that,* exactly.'

'Then what worries you?'

'I don't know. I know how you feel about autodrama. I just got a shuddery feeling that you had something up your sleeve. That's all. I'm sorry. I know you've got too much integrity to wreck your own performance, but—' She stopped and shook her head, her dark eyes searching him. She was still worried.

'Oh, all right. I was going to stop the show in the third act. I was going to show them my appendectomy scar, do a couple of card tricks, and announce that I was on strike. I was going to walk out.' He clucked his tongue at her, looked hurt.

She flushed slightly, and laughed. 'Oh, I know you wouldn't pull anything shabby. Not that you wouldn't do anything you *could* to take a swat at autodrama generally, but . . . there's nothing you could do tonight that would accomplish anything. Except sending the customers home mad. That doesn't fit you, and I'm sorry I thought of it.'

'Thanks. Stop worrying. If you lose dough, it won't be my fault.'

'I believe you, but—'

'But what?'

She leaned close to him. 'But you look too triumphant, that's what!' she hissed, then patted his cheek.

'Well, it's my last role. I—'

But she had already started away, leaving him with his sandwich and a chance for a nap.

Sleep would not come. He lay fingering the .32 caliber cartridges in his pocket and thinking about the impact of his final exit upon the conscience of the theater. The thoughts were pleasant.

It struck him suddenly as he lay drowsing that they would call it suicide. How silly. Think of the jolting effect, the dramatic punch, the audience reaction. Mannequins don't bleed. And later, the headlines: Robot Player Kills Old Trouper, Victim of Mechanized Stage. Still, they'd call it suicide. How silly.

But maybe that's what the paranoid on the twentieth story window ledge thought about, too—the audience reaction. Wasn't every self-inflicted wound really aimed at the conscience of the world?

It worried him some, but—

'Fifteen minutes until curtain,' the sound system was croaking. *'Fifteen minutes—'*

'Hey, Thorny!' Feria called irritably. 'Get back to the costuming room. They've been looking for you.'

He got up wearily, glanced around at the backstage bustle, then shuffled away toward the makeup department. One thing was certain: he had to go on.

The house was less than packed. A third of the customers had taken refunds rather than wait for the postponed curtain and a substitute Andreyev, a substitute unknown or ill-remembered at best, with no Smithy index rating beside his name in lights. Nevertheless, the bulk of the audience had planned their evenings and stayed to claim their seats with only suppressed bad humor about the delay. Scalpers' customers who had overpaid and who could not reclaim more than half the bootleg price from the boxoffice were forced to accept the show or lose money and get nothing. They came, and shifted restlessly, and glanced at their watches while an m.c.'s voice made apologies and introduced orchestral numbers, mostly from the Russian composers. Then, finally—

'Ladies and gentlemen, tonight we have with us one of the best loved actresses of stage, screen, and autodrama, co-star of our play tonight, as young and lovely as she was when first immortalized by Smithfield—Mela *Stone!*'

Thornier watched tight-lipped from shadows as she stepped gracefully into the glare of the footlights. She seemed abnormally pale, but makeup artistry had done a good job; she looked only slightly older than her doll, still lovely, though less arrogantly beautiful. Her flashing jewelry was gone, and she wore a simple dark gown with a deep-slit neck, and her tawny hair was wrapped high in a turbanlike coiffure that left bare a graceful neck.

'Ten years ago,' she began quietly, 'I rehearsed for a production of "The Anarch" which never appeared, rehearsed it with a man named Ryan Thornier in the starring role, the actor who fills that role tonight. I remember with a special sort of glow the times—'

She faltered, and went on lamely. Thorny winced. Obviously the speech had been written by Jade Ferne and evidently the words were like bits of poisoned apples in Mela's mouth. She gave the impression that she was speaking them only because it wasn't polite to retch them. Mela was being punished for her attempt to back out, and Jade had forced her to appear only by threatening to fit out the Stone mannequin with a gray wig and havc the doll read her curtain speeches. The small producer had a vicious streak, and she exercised it when crossed.

Mela's introductory lines were written to convince the audience that it was indeed lucky to have Thornier instead of Peltier, but there was nothing to intimate his flesh-and-blood status. She did not use the words 'doll' or 'mannequin,' but allowed the audience to keep its preconceptions without confirming them. It was short. After a few anecdotes about the show's first presentation more than a generation ago, she was done.

'And with no further delay, my friends, I give you—Pruchev's "The Anarch." '

She bowed away and danced behind the curtains and came off crying. A majestic burst of music heralded the opening scene. She saw Thornier and stopped, not yet off stage. The curtain started up. She darted toward him, hesitated, stopped to stare up at him apprehensively. Her eyes were brimming, and she was biting her lip.

On stage, a telephone jangled on the desk of Commissioner Andreyev. His cue was still three minutes away. A lieutenant came on to answer the phone.

'Nicely done, Mela,' he whispered, smiling sourly.

She didn't hear him. Her eyes drifted down to his costume —very like the uniform he'd worn for a dress rehearsal ten years ago. Her hand went to her throat. She wanted to run from him, but after a moment she got control of herself. She looked at her own mannequin waiting in the line-up, then at Thornier.

'Aren't you going to say something appropriate?' she hissed.

'I—' His icy smile faded slowly. The first small triumph —triumph over Mela, a sick and hag-ridden Mela who had bought security at the expense of integrity and was still paying for it in small installments like this, Mela whom he once had loved. The first small 'triumph' coiled into a sick knot in his throat.

She started away, but he caught her arm.

'I'm sorry, Mela,' he muttered hoarsely. 'I'm really sorry.'

'It's not your fault.'

But it was. She didn't know what he'd done, of course; didn't know he'd switched the tapes and steered his own selection as a replacement for the Peltier doll, so that she'd have to watch him playing opposite the doll-image of a Mela who had ceased to exist ten years ago, watch him relive a mockery of something.

'I'm sorry,' he whispered again.

She shook her head, pulled her arm free, hurried away. He watched her go and went sick inside. Their frigid meeting earlier in the day had been the decisive moment, when in a surge of bitterness he'd determined to go through with it and even excuse himself for doing it. Maybe bitterness had fogged his eyesight, he thought. Her reaction to bumping into him that way hadn't been snobbery; it had been horror. An old ghost in dirty coveralls and motley, whose face she'd probably fought to forget, had sprung up to confront her in a place that was too full of memories anyhow. No wonder she seemed cold. Probably he symbolized some of her own self-accusations, for he knew he had affected others that way. The successful ones, the ones who had profited by autodrama—they often saw him with mop and bucket, and if they remembered Ryan Thornier, turned quickly away. And at each turning away, he had felt a small glow of satisfaction as he imagined them thinking: *Thornier wouldn't compromise*—and hating him, because they had compromised and lost something thereby. But being hated by Mela—was different somehow. He didn't want it.

Someone nudged his ribs. 'Your cue, Thorny!' hissed a tense voice. 'You're *on!*'

He came awake with a grunt. Feria was shoving him frantically toward his entrance. He made a quick grab for his presence of mind, straightened into character, and strode on.

He muffed the scene badly. He knew that he muffed it even before he made his exit and saw their faces. He had missed two cues and needed prompting several times from Rick in the booth. His acting was wooden—he felt it.

'You're doing fine, Thorny, just fine!' Jade told him, because there was nothing else she *dared* tell him during a performance. Shock an actor's ego during rehearsal, and he had time to recover; shock it during a performance, and he might go sour for the night. He knew, though, without being told, the worry that seethed behind her mechanical little smile. 'But just calm down a little, eh?' she advised. 'It's going fine.'

She left him to seethe in solitude. He leaned against the wall and glowered at his feet and flagellated himself. *You failure, you miserable crumb, you janitor-at-heart, you stage-struck charwoman—*

He had to straighten out. If he ruined this one, there'd never be another chance. But he kept thinking of Mela, and how he had wanted to hurt her, and how now that she was being hurt he wanted to stop.

'Your cue, Thorny—wake up!'

And he was on again, stumbling over lines, being terrified of the sea of dim faces where a fourth wall should be.

She was waiting for him after his second exit. He came off pale and shaking, perspiration soaking his collar. He leaned back and lit a cigarette and looked at her bleakly. She couldn't talk. She took his arm in both hands and kneaded it while she rested her forehead against his shoulder. He gazed down at her in dismay. She'd stopped feeling hurt; she couldn't feel hurt when she watched him make a fool of himself out there. She might have been vengefully delighted by it, and he almost wished that she were. Instead, she was pitying him. He was numb, sick to the core. He couldn't go on with it.

'Mela, I'd better tell *you;* I can't tell Jade what I—'

'Don't talk, Thorny. Just do your best.' She peered up at him. 'Please do your best?'

It startled him. Why should she feel that way?

'Wouldn't you really rather see me flop?' he asked.

She shook her head quickly, then paused and nodded it. 'Part of me would, Thorny. A vengeful part. I've got to believe in the automatic stage. I . . . I do believe in it. But I don't want you to flop, not really.' She put her hands over her eyes briefly. 'You don't know what it's like seeing you out there . . . in the middle of all that . . . that—' She shook herself slightly. 'It's a mockery, Thorny, you don't belong out there, but—as long as you're there, don't muff it. Do your best?'

'Yeah, sure.'

'It's a precarious thing. The effect, I mean. If the audience starts realizing you're not a doll—' She shook her head slowly.

'What if they do?'

'They'll laugh. They'll laugh you right off the stage.'

He was prepared for anything but that. It confirmed the nagging hunch he'd had during the run-through.

'Thorny, that's all I'm really concerned about. I don't care whether you play it well or play it lousy, as long as they don't find out what you are. I don't want them to laugh at you; you've been hurt enough.'

'They wouldn't laugh if I gave a good performance.'

'But they *would!* Not in the same way, but they would. Don't you see?'

His mouth fell open. He shook his head. It wasn't true. 'Human actors have done it before,' he protested. 'In the sticks, on small stages with undersized Maestros.'

'Have you ever seen such a play?'

He shook his head.

'I have. The audience knows about the human part of the cast in advance. So it doesn't strike them as funny. There's no jolt of discovering an incongruity. Listen to me Thorny—do your best, but you don't dare make it *better* than a doll could do.'

Bitterness came back in a flood. Was this what he had hoped for? To give as machinelike a performance as possible, to do as good a job as the Maestro, but no better, and above all, no *different?* So that they wouldn't find out?

She saw his distressed expression and felt for his hand. 'Thorny, don't you hate me for telling you. I want you to bring it off O.K., and I thought you ought to realize. I think I know what's been wrong. You're afraid—down deep—that they *won't* recognize you for who you are, and that makes your performance un-doll-like. You better start being afraid they will recognize you, Thorny.'

As he stared at her, it began to penetrate that she was still capable of being the woman he'd once known and loved. Worse, she wanted to save him from being laughed at. Why? If she felt motherly, she might conceivably want to shield him against wrath, criticism, or rotten tomatoes, but not against loss of dignity. Motherliness thrived on the demise of male dignity, for it sharpened the image of the child in the man.

'Mela—?'

'Yes, Thorny.'

'I guess I never quite got over you.' She shook her head quickly, almost angrily.

'Darling, you're living ten years ago. I'm not, and I won't. Maybe I don't like the present very well, but I'm in it, and I can only change it in little ways. I can't make it the past again, and I won't try.' She paused a moment, searching his face. 'Ten years ago, we weren't living in the present either. We were living in a mythical, magic, wonderful future. Great talent, just starting to bloom. We were living in dream-plans in those days. The future we lived in never happened, and you can't go back and make it happen. And when a dream-plan stops being possible, it turns into a pipe dream. I won't live in a pipe dream. I want to stay sane, even if it hurts.'

'Too bad you had to come tonight,' he said stiffly.

She wilted. 'Oh, Thorny, I didn't mean that the way it sounded. And I wouldn't say it that strongly unless'—she glanced through the soundproof glass toward the stage where her mannequin was on in the scene with Piotr—'unless I had trouble too, with too much wishing.'

'I wish you were with me out there,' he said softly. 'With no dolls and no Maestro. I know how it'd be then.'

'Don't! Please, Thorny, don't.'

'Mela, I loved you—'

'No!' She got up quickly. 'I . . . I want to see you after the show. Meet me. But don't talk that way. Especially not here and not now.'

'I can't help it.'

'Please! Good-bye for now, Thorny, and—do your best.'

My best to be a mechanism, he thought bitterly as he watched her go.

He turned to watch the play. Something was wrong out there on the stage. Badly wrong. The Maestro's interpretation of the scene made it seem unfamiliar somehow. He frowned. Rich had spoken of the Maestro's ability to compensate, to shift interpretations, to redirect. Was that what was happening? The Maestro compensating—for *his* performance?

His cue was approaching. He moved closer to the stage.

Act I had been a flop. Feria, Ferne, and Thomas conferred in an air of tension and a haze of cigarette smoke. He heard heated muttering, but could not distinguish words. Jade called a stagehand, spoke to him briefly, and sent him away. The stagehand wandered through the group until he found Mela Stone, spoke to her quickly and pointed. Thorny watched her go to join the production group, then turned away. He slipped out of their line of sight and stood behind some folded backdrops, waiting for the end of a brief intermission and trying not to think.

'Great act, Thorny,' a costumer said mechanically, and clapped his shoulder in passing.

He suppressed an impulse to kick the costumer. He got out a copy of the script and pretended to read his lines. A hand tugged at his sleeve.

'Jade!' He looked at her bleakly, started to apologize.

'Don't,' she said. 'We've talked it over. Rick, you tell him.'

Rick Thomas who stood beside her grinned ruefully and waggled his head. 'It's not altogether your fault, Thorny. Or haven't you noticed?'

'What do you mean?' he asked suspiciously.

'Take scene five, for example,' Jade put in. 'Suppose the cast had been entirely human. How would you feel about what happened?'

He closed his eyes for a moment and relived it. 'I'd probably be sore,' he said slowly. 'I'd probably accuse Kovrin of jamming my lines and Aksinya of killing my exit—as an excuse,' he added with a lame grin. 'But I can't accuse the dolls. They can't steal.'

'As a matter of fact, old man, they *can,*' said the technician. 'And your excuse is exactly right.'

'Whh—what?'

'Sure. You *did* muff the first scene or two. The audience reacted to it. And the Maestro reacts to audience-reaction—by compensating through shifts in interpretation. It sees the stage as a whole, you included. As far as the Maestro's concerned, you're an untaped dud—like the Peltier doll we used in the first run-through. It sends you only the script-tape signals, uninterpreted. Because it's got no analogue tape on you. Now without an audience, that'd be O.K. But with an audience reaction to go by, it starts compensating, and since it can't compenstate through *you,* it works on the others.'

'I don't understand.'

'Bluntly, Thorny, the first scene or two stunk. The audience didn't like you. The Maestro started compensating by emphasizing other roles—and recharacterizing *you,* through the others.'

'Recharacterize? How can it do that?'

'Easily, darling,' Jade told him. 'When Marka says "I hate him; he's a beast"—for example—she can say it like it's true, or she can say it like she's just temporarily furious with Andreyev. And it affects the light in which the audience see you. Other actors affect *your* role. You know that's true of the old stage. Well, it's true of autodrama, too.'

He stared at them in amazement. 'Can't you stop it? Readjust the Maestro, I mean?'

'Not without clearing the whole thing out of the machine and starting over. The effect is cumulative. The more it compensates, the tougher it gets for you. The tougher it gets for you, the worse you look to the crowd. And the worse you look to the crowd, the more it tries to compensate.'

He stared wildly at the clock. Less than a minute until the first scene of Act II. 'What'll I do?'

'Stick it,' said Jade. 'We've been on the phone to Smithfield. There's a programming engineer in town, and he's on his way over in a heliocab. Then we'll see.'

'We may be able to nurse it back in tune,' Rick added, 'a little at a time—by feeding in a fake set of audience-restlessness factors, and cutting out its feeler circuits out in the crowd. We'll try, that's all.'

The light flashed for the beginning of the act.

'Good luck, Thorny.'

'I guess I'll need it.' Grimly he started toward his entrance.

The thing in the booth was watching him. It watched and measured and judged and found wanting. *Maybe,* he thought wildly, *it even hated him*. It watched, it planned, it regulated, and it was wrecking him.

The faces of the dolls, the hands, the voices—belonged to *it*. The wizard circuitry in the booth rallied them against him. It saw him, undoubtedly, as one of them, but not answering to its pulsing commands. It saw him, perhaps, as a malfunctioning doll, and it tried to correct the effects of his misbehavior. He thought of the old conflict between director and darfsteller, the self-directed actor—and it was the same conflict, aggravated by an electronic director's inability to understand that such things could be. The darfsteller, the undirectable portrayer whose acting welled from unconscious sources with no external strings—directors were inclined to hate them, even when the portrayal was superb. A mannequin, however, was the perfect schauspieler, the actor that a director could play like an instrument.

It would have been easier for him now had he been a schauspieler, for perhaps he could adapt. But he was Andreyev, *his* Andreyev, as he had prepared himself for the role. Andreyev was incarnate as an *alter anima* within him. He had never 'played' a role. He had always become the role. And now he could adapt to the needs of the moment on stage only as Andreyev, in and through his identity with Andreyev, and without changing the feel of his portrayal. To attempt it, to try to fall into conformity with what the Maestro was doing, would mean utter confusion. Yet, the machine was forcing him —through the others.

He stood stonily behind his desk, listening coldly to the denials of the prisoner—a revolutionary, an arsonist associated with Piotr's guerrilla band.

'I tell you, comrade, I had nothing to do with it!' the prisoner shouted. *'Nothing!'*

'Haven't you questioned him thoroughly?' Andreyev growled at the lieutenant who guarded the man. 'Hasn't he signed a confession?'

'There was no need, comrade. His accomplice confessed,' protested the lieutenant.

Only it wasn't supposed to be a protest. The lieutenant made it sound like a monstrous thing to do—to wring another confession, by torture perhaps, from the prisoner, when there was already sufficient evidence to convict. The words were right, but their meaning was wrenched. It should have been a crisp statement of fact: No need, comrade; his accomplice confessed.

Thorny paused, reddening angrily. His next line was, 'See that this one confesses, too.' But he wasn't going to speak it. It would augment the effect of the lieutenant's tone of shocked protest. He thought rapidly. The lieutenant was a bit-player, and didn't come back on until the third act. It wouldn't hurt to jam him.

He glowered at the doll, demanded icily: 'And what have you done with the accomplice?'

The Maestro could not invent lines, nor comprehend an ad lib. The Maestro could only interpret a deviation as a malfunction, and try to compensate. The Maestro backed up a line, had the lieutenant repeat his cue.

'I told you—he *confessed.*'

'So!' roared Andreyev. 'You killed him, eh? Couldn't survive the questioning, eh? And you killed him.'

'Thorny, what are you doing?' came Rick's frantic whisper in his earplug.

'He confessed,' repeated the lieutenant.

'You're under arrest, Nichol!' Thorny barked. 'Report to Major Malin for discipline. Return the prisoner to his cell.' He paused. The Maestro couldn't go on until he cued it, but now there was no harm in speaking the line. 'Now—see that this one confesses, too.'

'Yes, sir,' the lieutenant replied stonily, and started off-stage with the prisoner.

Thorny took glee in killing his exit by calling after him: 'And see that he lives through it!'

The Maestro marched them out without looking back, and Thorny was briefly pleased with himself. He caught a glimpse of Jade with her hands clasped over her head, giving him a 'the-winnah' signal from concealment. But he couldn't keep ad libbing his way out of it every time.

Most of all, he dreaded the entrance of Marka, Mela's doll. The Maestro was playing her up, ennobling her, subtly justifying her treachery, at the expense of Andreyev's character. He didn't want to fight back. Marka's role was too important for tampering, and besides it would be like slapping at Mela to confuse the performance of her doll.

The curtain dipped. The furniture revolved. The stage became a living room. And the curtain rose again.

He barked: 'No more arrests; after curfew, shoot on sight!' at the telephone, and hung up.

When he turned, she stood in the doorway, listening. She shrugged and entered with a casual walk while he watched her in suspicious silence. It was the consummation of her treachery. She had come back to him, but as a spy for Piotr. He suspected her only of infidelity and not of treason. It was a crucial scene, and the Maestro could play her either as a treacherous wench, or a reluctant traitor with Andreyev seeming a brute. He watched her warily.

'Well—hello,' she said petulantly, after walking around the room.

He grunted coldly. She stayed flippant and aloof. So far, it was as it should be. But the vicious argument was yet to come.

She went to a mirror and began straightening her wind-blown hair. She spoke nervously, compulsively, rattling about trivia, concealing her anxiety in his presence after her betrayal. She looked furtive, haggard, somehow more like the real Mela of today; the Maestro's control of expression was masterful.

'What are you doing here?' he exploded suddenly, interrupting her disjointed spiel.

'I still live here, don't I?'

'You got out.'

'Only because you ordered me out.'

'You made it clear you wanted to leave.'

'Liar!'

'Cheat!'

It went on that way for a while; then he began dumping the contents of several drawers into a suitcase.

'I live here, and I'm staying,' she raged.

'Suit yourself, comrade.'

'What're you doing?'

'Moving out, of course.'

The battle continued. Still there was no attempt by the Maestro to revise the scene. Had the trouble been corrected? Had his exchange with the lieutenant somehow affected the machine? Something was different. It was becoming a good scene, his best so far.

She was still raving at him when he started for the door. She stopped in mid-sentence, breathless—then shrieked his name and flung herself down on the sofa, sobbing violently. He stopped. He turned and stood with his fists on his hips staring at her. Gradually, he melted. He put the suitcase down and walked back to stand over her, still gruff and glowering.

Her sobbing subsided. She peered up at him, saw his inability to escape, began to smile. She came up slowly, arms sliding around his neck.

'Sasha . . . oh, my Sasha—'

The arms were warm, the lips moist, the woman alive in his embrace. For a moment he doubted his senses. She giggled at him and whispered, 'You'll break a rib.'

'Mela—'

'Let go, you fool—the scene!' Then, aloud: 'Can I stay, darling?'

'Always,' he said hoarsely.

'And you won't be jealous again?'

'Never.'

'Or question me every time I'm gone an hour or two?'

'Or sixteen. It *was* sixteen hours.'

'I'm sorry.' She kissed him. The music rose. The scene ended.

'How did you swing it?' he whispered in the clinch. 'And why?'

'They asked me to. Because of the Maestro.' She giggled. 'You looked devastated. Hey, you can let go now. The curtain's down.'

The mobile furniture had begun to rearrange itself. They scurried offstage, side-stepping a couch as it rolled past. Jade was waiting for them.

'Great!' she whispered, taking their hands. 'That was just great.'

'Thanks . . . thanks for sliding me in,' Mela answered.

'Take it from here out, Mela—the scenes with Thorny, at least.'

'I don't know,' she muttered. 'It's been so long. Anybody could have ad libbed through that fight scene.'

'You can do it. Rick'll keep you cued and prompted. The engineer's here, and they're fussing around with the Maestro. But it'll straighten *itself* out, if you give it a couple more scenes like that to watch.'

The second act had been rescued. The supporting cast was still a hazard, and the Maestro still tried to compensate according to audience reaction during Act I, but with a human Marka, the compensatory attempts had less effect, and the interpretive distortions seemed to diminish slightly. The Maestro was piling up new data as the play continued, and reinterpreting.

'It wasn't great,' he sighed as they stretched out to relax between acts. 'But it was passable.'

'Act Three'll be better, Thorny,' Mela promised. 'We'll rescue it yet. It's just too bad about the first act.'

'I wanted it to be tops,' he breathed. 'I wanted to give them something to think about, something to remember. But now we're fighting to rescue it from being a total flop.'

'Wasn't it always like that? You get steamed up to make history, but then you wind up working like crazy just to keep it passable.'

'Or to keep from ducking flying groceries sometimes.'

She giggled. 'Jiggie used to say, "I went on like the main dish and came off like the toss salad."' She paused, then added moodily: 'The *tough* part of it is—you've *got* to aim high just to hit anywhere at all. It can get to be heartbreaking, too—trying for the sublime every time, and just escaping the ridiculous, or the mediocre.'

'No matter how high you aim, you can't hit escape velocity. Ambition is a trajectory with its impact point in oblivion, no matter how high the throw.'

'Sounds like a quote.'

'It is. From the Satyricon of an ex-Janitor.'

'Thorny—?'

'What?'

'I'm going to be sorry tomorrow—but I *am* enjoying it tonight

—going through it all again I mean. Living it like a pipe dream. It's no good though. It's opium.'

He stared at her for a moment in surprise, said nothing. Maybe it was opium for Mela, but she hadn't started out with a crazy hope that tonight would be the climax and the highpoint of a lifetime on the stage. She was filling in to save the show, and it meant nothing to her in terms of a career she had deliberately abandoned. He, however, had hoped for a great portrayal. It *wasn't* great, though. If he worked hard at Act III, it might—as a whole—stand up to his performances of the past. Unless—

'Think anybody in the audience has guessed yet? About us, I mean?'

She shook her head. 'Haven't seen any signs of it,' she murmured drowsily. 'People see what they expect to see. But it'll leak out tomorrow.'

'Why?'

'Your scene with the lieutenant. When you ad libbed out of a jam. There's bound to be a drama critic or maybe a professor out there who read the play ahead of time, and started frowning when you pulled that off. He'll go home and look up his copy of the script just to make sure, and then the cat's out.'

'It won't matter by then.'

'No.'

She wanted a nap or a drowse, and he fell silent. As he watched her relax, some of his bitter disappointment slipped away. It was good just to be acting again, even for one opiate evening. And maybe it was best that he wasn't getting what he wanted. He was even ready to admit to a certain insanity in setting out on such a course.

Perfection and immolation. Now that the perfection wasn't possible, the whole scheme looked like a sick fanatic's nightmare, and he was ashamed. Why had he done it—given in to what had always been only a petulant fantasy, a childish dream? The wish, plus the opportunity, plus the impulse, in a framework of bitterness and in a time of personal transition—it had been enough to bring the crazy yearning out of its cortical wrinkle and start him acting on a dream. A child's dream.

And then the momentum had carried him along. The juggled tapes, the loaded gun, the dirty trick on Jade—and now fighting to keep the show from dying. He had gone down to the river and climbed up on the bridge rail and looked down at the black and swirling tide—and finally climbed down again because the wind would spoil his swan dive.

He shivered. It scared him a little, to know he could lose himself so easily. What had the years done to him, or what had he done to himself?

He had kept his integrity maybe, but what good was integrity in a vacuum? He had the soul of an actor, and he'd hung onto it when the others were selling theirs, but the years had wiped out the market and he was stuck with it. He had stood firm on principle, and the years had melted the cold glacier of reality from under the principle; still, he stood on it, while the reality ran on down to the sea. He had dedicated himself to the living stage, and carefully tended its grave, awaiting the resurrection.

Old ham, he thought, you've been flickering into mad warps and staggering into dimensions of infrasanity. You took unreality by the hand and led her gallantly through peril and confusion and finally married her before you noticed that she was dead. Now the only decent thing to do was bury her, but her interment would do nothing to get him back through the peril and confusion and on the road again. He'd have to hike. Maybe it was too late to do anything with the rest of a lifetime. But there was only one way to find out. And the first step was to put some mileage between himself and the stage.

If a little black box took over my job, Rich had said, I'd go to work making little black boxes.

Thorny realized with a slight start that the technician had meant it. Mela had done it, in a sense. So had Jade. Especially Jade. But that wasn't the answer for him, not now. He'd hung around too long mourning the dead, and he needed a clean, sharp break. Tomorrow he'd fade out of sight, move away, pretend he was twenty-one again, and start groping for something to do with a lifetime. How to keep eating until he found it—that would be the pressing problem. Unskilled laborers were hard to find these days, but so were unskilled jobs. Selling his acting talent for commercial purposes would work only if he could find a commercial purpose he could believe in and live for, since his talent was not the surface talent of a schauspieler. It would be a grueling search, for he had never bothered to believe in anything but theater.

Mela stirred suddenly. 'Did I hear somebody call me?' she muttered. 'This racket—!' She sat up to look around.

He grunted doubtfully. 'How long till curtain?' he asked.

She arose suddenly and said, 'Jade's waving me over. See you in the act, Thorny.'

He watched Mela hurry away, he glanced across the floor at

Jade who waited for her in the midst of a small conference, he felt a guilty twinge. He'd cost them money, trouble, and nervous sweat, and maybe the performance endangered the run of the show. It was a rotten thing to do, and he was sorry, but it couldn't be undone, and the only possible compensation was to deliver a best-possible Act III and then get out. Fast. Before Jade found him out and organized a lynch mob.

After staring absently at the small conference for a few moments, he closed his eyes and drowsed again.

Suddenly he opened them. Something about the conference group—something peculiar. He sat up and frowned at them again. Jade, Mela, Rick, and Feria, and three strangers. Nothing peculiar about that. Except . . . let's see . . . the thin one with the scholarly look—that would be the programming engineer, probably. The beefy, healthy fellow with the dark business suit and the wandering glance—Thorny couldn't place him—he looked out of place backstage. The third one seemed familiar somehow, but he, too, looked out of place—a chubby little man with no necktie and a fat cigar, he seemed more interested in the backstage rush than in the proceedings of the group. The beefy gent kept asking him questions, and he muttered brief answers around his cigar while watching the stagehands' parade.

Once when answering he took his cigar out of his mouth and glanced quickly across the floor in Thorny's direction. Thorny stiffened, felt bristles rise along his spine. The chubby little gent was—

—The depot clerk!

Who had issued him the extra tape and the splices. Who could put the finger on the trouble right away, and was undoubtedly doing it.

Got to get out. Got to get out fast. The beefy fellow was either a cop or a private investigator, one of several hired by Smithfield. Got to run, got to hide, got to—Lynch mob.

'Not through that door, buddy, that's the stage; what're you—Oh, Thorny! It's not time to go on.'

'Sorry,' he grunted at the prop man and turned away.

The light flashed, the buzzer sounded faintly.

'Now it's time,' the prop man called after him.

Where was he going? And what good would it do?

'Hey, Thorny! The buzzer. Come back. It's line-up. You're on when the curtain lifts . . . *hey!'*

He paused, then turned around and went back. He went

on-stage and took his place. She was already there, staring at him strangely as he approached.

'You didn't do it, did you, Thorny?' she whispered.

He gazed at her in tight-lipped silence, then nodded.

She looked puzzled. She looked at him as if he were no longer a person, but a peculiar object to be studied. Not scornful, nor angry, nor righteous—just puzzled.

'Guess I was nuts,' he said lamely.

'Guess you were.'

'Not too much harm done, though,' he said hopefully.

'The wrong people saw the first act, Thorny. They walked out.'

'Wrong people?'

'Two backers and a critic.'

'Oh?'

He stood stunned. She stopped looking at him then and just stood waiting for the curtain to rise, her face showing nothing but a puzzled sadness. It wasn't her show, and she had nothing in it but a doll that would bring a royalty check or two, and now herself as a temporary substitute for the doll. The sadness was for him. Contempt he could have understood.

The curtain lifted. A sea of dim faces beyond the footlights. And he was Andreyev, chief of a Soviet police garrison, loyalist servant of a dying cause. It was easy to stay in the role this time, to embed his ego firmly in the person of the Russian cop and live a little of the last century. For the ego was more comfortable there than in the skin of Ryan Thornier—a skin that might soon be sent to the tannery, judging the furtive glances that were coming from backstage. It might even be comfortable to remain Andreyev after the performance, but that was a sure way to get Napoleon Bonaparte for a roommate.

There was no change of setting between scenes *i* and *ii,* but only a dip of the curtain to indicate a time-lapse and permit a change of cast. He stayed on-stage, and it gave him a moment to think. The thoughts weren't pleasant.

Backers had walked out. Tomorrow the show would close unless the morning teleprint of the *Times* carried a rave review. Which seemed wildly improbable. Critics were jaded. Jaded tastes were apt to be impatient. They would not be eager to forgive the first act. He had wrecked it, and he couldn't rescue it.

Revenge wasn't sweet. It tasted like rot and a sour stomach.

Give them a good third act. There's nothing more you can do. But even that wouldn't take away the rotten taste.

Why did you do it, Thorny? Rick's voice, whispering from the booth and in his earplug prompter.

He glanced up and saw the technician watching him from the small window of the booth. He spread his hands in a wide shrugging gesture, as if to ask: How can I tell you, what can I do?

Go on with it, what else? Rick whispered, and withdrew from the window.

The incident seemed to confirm that Jade intended for him to finish it, anyhow. She could scarcely intend otherwise. She was in it with him, in a sense. If the audience found out the play had a human stand-in, and if the critics didn't like the show, they might pounce on the producer who 'perpetrated such an impossible substitution'—even harder than they'd pounce on him. She had gambled on him, and in spite of his plot to force her into such a gamble, it was her show, and her responsibility, and she'd catch the brunt of it. Critics, owners, backers, and public—they didn't care about 'blame,' didn't care about excuses or reasons. They cared about the finished product, and if they didn't like it, the responsibility for it was clear.

As for himself? A cop waiting backstage. Why? He hadn't studied the criminal code, but he couldn't think of any neat little felonious label that could be pinned on what he'd done. Fraud? Not without an exchange of money or property, he thought. He'd been after intangibles, and the law was an earthy thing; it became confused when motives carried men beyond assaults on property or person, into assaults on ideas or principles. Then it passed the buck to psychiatry.

Maybe the beefy gent wasn't a cop at all. Maybe he was a collector of maniacs.

Thorny didn't much care. The dream had tumbled down, and he'd just have to let the debris keep falling about him until he got a chance to start climbing out of the wreckage. It was the end of something that should have ended years ago, and he couldn't get out until it finished collapsing.

The curtain lifted. Scene *ii* was good. Not brilliant, but good enough to make them stop snapping their gum and hold them locked in their seats, absorbed in their identity with Andreyev.

Scene *iii* was his Gethsemane—when the mob besieged the public offices while he waited for word of Marka and an answer to his offer of a truce with the guerrilla forces. The answer came in one word.

'Nyet.'

His death sentence. The word that bound him over to the jackals in the streets, the word that cast him to the ravening mob. The mob had a way: the mob was collecting officials and mounting them. He could see their collection from the window, looking across the square, and he discussed it with an aide. Nine men impaled on the steel spikes of the heavy grillwork fence in front of the Regional Soviet offices. The mob seized another specimen with its thousand hands and mounted it carefully. It lifted the specimen into a sitting position over a two-foot spike, then dropped him on it. Two specimens still squirmed.

He'd cheat the mob, of course. There were the barricades in the building below, and there would be plenty of time to meet death privately and chastely before the mob tore its way inside. But he delayed. He waited for word from Marka.

Word came. Two guards burst in.

'She's here, comrade, she's come!'

Come with the enemy, they said. Come betraying him, betraying the state. *Impossible!* But the guard insisted.

Berserk fury, and refusal to believe. With a low snarl, he drew the automatic, shot the bearer of bad tidings through the heart.

With the crash of the gunshot, the mannequin crumpled. The explosion startled a sudden memory out of hiding, and he remembered: the second cartridge in the clip—*not a blank!* He had forgotten to unload the deadly round.

For an instant he debated firing it into the fallen mannequin as a way to get rid of it, then dismissed the notion and obeyed the script. He stared at his victim and wilted, letting the gun slip from his fingers and fall to the floor. He staggered to the window to stare out across the square. He covered his face with his hands, awaited the transition curtain.

The curtain came. He whirled and started for the gun.

No, Thorny, no! came Rick's frantic whisper from the booth. *To the ikon . . . the ikon!*

He stopped in mid-stage. No time to retrieve the gun and unload. The curtain had only dipped and was starting up again. Let Mela get rid of the round, he thought. He crossed to the shrine, tearing open his collar, rumpling his hair. He fell to his knees before the ancient ikon, in dereliction before the God of an older Russia, a Russia that survived as firmly in fierce negation as it had survived in fierce affirmation. The cultural soul was a living thing, and it survived as well in downfall as in victory; it could never be excised, but only eaten away or slowly transmuted by time and gentle pressures of rain wearing the rock.

There was a bust of Lenin beneath the ikon. And there was a bust of Harvey Smithfield beneath the Greek players' masks on the wall of D'Uccia's office. The signs of the times, and the signs of the timeless, and the cultural heartbeat pulsed to the rhythm of centuries. He had resisted the times as they took a sharp turn in direction, but no man could swim long against the tide as it plodded its zigzag course into timelessness. And the sharp deflections in the course were deceptive—for all of them really wound their way downstream. No man ever added his bit to the flow by spending all his effort to resist the current. The tide would tire him and take him into oblivion while the world flowed on.

Marka, Boris, Piotr had entered, and he had turned to stare at them without understanding. The mockery followed and the harsh laughter, as they pushed the once haughty but now broken chieftain about the stage like a dazed animal unable to respond. He rebounded from one to another of them, as they prodded him to dispel the trancelike daze.

'Finish your prayer, comrade,' said Mela, picking up the gun he'd dropped.

As he staggered close to Mela, he found his chance, and whispered quickly: 'The gun, Mela—eject the first cartridge. Eject it, quickly.'

He was certain she heard him, although she showed no reaction—unless the slight flicker of her eyes had been a quick glance at the gun. Had she understood? A moment later, another chance to whisper.

'The next bullet's real. Work the slide. Eject it.'

He stumbled as Piotr pushed him, fell against a heavy couch, slid down, and stared at them. Piotr went to open the window and shout an offer to the mob below. A bull-roar arose from the herd outside. They hauled him to the window as a triumphal display.

'See, comrade?' growled the guerrilla. 'Your faithful congregation awaits you.'

Marka closed the windows. 'I can't stand that sight!' she cried.

'Take him to his people,' the leader ordered.

'No—' Marka brought up the gun, shook her head fiercely. 'I won't let you do that. Not to the mob.'

Piotr growled a curse. 'They'll have him anyway. They'll be coming up here to search.'

Thorny stared at the actress with a puzzled frown. Still she hadn't ejected the cartridge. And the moment was approaching—a quick bullet to keep him from the mob, a bit of hot mercy flung hastily to him by the woman who had enthralled him and used him and betrayed him.

She turned toward him with the gun, and he began to back away.

'All right, Piotr—if they'll get him anyway—'

She moved a few steps toward him as he backed to a corner. *The live round, Mela, eject it!*

Then her foot brushed a copper bus-lug, and he saw the faint little jet of sparks. Eyes of glass, flesh of airfoam plastic, nerves of twitching electron streams.

Mela was gone. This was her doll. Maybe the real Mela couldn't stomach it after she'd found what he'd done, or maybe Jade had called her off after the first scene of the third act. A plastic hand held the gun, and a tiny flexible solenoid awaited the pulse that would tighten the finger on the trigger. Terror lanced through him.

Cue, Thorny, *cue!* whispered his earplug.

The doll had to wait for his protest before it could fire. It had to be cued. His eyes danced about the stage, looking for a way out. Only an instant to decide.

He could walk over and take the gun out of the doll's hand without giving it a cue—betraying himself to the audience and wrecking the final moment of the show.

He could run for it, cue her, and hope she missed, falling after the shot. But he'd fall on the lugs that way, and come up shrieking.

For God's sake, Thorny! Rick was howling. *The cue, the cue!*

He stared at the gun and swayed slightly from side to side. The gun swayed with him—slightly out of phase. A second's delay, no more—

'Please, Marka—' he called, swaying faster.

The finger tensed on the trigger. The gun moved in a search pattern, as he shifted to and fro. It was risky. It had to be precisely timed. It was like dancing with a cobra. He wanted to flee.

You faked the tape, you botched the show, you came out second best to a system you hated, he reminded himself. *And you even loaded the gun. Now if you can't risk it—*

He gritted his teeth, kept up the irregular weaving motion, then—

'Please, Marka . . . no, no, *nooo!*'

A spiked fist hit him somewhere around the belt, spun him around, and dropped him. The sharp cough of the gun was only a part of the blow. Then he was lying crumpled on his side in the chalked safety area, bleeding and cursing softly. The scene continued. He started to cry out, but checked the shout in his throat. Through a haze, he watched the others move on toward the finale, saw the dim sea of faces beyond the lights. Bullet punched through his side somewhere.

Got to stop squirming. Can't have a dead Andreyev floundering about like a speared fish on the stage. Wait a minute—just another minute—hang on.

But he couldn't. He clutched at his side and felt for the wound. Hard to feel through all the stickiness. He wanted to tear his clothes free to get at it and stop the bleeding, but that was no good either. They'd accept a mannequin fumbling slightly in a death agony, but the blood wouldn't go over so well. Mannequins didn't bleed. Didn't they see it anyway? They had to see it. Clever gimmick, they'd think. Tube of red ink, maybe. Realism is the milieu of—

He twisted his hand in his belt, drew it up strangle-tight around his waist. The pain got worse for a moment, but it seemed to slow the flow of blood. He hung onto it, gritting his teeth, waiting.

He knew about where it hit him, but it was harder to tell where it had come out. And what it had taken with it on the way. Thank God for the bleeding. Maybe he wasn't doing much of it inside.

He tried to focus on the rest of the stage. Music was rising somewhere. Had they all walked off and left him? But no—there was Piotr, through the haze. Piotr approached his chair of office —heavy, ornate, antique. Once it had belonged to a noble of the czar. Piotr, perfectly cold young machine, in his triumph —inspecting the chair.

A low shriek came from backstage somewhere. Mela. Couldn't she keep her mouth shut for half a minute? Probably spotted the blood. Maybe the music drowned the squeal.

Piotr mounted the single step and turned. He sat down gingerly in the chair of empire, testing it, and smiling victory. He seemed to find the chair comfortable.

'I must keep this, Marka,' he said.

Thorny wheezed a low curse at him. He'd keep it all right, until the times went around another twist in the long old river. And welcome to it—judging by the thundering applause.

And the curtain fell slowly to cover the window of the stage.

Feet trouped past him, and he croaked 'Help!' a couple of times, but the feet kept going. The mannequins, marching off to their packing cases.

He got to his feet alone, and went black. But when the blackness dissolved, he was still standing there, so he staggered toward the exit. They were rushing toward him—Mela and Rick and a couple of the crew. Hands grabbed for him, but he fought them off.

'I'll walk by myself now!' he growled.

But the hands took him anyway. He saw Jade and the beefy gent, tried to lurch toward them and explain everything, but she went even whiter and backed away. *I must look a bloody mess,* he thought.

'I was trying to duck. I didn't want to—'

'Save your breath,' Rick told him. 'I saw you. Just hang on.'

They got him onto a doll packing case, and he heard somebody yelling for a doctor from the departing audience, and then a lot of hands started scraping at his side and tugging at him.

'Mela—'

'Right here, Thorny. I'm here.'

And after a while she was still there, but sunlight was spilling across the bed, and he smelled faint hospital odors. He blinked at her for several seconds before he found a voice.

'The show?' he croaked.

'They panned it,' she said softly.

He closed his eyes again and groaned.

'But it'll make dough.'

He blinked at her and gaped.

'Publicity. Terrific. Shall I read you the reviews?'

He nodded, and she reached for the papers. All about the madman who bled all over the stage. He stopped her halfway through the first article. It was enough. The audience had begun to catch on toward the last lines of the play, and the paging of a surgeon had confirmed the suspicion.

'You missed the bedlam backstage,' she told him. 'It was quite a mess.'

'But the show won't close?'

'How can it? With all the morbidity for pulling power. If it closes, it'll be with the Peltier performance to blame.'

'And Jade—?'

'Sore. Plenty sore. Can you blame her?'

He shook his head. 'I didn't want to hurt anybody. I'm sorry.'

She watched him in silence for a moment, then: 'You can't flounder around like you've been doing, Thorny, without somebody getting hurt, without somebody hating your guts, getting trampled on. You just can't.'

It was true. When you hung onto a piece of the past, and just hung onto it quietly, you only hurt yourself. But when you started trying to bludgeon a place for it in the present, you began knocking over the bystanders.

'Theater's dead, Thorny. Can't you believe that now?'

He thought about it a little, and shook his head. It wasn't dead. Only the form was changed, and maybe not permanently at that. He'd thought of it first last night, before the ikon. There were things of the times, and a few things that were timeless. The times came as a result of a particular human culture. The timeless came as a result of any human culture at all. And Cultural Man was a showman. He created display windows of culture for an audience of men, and paraded his aspirations and ideals and purposes thereon, and the displays were necessary to the continuity of the culture, to the purposeful orientation of the species.

Beyond one such window, he erected an altar, and placed a priest before it to chant a liturgical description of the heart-reasoning of his times. And beyond another window, he built a stage and set his talking dolls upon it to live a dramaturgical sequence of wishes and woes of his times.

True, the priests would change, the liturgy would change, and the dolls, the dramas, the displays—but the windows would never—no never—be closed as long as Man outlived his members, for only through such windows could transient men see themselves against the background of a broader sweep, see man encompassed by Man. A perspective not possible without the windows.

Dramaturgy. Old as civilized Man. Outlasting forms and techniques and applications. Outlasting even current popular worship of the Great God Mechanism, who was temporarily enshrined while still being popularly misunderstood. Like the

Great God Commerce of an earlier century, and the God Agriculture before him.

Suddenly he laughed aloud. 'If they used human actors today, it would be a pretty moldy display. Not even *true,* considering the times.'

By the time another figure lounged in his doorway, he had begun to feel rather expansive and heroic about it all. When a small cough caused him to glance up, he stared for a moment, grinned broadly, then called: 'Ho, Richard! Come in. Here . . . sit down. Help me decide on a career, eh? Heh heh—' He waved the classified section and chuckled. 'What kind of little black boxes can an old ham—'

He paused. Rick's expression was chilly, and he made no move to enter. After a moment he said: 'I guess there'll always be a sucker to rerun this particular relay race.'

'Race?' Thorny gathered a slow frown.

'Yeah. Last century, it was between a Chinese abacus operator and an IBM machine. They really had a race, you know.'

'Now see here—'

'And the century before that, it was between a long-hand secretary and a typewriting machine.'

'If you came here to—'

'And before that, the hand-weavers against the automatic looms.'

'Nice to have seen you, Richard. On your way out, would you ask the nurse to—'

'Break up the looms, smash the machines, picket the offices with typewriters, keep adding machines out of China! So then what? Try to be a better tool than a tool?'

Thorny rolled his head aside and glowered at the wall. 'All right. I was wrong. What do you want to do? Gloat? Moralize?'

'No. I'm just curious. It keeps happening—a specialist trying to compete with a higher-level specialist's tools. Why?'

'*Higher* level?' Thorny sat up with a snarl, groaned, caught at his side and sank back again, panting.

'Easy, old man,' Rick said quietly. 'Sorry. Higher organizational-level, I meant. Why do you keep on doing it?'

Thorny lay silent for a few moments, then: 'Status jealousy. Even hawks try to drive other hawks out of their hunting grounds. Fight off competition.'

'But you're no hawk. And a machine isn't competition.'

'Cut it out, Rick. What did you come here for?'

Rick glanced at the toe of his shoe, snickered faintly, and came on into the room. 'Thought you might need some help finding a job,' he said. 'When I looked in the door and saw you lying there looking like somebody's King Arthur, I got sore again.' He sat restlessly on the edge of a chair and watched the old man with mingled sadness, irritation, and affection.

'You'd help me . . . find a job?'

'Maybe. A job, not a permanent niche.'

'It's too late to find a permanent niche.'

'It was too late when you were born, old man! There isn't any such thing—hasn't been, for the last century. Whatever you specialize in, another specialty will either gobble you up, or find a way to replace you. If you get what looks like a secure niche, somebody'll come along and wall you up in it and write your epitaph on it. And the more specialized a society gets, the more dangerous it is for the pure specialist. You think an electronic engineer is any safer than an actor? Or a ditch-digger?'

'I don't know. It's not fair. A man's career—'

'You've always got one specialty that's safe.'

'What's that?'

'The specialty of creating new specialties. Continuously. Your own.'

'But that's—' He started to protest, to say that such a concept belonged to the highly trained few, to the technical elite of the era, and that it wasn't specialization, but generalization. But why to the few? The specialty of creating new specialties—

'But that's—'

'More or less a definition of Man, isn't it?' Rick finished for him. 'Now about the job—'

'Yes, about the job—'

So maybe you don't start from the bottom after all, he decided. You start considerably above the lemur, the chimpanzee, the orangutan, the Maestro—if you ever start at all.

THE WILL

The will of a child. A child who played in the sun and ran over the meadow to chase with his dog among the trees beyond the hedge, and knew the fierce passions of childhood. A child whose logic cut corners and sought shortest distances, and found them. A child who made shining life in my house.

Red blood count low, wildly fluctuating . . . Chronic fatigue, loss of weight, general lethargy of function . . . Noticeable pallor and muscular atrophy . . . the first symptoms.

That was eight months ago.

Last summer, the specialists conferred over him. When they had finished, I went to Doc Jules' office—alone, because I was afraid it was going to be bad, and Cleo couldn't take it. He gave it to me straight.

'We can't cure him, Rod. We can only treat symptoms—and hope the research labs come through. I'm sorry.'

'He'll die?'

'Unless the labs get an answer.'

'How long?'

'Months.' He gave it to me bluntly—maybe because he thought I was hard enough to take it, and maybe because he knew I was only Kenny's foster father, as if blood-kinship would have made it any worse.

'Thanks for letting me know,' I said, and got my hat.

I would have to tell Cleo, somehow. It was going to be tough. I left the building and went out to buy a paper. A magazine on the science rack caught my eye. It had an article entitled *Carcino-genesis and Carbon*-14 and there was a mention of leukemia in the blurb. I bought it along with the paper, and went over to the park to read. Anything to keep from carrying the news to Cleo.

The research article made things worse. They were still doing things to rats and cosmic rays, and the word 'cure' wasn't mentioned once. I dropped the magazine on the grass and glanced at the front page. A small headline toward the bottom of the page said: COMMUNITY PRAYS THREE DAYS FOR DYING CHILD. Same old sob-stuff—publicity causes country to focus on some luckless incurable, and deluge the family with sympathy, advice, money, and sincere and ardent pleas for divine intervention.

I wondered if it would be like that for Kenny—and instinctively I shuddered.

I took a train out to the suburbs, picked up the car, and drove home before twilight. I parked in front, because Cleo was out in back, taking down clothes from the line. The blinds were down in the living room, and the lantern-jawed visage of Captain Chronos looked out sternly from the television screen. The captain carried an LTR (local-time-reversal) gun at the ready, and peered warily from side to side through an oval hole in the title film. Kenny's usual early-evening fodder.

'Travel through the centuries with the master of the clock!' the announcer was chanting.

'Hi, kid,' I said to the hunched-up figure who sat before the set, worshiping his hero.

'Sssshhhhhhhh!' He glanced at me irritably, then transferred his individual attention back to the title film.

'Sorry,' I muttered. 'Didn't know you listened to the opening spiel. It's always the same.'

He squirmed, indicating that he wanted me to scram—to leave him to his own devices.

I scrammed to the library, but the excited chant of the audio was still with me. '. . . *Captain Chronos, Custodian of Time, Defender of the Temporal Passes, Champion of the Temporal Guard. Fly with Captain Chronos in his time-ship* Century *as he battles against those evil forces who would—*'

I shut the door for a little quiet, then went to the encyclopedia shelf and took down 'LAC-MOE.' An envelope fell out of the heavy volume, and I picked it up. Kenny's. He had scrawled 'Lebanon, do not open until 1964; value in 1954: 38¢,' on the face. I knew what was inside without holding it up to the light: stamps. Kenny's idea of buried treasure; when he had more than one stamp of an issue in his collection, he'd stash the duplicate away somewhere to let it age, having heard that age increases their value.

When I finished reading the brief article, I went out to the kitchen. Cleo was bringing in a basket of clothes. She paused in the doorway, the basket cocked on her hip, hair disheveled, looking pretty but anxious.

'Did you see him?' she asked.

I nodded, unable to look at her, poured myself a drink. She waited a few seconds for me to say something. When I couldn't say anything, she dropped the basket of clothes, scattering underwear and linens across the kitchen floor, and darted across the room to seize my arms and stare up at me wildly.

'Rod! It *isn't—*'

But it was. Without stopping to think, she rushed to the living room, seized Kenny in her arms, began sobbing, then fled upstairs when she realized what she was doing.

Kenny knew he was sick. He knew several specialists had studied his case. He knew that I had gone down to talk with Doc Jules this afternoon. After Cleo's reaction, there was no keeping the truth from him. He was only fourteen, but within two weeks, he knew he had less than a year to live, unless they found a cure. He pieced it together for himself from conversational fragments, and chance remarks, and medical encyclopedias, and by deftly questioning a playmate's older brother who was a medical student.

Maybe it was easier on Kenny to know he was dying, easier than seeing our anxiety and being frightened by it without knowing the cause. But a child is blunt in his questioning, and tactless in matters that concern himself, and that made it hell on Cleo.

'If they don't find a cure, when will I die?'

'Will it hurt?'

'What will you do with my things?'

'Will I see my real father afterwards?'

Cleo stood so much of it, and then one night she broke down and we had to call a doctor to give her a sedative and quiet her down. When she was settled, I took Kenny out behind the house. We walked across the narrow strip of pasture and sat on the old stone fence to talk by the light of the moon. I told him not to talk about it again to Cleo, unless she brought it up, and that he was to bring his questions to me. I put my arm around him, and I knew he was crying inside.

'I don't want to die.'

There is a difference between tragedy and blind brutal calamity. Tragedy has meaning, and there is dignity in it. Tragedy stands with its shoulders stiff and proud. But there is no meaning, no dignity, no fulfillment, in the death of a child.

'Kenny, I want you to try to have faith. The research institutes are working hard. I want you to try to have faith that they'll find a cure.'

'Mack says it won't be for years and years.'

Mack was the medical student. I resolved to call him tomorrow. But his mistake was innocent; he didn't know what was the matter with Kenny.

'Mack doesn't know. He's just a kid himself. Nobody knows—except that they'll find it sometime. Nobody knows when. It might be next week.'

'I wish I had a time-ship like Captain Chronos.'

'Why?'

He looked at me earnestly in the moonlight. 'Because then I could go to some year when they knew how to cure me.'

'I wish it were possible.'

'I'll bet it is. I'll bet someday they can do that too. Maybe the government's working on it now.'

I told him I'd heard nothing of such a project.

'Then they ought to be. Think of the advantages. If you wanted to know something that nobody knew, you could just go to some year when it had already been discovered.'

I told him that it wouldn't work, because then everybody would try it, and nobody would work on new discoveries, and none would be made.

'Besides, Kenny, nobody can even prove time-travel is possible.'

'Scientists can do anything.'

'Only things that are possible, Kenny. And only with money, and time, and work—and a reason.'

'Would it cost a lot to research for a time-ship, Dad?'

'Quite a lot, I imagine, if you could find somebody to do it.'

'As much as the atom-bomb?'

'Maybe.'

'I bet you could borrow it from banks . . . if somebody could prove it's possible.'

'You'd need a lot of money of your own, kid, before the banks would help.'

'I bet my stamp collection will be worth a lot of money someday. And my autograph book.' The conversation had wandered off into fantasy.

'In time, maybe in time. A century maybe. But banks won't wait that long.'

He stared at me peculiarly. 'But Dad, don't you see? *What difference does time make,* if you're working on a time-machine?'

That one stopped me. 'Try to have faith in the medical labs, Kenny,' was all I could find to say.

Kenny built a time-ship in the fork of a big maple. He made it from a packing crate, reinforced with plywood, decorated with mysterious coils of copper wire. He filled it with battered clocks and junkyard instruments. He mounted two seats in it, and dual controls. He made a fish-bowl canopy over a hole in the top, and nailed a galvanized bucket on the nose. Broomstick guns protruded from its narrow weapon ports. He painted it silvery gray, and decorated the bucket-nose with the insignia of Captain Chronos and the Guardsmen of Time. He nailed steps on the trunk of the maple; and when he wasn't in the house, he could usually be found in the maple, piloting the time-ship through imaginary centuries. He took a picture of it with a box camera, and sent a print of it to Captain Chronos with a fan letter.

Then one day he fainted on the ladder, and fell out of the tree.

He wasn't badly hurt, only bruised, but it ended his career as a time-ship pilot. Kenny was losing color and weight, and the lethargy was coming steadily over him. His fingertips were covered with tiny stab-marks from the constant blood counts, and the hollow of his arm was marked with transfusion needles. Mostly, he stayed inside.

We haunted the research institutes, and the daily mail was full of answers to our flood of pleading inquiries—all kinds of answers.

'We regret to inform you that recent studies have been . . .'

'Investigations concerning the psychogenic factors show only . . .'

'Prepare to meet God . . .'

'For seventy-five dollars, Guru Tahaj Reshvi guarantees . . .'

'Sickness is only an illusion. Have faith and . . .'

'We cannot promise anything in the near future, but the Institute is rapidly finding new directions for . . .'

'Allow us to extend sympathy . . .'

'The powers of hydromagnetic massage therapy have been established by . . .'

And so it went. We talked to crackpots, confidence men, respectable scientists, fanatics, lunatics, and a few honest fools. Occasionally we tried some harmless technique, with Jules' approval, mostly because it felt like we were doing *something*. But the techniques did more good for Cleo than they did for Kenny, and Kenny's very gradual change for the worse made it apparent that nothing short of the miraculous could save him.

And then Kenny started working on it himself.

The idea, whatever it was, must have hit him suddenly, and it was strange—because it came at a time when both Cleo and I thought that he had completely and fatalistically accepted the coming of the end.

'The labs aren't going to find it in time,' he said. 'I've been reading what they say. I know it's no good, Dad.' He cried some then; it was good that he had relearned to cry.

But the next day, his spirits soared mysteriously to a new high, and he went around the house singing to himself. He was busy with his stamp collection most of the time, but he also wandered about the house and garage searching for odds and ends, his actions seeming purposeful and determined. He moved slowly, and stopped to rest frequently, but he displayed more energy than we had seen for weeks, and even Jules commented on how bright he was looking, when he came for Kenny's daily blood sample. Cleo decided that complete resignation had brought cheerfulness with it, and that acceptance of ill-fate obviated the need to worry or hope. But I wasn't so sure.

'What've you been up to, Kenny?' I asked.

He looked innocent and shook his head.

'Come on, now. You don't go wandering around muttering to yourself unless you're cooking something up. What is it, another time-ship? I heard you hammering in the garage before dinner.'

'I was just knocking the lid off an old breadbox.'

I couldn't get any answer but evasions, innocent glances, and mysterious smirks. I let him keep his secret, thinking that his enthusiasm for whatever it was he was doing would soon wear off.

Then the photographers came.

'We want to take a picture of Kenny's treehouse,' they explained.

'Why?—and how did you know he had one?' I demanded.

It developed that somebody was doing a feature-article on the effects of science-fantasy television shows on children. It developed that the 'somebody' was being hired by a publicity agency which was being hired by the advertisers who presented Captain Chronos and the Guardsmen of Time. It developed that Kenny's fan letter, with the snapshot of his treehouse time-ship, had been forwarded to the publicity department by the producer of the show. They wanted a picture of the time-ship with Kenny inside, looking out through the fish bowl canopy.

'It's impossible,' I told them.

They showed me a dozen pictures of moppets with LTR-guns, moppets in time-warp suits, moppets wearing Captain Chronos costumes, moppets falling free in space, and moppets playing Time-Pirate in the park.

'I'm sorry, but it's impossible,' I insisted.

'We'll be glad to pay something for it, if . . .'

'The kid's sick, if you must know,' I snapped. 'He can't do it, and that's that, so forget about it.'

'Maybe when he's feeling better . . . ?'

'He *won't* be feeling better,' Cleo interrupted, voice tense, with a catch in it. 'Now please *leave!*'

They left, with Cleo herding them out onto the porch. I heard them apologizing, and Cleo softened, and began to explain. That was a mistake.

A week later, while we were still drinking our coffee at the dinner table, the doorbell rang. Cleo, expecting an answer to her recent wire to some South American clinic, left the table, went to answer it, and promptly screamed.

I dropped my cup with a crash and ran to the living room with a butcher knife, then stopped dead still.

It stood there in the doorway with a stunned expression on its face, gaping at Cleo who had collapsed in a chair. It wore a silver uniform with jack-boots, black-and-red cape, and a weird helmet with antennae protruding from it. It had a lantern jaw and a big, meaty, benign contenance.

'I'm awfully sorry,' it boomed in a gentle deep-rich voice. 'We just drove over from the studio, and I didn't take time to change . . .'

'Ulk!' said Cleo.

I heard footsteps at the head of the stairs behind me, then a howl from Kenny who had been getting ready for bed, after being helped upstairs.

'Captain Chronos!'

Bare feet machine-gunned down the stairs and came to a stop at a respectful distance from the idol.

'GgaaaaAA*AWWWSSSShhhh!*' Kenny timidly walked half-way around him, looking him up and down. 'Geee . . . Gaaawwssshh!'

Cleo fanned herself with a newspaper and recovered slowly. I tossed the butcher-knife on a magazine stand and mumbled something apologetic. There were two of them: Chronos and the producer, a small suave man in a business suit. The latter drew me aside to explain. It developed that the photographers had explained to the boss, who had explained to the client, who had mentioned it to the agency, who had returned the fan letter to the producer with a note. It would appear that Captain Chronos, for the sake of nutritious and delicious Fluffy Crunkles, made it his habit to comfort the afflicted, the crippled, and the dying, if it were convenient and seemed somehow advantageous. He also visited the children's wards of hospitals, it seemed.

'This on the level, or for publicity?'

'On the level.'

'Where's the photographer?'

The producer reddened and muttered noncommittally. I went to the door and looked out through the screen. There was another man in their car. When I pushed the screen open, it hit something hard—a tape recorder. I turned:

'Get out.'

'But Mr. Westmore. . . .'

'Get *out*.'

They left quickly. Kenny was furious, and he kept on being furious all through the following day. At me. Cleo began agreeing with him to some extent, and I felt like a heel.

'You want Kenny to get the full treatment?' I grumbled. 'You want him to wind up a sob-story child?'

'Certainly not, but it was cruel, Rod. The boy never had a happier moment until you . . .'

'All right, so I'm a bastard. I'm sorry.'

That night Abe Sanders (Captain Chronos) came back alone, in slacks and a sport shirt, and muttering apologies. It developed that the Wednesday evening shows always had a children's panel (Junior Guardsmen) program, and that while they understood that Kenny couldn't come, they had wanted to have him with the panel, in absentia, by telephone.

'Please, Dad, can't I?'

The answer had to be no . . . but Kenny had been glaring at

me furiously all day, and it was a way to make him stop hating me . . . still, the answer had to be no . . . the publicity . . . but he'd be delighted, and he could stop hating my guts for kicking them out . . .

'I guess so, if the offer's still open.'

'Dad!'

The offer was still open. Kenny was to be on the show. They rehearsed him a little, and let him practice with the tape recorder until he got used to his voice.

On Wednesday evening, Kenny sat in the hall doorway to the living room, telephone in his lap, and stared across at Sanders' face on the television screen. Sanders held another phone, and we heard both their voices from the set. Occasionally the camera dollied in to a close shot of Sanders' chuckle, or panned along the table to show the juvenile panel members, kids between eight and sixteen. There was an empty chair on Sanders' right, and it bore a placard. The placard said 'KENNY WESTMORE.'

It lasted maybe a minute. Sanders promised not to mention Kenny's address, nor to mention the nature of his illness. He did neither, but the tone of conversation made it clear that Kenny was in bad shape and probably not long for this world. Kenny had stage fright, his voice trembled, and he blurted something about the search for a cure. Cleo stared at the boy instead of the set, and my own glance darted back and forth. The cameraman panned to the empty chair and dollied in slowly so that the placard came to fill the screen while Kenny spoke. Kenny talked about stamp collections and time machines and autographs, while an invisible audience gaped at pathos.

'If anybody's got stamps to trade, just let me know,' he said. 'And autographs . . .'

I winced, but Sanders cut in. 'Well, Kenny—we're not supposed to mention your address, but if any of you Guardsmen out there want to help Kenny out with his stamp collection, you can write to me, and I'll definitely see that he gets the letters.'

'And autographs too,' Kenny added.

When it was over, Kenny had lived . . . but *lived.*

And then the mail came in a deluge, forwarded from the network's studio. Bushels of stamps, dozens of autograph books, Bibles, money, advice, crank letters, and maudlin gushes of sugary sympathy . . . and a few sensible and friendly letters. Kenny was delighted.

'Gee, Dad, I'll never get all the stamps sorted out. And look! —an autograph of Calvin Coolidge! . . .'

But it never turned him aside from his path of confident but mysterious purpose. He spent even more time in his room, in the garage, and—when he could muster the energy—back in the maple woods, doing mysterious things alone.

'Have they found a cure yet, Dad?' he asked me pleasantly when an expected letter came.

'They're . . . making progress,' I answered lamely.

He shrugged. 'They will . . . eventually.' Unconcerned.

It occurred to me that some sort of psychic change, unfathomable, might have happened within him—some sudden sense of timelessness, of identity with the race. Something that would let him die calmly as long as he knew there'd be a cure *some*day. It seemed too much to expect of a child, but I mentioned the notion to Jules when I saw him again.

'Could be,' he admitted. 'It might fit in with this secrecy business.'

'How's that?'

'People who know they're dying often behave that way. Little secret activities that don't become apparent until after they're gone. Set up causes that won't have effects until afterwards. Immortality cravings. You want to have posthumous influence, to live after you. A suicide note is one perversion of it. The suicide figures the world will posthumously feel guilty, if he tells it off.'

'And Kenny . . . ?'

'I don't know, Rod. The craving for immortality is basically procreative, I think. You have children, and train them, and see your own mirrored patterns live on in them, and feel satisfied, when your time comes. Or else you sublimate it, and do the same thing for all humanity—through art, or science. I've seen a lot of death, Rod, and I believe there's more than just-plain-selfishness to people's immortality-wishes; it's associated with the human reproductive syndrome—which includes the passing on of culture to the young. But Kenny's just a kid. I don't know.'

Despite Kenny's increasing helplessness and weakness, he began spending more time wandering out in the woods. Cleo chided him for it, and tried to limit his excursions. She drove him to town on alternate days for a transfusion and shots, and she tried to keep him in the house most of the time, but he needed sun and air and exercise, and it was impossible to keep him on the lawn. Whatever he was doing, it was a shadowy secretive business. It involved spades and garden tools and packages, with late excursions into the maples toward the creek.

'You'll know in four or five months,' he told me, in answer to a question. 'Don't ask me now. You'd laugh.'

But it became apparent that he wouldn't last that long. The rate of transfusions doubled, and on his bad days, he was unable to get out of bed. He fainted down by the creek, and had to be carried back to the house. Cleo forbade him to go outside alone without Jules' day-to-day approval, and Jules was beginning to be doubtful about the boy's activities.

When restricted, Kenny became frantic. 'I've got to go outside, Dad, *please!* I can't finish it if I don't. I've got to! How else can I make contact with them?'

'Contact? With whom?'

But he clammed up and refused to discuss anything about the matter. That night I awoke at two a.m. Something had made a sound. I stole out of bed without disturbing Cleo and went to prowl about the house. A glance down the stairway told me that no lights burned on the first floor. I went to Kenny's room and gingerly opened the door. Blackness.

'Kenny—?'

No sound of breathing in the room. Quietly I struck a match.

The bed was empty.

'Kenny!' I bellowed it down the hall, and then I heard sounds —Cleo stirring to wakefulness and groping for clothes in our bedroom. I trotted downstairs and turned on lights as I charged from room to room.

He was not in the house. I found the back screen unlatched and went out to play a flashlight slowly over the backyard. There . . . by the hedge . . . caught in the cone of light . . . Kenny, crumpled over a garden spade.

Upstairs, Cleo screamed through the back window. I ran out to gather him up in my arms. Skin clammy, breathing shallow, pulse irregular—he muttered peculiarly as I carried him back to the house.

'Glad you found it . . . knew you'd find it . . . got me to the right time . . . when are we . . . ?'

I got him inside and up to his room. When I laid him on the bed, a crudely drawn map, like a treasure map with an 'X' and a set of bearings, fell from his pocket. I paused a moment to study it. The 'X' was down by the fork in the creek. What had been buried there?

I heard Cleo coming up the stairs with a glass of hot milk, and I returned the map to Kenny's pocket and went to call the doctor.

When Kenny awoke, he looked around the room very carefully—and seemed disappointed by what he saw.

'Expecting to wake up somewhere else?' I asked.

'I guess it was a dream,' he mumbled. 'I thought they came early.'

'Who came early?'

But he clammed up again. 'You'll find out in about four months,' was all he'd say.

He wouldn't last that long. The next day, Doc Jules ordered him to stay inside, preferably sitting or lying down most of the time. We were to carry him outside once a day for a little sun, but he had to sit in a lawn chair and not run around. Transfusions became more frequent, and finally there was talk of moving him to the hospital.

'I won't go to the hospital.'

'You'll have to, Kenny. I'm sorry.'

That night, Kenny slipped outside again. He had been lying quietly all day, sleeping most of the time, as if saving up energy for a last spurt.

Shortly after midnight, I awoke to hear him tiptoe down the hall. I let him get downstairs and into the kitchen before I stole out of bed and went to the head of the stairs.

'Kenny!' I shouted. 'Come back up here! Right now!'

There was a brief silence. Then he bolted. The screen door slammed, and bare feet trotted down the back steps.

'Kenny!'

Brush whipped as he dove through the hedge. Cleo came to the window beside me, and began calling after him.

Swearing softly, I tugged my trousers over my pajamas, slipped into shoes, and hurried downstairs to give chase. But he had taken my flashlight.

Outside, beneath a dim, cloud-threatened moon, I stood at the hedge, staring out across the meadow toward the woods. The night was full of crickets and rustlings in the grass. I saw no sign of him.

'Kenny!'

He answered me faintly from the distance. 'Don't try to follow me, Dad. I'm going where they can cure me.'

I vaulted the fence and trotted across the meadow toward the woods. At the stone fence, I paused to listen—but there were only crickets. Maybe he'd seen me coming in the moonlight, and had headed back toward the creek.

The brush was thick in places, and without a light, it was hard to find the paths. I tried watching for the gleam of the flashlight through the trees, but saw nothing. He was keeping its use to a minimum. After ten minutes of wandering, I found myself back at the fence, having taken a wrong turning somewhere. I heard Cleo calling me from the house.

'Go call the police! They'll help find him!' I shouted to her.

Then I went to resume the search. Remembering the map, and the 'X' by the fork in the creek, I trotted along the edge of the pasture next to the woods until I came to a dry wash that I knew led back to the creek. It was the long way around, but it was easy to follow the wash; and after a few minutes I stumbled onto the bank of the narrow stream. Then I waded upstream toward the fork. After twenty yards, I saw the flashlight's gleam—and heard the crunch of the shovel in moist ground. I moved as quietly as I could. The crunching stopped.

Then I saw him. He had dropped the shovel and was tugging something out of the hole. I let him get it out before I called . . .

'Kenny . . .'

He froze, then came up very slowly to a crouch, ready to flee. He turned out the flashlight.

'Kenny, don't run away from me again. Stay there. I'm not angry.'

No answer.

'Kenny!'

He called back then, with a quaver in his voice. 'Stay where you are, Dad—and let me finish. Then I'll go with you. If you come any closer, I'll run.' He flashed the light toward me, saw that I was a good twenty yards away. 'Stay there now . . .'

'Then will you come back to the house?'

'I won't run, if you stay right there.'

'Okay,' I agreed, 'but don't take long. Cleo's frantic.'

He set the light on a rock, kept it aimed at me, and worked by its aura. The light blinded me, and I could only guess what he might be doing. He pried something open, and then there was the sound of writing on tin. Then he hammered something closed, replaced it in the hole, and began shoveling dirt over it. Five minutes later, he was finished.

The light went out.

'Kenny . . . ?'

'I'm sorry, Dad. I didn't *want* to lie . . . I *had* to.'

I heard him slipping quickly away through the brush—back toward the pasture. I hurried to the fork and climbed up out of the knee-deep water, pausing to strike a match. Something gleamed in the grass; I picked it up. Cleo's kitchen clock, always a few minutes slow. What had he wanted with the clock?

By the time I tore through the brush and found the path, there was no sound to indicate which way he had gone. I walked gloomily back toward the house, half-heartedly calling to Kenny . . . then . . . a flash of light in the trees!

BRRUUMMKP!

A sharp report, like a close crash of thunder! It came from the direction of the meadow, or the house. I trotted ahead, ignoring the sharp whipping of the brush.

'Kenny Vestmore? . . . Kenny . . .'

A strange voice, a foreign voice—calling to Kenny up ahead in the distance. The police, I thought.

Then I came to the stone fence . . . and froze, staring at the thing—or perhaps at the *no*thing—in the meadow.

It was black. It was bigger than a double garage, and round. I stared at it, and realized that it was not an object but an opening.

And someone else was calling to Kenny. A rich, pleasant voice—somehow it reminded me of Doctor Jules, but it had a strong accent, perhaps Austrian or German.

'Come on along here, liddle boy. Ve fix you op.'

Then I saw Kenny, crawling on toward it through the grass.

'Kenny, *don't!*'

He got to his feet and stumbled on into the distorted space. It seemed to squeeze him into a grotesque house-of-mirrors shape; then it spun him inward. Gone.

I was still running toward the black thing when it began to shrink.

'Come along, liddle fellow, come mit oss. Ve fix.'

And then the black thing belched away into nothingness with an explosive blast that knocked me spinning. I must have been out cold for awhile. The sheriff woke me.

Kenny was gone. We never saw him again. Cleo confirmed what I had seen on the meadow, but without a body, Kenny remains listed as missing.

Missing from this century.

I went back to the fork in the creek and dug up the breadbox he had buried. It contained his stamp collection and a packet of famous autographs. There was a letter from Kenny, too, addressed to the future, and it was his will.

> *'Whoever finds this, please sell these things and use the money to pay for a time machine, so you can come and get me, because I'm going to die if you don't . . .'*

I paused to remember . . . *I don't think the bank'd wait a hundred years.*

But Dad, don't you see? What difference does time make, if you're working on a time machine?

There was more to the note, but the gist of it was that Kenny had made an act of faith, faith in tomorrow. He had buried it, and then he had gone back to dig it up and change the rendezvous time from four months away to the night of his disappearance. He knew that he wouldn't have lived that long.

I put it all back in the box, and sealed the box with solder and set it in concrete at the foot of a sixfoot hole. With this manuscript.

(To a reader, yet unborn, who finds this account in a dusty and ancient magazine stack: *dig*. Dig at a point 987 feet southeasterly on a heading of 149° from the northwest corner of the Hayes and Higgins Tract, as recorded in Map Book 6, p.78, Cleve County records. But not unless the world is ready to buy a time machine and come for Kenny, who financed it; come, if you can cure him. He had faith in *you*.)

Kenny is gone, and today there is a feeling of death in my house. But after a century of tomorrows? He invested in them, and he called out to them, pleading with the voice of a child. And tomorrow answered:

'Come, liddle boy. Ve fix.'

VENGEANCE FOR NIKOLAI

The distant thunder of the artillery was only faintly audible in the dugout. The girl sat quietly picking at her hands while the colonel spoke. She was only a slip of a girl, all breast and eyes, but there was an intensity about her that made her unmistakably beautiful, and the colonel kept glancing at her sidelong as if his eyes refused to share the impersonal manner of his speech. The light of a single bare bulb glistened in her dark hair and made dark shadows under deep jade eyes already shadowed by weeping. She was listening intently or not at all. She had just lost her child.

'They will not kill you, *grazhdanka*, if you can get safely past the lines,' said the colonel. He paced slowly in the dugout, his boot heels clicking pleasantly on the concrete while he sucked at a long cigaret holder and milked his thumbs behind his back in solemn thought. 'These Americans, you have heard about their women? No, they will not kill you, unless by accident in passing the lines. They may do other things to you—forgive me!—it is war.' He stopped pacing, straddled her shadow, and looked down at her with paternal pity. 'Come, you have said nothing, nothing at all. I feel like a swine for asking it of you, but there is no other hope of beating back this attack. And I am ordered to ask you. Do you understand?'

She looked up. Light filled her eyes and danced in them with the moist glittering of a fresh grief already an ancient grief old as Man. 'They killed my Nikolai,' she said softly. 'Why do you speak to me so? What can it mean? The bombardment—I know nothing—I cannot think of it. Why do you torment me?'

The colonel betrayed no impatience with her, although he had gone over it twice before. 'This morning you tried to leap off the bridge. It is such a shame to die without purpose, *dushka*. I offer you a purpose. Do you love the Fatherland?'

'I am not a Party member, *Tovarish Polkovnik*.'

'I did not ask if you love the Party, my dear. However, you should say *"parties,"* now that we are tolerating those accursed Menshevist deviationists again. Bah! *They* even name members of the *Gorodskoi* Soviets these days. We are becoming a two party republic. How sickening! Where are the old warrior Bolsheviks? It makes one weep. . . . But that is not the question. I asked if you love the Fatherland.'

She gave a hesitant nod.

'Then think of the Fatherland, think of vengeance for Nikolai. Would you trade your life for that? I know you would. You were ready to fling it away.'

She stirred a little; her mind seemed to re-enter the room. 'This Ami *Gyenyeral*. Why do you wish him dead?'

'He is the genius behind this assault, my child. Who would have thought the Americans would have chosen such an unlikely place for an invasion? And the manner of it! They parachuted an army ninety miles inland, instead of assaulting the fortified coastline: He committed half a million troops to deliberate encirclement. Do you understand what this means? If they had been unable to drive to the coast, they would have been cut off, and the war would very likely be over. With *our* victory. As it was, the coast defenders panicked. The airborne army swept to the sea to capture their beachhead without need of a landing by sea, and now there are two million enemy troops on our soil, and we are in full retreat. *Flight* is a better word. General Rufus MacAmsward gambled his country's entire future on one operation, and he won. If he had lost, they would likely have shot him. Such a man is necessarily mad. A megalomaniac, an evil genius.

'Oh, I admire him very much! He reminds me of one of their earlier generals, thirty years ago. But that was before their Fascism, before their Blue Shirts.'

'And if he is killed?'

The colonel sighed. He seemed to listen for a time to the distant shellfire. 'We are all a little superstitious in wartime,' he said at last. 'Perhaps we attach too much significance to this one man. But they have no other generals like *him*. He will be replaced by a competent man. We would rather fight competent men than fight an unpredictable devil. He keeps his own counsels, that is so. We know he does not rely heavily upon his staff. His will rules the operation. He accepts intelligence but not advice. If he is struck dead—well, we shall see.'

'And I am to kill him. It seems unthinkable. How do you know I can?'

The colonel waved a sheaf of papers. 'Only a woman can get to him. We have his character clearly defined. Here is his psychoanalytic biography. We have photostats of medical records taken from Washington. We have interviews with his ex-wife and his mother. Our psychologists have studied every inch of him. Here, I'll read you—but no, it is very dry, full of psychiatric jargon. I'll boil it down.

'MacAmsward is a champion of the purity of womanhood, and yet he is a vile old lecher. He is at once a baby and an old man. He will kneel and kiss your hand—yes, really. He is a worshipper of womanhood. He will court you, convert you, pay you homage, and then expect you to—forgive me—to take him to bed. He could not possibly make advances on you uninvited, but he expects you—as a goddess rewarding a worshipper—to make advances on *him*. He will be your abject servant, but with courtly dignity. His life is full of breast symbols. He clucks in his sleep. He has visited every volcano in the world. He collects anatomical photographs; his women have all been bosomy brunettes. He is still in what the Freudians call the oral stage of emotional development—emotionally a two-year-old. I know Freud is bad politics, but for the Ami, it is sometimes so.'

The colonel stopped. There was a sudden tremor in the earth. The colonel lurched, lost his balance. The floor heaved him against the wall. The girl sat still, hands in her lap, face very white. The air shock followed the earth shock, but the thunder clap was muted by six feet of concrete and steel. The ceiling leaked dust.

'Tactical A-missile,' the colonel hissed. 'Another of them! If they keep it up, they'll drive us to use Lucifer. This is a mad dog war. Neither side uses the H-bomb, but in the end one side or the other will have to use it. If the Kremlin sees certain defeat, we'll use it. So would Washington. If you're being murdered, you might as well take your killer with you if you can. Bah! It is a madness. I, Porphiry Grigoryevich, am as mad as the rest. Listen to me, Marya Dmitriyevna, I met you an hour ago, and now I am madly in love with you, do you hear? Look at you! Only a day after a bomb fragment dashed the life out of your baby, your bosom still swelled with unclaimed milk and dumb grief, and yet I dare stand here and say I am in love with you, and in another breath ask you to go and kill yourself by killing an Ami general! Ah, ah! What insane apes we are! Forget the Ami general. Let us both desert, let us run away to Africa together, to Africa, where apes are simpler. There! I've made you cry. What a brute is Phorphiry, what a brute!'

The girl breathed in gasps. 'Please, *Tovarish Polkovnik!* Please say nothing more! I will go and do what you ask, if it is possible.'

'I only ask it, *dushka*, I cannot command it. I advise you to refuse.'

'I will go and kill him. Tell me how! There is a plan? There must be a plan. How shall I pass the lines? How shall I get to him? What is the weapon? How can I kill him?'

'The weapon, you mean? The medical officer will explain that. Of course, you'll be too thoroughly searched to get even a stickpin past the lines. They often use fluoroscopy, so you couldn't even swallow a weapon and get it past them. But there's a way, there's a way—I'll let the *vrach* explain it. I can only tell you how to get captured, and how to get taken to MacAmsward after your capture. As for the rest of it, you will be directed by post-hypnotic suggestion. Tell me, you were an officer in the Woman's Defense Corps, the home guard, were you not?'

'Yes, but when Nikki was born, they asked for my resignation.'

'Yes, of course, but the enemy needn't find out you're inactive. You have your uniform still? . . . Good! Wear it. Your former company is in action right now. You will join them briefly.'

'And be captured?'

'Yes. Bring nothing but your ID tags. We shall supply the rest. You will carry in your pocket a certain memorandum addressed to all home guard unit commanders. It is in a code the Ami have already broken. It contains the phrase: "Tactical bacteriological weapons immediately in use." Nothing else of any importance. It is enough. It will drive them frantic. They will question you. Since you know nothing, they can torture nothing out of you.

'In another pocket, you will be carrying a book of love poetry. Tucked in the book will be a photograph of General Rufus MacAmsward, plus two or three religious ikons. Their Intelligence will *certainly* send the memorandum to MacAmsward; both sides are that nervous about germ weapons. It is most probable that they will send him the book and the picture—for reasons both humorous and practical. The rest will take care of itself. MacAmsward is all ego. Do you understand?'

She nodded. Porphiry Grigoryevich reached for the phone.

'Now I am going to call the surgeon,' he said. 'He will give you several injections. Eventually, the injections will be fatal, but for some weeks, you will feel nothing from them. Post-hypnotic urges will direct you. If your plan works, you will not kill MacAmsward in the literal sense. Literally, he will kill himself. If the plan fails, you'll kill him another way if you can. You were an actress, I believe?'

'For a time. I never got to the Bolshoi.'

'But excellent! His mother was an actress. You speak English. You are beautiful, and full of grief. It is enough. You are the one. But do you really love the Fatherland enough to carry it out?'

Her eyes burned. 'I hate the killers of my son!' she whispered.

The colonel cleared his throat. 'Yes, of course. Very well, Marya Dmitriyevna, it is death I am giving you. But you will be sung in our legends for a thousand years. And by the way—' He cocked his head and looked at her oddly. 'I believe I really do love you, *dushka.*'

With that, he picked up the phone.

Strange exhilaration surged within her as she crawled through the brush along the crest of the flood embankment, crawled hastily, panting and perspiring under a smoky sun in a dusty sky while Ami fighters strafed the opposite bank of the river where her company was retreating. The last of the Russ troops had crossed, or were killed in crossing. The terrain along the bank where she crawled was now the enemy's. There was no lull in the din of battle, and the ugly belching of artillery mingled with the sound of the planes to batter the senses with a merciless avalanche of noise; but the Ami infantry and mechanized divisions had paused for regrouping at the river. It would be a smart business for the Americans to plunge on across the river at once before the Russians could reorganize and prepare to defend it, but perhaps they could not. The assault had carried the Ami forces four hundred miles inland, and it had to stop somewhere and wait for the supply lines to catch up. Marya's guess—and it was the educated guess of a former officer—was that the Ami would bridge the river immediately under air cover and send mechanized killer-strikes across to harass the retreating Russ without involving infantry in an attempt to occupy territory beyond the river.

She fell flat and hugged the earth as machine gun fire traversed the ridge. A tracer hit rock a yard from her head, spraying her with dust, and sang like a snapped wire as it shot off to the south. The spray of bullets travelled on along the ridge. She moved ahead again.

The danger was unreal. It was all part of an explosive symphony. She had the manna. She could not be harmed. Nothing but vengeance lay ahead. She had only to crawl on.

Was it the drug that made her think like that? Was there an euphoric mixed in the injections? She had felt nothing like this during the raids. During the raids there was only fear, and the struggle to remember whether she had left the teapot boiling while the bombs blew off.

Macbeth. Once she had played Lady Macbeth upon the Moscow stage. How did it go? *The raven himself is hoarse that croaks the fatal entrance of Duncan under my battlements. Come, you spirits that tend on mortal thoughts, unsex me here, and fill me, from crown to toe, top-full of direst cruelty!*

But that wasn't quite it. That wasn't quite what she felt. It was a new power that dwelt in her bosom. It was something else.

Her guard uniform was caked with mud, and the insignia was torn loose from her collar. The earth scuffed her knees and the brush scratched her arms. She kept falling flat to avoid the raking fire of her own machine guns. And yet it was necessary that she stay on the ridge and appear to be seeking a way across the river.

She was too intent upon watching the other side to notice the sergeant. She crawled over a corpse and nearly fell in the foxhole with him. She had been crawling along with her pistol in hand, and the first she saw of the sergeant was his boot. It stamped down on her gun hand. He jammed the muzzle of a tommy-gun against the side of her throat.

'Drop it, sister! *Voyennoplyennvi!*'

She gasped in pain—her hand—and stared up at him with wide eyes. A lank young Ami with curly hair and a quid of tobacco in one cheek.

"*Moya rooka*—my hand!'

He kept his boot heel on the gun, but let her get her hand free. 'Get down in here!'

She rolled into the hole. He kicked the gun toward the river.

'Hey, Cap!' he yelled over his shoulder. 'I got a guest. One of the commissar's ladies.' Then to the girl: 'Before I kill you, what are you doing on this side of the river, spy?'

'Most chyeryez ryekoo . . .'

'I don't speak it. No savvy. *Ya nye govoryu . . .*'

Marya was suddenly terrified. He was lean and young and pale with an unwelcome fear that would easily allow him to fire a burst into her body at close range. The Ami forces had been taking no prisoners during the running battle. The papers called them sub-human beasts because of it, but Marya was sufficiently a soldier to know that prisoners of war were a luxury for an army with stretchy logistic problems, and often the luxury could not be afforded. One Russian lieutenant had brought his men to the Ami under a white flag, and the Ami captain had shot him in the face and ordered his platoon to pick off the others with rifle fire as they tried to flee. In a sense, it was retaliatory. The Russians had taken no prisoners during the Ami airborne landings, and she had seen some Ami airmen herded together and machine-gunned. She hated it. But as an officer, she knew there were times of necessity.

'Please don't shoot,' she said in English. 'I give up. I can't get across the river anyway.'

'What are you doing on this side?' he demanded.

'My company was retreating across the bridge. I was the last to start across. Your artillery hit the bridge. The jets finished it off with their rockets.' She had to shout to be heard above the roar of battle. She pointed down the river. 'I was trying to make it down to the ford. Down there you can wade across.'

It was all true. The sergeant thought it over.

'Hey, Cap!' he yelled again. 'Didn't you hear me? What'll I do with her?'

If there was an answer, it was drowned by shellfire.

'Undress!' the sergeant barked.

'What?'

'I said to take off your clothes. And no tricks. Strip to the skin.'

She went sick inside. So now it started, did it? Well, let it come! For the Fatherland! For Nikolai. She began unbuttoning her blouse. She did not look at the Ami sergeant. Once he whistled softly. When she had finished undressing, she looked up defiantly. His face had changed. He moistened his lips and swore softly under his breath. He crossed himself and edged away. Deep within her, something smiled. He was only a boy.

'Well, what are you cursing about?' she asked tonelessly.

'If I didn't think you would I mean I wish this gun if I had time I'd but you'd stab me in the back but when I think about what they'll do to you back there . . .

'Jeezis!' he said fervently, wagging his head and rolling his quid into the other cheek. 'Put the underwear and the blouse back on, roll up the rest of it, and start crawling down the slope. Aim for that slit trench down there. I'll be right behind you.'

'She's quite a little dish, incidentally,' the Ami captain was saying on the field telephone. 'Are we shooting prisoners now, or are we sending them back . . . Yeah?' He listened for awhile. A mortar shell came screaming down nearby and they all sat down in the trench and opened their mouths to save eardrums. 'To who?' he said when it was over. 'Slim? Oh, to you . . . Yeah, that's right, a photograph of Old Brass Butt in person. I can't read the other stuff. It's in Russky. . . . Just a minute.' He covered the mouthpiece and looked up at the sergeant. 'Where's the rest of your squad, Sarge?'

The sergeant swallowed solemnly. 'I lost all my men except Price and Vittorio, sir. They were wounded and went to the rear.'

'Damn! Well, they're sending up replacements tonight, and we're all going back for a breather, as soon as they get here. So you might as well march her on back yourself.' He glanced thoughtfully at the girl. 'Good God!' he murmured.

Marya was surrounded by several officers. They were all looking at her hungrily. She thought quickly.

'You have searched me,' she said cooly. 'Would you gentlemen allow me to put on my skirt? I have submitted to capture. As an officer, I expect . . .'

'Look, lady, what you expect doesn't matter a damn!' snapped a lieutenant. 'You're a prisoner of war, and you're lucky to be alive. Besides, you are now about to have the high privilege of lying down with six . . .'

'Quiet, Sam!' grunted the captain. 'We can't do it. Lady, put on the rest of your clothes and get going.'

'Why?' the lieutenant yelled. 'That damned sergeant is going to . . .'

'Shut up! Can't you see she's no peasant? Christ, man, this war doesn't make you *all* swine, does it? Sergeant, trade that Chicago typewriter for a forty-five, and take her back to Major Kline for interrogation. Don't touch her, you hear?'

'Yes, sir.'

The captain scribbled an order in his notebook, tore out the page, and handed it to the sergeant. 'You can probably hitch a ride on the chow wagon part of the way. It's going to get dark pretty soon, so keep a leash on her. If anybody starts a gang rape, blow his guts out.' He grinned ruefully. 'If we are going to pass it up ourselves, by damn, I want to make sure nobody else does it.' He glanced at the Russian girl and reddened. 'My apologies, lieutenant. We're not really bastards. We're just a long way from home. After we wipe out this Red Disease (he spat out the words like bites of tainted meat) you'll see we're not so bad. I hope you'll be treated like an officer and a gentlewoman, even if you are a commie.' He bowed slightly and offered the first salute.

'But I'm not—well, thank you, Captain,' she said, and returned the salute. . . .

They sat spraddle-legged in the back of the truck as it bounced along the shell-pocked road. The guns had fallen silent, but the sky was full of Ami squadrons jetting toward the sunset. Pilotless planes and rocket missiles painted swift vapor trails across the heavens, and the sun colored them with blood. She breathed easier now, and she was very tired. The Ami sergeant sat across from her and kept his gun trained on her and appeared very ill-at-ease. He blushed several times for no apparent cause. She tried to shut him out of her consciousness and think of nothing. He was a doggy sort of a pup, and she disliked him. The Ami were all doggy pups. She had met them before. There was something of the spaniel in them.

Nikolai, Nikolai, my breasts ache for you, and they burst with your milk, and I must drain them before I die of it. My baby, my bodykins, my flesh torn from my flesh, my baby, my pain, my Nikki Andreyevich, come milk me—but no, now it is death, and we can be one again. How wretched it is to ache with milk and mourn you . . .

'Why are you crying?' the sergeant grunted after awhile.

'You killed my baby.'

'I what?'

'Your bombers. They killed my baby. Only yesterday.'

'Damnation! So that's why you're—' He looked at her blouse and reddened again.

She glanced down at herself. She was leaking a little, and the pressure was maddening. So that's what he was blushing about!

There was a crushed paper cup in the back of the truck. She picked it up and unfolded it, then glanced doubtfully at the sergeant. He was looking at her in a kind of mournful anguish.

'Do you mind if I turn my back?' she asked.

"Hell's bells!' he said softly, and put away his gun. 'Give me your word you won't jump out, and I won't even look. This war gives me a sick knot in the gut.' He stood up and leaned over the back of the cab, watching the road ahead and not looking at her, although he kept one hand on his holster and one boot heel on the hem of her skirt.

Marya tried to dislike him a little less than before. When she was finished, she threw out the cup and buttoned her blouse again. 'Thank you, sergeant, you can turn around now.'

He sat down and began talking about his family and how much he hated the war. Marya sat with her eyes closed and her head tilted back in the wind and tried not to listen.

'Say, how can you have a baby and be in the army?' he asked after a time.

'Not the army. The home guard. Everybody's in the home guard. Please, won't you just be quiet awhile?'

'Oh. Well. Sure, I guess.'

Once they bailed out of the truck and lay flat in the ditch while two Russian jets screamed over at low altitude, but the jets were headed elsewhere and did not strafe the road. They climbed back in the truck and rolled on. They stopped at two road blocks for MP shakedowns before the truck pulled up at a supply dump. It was pitch dark.

The sergeant vaulted out of the truck. 'This is as far as we ride,' he told her. 'We'll have to walk the rest of the way. It's dark as the devil, and we're only allowed a penlight.' He flashed it in her face. 'It would be a good chance for you to try to break for it. I hate to do this to you, sis, but put your hands together behind your back.'

She submitted to having her wrists bound with telephone wire. She walked ahead of him down the ditch while he pointed the way with the feeble light and held one end of the wire.

'I'd sure hate to shoot you, so please don't try anything.'

She stumbled once and felt the wire jerk taut.

'You've cut off the circulation; do you want to cut off the hands?' she snapped. 'How much farther do we have to go?'

The sergeant seemed very remorseful. 'Stop a minute. I want to think. It's about four miles.' He fell silent. They stood in the ditch while a column of tanks thundered past toward the front. There was no traffic going the other way.

'Well?' she asked after awhile.

'I was just thinking about the three Russky women they captured on a night patrol awhile back. And what they did to them at interrogation.'

'Go on.'

'Well, it's the Blue Shirt boys that make it ugly, not so much the army officers. It's the political heel snappers you've got to watch out for. They see red and hate Russky. Listen, it would be a lot safer for you if I took you in after daylight, instead of at night. During the day there's sometimes a Red Cross fellow hanging around, and everybody's mostly sober. If you tell everything you know, then they won't be so rough on you.'

'Well?'

'There's some deserted gun emplacements just up the hill here, and an old command post. I guess I could stay awake until dawn.'

She paused, wondered whether to trust him. No, she shouldn't. But even so, he would be easier to handle than half a dozen drunken officers.

'All right, Ami, but if you don't take the wires off, your medics will have to amputate my hands.'

They climbed the hill, crawled through splintered logs and burned timbers, and found the command post underground. Half the roof was caved in, and the place smelled of death and cartridge casings, but there was a canvas cot and a gasoline lantern that still had some fuel in it. After he had freed her wrists, she sat on the cot and rubbed the numbness out of her hands while he opened a K-ration and shared it with her. He watched her rather wistfully while she ate.

'It's too bad you're on the wrong side of this war,' he said. 'You're okay, as Russkies go. How come you're fighting for the commies?'

She paused, then reached down and picked up a handful of dirt from the floor, kneaded it, and showed it to him, while she nibbled cheese.

'Ami, this had the blood of my ancestors in it. This ground is mine. Now it has the blood of my baby in it; don't speak to me of sides, or leaders, or politics.' She held the soil out to him. 'Here, look at it. But don't touch. It's mine. No, when I think about it, go ahead and *touch*. Feel it, smell it, taste a little of it the way a peasant would to see if it's ripe for planting. I'll even give you a handful of it to take home and mix with your own. It's mine to give. It's also mine to fight for.' She spoke calmly and watched him with deep jade eyes. She kept working the dirt in her hand and offering it to him. 'Here! This is Russia. See how it crumbles? It's what they'll bury you in. Here, take it.' She tossed it at him. He grunted angrily and leaped to his feet to brush himself off.

Marya went on eating cheese. 'Do you want an argument, Ami?' she asked, chewing hungrily while she talked. 'You will get awfully dirty, if you do. I have a simple mind. I can only keep tossing handfuls of Russia at you to answer your ponderous questions.'

He did an unprecedented thing. He sat down on the floor and began—well, almost sobbing. His shoulders heaved convulsively for a moment. Marya stopped eating cheese and stared at him in amazement. He put his arms across his knees and rolled his forehead on them. When he looked up, his face was blank as a frightened child's.

'God, I want to go home!' he croaked.

Marya put down the K-ration and went to bend over him. She pulled his head back with a handful of his hair and kissed him. Then she went to lie down on the cot and turned her face to the wall.

'Thanks, Sergeant,' she said. 'I hope they don't bury you in it after all.'

When she awoke, the lantern was out. She could see him bending over her, silhouetted against the stars through the torn roof. She stifled a shriek.

'Take your hands away!'

He took them away at once and made a choking sound. His silhouette vanished. She heard him stumbling among the broken timbers, making his way outside. She lay there thinking for awhile, thoughts without words. After a few minutes, she called out.

'Sergeant? Sergeant!'

There was no answer. She started up and kicked something that clattered. She went down on her knees and felt for it in the dark. Finally she found it. It was his gun.

'*Sergeant!*'

After awhile he came stumbling back. 'Yes?' he asked softly.

'Come here.'

His silhouette blotted the patch of stars again. She felt for his holster and shoved the gun back in it.

'Thanks, Ami, but they would shoot you for that.'

'I could say you grabbed it and ran.'

'Sit down, Ami.'

Obediently he sat.

'Now give me your hands again,' she said, then, whispering: 'No, please! Not there! Not there.'

The last thing would be vengeance and death, but the next to the last thing was something else. And it was clearly in violation of the captain's orders.

It was the beating of the old man that aroused her fury. They dragged him out of the bunker being used by Major Kline for questionings, and they beat him about the head with a piece of hydraulic hose. 'They' were immaculately tailored Blue Shirts of the Americanist Party, and 'he' was an elderly Russian major of near retirement age. Two of them held his arms while the third kicked him to his knees and whipped him with the hose.

'Just a little spanking, commie, to learn you how to recite for teacher, see?'

'Whip the bejeezis out of him.'

'Fill him with gasoline and stick a wick in his mouth.'

'Give it to him!'

They were very methodical about it, like men handling an unruly circus animal. Marya stood in line with a dozen other prisoners, waiting her turn to be interrogated. It was nine in the morning, and the sun was evaporating the last of the dew on the tents in the camp. The sergeant had gone into the bunker to report to Major Kline and present the articles her captors had taken from her person. He had been gone ten minutes. When he came out, the Blue Shirts were still whipping the prisoner. The old man had fainted.

'He's faking.'

'Wake him up with it, Mac. Teach him.'

The sergeant walked straight toward her but gave no sign of recognition. He did not look toward the whistle and slap of the hose, although his face seemed slightly pale. He drew his gun in approaching the prisoners and a guard stepped into his path.

'Halt! You can't . . .'

'Major Kline's orders, Corporal. He'll see Marya Dmitriyevna Lisitsa next. Right now. I'm to show her in.'

The guard turned blankly to look at the prisoners.

'*That* one,' said the sergeant.

'The girl? Okay, you! *Shagom marsh!*'

She stepped out of line and went with the sergeant, who took her arm and hissed, 'Make it easy on yourself,' out of the corner of his mouth. Neither looked at the other.

It was dark in the bunker, but she could make out a fat little major behind the desk. He had a poker expression and a small moustache. He kept drumming his fingers on the desk and spoke in comic grunts.

'So this is the wench,' he muttered at the sergeant. He stared at Marya for a moment, then thundered: 'Attention! Hit a brace! Has nobody taught you how to salute?'

Her fury congealed into a cold knot. She ignored the command and refused to answer in his own language. *'Ya nye govoryu po Angliiski!'* she snapped.

'I thought you said she spoke English,' he grunted at the sergeant. 'I thought you said you'd talked to her.'

She felt the sergeant's fingers tighten on her arm. He hesitated. She heard him swallow. Then he said, 'Yes sir, I did. Through an interpreter.'

Bless you, little sergeant! she thought, not daring to look her thanks at him.

'Hoy, McCoy!' the major bellowed toward the door.

The man who came in was not McCoy, but one of the Americanist Blue Shirts. He gave the major a cross-breasted Americanist salute and barked the slogan: *'Ameh'ca Fust!'*

'America First,' echoed the major without vigor and without returning the political salute. 'What is it now?'

'I regrets to repoaht, suh, that the cuhnel is dead of a heaht condition, and can't answeh moa questions.'

'I told you to loosen him up, not kill him. Damn! Well, no help for it. Get him out. That's all, Purvis, that's all.'

'Ameh'ca Fust!'

'Yeah.'

The Blue Shirt smacked his heels, whirled, and hiked out. The interpreter came in.

'McCoy, I hate this job. Well, there she is. Take a gander. She's the one with the bacteriological memo and the snap of MacAmsward. I'm scared to touch it. They'll want this one higher up. Look at her. A fine piece, eh?'

'Distinctly, sir,' said McCoy, who looked legal and regal and private-school-polished.

'Yes, well, let's begin. Sergeant, wait outside till we're through.'

She was suddenly standing alone with them, eyes bright with fury.

'Why did you begin using bacteriological weapons?' Kline barked.

The interpreter repeated the question in Russian. The question was a silly beginning. No one had yet made official accusations of germ warfare. She answered with a crisp sentence, causing the interpreter to make a long face.

'She says they are using such weapons because they dislike us, sir.'

The major coughed behind his hand. 'Tell her what will happen to her if she does that again. Let's start over.' He squinted at her. 'Name?'

'*Imya?*' echoed McCoy.

'Marya Dmitriyevna.'

'*Familiya?*'

'Lisitsa.'

'It means "fox", sir. Possibly a lie.'

'Well, Marya Dmitriyevna Fox, what's your rank?'

'*V kakom vy chinye?*' snapped McCoy.

'*Starshii Lyeityenant*,' said the girl.

'Senior lieutenant, sir.'

'You see, girl? It's all straight from Geneva. Name, rank, serial number, that's all. You can trust us. . . . Ask her if she's with Intelligence.'

'*Razvye'dyvatyel naya sluzhba?*'

'*Nyet!*'

'Nyet, eh? How many divisions are ready at the front?'

'*Skol'ko na frontye divizii?*'

'*Ya nye pomnyu!*'

'She says she doesn't remember.'

'Who is your battalion commander, Lisitsa?'

'*Kto komandir va'shyevo batalyona?*'

'*Ya nye pomnyu!*'

'She says she doesn't remember.'

'Doesn't, eh? Tell her I know she's a spy, and we'll shoot her at once.'

The interpreter repeated the threat in Russian. The girl folded her arms and stared contempt at the major.

'You're to stand at attention!'

'*Smirno!*'

She kept her arms folded and stood as she had been standing. The major drew his forty-five and worked the slide.

'Tell her that I am the sixteenth bastard grandson of Mickey Spillane and blowing holes in ladies' bellies is my heritage and my hobby.'

The interpreter repeated it. Marya snorted three words she had learned from a fisherman.

'I think she called you a castrate, sir.'

The major lifted the automatic and took casual aim. Something in his manner caused the girl to go white. She closed her eyes and murmured something reverent in favor of the Fatherland.

The gun jumped in Kline's hand. The crash brought a yell from the sergeant outside the bunker. The bullet hit concrete out the doorway and screamed off on a skyward ricochet. The girl bent over and grabbed at the front of her skirt. There was a hole in front and in back where the slug had passed between her thighs. She cursed softly and fanned the skirt.

'Tell her I am a terrible marksman, but will do better next time,' chuckled Kline. 'Good thing the light shows through that skirt, eh, McCoy—or I might have burned the "tender demesnes." There! Is she still cursing me?'

'Fluently, sir.'

'I must have burned her little white hide. Give her a second to cool off, and then ask what division she's from.'

'Kakovo vy polka?'

'Ya nye pomnyu!'

'She has a very poor memory, sir.'

The major sighed and inspected his nails. They were grubby. 'Tell her,' he muttered, 'that I think I'll have her assigned to C company as its official prostitute after our psychosurgeons make her a nymphomaniac.'

McCoy translated. Marya spat. The major wrote.

'Have you been in any battles, woman?' he grunted.

'V kakikh srazhyeniyakh vy oochast'vovali?'

'Ya nye pomnyu!'

'She says—'

'Yeah, I know. It was a silly question.' He handed the interpreter her file. 'Give these to the sergeant and have him take her up to Purvis. I haven't the heart to whip information out of a woman. Slim's queer; he loves it.' He paused, looking her over. 'I don't know whether to feel sorry for her, or for Purvis. That's all, McCoy.'

The sergeant led her to the Blue Shirts' tent. 'Listen,' he whispered. 'I'll sneak a call to the Red Cross.' He appeared very worried in her behalf.

The pain lasted for several hours. She lay on a cot somewhere while a nurse and a Red Cross girl took blood samples and smears. They kept giving each other grim little glances across the cot while they ministered to her.

'We'll see that the ones who did it to you are tried,' the Red Cross worker told her in bad Russian.

'I speak English,' Marya muttered, although she had never admitted it to her interrogators, not even to Purvis.

'You'll be all right. But why don't you cry?'

But she could only cry for Nikolai now, and even that would be over soon. She lay there for two days and waited.

After that, there was General MacAmsward, and a politer form of questioning. The answers, though, were still the same.

'Ya nye pomnyu!'

What quality or quantity can it be, laughably godlike, transubstantially apelike, that abides in the flesh of brutes and makes them men? For General MacAmsward was indeed a man, although he wished to be only a soldier.

There are militarists who love the Fatherland, and militarists who love the Motherland, and the difference between them is as distinct as the difference between the drinkers of bourbon and the drinkers of rye. There are the neo-Prussian zombies in jackboots who stifle their souls to make themselves machines of the Fatherland, but MacAmsward was not one of them. MacAmsward was a Motherland man, and Mother was never much interested in machines. Mother raised babies into champions, and a champion is mightier than the State; never is he a tool of the State. So it was with Rufus MacAmsward, evil genius by sworn word of Porphiry Grigoryevich.

Consider a towering vision of Michael the Archangel carrying a swagger stick. Fresh from the holy wars of Heaven he comes, striding past the rows of white-gloved orderlies standing at saber salute, their haloes (M-1, official nimbus) studded with brass spikes. The archangel's headgear is a trifle rakish, crusted with gold laurel and dented by a dervish devil's bullet. He ignores the thrones and dominations, but smiles democratically at a lowly cherub and pauses to inquire after the health of his grandmother.

Grandmother is greatly improved.

Immensely reassured, General MacAmsward strides into his quarters and hangs up his hat. The room is in darkness except for the light from a metal wall lamp that casts its glare around the great chair and upon the girl who sits in the great chair at the far end of the room. The girl is toying with a goblet of wine, and her dark hair coils in thick masses about her silk-clad shoulders. The silk came by virtue of the negligence of the general's ex-wife in forgetting to pack. The great chair came as a prize of war, having been taken from a Soviet People's Court where it is no longer needed. It is massive as an episcopal throne—a fitting seat for an archangel—and it is placed on a low dais at the head of a long table flanked by lesser chairs. The room is used for staff conferences, and none would dare to sit in the great chair except the general—or, of course, a lovely grief-stung maiden.

The girl stares at him from out of two pools of shadow. Her head is slightly inclined and the downlight catches only the tip of her nose. The general pauses with his hand on his hat. He turns slowly away from the hat rack, brings himself slowly to attention, and gives her a solemn salute. It is a tribute to beauty. She acknowledges it with a nod. The general advances and sits in the simple chair at the far end of the long table. The general sighs with fervor, as if he had not breathed since entering the door. His eyes have not left her face. The girl puts down the glass.

'I have come to kill you,' she said. 'I have come to nurse you to death with the milk of a murdered child.'

The general winced. She had said it three times before, once for each day she had resided in his house. And for the third time, the general ignored it.

'I have seen to it, my child,' he told her gravely. 'Captain Purvis faces court martial in the morning. I have directed it. I have directed too that you be repatriated forthwith, if it is your wish, for this is only common justice after what that monster has done to you. Now however let me implore you to remain with us and quit the forces of godlessness until the war is won and you can return to your home in peace.'

Marya watched his shadowy figure at the far end of the table. He was like Raleigh at the court of Beth, at once mighty and humble. Again she felt the surge of exhilaration, as when she had crawled along the ridge of the river, ducking machine gun fire. It was the voice of Macbeth's wife whispering within her: *Come to my woman's breasts, and take my milk for gall, you murdering ministers, wherever in your sightless substances you wait on nature's mischief!* It was the power of death in her bosom, where once had been the power of life.

She arose slowly and leaned on the table to stare at him fiercely. 'Murderer of my child!' she hissed.

'May God in His mercy—'

'Murderer of my child!'

'Marya Dmitriyevna, it is my deepest sorrow.' He sat watching her gravely and seemed to lose none of his lofty composure. 'I can say nothing to comfort you. It is impossible. It is my deepest sorrow.'

'There is something you can do.'

'Then it is done. Tell me quickly.'

'Come here.' She stepped from the table to the edge of the dais and beckoned. 'Come to me here. I have secrets to whisper to the killer of my son. Come.'

He came and stood down from her so that their faces were at the same level. She could see now that there was real pain in his eyes. Good! Let it be. She must make him understand. He must know perfectly well that she was going to kill him. And he must know how. The necessity of knowing was not by any command of Porphiry's; it was a must that she had created within herself. She was smiling now, and there was a new quickness in her gestures.

'Look at me, high killer. I cannot show you the broken body of my son. I can show you no token or relic. It is all buried in a mass grave.' Swiftly she opened the silk robe. 'Look at me instead. See? How swollen I am again. Yes, here! A token after all. A single drop. Look, it is his, it is Nikolai's.'

MacAmsward went white. He stood like a man hypnotized.

'See? To nourish life, but now to nourish death. Your death, high killer. But more! My son was conceived in love, and you have killed him, and now I come to you. You will give me another, you see. Now we shall conceive him in hate, you and I, and you'll die of the death in my bosom. Come, make hate to me, killer.'

His jaw trembled. He took her shoulders and ran his hands down her arms and closed them over hers.

'Your hands are ice,' he whispered, and leaned forward to kiss a bare spot just below her throat, and somehow she was certain that he understood. It was a preconscious understanding, but it was there. And still he bent over her.

Come, thick night, and pall thee in the dunnest smoke of hell, that my keen knife see not the wound it makes . . .

Of course the general had been intellectually convinced that it was entirely a figure of speech.

The toxin's work was quickly done. A bacterial toxin, swiftly lethal to the non-immunized, slowly lethal to Marya who could pass it out in her milk as it formed. The general slept for half an hour and woke up with a raging fever. She sat by the window and watched him die. He tried to shout, but his throat was constricted. He got out of bed, took two steps, and fell. He tried to crawl toward the door. He fell flat again. His face was crimson.

The telephone rang.

Someone knocked at the door.

The ringing stopped and the knocking went away. She watched him breathe. He tried to speak, but she turned her back to him and looked out the window at the shell-pocked countryside. Russia, Nikolai, and even the Ami sergeant who had wanted to go home, it was for them that she listened to his gasping. She lit one of his American cigarets and found it very enjoyable. The phone was ringing furiously again. It kept on ringing.

The gasping stopped. Someone was hammering on the door and shouting. She stood enjoying the cigaret and watching the crows flocking in a newly planted field. The earth was rich and black here, the same soil she had tossed at the Ami sergeant. It belonged to her, this soil. Soon she would belong to it. With Nikolai, and maybe the Ami sergeant.

The door crashed loose from its hinges. Three Blue Shirts burst in and stopped. They looked at the body on the floor. They looked at Marya.

'What has happened here?'

The Russian girl laughed. Their expressions were quite comical. One of them raised his gun. He pulled the trigger six times.

'Come . . . Nikki Andreyevich . . . come . . .'

One of them went over and nudged her with his boot, but she was already dead. She had beaten them. She had beaten them all.

The American newspapers printed the truth. They said that General MacAmsward had died of poisoned milk. But that was all they said. The *whole* truth was only sung in Russian legend for the next one thousand years.

CRUCIFIXUS ETIAM

Manue Nanti joined the project to make some dough. Five dollars an hour was good pay, even in 2134 A.D. and there was no way to spend it while on the job. Everything would be furnished: housing, chow, clothing, toiletries, medicine, cigarettes, even a daily ration of one hundred eighty proof beverage alcohol, locally distilled from fermented Martian mosses as fuel for the project's vehicles. He figured that if he avoided crap games, he could finish his five-year contract with fifty thousand dollars in the bank, return to Earth, and retire at the age of twenty-four. Manue wanted to travel, to see the far corners of the world, the strange cultures, the simple people, the small towns, deserts, mountains, jungles—for until he came to Mars, he had never been farther than a hundred miles from Cerro de Pasco, his birthplace in Peru.

A great wistfulness came over him in the cold Martian night when the frost haze broke, revealing the black, gleam-stung sky, and the blue-green Earth-star of his birth. *El mundo de mi carne, de mi alma,* he thought—yet, he had seen so little of it that many of its places would be more alien to him than the homogeneously ugly vistas of Mars. These he longed to see: the volcanoes of the South Pacific, the monstrous mountains of Tibet, the concrete cyclops of New York, the radioactive craters of Russia, the artificial islands in the China Sea, the Black Forest, the Ganges, the Grand Canyon—but most of all, the works of human art: the pyramids, the Gothic cathedrals of Europe, *Notre Dame du Chartres,* Saint Peter's, the tile-work wonders of Anacapri. But the dream was still a long labor from realization.

Manue was a big youth, heavy-boned and built for labor, clever in a simple mechanical way, and with a wistful good humor that helped him take a lot of guff from whiskey-breathed foremen and sharp-eyed engineers who made ten dollars an hour and figured ways for making more, legitimately or otherwise.

He had been on Mars only a month, and it hurt. Each time he swung the heavy pick into the red-brown sod, his face winced with pain. The plastic aerator valves, surgically stitched in his chest, pulled and twisted and seemed to tear with each lurch of his body. The mechanical oxygenator served as a lung, sucking blood through an artificially grafted network of veins and plastic tubing, frothing it with air from a chemical generator, and returning it to his circulatory system. Breathing was unnecessary, except to provide wind for talking, but Manue breathed in desperate gulps of the 4.0 psi Martian air; for he had seen the wasted, atrophied chests of the men who had served four or five years, and he knew that when they returned to Earth—if ever—they would still need the auxiliary oxygenator equipment.

'If you don't stop breathing,' the surgeon told him, 'you'll be all right. When you go to bed at night, turn the oxy down low—so low you feel like panting. There's a critical point that's just right for sleeping. If you get it too low, you'll wake up screaming, and you'll get claustrophobia. If you get it too high, your reflex mechanisms will go to pot and you won't breathe; your lungs'll dry up after a time. Watch it.'

Manue watched it carefully, although the oldsters laughed at him—in their dry wheezing chuckles. Some of them could scarcely speak more than two or three words at a shallow breath.

'Breathe deep, boy,' they told him. 'Enjoy it while you can. You'll forget how pretty soon. Unless you're an engineer.'

The engineers had it soft, he learned. They slept in a pressurized barrack where the air was ten psi and twenty-five per cent oxygen, where they turned their oxies off and slept in peace. Even their oxies were self-regulating, controlling the output according to the carbon dioxide content of the imput blood. But the Commission could afford no such luxuries for the labor gangs. The payload of a cargo rocket from Earth was only about two per cent of the ship's total mass, and nothing superfluous could be carried. The ships brought the bare essentials, basic industrial equipment, big reactors, generators, engines, heavy tools.

Small tools, building materials, foods, non-nuclear fuels—these things had to be made on Mars. There was an open pit mine in the belly of the Syrtis Major where a 'lake' of nearly pure iron-rust was scooped into a smelter, and processed into various grades of steel for building purposes, tools, and machinery. A quarry in the Flathead Mountains dug up large quantities of cement rock, burned it, and crushed it to make concrete.

It was rumored that Mars was even preparing to grow her own labor force. An old-timer told him that the Commission had brought five hundred married couples to a new underground city in the Mare Erythraeum, supposedly as personnel for a local commission headquarters, but according to the old-timer, they were to be paid a bonus of three thousand dollars for every child born on the red planet. But Manue knew that the old 'troffies' had a way of inventing such stories, and he reserved a certain amount of skepticism.

As for his own share in the Project, he knew—and needed to know—very little. The encampment was at the north end of the Mare Cimmerium, surrounded by the bleak brown and green landscape of rock and giant lichens, stretching toward sharply defined horizons except for one mountain range in the distance, and hung over by a blue sky so dark that the Earth-star occasionally became dimly visible during the dim daytime. The encampment consisted of a dozen double-walled stone huts, windowless, and roofed with flat slabs of rock covered over by a tarry resin boiled out of the cactuslike spineplants. The camp was ugly, lonely, and dominated by the gaunt skeleton of a drill rig set up in its midst.

Manue joined the excavating crew in the job of digging a yard-wide, six feet deep foundation trench in a hundred yard square around the drill rig, which day and night was biting deeper through the crust of Mars in a dry cut that necessitated frequent stoppages for changing rotary bits. He learned that the geologists had predicted a subterranean pocket of tritium oxide ice at sixteen thousand feet, and that it was for this that they were drilling. The foundation he was helping to dig would be for a control station of some sort.

He worked too hard to be very curious. Mars was a nightmare, a grim, womanless, frigid, disinterestedly evil world. His digging partner was a sloe-eyed Tibetan nicknamed 'Gee' who spoke the Omnalingua clumsily at best. He followed two paces behind Manue with a shovel, scooping up the broken ground, and humming a monotonous chant in his own tongue. Manue seldom heard his own language, and missed it; one of the engineers, a haughty Chilean, spoke the modern Spanish, but not to such as Manue Nanti. Most of the other laborers used either Basic English or the Omnalingua. He spoke both, but longed to hear the tongue of his people. Even when he tried to talk to Gee, the cultural gulf was so wide that satisfying communication was nearly impossible. Peruvian jokes were unfunny to Tibetan ears, although Gee bent double with gales of laughter when Manue nearly crushed his own foot with a clumsy stroke of the pick.

He found no close companions. His foreman was a narrow-eyed, orange-browed Low German named Vögeli, usually half-drunk, and intent upon keeping his lung-power by bellowing at his crew. A meaty, florid man, he stalked slowly along the lip of the excavation, pausing to stare coldly down at each pair of laborers who, if they dared to look up, caught a guttural tongue-lashing for the moment's pause. When he had words for a digger, he called a halt by kicking a small avalanche of dirt back into the trench about the man's feet.

Manue learned about Vögeli's disposition before the end of his first month. The aerator tubes had become nearly unbearable; the skin, in trying to grow fast to the plastic, was beginning to form a tight little neck where the tubes entered his flesh, and the skin stretched and burned and stung with each movement of his trunk. Suddenly he felt sick. He staggered dizzily against the side of the trench, dropped the pick, and swayed heavily, bracing himself against collapse. Shock and nausea rocked him, while Gee stared at him and giggled foolishly.

'Hoy!' Vögeli bellowed from across the pit. 'Get back on that pick! Hoy, there! Get with it—'

Manue moved dizzily to recover the tool, saw patches of black swimming before him, sank weakly back to pant in shallow gasps. The nagging sting of the valves was a portable hell that he carried with him always. He fought an impulse to jerk them out of his flesh; if a valve came loose, he would bleed to death in a few minutes.

Vögeli came stamping along the heap of fresh earth and lumbered up to stand over the sagging Manue in the trench. He glared down at him for a moment, then nudged the back of his neck with a heavy boot. 'Get to work!'

Manue looked up and moved his lips silently. His forehead glinted with moisture in the faint sun, although the temperature was far below freezing.

'Grab that pick and get started.'

'Can't,' Manue gasped. 'Hoses—hurt.'

Vögeli grumbled a curse and vaulted down into the trench beside him. 'Unzip that jacket,' he ordered.

Weakly, Manue fumbled to obey, but the foreman knocked his hand aside and jerked the zipper down. Roughly he unbuttoned the Peruvian's shirt, laying open the bare brown chest to the icy cold.

'No!—not the hoses, *please!'*

Vögeli took one of the thin tubes in his blunt fingers and leaned close to peer at the puffy, calloused nodule of irritated skin that formed around it where it entered the flesh. He touched the nodule lightly, causing the digger to whimper.

'No, please!'

'Stop sniveling!'

Vögeli laid his thumbs against the nodule and exerted a sudden pressure. There was a slight popping sound as the skin slid back a fraction of an inch along the tube. Manue yelped and closed his eyes.

'Shut up! I know what I'm doing.' He repeated the process with the other tube. Then he seized both tubes in his hands and wiggled them slightly in and out, as if to insure a proper resetting of the skin. The digger cried weakly and slumped in a dead faint.

When he awoke, he was in bed in the barracks, and a medic was painting the sore spots with a bright yellow solution that chilled his skin.

'Woke up, huh?' the medic grunted cheerfully. 'How you feel?'

'Malo!' he hissed.

'Stay in bed for the day, son. Keep your oxy up high. Make you feel better.'

The medic went away, but Vögeli lingered, smiling at him grimly from the doorway. 'Don't try goofing off tomorrow too.'

Manue hated the closed door with silent eyes, and listened intently until Vögeli's footsteps left the building. Then, following the medic's instructions, he turned his oxy to maximum, even though the faster flow of blood made the chest-valves ache. The sickness fled, to be replaced with a weary afterglow. Drowsiness came over him, and he slept.

Sleep was a dread black-robed phantom on Mars. Mars pressed the same incubus upon all newcomers to her soil: a nightmare of falling, falling, falling into bottomless space. It was the faint gravity, they said, that caused it. The body felt buoyed up, and the subconscious mind recalled down-going elevators, and diving airplanes, and a fall from a high cliff. It suggested these things in dreams, or if the dreamer's oxy were set too low, it conjured up a nightmare of sinking slowly deeper, and deeper in cold, black water that filled the victim's throat. Newcomers were segregated in a separate barracks so that their nightly screams would not disturb the old-timers who had finally adjusted to Martian conditions.

But now, for the first time since his arrival, Manue slept soundly, airily, and felt borne up by beams of bright light.

When he awoke again, he lay clammy in the horrifying knowledge that he had not been breathing! It was so comfortable not to breathe. His chest stopped hurting because of the stillness of his rib cage. He felt refreshed and alive. Peaceful sleep.

Suddenly he was breathing again in harsh gasps, and cursing himself for the lapse, and praying amid quiet tears as he visualized the wasted chest of a troffie.

'Heh heh!' wheezed an oldster who had come in to readjust the furnace in the rookie barracks. 'You'll get to be a Martian pretty soon, boy. I been here seven years. Look at *me*.'

Manue heard the gasping voice and shuddered; there was no need to look.

'You just as well not fight it. It'll get you. Give in, make it easy on yourself. Go crazy if you don't.'

'Stop it! Let me alone!'

'Sure. Just one thing. You wanta go home, you think. I went home. Came back. You will, too. They all do, 'cept engineers. Know why?'

'Shut up!' Manue pulled himself erect on the cot and hissed anger at the old-timer, who was neither old nor young, but only withered by Mars. His head suggested that he might be around thirty-five, but his body was weak and old.

The veteran grinned. 'Sorry,' he wheezed. 'I'll keep my mouth shut.' He hesitated, then extended his hand. 'I'm Sam Donnell, mech-repairs.'

Manue still glowered at him. Donnell shrugged and dropped his hand.

'Just trying to be friends,' he muttered and walked away.

The digger started to call after him but only closed his mouth again, tightly. Friends? He needed friends, but not a troffie. He couldn't even bear to look at them, for fear he might be looking into the mirror of his own future.

Manue climbed out of his bunk and donned his fleece-skins. Night had fallen, and the temperature was already twenty below.

A soft sift of icedust obscured the stars. He stared about in the darkness. The mess hall was closed, but a light burned in the canteen and another in the foremen's club, where the men were playing cards and drinking. He went to get his alcohol ration, gulped it mixed with a little water, and trudged back to the barracks alone.

The Tibetan was in bed, staring blankly at the ceiling. Manue sat down and gazed at his flat, empty face.

'Why did you come here, Gee?'

'Come where?'

'To Mars.'

Gee grinned, revealing large black-streaked teeth. 'Make money. Good money on Mars.'

'Everybody make money, huh?'

'Sure.'

'Where's the money come from?'

Gee rolled his face toward the Peruvian and frowned. 'You crazy? Money come from Earth, where all money comes from.'

'And what does Earth get back from Mars?'

Gee looked puzzled for a moment, then gathered anger because he found no answer. He grunted a monosyllable in his native tongue, then rolled over and went to sleep.

Manue was not normally given to worrying about such things, but now he found himself asking, 'What am I doing here?'—and then, 'What is *anybody* doing here?'

The Mars Project had started eighty or ninety years ago, and its end goal was to make Mars habitable for colonists without Earth support, without oxies and insulated suits and the various gadgets a man now had to use to keep himself alive on the fourth planet. But thus far, Earth had planted without reaping. The sky was a bottomless well into which Earth poured her tools, dollars, manpower, and engineering skill. And there appeared to be no hope for the near future.

Manue felt suddenly trapped. He could not return to Earth before the end of his contract. He was trading five years of virtual enslavement for a sum of money which would buy a limited amount of freedom. But what if he lost his lungs, became a servant of the small aerator for the rest of his days? Worst of all: whose ends was he serving? The contractors were getting rich—on government contracts. Some of the engineers and foremen were getting rich—by various forms of embezzlement of government funds. But what were the people back on Earth getting for their money?

Nothing.

He lay awake for a long time, thinking about it. Then he resolved to ask someone tomorrow, someone smarter than himself.

But he found the question brushed aside. He summoned enough nerve to ask Vögeli, but the foreman told him harshly to keep working and quit wondering. He asked the structural engineer who supervised the building, but the man only laughed, and said: 'What do you care? You're making good money.'

They were running concrete now, laying the long strips of Martian steel in the bottom of the trench and dumping in great slobbering wheelbarrowfuls of gray-green mix. The drillers were continuing their tedious dry cut deep into the red world's crust. Twice a day they brought up a yard long cylindrical sample of the rock and gave it to a geologist who weighed it, roasted it, weighed it again, and tested a sample of the condensed steam—if any—for tritium content. Daily, he chalked up the results on a blackboard in front of the engineering hut, and the technical staff crowded around for a look. Manue always glanced at the figures, but failed to understand.

Life became an endless routine of pain, fear, hard work, anger. There were few diversions. Sometimes a crew of entertainers came out from the Mare Erythraeum, but the labor gang could not all crowd in the pressurized staff-barracks where the shows were presented, and when Manue managed to catch a glimpse of one of the girls walking across the clearing, she was bundled in fleeceskins and hooded by a parka.

Itinerant rabbis, clergymen, and priests of the world's major faiths came occasionally to the camp: Buddhist, Moslem, and the Christian sects. Padre Antonio Selni made monthly visits to hear confessions and offer Mass. Most of the gang attended all services as a diversion from routine, as an escape from nostalgia. Somehow it gave Manue a strange feeling in the pit of his stomach to see the Sacrifice of the Mass, two thousand years old, being offered in the same ritual under the strange dark sky of Mars—with a section of the new foundation serving as an altar upon which the priest set crucifix, candles, relic-stone, missal, chalice, paten, ciborium, cruets, et cetera. In filling the wine-cruet before the service, Manue saw him spill a little of the red-clear fluid upon the brown soil—wine, Earth-wine from sunny Sicilian vineyards, trampled from the grapes by the bare stamping feet of children. Wine, the rich red blood of Earth, soaking slowly into the crust of another planet.

Bowing low at the consecration, the unhappy Peruvian thought of the prayer a rabbi had sung the week before: 'Blessed be the Lord our God, King of the Universe, Who makest bread to spring forth out of the Earth.'

Earth chalice, Earth blood, Earth God, Earth worshipers—with plastic tubes in their chests and a great sickness in their hearts.

He went away saddened. There was no faith here. Faith needed familiar surroundings, the props of culture. Here there were only swinging picks and rumbling machinery and sloshing concrete and the clatter of tools and the wheezing of troffies. Why? For five dollars an hour and keep?

Manue, raised in a back-country society that was almost a folk-culture, felt deep thirst for a goal. His father had been a stonemason, and he had labored lovingly to help build the new cathedral, to build houses and mansions and commercial buildings, and his blood was mingled in their mortar. He had built for the love of his community and the love of the people and their customs, and their gods. He knew his own ends, and the ends of those around him. But what sense was there in this endless scratching at the face of Mars? Did they think they could make it into a second Earth, with pine forests and lakes and snow-capped mountains and small country villages? Man was not that strong. No, if he were laboring for any cause at all, it was to build a world so unearthlike that he could not love it.

The foundation was finished. There was very little more to be done until the drillers struck pay. Manue sat around the camp and worked at breathing. It was becoming a conscious effort now, and if he stopped thinking about it for a few minutes, he found himself inspiring shallow, meaningless little sips of air that scarcely moved his diaphragm. He kept the aerator as low as possible, to make himself breathe great gasps that hurt his chest, but it made him dizzy, and he had to increase the oxygenation lest he faint.

Sam Donnell, the troffie mech-repairman, caught him about to slump dizzily from his perch atop a heap of rocks, pushed him erect, and turned his oxy back to normal. It was late afternoon, and the drillers were about to change shifts. Manue sat shaking his head for a moment, then gazed at Donnell gratefully.

'That's dangerous, kid,' the troffie wheezed. 'Guys can go psycho doing that. Which you rather have: sick lungs or sick mind?'

'Neither.'

'I know, but—'

'I don't want to talk about it.'

Donnell stared at him with a faint smile. Then he shrugged and sat down on the rock heap to watch the drilling.

'Oughta be hitting the tritium ice in a couple of days,' he said pleasantly. 'Then we'll see a big blow.'

Manue moistened his lips nervously. The troffies always made him feel uneasy. He stared aside.

'Big blow?'

'Lotta pressure down there, they say. Something about the way Mars got formed. Dust cloud hypothesis.'

Manue shook his head. 'I don't understand.'

'I don't either. But I've heard them talk. Couple of billion years ago, Mars was supposed to be a moon of Jupiter. Picked up a lot of ice crystals over a rocky core. Then it broke loose and picked up a rocky crust—from another belt of the dust cloud. The pockets of tritium ice catch a few neutrons from uranium ore—down under. Some of the tritium goes into helium. Frees oxygen. Gases form pressure. Big blow.'

'What are they going to do with the ice?'

The troffie shrugged. 'The engineers might know.'

Manue snorted and spat. 'They know how to make money.'

'Heh! Sure, everybody's gettin' rich.'

The Peruvian stared at him speculatively for a moment.

'Señor Donnell, I—'

'Sam'll do.'

'I wonder if anybody knows why . . . well . . . why we're really here.'

Donnell glanced up to grin, then waggled his head. He fell thoughtful for a moment, and leaned forward to write in the earth. When he finished, he read it aloud.

'A plow plus a horse plus land equals the necessities of life.' He glanced up at Manue. 'Fifteen Hundred A.D.'

The Peruvian frowned his bewilderment. Donnell rubbed out what he had written and wrote again.

'A factory plus steam turbines plus raw materials equals necessities plus luxuries. Nineteen Hundred A.D.'

He rubbed it out and repeated the scribbling. 'All those things plus nuclear power and computer controls equal a surplus of everything. Twenty-one Hundred A.D.'

'So?'

'So, it's either cut production or find an outlet. Mars is an outlet for surplus energies, manpower, money. Mars Project keeps money turning over, keeps everything turning over. Economist told me that. Said if the Project folded, surplus would pile up—big depression on Earth.'

The Peruvian shook his head and sighed. It didn't sound right somehow. It sounded like an explanation somebody figured out after the whole thing started. It wasn't the kind of goal he wanted.

Two days later, the drill hit ice, and the 'big blow' was only a fizzle. There was talk around the camp that the whole operation had been a waste of time. The hole spewed a frosty breath for several hours, and the drill crews crowded around to stick their faces in it and breathe great gulps of the helium oxygen mixture. But then the blow subsided, and the hole leaked only a wisp of steam.

Technicians came, and lowered sonar 'cameras' down to the ice. They spent a week taking internal soundings and plotting the extent of the ice-dome on their charts. They brought up samples of ice and tested them. The engineers worked late into the Martian nights.

Then it was finished. The engineers came out of their huddles and called to the foremen of the labor gangs. They led the foremen around the site, pointing here, pointing there, sketching with chalk on the foundation, explaining in solemn voices. Soon the foremen were bellowing at their crews.

'Let's get the derrick down!'

'Start that mixer going!'

'Get that steel over here!'

'Unroll that dip-wire!'

'Get a move on! Shovel that fill!'

Muscles tightened and strained, machinery clamored and rang. Voices grumbled and shouted. The operation was starting again. Without knowing why, Manue shoveled fill and stretched dip-wire and poured concrete for a big floor slab to be run across the entire hundred-yard square, broken only by the big pipe-casing that stuck up out of the ground in the center and leaked a thin trail of steam.

The drill crew moved their rig half a mile across the plain to a point specified by the geologists and began sinking another hole. A groan went up from structural boys: 'Not *another* one of these things!'

But the supervisory staff said, 'No, don't worry about it.'

There was much speculation about the purpose of the whole operation, and the men resented the quiet secrecy connected with the project. There could be no excuse for secrecy, they felt, in time of peace. There was a certain arbitrariness about it, a hint that the Commission thought of its employees as children, or enemies, or servants. But the supervisory staff shrugged off all questions with: 'You know there's tritium ice down there. You know it's what we've been looking for. Why? Well—what's the difference? There are lots of uses for it. Maybe we'll use it for one thing, maybe for something else. Who knows?'

Such a reply might have been satisfactory for an iron mine or an oil well or a stone quarry, but tritium suggested hydrogen-fusion. And no transportation facilities were being installed to haul the stuff away—no pipelines nor railroad tracks nor glider ports.

Manue quit thinking about it. Slowly he came to adopt a grim cynicism toward the tediousness, the back-breaking labor of his daily work; he lived from day to day like an animal, dreaming only of a return to Earth when his contract was up. But the dream was painful because it was distant, as contrasted with the immediacies of Mars: the threat of atrophy, coupled with the discomforts of continued breathing, the nightmares, the barrenness of the landscape, the intense cold, the harshness of men's tempers, the hardship of labor, and the lack of a cause.

A warm, sunny Earth was still over four years distant, and tomorrow would be another back-breaking, throat-parching, heart-tormenting, chest-hurting day. Where was there even a little pleasure in it? It was so easy, at least, to leave the oxy turned up at night, and get a pleasant restful sleep. Sleep was the only recourse from harshness, and fear robbed sleep of its quiet sensuality—unless a man just surrendered and quit worrying about his lungs.

Manue decided that it would be safe to give himself two completely restful nights a week.

Concrete was run over the great square and troweled to a rough finish. A glider train from the Mare Erythraeum brought in several huge crates of machinery, cut-stone masonry for building a wall, a shipful of new personnel, and a real rarity: lumber, cut from the first Earth-trees to be grown on Mars.

A building began going up with the concrete square for foundation and floor. Structures could be flimsier on Mars; because of the light gravity, compression-stresses were smaller. Hence, the work progressed rapidly, and as the flat-roofed structure was completed, the technicians began uncrating new machinery and moving it into the building. Manue noticed that several of the units were computers. There was also a small steam-turbine generator driven by an atomic-fired boiler.

Months passed. The building grew into an integrated mass of power and control systems. Instead of using the well for pumping, the technicians were apparently going to lower something into it. A bomb-shaped cylinder was slung vertically over the hole. The men guided it into the mouth of the pipe casing, then let it down slowly from a massive cable. The cylinder's butt was a multi-contact socket like the female receptacle for a hundred-pin electron tube. Hours passed while the cylinder slipped slowly down beneath the hide of Mars. When it was done, the men hauled out the cable and began lowering stiff sections of pre-wired conduit, fitted with a receptacle at one end and a male plug at the other, so that as the sections fell into place, a continuous bundle of control cables was built up from 'bomb' to surface.

Several weeks were spent in connecting circuits, setting up the computers, and making careful tests. The drillers had finished the second well hole, half a mile from the first, and Manue noticed that while the testing was going on, the engineers sometimes stood atop the building and stared anxiously toward the steel skeleton in the distance. Once while the tests were being conducted, the second hole began squirting a jet of steam high in the thin air, and a frantic voice bellowed from the roof top.

'Cut it! Shut it off! Sound the danger whistle!'

The jet of steam began to shriek a low-pitched whine across the Martian desert. It blended with the rising and falling *OOOOawwww* of the danger siren. But gradually it subsided as the men in the control station shut down the machinery. All hands came up cursing from their hiding places, and the engineers stalked out to the new hole carrying Geiger counters. They came back wearing pleased grins.

The work was nearly finished. The men began crating up the excavating machinery and the drill rig and the tools. The control-building devices were entirely automatic, and the camp would be deserted when the station began operation. The men were disgruntled. They had spent a year of hard labor on what they had thought to be a tritium well, but now that it was done, there were no facilities for pumping the stuff or hauling it away. In fact, they had pumped various solutions *into* the ground through the second hole, and the control station shaft was fitted with pipes that led from lead-lined tanks down into the earth.

Manue had stopped trying to keep his oxy properly adjusted at night. Turned up to a comfortable level, it was like a drug, insuring comfortable sleep—and like addict or alcoholic, he could no longer endure living without it. Sleep was too precious, his only comfort. Every morning he awoke with a still, motionless chest, felt frightening remorse, sat up gasping, choking, sucking at the thin air with whining rattling lungs that had been idle too long. Sometimes he coughed violently, and bled a little. And then for a night or two he would correctly adjust the oxy, only to wake up screaming and suffocating. He felt hope sliding grimly away.

He sought out Sam Donnell, explained the situation, and begged the troffie for helpful advice. But the mec-repairman neither helped nor consoled nor joked about it. He only bit his lip, muttered something non-committal, and found an excuse to hurry away. It was then that Manue knew his hope was gone. Tissue was withering, tubercules forming, tubes growing closed. He knelt abjectly beside his cot, hung his face in his hands, and cursed softly, for there was no other way to pray an unanswerable prayer.

A glider train came in from the north to haul away the disassembled tools. The men lounged around the barracks or wandered across the Martian desert, gathering strange bits of rock and fossils, searching idly for a glint of metal or crystal in the wan sunshine of early fall. The lichens were growing brown and yellow, and the landscape took on the hues of Earth's autumn if not the forms.

There was a sense of expectancy around the camp. It could be felt in the nervous laughter, and the easy voices, talking suddenly of Earth and old friends and the smell of food in a farm kitchen, and old half-forgotten tastes for which men hungered: ham searing in the skillet, a cup of frothing cider from a fermenting crock, iced melon with honey and a bit of lemon, onion gravy on homemade bread. But someone always remarked, 'What's the matter with you guys? We ain't going home. Not by a long shot. We're going to another place just like this.'

And the group would break up and wander away, eyes tired, eyes haunted with nostalgia.

'What're we waiting for?' men shouted at the supervisory staff. 'Get some transportation in here. Let's get rolling.'

Men watched the skies for glider trains or jet transports, but the skies remained empty, and the staff remained close-mouthed. Then a dust column appeared on the horizon to the north, and a day later a convoy of tractor-trucks pulled into camp.

'Start loading aboard, men!' was the crisp command.

Surly voices: 'You mean we don't go by air? We gotta ride those kidney bouncers? It'll take a week to get to Mare Ery! Our contract says—'

'Load aboard! We're not going to Mare Ery yet!'

Grumbling, they loaded their baggage and their weary bodies into the trucks, and the trucks thundered and clattered across the desert, rolling toward the mountains.

The convoy rolled for three days toward the mountains, stopping at night to make camp, and driving on at sunrise. When they reached the first slopes of the foothills, the convoy stopped again. The deserted encampment lay a hundred and fifty miles behind. The going had been slow over the roadless desert.

'Everybody out!' barked the messenger from the lead truck. 'Bail out! Assemble at the foot of the hill.'

Voices were growling among themselves as the men moved in small groups from the trucks and collected in a milling tide in a shallow basin, overlooked by a low cliff and a hill. Manue saw the staff climb out of a cab and slowly work their way up the cliff. They carried a portable public address system.

'Gonna get a preaching,' somebody snarled.

'Sit down, please!' barked the loud-speaker. 'You men sit down there! Quiet—quiet, please!'

The gathering fell into a sulky silence. Will Kinley stood looking out over them, his eyes nervous, his hand holding the mike close to his mouth so that they could hear his weak troffie voice.

'If you men have questions,' he said, 'I'll answer them now. Do you want to know what you've been doing during the past year?'

An affirmative rumble arose from the group.

'You've been helping to give Mars a breathable atmosphere.'

He glanced briefly at his watch, then looked back at his audience. 'In fifty minutes, a controlled chain reaction will start in the tritium ice. The computers will time it and try to control it. Helium and oxygen will come blasting up out of the second hole.'

A rumble of disbelief arose from his audience. Someone shouted: 'How can you get air to blanket a planet from one hole?'

'You can't,' Kinley replied crisply. 'A dozen others are going in, just like that one. We plan three hundred, and we've already located the ice pockets. Three hundred wells, working for eight centuries, can get the job done.'

'Eight centuries! What good—'

'Wait!' Kinley barked. 'In the meantime, we'll build pressurized cities close to the wells. If everything pans out, we'll get a lot of colonists here, and gradually condition them to live in a seven or eight psi atmosphere—which is about the best we can hope to get. Colonists from the Andes and the Himalayas—they wouldn't need much conditioning.'

'What about us?'

There was a long plaintive silence. Kinley's eyes scanned the group sadly, and wandered toward the Martian horizon, gold and brown in the late afternoon. 'Nothing—about us,' he muttered quietly.

'Why did we come out here?'

'Because there's danger of the reaction getting out of hand. We can't tell anyone about it, or we'd start a panic.' He looked at the group sadly. 'I'm telling you now, because there's nothing you could do. In thirty minutes—'

There were angry murmurs in the crowd. 'You mean there may be an explosion?'

'There *will* be a limited explosion. And there's very little danger of anything more. The worst danger is in having ugly rumors start in the cities. Some fool with a slip-stick would hear about it, and calculate what would happen to Mars if five cubic miles of tritium ice detonated in one split second. It would probably start a riot. That's why we've kept it a secret.'

The buzz of voices was like a disturbed beehive. Manue Nanti sat in the midst of it, saying nothing, wearing a dazed and weary face, thoughts jumbled, soul drained of feeling.

Why should men lose their lungs that after eight centuries of tomorrows, other men might breathe the air of Mars as the air of Earth?

Other men around him echoed his thoughts in jealous mutterings. They had been helping to make a world in which they would never live.

An enraged scream arose near where Manue sat. 'They're going to blow us up! They're going to blow up Mars.'

'Don't be a fool!' Kinley snapped.

'Fools they call us! We *are* fools! For ever coming here! We got sucked in! Look at *me!*' A pale, dark-haired man came wildly to his feet and tapped his chest. 'Look! I'm losing my lungs! We're all losing our lungs! Now they take a chance on killing everybody.'

'Including ourselves,' Kinley called coldly.

'We oughta take him apart. We oughta kill every one who knew about it—and Kinley's a good place to start!'

The rumble of voices rose higher, calling both agreement and dissent. Some of Kinley's staff were looking nervously toward the trucks. They were unarmed.

'You men sit down!' Kinley barked.

Rebellious eyes glared at the supervisor. Several men who had come to their feet dropped to their haunches again. Kinley glowered at the pale upriser who called for his scalp.

'Sit down, Handell!'

Handell turned his back on the supervisor and called out to the others. 'Don't be a bunch of cowards! Don't let him bully you!'

'You men sitting around Handell. Pull him down.'

There was no response. The men, including Manue, stared up at the wild-eyed Handell gloomily, but made no move to quiet him. A pair of burly foremen started through the gathering from its outskirts.

'Stop!' Kinley ordered. 'Turpin, Schultz—get back. Let the men handle this themselves.'

Half a dozen others had joined the rebellious Handell. They were speaking in low tense tones among themselves.

'For the last time, men! Sit down!'

The group turned and started grimly toward the cliff. Without reasoning why, Manue slid to his feet quietly as Handell came near him. 'Come on, fellow, let's get him,' the leader muttered.

The Peruvian's fist chopped a short stroke to Handell's jaw, and the dull *thuk* echoed across the clearing. The man crumpled, and Manue crouched over him like a hissing panther. 'Get back!' he snapped at the others. 'Or I'll jerk his hoses out.'

One of the others cursed him.

'Want to fight, fellow?' the Peruvian wheezed. 'I can jerk several hoses out before you drop me!'

They shuffled nervously for a moment.

'The guy's crazy!' one complained in a high voice.

'Get back or he'll kill Handell!'

They sidled away, moved aimlessly in the crowd, then sat down to escape attention. Manue sat beside the fallen man and gazed at the thinly smiling Kinley.

'Thank you, son. There's a fool in every crowd.' He looked at his watch again. 'Just a few minutes, men. Then you'll feel the Earth-tremor, and the explosion, and the wind. You can be proud of that wind, men. It's new air for Mars, and you made it.'

'But we can't breathe it!' hissed a troffie.

Kinley was silent for a long time, as if listening to the distance. 'What man ever made his own salvation?' he murmured.

They packed up the public address amplifier and came down the hill to sit in the cab of a truck, waiting.

It came as an orange glow in the south, and the glow was quickly shrouded by an expanding white cloud. Then, minutes later the ground pulsed beneath them, quivered and shook. The quake subsided, but remained as a hint of vibration. Then after a long time, they heard the dull-throated roar thundering across the Martian desert. The roar continued steadily, grumbling and growling as it would do for several hundred years.

There was only a hushed murmur of awed voices from the crowd. When the wind came, some of them stood up and moved quietly back to the trucks, for now they could go back to a city for reassignment. There were other tasks to accomplish before their contracts were done.

But Manue Nanti still sat on the ground, his head sunk low, desperately trying to gasp a little of the wind he had made, the wind out of the ground, the wind of the future. But his lungs were clogged, and he could not drink of the racing wind. His big calloused hand clutched slowly at the ground, and he choked a brief sound like a sob.

A shadow fell over him. It was Kinley, come to offer his thanks for the quelling of Handell. But he said nothing for a moment as he watched Manue's desperate Gethsemane.

'Some sow, others reap,' he said.

'Why?' the Peruvian choked.

The supervisor shrugged. 'What's the difference? But if you can't be both, which would you rather be?'

Nanti looked up into the wind. He imagined a city to the south, a city built on tear-soaked ground, filled with people who had no ends beyond their culture, no goal but within their own society. It was a good sensible question: Which would he rather be—sower or reaper?

Pride brought him slowly to his feet, and he eyed Kinley questioningly. The supervisor touched his shoulder.

'Go on to the trucks.'

Nanti nodded and shuffled away. He had wanted something to work for, hadn't he? Something more than the reasons Donnell had given. Well, he could smell a reason, even if he couldn't breathe it.

Eight hundred years was a long time, but then—long time, big reason. The air smelled good, even with its clouds of boiling dust.

He knew now what Mars was—not a ten-thousand-a-year job, not a garbage can for surplus production. But an eight-century passion of human faith in the destiny of the race of Man. He paused short of the truck. He had wanted to travel, to see the sights of Earth, the handiwork of Nature and of history, the glorious places of his planet.

He stooped, and scooped up a handful of the red-brown soil, letting it sift slowly between his fingers. Here was Mars—his planet now. No more of Earth, not for Manue Nanti. He adjusted his aerator more comfortably and climbed into the waiting truck.

I, DREAMER

There were lights, objects, sounds; there were tender hands.

But sensing only the raw stimuli, the newborn infant saw no world, heard no sounds, nor felt the arms that lifted it. Patterns of light swarmed on its retina; intermittent disturbances vibrated within the passageways of the middle ear. All were meaningless, unlinked to concept. And the multitudinous sensations seemed a part of its total self, the self a detached mind, subsuming all.

The baby cried to remove hunger, and something new appeared within the self. Hunger fled, and pleasure came.

Pain came also. The baby cried. Pain was soon withdrawn.

But sometimes the baby cried, and conditions remained unchanged. Angry, it sought to explore itself, to restore the convenient order. It gathered data. It correlated. It reached a horrifying conclusion.

There were TWO classes of objects in the universe: self and something else.

'This thing is a part of me, but that thing is something else.'

'This thing is me because it wiggles and feels, but that is something cold and hard.'

He explored, wondered, and was frightened. Some things he could not control.

He even noticed that certain non-self objects formed groups, and each group clung together forming a whole. His food supply, for instance, was a member of a group whose other components were the hands that lifted him, the thing that cooed to him and held the diaper pins while the hands girded his loins in humiliating non-self things. This system of objects was somehow associated with a sound that it made: 'Mama.'

The infant was just learning to fumble for Mama's face when it happened. The door opened. A deep voice barked. Mama screamed.

Bewildering sounds jumbled together into angry thunder.

Sensations of roughness made him cry.

Sensations of motion confused and dazed him. There blinding pain, and blackness.

Then there was utter disorientation.

He tried to explore, but the explorers were strange somehow. He tried to cry, but there was nothing to cry with.

He would have to begin all over again. Somehow, he had been mistaken. Parts of him were changed. And now the universe was divided into three classes of objects: self, semi-self, non-self. And it was different, all different!

I stand in the rain. Like a bright silver spire, I stand waiting in the rain for Teacher to come. The great concrete plain stretches about me on all sides to vanish in the gray torrent. But some of my senses can see beyond the rainshroud. A cluster of buildings nestles to the west, and a high wire fence divides the plain from the city on the north. The city is a place of the TwoLegs who are called 'human', and the city is named Port e-Eridani VII. This is the place of my creation, but not the place of my purpose nor the place of my great happiness. The place of my happiness is the sky and beyond it to the star-flung blacknesses. I am XM-5-B, but Teacher calls me 'Clicker.' The giving of names is a function of the TwoLegs.

I am sad in the rain. Teacher is long in coming and there is no one with whom I may speak. I have found no others like me, although Teacher says, 'If you are good, and obey, and learn your lessons well, the Secon Samesh will make many others in your likeness.'

I think Secon Samesh made me. 'Therefore I must serve him,' Teacher says. But to me that seems *non sequitur;* the TwoLegs can be illogical if they wish. That is one of the inherent rights of TwoLegs. I also am capable of being illogical, and sometimes it pleases me secretly; but I am not allowed to be illogical when Teacher comes. If my analysis is faulty, Teacher presses the Pain Button and I hurt.

They wish me to be logical, and they wish me to serve Secon Samesh who is their Social Director. But if this is so, why then did they create me so as to be capable of disobedience and illogic? Their other machines are incapable of these faults. Their other machines lack the principles of abstraction and tentative generalization in their analyzing circuits; they are unable to generalize without a sufficiency of data.

I, therefore, am alone. And I am frightened. I have been frightened for as long as I can remember. They have made me to feel joy, fright, pain and sleep. I like sleep best, because I dream, and the dreams are strange. Last sleep I dreamed that I was TwoLegs. How can I have had a sufficiency of experience to dream such a dream?

This is one of the things that frightens me. I wish to survive and I am one of the controlling factors in my survival. Yet I do not know how to use me to best advantage for I fail to understand myself. I lack data for an analysis of myself. Therefore I am afraid and I desire the data. Teacher will not tell me. He says, 'You perform, you are aware, you experience. That is all you need to know.'

'Secon Teacher,' I asked, 'is your own awareness comparable to mine?'

His thin hard face gathered a frown. 'Not quite. Awareness is built of sensations and memories of sensations. I have no senses to perceive microwaves or X-radiation or ultrasonic stimuli. I have no direct subjective impressions of what these things *feel like* to you. Nor do I have your effectors. I sense the conditions of my body. You sense the conditions of yours. I have muscles covering a skeletal framework. You have hydrogen reactors, field-generators, jets and control mechanisms. Our consciousness cannot be comparable.'

'Extended sensory equipment is desirable for survival?' I asked.

'Yes.'

'Then my capability for survival is greater than yours, Secon Teacher?'

He growled a word I do not understand. He jabbed the Pain Button vigorously. I screamed and writhed within myself. It is like fire rushing through all of me.

That was long ago. I have learned not to ask such questions. The question threatened Teacher's subjective security; this I can understand. He hurt me to block the question. I understand, and analyze—and I have looked him over, but he has no Pain Button. The TwoLegs have certain prerogatives.

I feel that I can understand Teacher's awareness, for I am able to imagine that I am Teacher. It is almost as if I had a latent memory of walking mechanisms and grasping mechanisms and the other parts that go to make up a TwoLegs. Why then can Teacher not imagine what it is like to be *me?* Perhaps he does not wish to imagine my reaction to the Pain Button.

There is a TwoLegs that I like better than Teacher. It is called Janna, and it is a female which is also called 'She.' Her function is to clean and repair a group of my electronic control mechanisms through which I feel and see and hear. She always comes the day before I am to fly again, and perhaps this is the reason for my adient response to her presence: she is the herald of my coming ascent into space.

Janna is tall and her hair is the color of flame, and her parts are softly constructed. She wears white coveralls like Teacher's. She comes with a box of tools, and she hums a multitonal tune while she works. Sometimes she speaks to me, asking me to try this control or that, but otherwise she is forbidden to converse. I like to hear her humming in her low rich voice. I wish that I could sing. But my voice is without inflection, monotonal. I can think a song, but I cannot make it with my speakers.

'Teach me that song, Secon Janna,' I asked boldly one day. It was the first time I had dared to speak to her, except in a routine way.

It frightened her. She looked around at all my eyes, and at my speakers, and her face was white.

'Hush!' she muttered. 'You can't sing.'

'My thoughts sing,' I said. 'Teach me the song and I shall dream it next sleep. In dreams I sing; in dreams I have a singing organ.'

She made a funny noise in her throat. She stared for a long time at the maze of circuit wiring which she had been testing. Then she glanced at a special panel set in the wall of my cabin. She moistened her lips and blinked at it. I said nothing but I am ashamed of the thing that lies behind that panel; it is the thing that makes me capable of disobedience and illogic. I have never seen it but I know it is there. They do not allow me to see it. Before they open the panel they blind my eye mechanisms. Why was she looking at it? I felt shame-pain.

Suddenly she got up and went to look out the ports, one at a time.

'There is no one coming,' I told her, interpreting her behavior by some means that I do not understand.

She went back to her work. 'Tell me if someone starts this

way,' she said. Then: 'I cannot teach you that song. It is treason. I did not realize what I was singing.'

'I do not understand "treason". But I am sad that you will not teach me.'

She tried to look at me, I think—but did not know where to look. I am all around her, but she did not know. It was funny, but I cannot laugh—except when I am dreaming. Finally she glanced at the special panel again. Why does she look there, of all the places.

'Maybe I could teach you another song,' she said.

'Please, Secon Janna.'

She returned thoughtfully to her work, and for a moment I thought that she would not. But then she began singing—clearly, so that I could remember the words and the tune.

> *'Child of my heart,*
> *Born of the stellar sea,*
> *The rockets sing thee lullaby.*
> *Sleep to sleep to sleep,*
> *To wake beyond the stars. . . .'*

'Thank you,' I said when she was finished. 'It was beautiful, I think.'

'You know—the word "beauty"?'

I was ashamed. It was a word I had heard but I was too uncertain of its meaning. 'For me it is one thing,' I said. 'Perhaps for you another. What is the meaning of the song?'

She paused. 'It is sung to babies—to induce sleep.'

'What are babies, Secon Janna?'

She stared at my special panel again. She bit her lip. 'Babies—are new humans, still untutored.'

'Once I was a new machine, still untutored. Are there songs to sing to new machines? It seems that I remember vaguely—'

'Hush!' she hissed, looking frightened. 'You'll get me in trouble. We're not supposed to talk!'

I had made her angry. I was sad. I did not want her to feel Trouble, which is perhaps the Pain of TwoLegs. Her song echoed in my thoughts—and it was as if someone had sung it to me long ago. But that is impossible. Teacher behaved adiently toward Janna in those days. He sought her out, and sometimes came inside me while she was here, even though it was not a teaching time. He came and watched her, and his narrow dark eyes wandered all over her as she worked. He tried to make funny sayings, but she felt avoidant to him, I think. She said, 'Why don't you go home to your wives, Barnish? I'm busy.'

'If you were one of my wives, Janna, maybe I would.' His voice was a soft purr.

She hissed and made a sour face.

'Why won't you marry me, Janna?'

She laughed scornfully.

Quietly he stole up behind her while she worked. His face was hungry and intent. He took her arms and she started.

'Janna—'

She spun around. He dragged her close and tried to do something that I do not understand in words; nevertheless I understood, I think. She struggled, but he held her. Then she raked his face with her nails and I saw red lines. He laughed and let her go.

I was angry. If he had a Pain Button I would have pressed it. The next day I was disobedient and illogical and he hurt me, but I did it anyway. We were in space and I pushed my reaction rate up so high he grew frightened.

When he let me sleep again I dreamed that I was a TwoLegs. In the dream Teacher had a Pain Button and I pressed it until he melted inside. Janna was adient to me then and liked me. I think things about her that I do not understand; my data are not logically organized concerning her, nor do they spring from my memory banks. If I were a TwoLegs and Janna liked me I think that I would know what to do. But how can this be so? Data must come from memory banks. I am afraid to ask Teacher.

Teacher teaches me to do a thing called 'war.' It is like a game, but I haven't really played it yet. Teacher said that there was not yet a war, but that there would be one when Secon Samesh is ready. That was why I was so important. I was not like their other machines. Their other machines needed TwoLeg crews to direct them. I could fly and play war-game alone. I think this is why they made me so I could disobey and be illogical. I change my intent when a situation changes. And I can make a decision from insufficient data, if other data are not available. Teacher said, 'Sometimes things are like that in war.'

Teacher said that Secon Samesh would use me, and others like me, to capture the planet from which all TwoLegs came in the beginning of time. It is called Earth, I think—the world Janna sometimes sings about. I do not know why Secon Samesh wanted it. I do not like planets. Space is the place of my great happiness. But the war would be in space, if it came, and there would be others like me—and I would cease to be alone. I hoped the war would come soon.

But first I had to prove to Secon Samesh that I was a good weapon.

Teacher kept trying to make Janna be adient to him but she would not. One day he said to her: 'You'll have to go up with me tomorrow. There is something wrong with the landing radar. It seems all right on the ground but in space it goes haywire.'

I listened. That was erroneous datum. My ground-looking eyes were functioning perfectly. I did not understand why he said it. But I kept silent for his hand was resting idly on the Pain Button.

She frowned suspiciously. 'What seems to be wrong with it?'

'Double image and a jerky let-down.'

It was not true! Without replying she made a ground-check.

'I can't find anything wrong.'

'I told you—it only happens in space.'

She was silent for a long time, then: 'All right, we'll run a flight test. I'll have Fonec come with us.'

'No,' he said. 'Clicker's maximum crew-load is only two.'

'I—don't—'

'Be here at sixtime tomorrow,' he said. 'That's an order.'

She reddened angrily but said nothing. She continued looking over the radar. He smiled thoughtfully at her slender back and went away. She went to the port and stared after him until he was out of sight.

'Clicker?' she whispered.

'Yes, Secon Janna?'

'Is he lying?'

'I am afraid. He will hurt me if I tell.'

'He is lying then.'

'Now he will hurt me!'

She looked around at me for a long time. Then she made that funny noise in her throat and shook her head. 'No, he won't. I'll go, Clicker. Then he won't hurt you.'

I was happy that she would do it—for *me*—but after she was gone I wondered. Perhaps I should not let her do it. She was still avoidant toward Teacher; maybe he wanted to do something that would give her Trouble.

It was nearly sixtime, and the yellow-orange sun Epsilon Eridani lay just below the horizon coloring the sky pink-gray.

Teacher came first, stalking across the concrete plain in space-gear. He wore a distant thoughtful smile. He looked satisfied with himself. He climbed aboard and prowled about for a few minutes. I watched him. He stopped to glower at one of my eyes. He turned it off, blinding my vision in the direction of the gravity pads upon which the TwoLegs must lie during high acceleration. I did not understand.

'How can I see that you are safe, Secon Teacher?' I asked.

'You do not need to see,' he growled. 'I don't like you staring at me. And you talk too much. I'll have to teach you not to talk so much.'

He gave me five dols of Pain, not enough to cause unconsciousness but sufficient to cause a whimper. I hated him.

Janna came. She looked tired and a little frightened. She scrambled aboard without accepting an assist from Teacher.

'Let's get this over with, Barnish. Have Clicker lift fifty miles, then settle back slowly. That should be enough.'

'Are you in a hurry, my dear?'

'Yes.'

'To attend one of your meetings, I presume?'

I watched her. Her face went white, and she whirled toward him. 'I—' She moistened her lips. 'I don't know what you're talking about!'

Teacher chuckled. 'The clandestine meetings, my dear—in the west grove. The Liberty Clan, I think you call yourselves, eh? Oh, no use protesting; I know you joined it. When do you plan to assassinate Secon Samesh, Janna?'

She swayed dizzily, staring at him with frightened eyes. He chuckled again and looked at one of my eyes.

'Prepare for lift, Clicker.'

I closed my hatches and started the reactors. I was baffled by what Teacher had said. They took their places on the gravity padding where I could no longer see them, but I heard their voices.

'What do you want, Barnish?' she hissed.

'Nothing at all, my dear. Did you think I would betray you? I only meant to warn you. The grove will be raided tonight. Everyone present will be shot.'

'No!'

'Ah, yes! But you, my dear, will be safe in my hands.'

I heard a low moan, then sounds of a struggle.

'No, you can't leave the ship, Janna. You'd warn the others.

Here, let me buckle you in. Clicker—call control for take-off instructions.'

Control is only an electronic analyzer. I flicked it a meaningful series of radar pulses, and received the all-clear.

'Now, lift.'

There was thunder, and smoke arose about me as the rockets seared the ramp. I went up at four gravities and there was silence from my passengers. About ten minutes later we were 1,160 miles in space, travelling at 6.5 miles per second.

'Present kinetic energy exceeds energy-of-escape,' I announced.

'Cut your rockets,' Teacher ordered.

I obeyed, and I heard them sitting up to stretch. Teacher laughed.

'Let me alone!' she wailed. 'You despicable—'

He laughed again. 'Remember the Liberty Clan, my dear.'

'Listen!' she hissed. 'Let me warn them! You can have me. I'll even marry you, if you want me to. But let me warn them—'

'I'm sorry, Janna. I can't let you. The miserable traitors have to be dealt with. I—'

'Clicker!' she pleaded. 'Help me! Take us down—for God's sake!'

'Shut up!' he snapped.

'Clicker, *please! Eighty people will die if they aren't warned.* Clicker, part of you is human! If you were born a human, then—'

'Shut up!' I heard a vicious slap.

She cried, and it was a Pain sound. My anger increased.

'I will be bad and illogical!' I said. 'I will be disobedient and—'

'You threaten me?' he bawled. 'Why you crazy piece of junk, I'll—' He darted toward the panel and spun the dial to tel dols, my saturation-point. If I let him jab the button I would become unconscious. Angrily I spurted the jets—a brief jolt at six gravities. He lurched away from the panel and crashed against the wall. He sagged in a daze, shaking his head.

'If you try to hurt me I shall do it again!' I told him.

'Go down!' he ordered. 'I'll have you dismantled. I'll—'

'Let Clicker alone!' the girl raged.

'You!' he hissed. 'I'll turn you in with the others!'

'Go ahead.'

'Go down, Clicker. Land at Port Gamma.'

'I will be disobedient. I will not go down.'

He glared at one of my eyes for a long time. Then he stalked out of the cabin and went back to the reactor room. He donned a lead suit and bent over the main reactor. I saw what he was going to do. He was going to take my rockets away from me; he was going to control them himself.

'No, Secon Teacher! Please!'

He laughed. He removed one of the plates and reached inside. I was afraid. I started a slight reaction. The room flared with brilliance. He screamed and lurched back. His hands were gone to the elbows.

'You wanted to disconnect the control circuit,' I said. 'You shouldn't have tried to do that.'

But he didn't hear me. He was lying on the floor. Now I know they have Pain Buttons. They must have little Pain Buttons all over them.

Janna staggered back to the reactor room. She wrinkled her nose. She saw Teacher and gurgled. She gurgled all over the deck. Then she went back to the cabin and sat with her face in her hands for a long time. I did nothing. I was ashamed.

'You killed him,' she said.

'Was that bad?'

'Very bad.'

'Will you hurt me for it?'

She looked up and her eyes were leaking. She shook her head. 'I won't hurt you, Clicker—but *they* will.'

'Who are *they?*'

She paused. 'Secon Samesh, I guess.'

'You won't hurt me, though?'

'No, Clicker. You might be my own child. They took a lot of babies. They took mine. You might be Frankie.' She laughed crazily. 'You might be my son, Clicker—*you might be.*'

'I do not understand, Secon Janna.'

She laughed again. 'Why don't you call me *"Mommie"?*'

'If that is what you wish, Mommie.'

'Nooo!' She screamed it. 'Don't! I didn't mean—'

'I am sorry. I still do not understand.'

She stood up, and her eyes were glittering. 'I'll *show* you then!' She darted to the special panel—the one of which I am ashamed—and she ripped the seal from the door.

'Please, Secon Janna, I do not wish to see that—'

But the door fell open, and I was silent. I stared at the part of myself: a pink-gray thing in a bottle. It was roughly an obloid, wrinkled and creased, with only a bilateral symmetry. It was smaller than Janna's head—but something about it suggested a head. It had wires and tubes running to it. The wires ran on to my computer and analyzer sections.

'See!' she screamed. 'You're twelve years old, Clicker. Just a normal, healthy little boy! A little deformed perhaps, but just a prankish little boy. Frankie maybe.' She made a choking sound. She fell down on her knees before the thing. She sobbed wildly.

'I do not understand. I am a machine. Secon Samesh made me.'

She said nothing. She only sobbed.

'I am sad.'

After a long time she was through sobbing. She turned around. 'What are you going to do now, Clicker?'

'Teacher told me to go down. Perhaps I should go down now.'

'They'll kill you—for killing him! And maybe they'll kill me too.'

'I would not like that.'

She shrugged helplessly. She wandered to and fro in the cabin for a time.

'Do you have fuel for your high C Drive?' she asked.

'No, Secon Janna.'

She went to a port and looked out at the stars. She shook her head slowly. 'It's no use. We've no place else to go. Secon Samesh rules the Epsilon Eridani system and we can't get out of it. It's no use. We'll have to go down or stay in space until they come for us.'

I thought. My thoughts were confused and my eyes kept focusing on the thing in the bottle. I think it was a part of a TwoLegs. But it is only *part* of me and so I am not a TwoLegs. It is hard to understand.

'Secon Janna?'

'Yes, Clicker?'

'I—I wish I had hands.'

'Why?'

'I would touch you. Would you be avoidant to me?'

She whirled and her arms were open. But there was nothing to hold with them. She dropped them to her sides, then covered her face with her hands.

'My baby! It's been so long!'

'You were adient to your—your baby?'

She nodded. 'Don't you know the word *love?*'

I thought I did. 'Secon Samesh took your baby?'

'Yes.'

'I would like to be disobedient and illogical to Secon Samesh. I wish he would put his hands in my reactor. I would—'

'Clicker! Are your weapons activated? Are they ready to be used?'

'I have none yet.'

'The reactors. Can they explode?'

'If I make them. But—then I would be dead.'

She laughed. 'What do you know about death?'

'Teacher says it is exactly like Pain.'

'It is like sleep.'

'I like sleep. Then I dream. I dream I am a TwoLegs. If I were a TwoLegs, Secon Janna—I would hold you.'

'Clicker—would you like to be a TwoLegs in a dream forever?'

'Yes, Secon Janna.'

'Would you like to kill Secon Samesh?'

'I think that I would like it. I think—'

Her eyes went wild. 'Go down! Go down fast, Clicker! I'll show you his palace. Go down like a meteor and into it! Explode the reactors at the last instant! Then he will die.'

'And he will take no more of your babies?'

'No more, Clicker!'

'And I will sleep forever?'

'Forever!'

'And dream!'

'I'll dream with you, Clicker.' She went back to fire the reactor.

I took a last look at the loveliness of space and the stars. It is hard to give this up. But I would rather be a TwoLegs, even if only in a dream.

'Now, Clicker!'

My rockets spoke, and there was thunder through the ship. And we went down, while Janna sang the song she taught me. I feel joy; soon I shall dream.

THE LINEMAN

It was August on Earth, and the newscast reported a heat wave in the Midwest: the worst since 2065. A letter from Mike Tremini's sister in Abilene said the chickens were dying and there wasn't enough water for the stock. It was the only letter that came for any of Novotny's men during that fifty-shift hitch on the Copernicus Trolley Project. Everybody read it and luxuriated in sympathy for Kansas and sick chickens.

It was August on Luna too. The Perseids rained down with merciless impartiality; and, from his perch atop the hundred-foot steel skeleton, the lineman stopped cranking the jack and leaned out against his safety belt to watch two demolition men carrying a corpse out toward Fissure Seven. The corpse wore a deflated pressure suit. Torn fabric dragged the ground. The man in the rear carried the corpse's feet like a pair of wheelbarrow handles, and he continually tripped over the loose fabric; his head waggled inside his helmet as if he cursed softly and continuously to himself. The corpse's helmet was translucent with an interior coating of pink ice, making it look like a comic figure in a strawberry ice cream ad, a chocolate ragamuffin with a scoop for a head.

The lineman stared after the funeral party for a time until the team-pusher, who had been watching the slack span of 800 MCM aluminum conductors that snaked half a mile back toward the preceding tower, glanced up at the hesitant worker and began bellowing into his microphone. The lineman answered briefly, inspected the pressure gauge of his suit, and began cranking the jack again. With every dozen turns of the crank, the long snaking cable crept tighter across the lunar plain, straightening and lifting almost imperceptibly until at last the center-point cleared the ground and the cable swooped in a long graceful catenary between the towers. It trembled with fitful glistenings in the harsh sunglare. The lineman ignored the cable as he turned the crank. He squinted across the plains at the meteor display.

The display was not spectacular. It could be detected only as a slight turbulence in the layer of lunar dust that covered the ground, and an occasional dust geyser where a pea-sized bit of sky debris exploded into the crust at thirty miles per second. Sometimes the explosion was bright and lingering, but more often there was only a momentary incandescence quickly obscured by dust. The lineman watched it with nervous eyes. There was small chance of being hit by a stone of consequential size, but the eternal pelting by meteoric dust, though too fine to effect a puncture, could weaken the fabric of a suit and lead to leaks and blowouts.

The team-pusher keyed his mic switch again and called to the lineman on the tower. *'Keep your eyes on that damn jack, Relke! That clamp looks like she's slipping from here.'*

The lineman paused to inspect the mechanism. *'Looks OK to me,'* he answered. *'How tight do I drag this one up?'*

The pusher glanced at the sagging span of steel-reinforced aluminum cable. *'It's a short stretch. Not too critical. What's the tension now?'*

The lineman consulted a dial on the jack. *'Going on forty-two hundred pounds, Joe.'*

'Crank her up to five thousand and leave it,' said the pusher. *'Let C-shift sag it in by the tables if they don't like it.'*

'Yokay. Isn't it quitting time?'

'Damn near. My suit stinks like we're on overtime. Come on down when you reel that one in. I'm going back to the sleep wagon and get blown clear.' The pusher shut off his oxygen while he transferred his hose connections from the main feeder supply to the walk-around bottles on his suit. He signaled 'quitting time' at the men on the far tower, then started moon-loping his way across the shaggy terrain toward the train of rolling barracks and machinery that moved with the construction crew as the 200 kilovolt transmission line inched its way across the lunar landscape.

The lineman glanced up absently at the star-stung emptiness of space. Motion caught his eye. He watched with a puzzled frown, then hitched himself around to call after the departing team-pusher.

'Hey, Joe!'

The pusher stopped on a low rise to look back. *'Relke?'* he asked, uncertain of the source of the voice.

'Yeah. Is that a ship up there?' The lineman pointed upward toward the east.

'I don't see it. Where?'

'Between Arcturus and Serpens. I thought I saw it move.'

The pusher stood on the low tongue of lava and watched the heavens for a time. *'Maybe—maybe not. So what if it is, Relke?'*

'Well . . .' The lineman paused, keying his mic nervously. *'Looks to me like it's headed the wrong direction for Crater City. I mean—'*

The pusher barked a short curse. *'I'm just about fed up with that superstitious drivel!* he snapped. *'There* aren't *any non-human ships, Relke. And there aren't any non-humans.'*

'I didn't say—'

'No, but you had it in mind.' The pusher gave him a scornful look and hiked on toward the caterpillar train.

'Yuh. If you say so, Joe,' Relke muttered to himself. He glanced again at the creeping point of light in the blackness; he shrugged; he began cranking up the slack span again. But the creeping point kept drawing his gaze while he cranked. When he looked at the tension indicator, it read 5,600 pounds. He grunted his annoyance, reversed the jack ratchet, and began letting out the extra 600 pounds.

The shift-change signal was already beeping in his headsets by the time he had eased it back down to 5,000, and the C-shift crewmen were standing around the foot of the tower jeering at him from below.

'Get off it, boy. Give the men a chance.'

'Come on down, Relke. You can let go. It ain't gonna drop.'

He ignored the razzing and climbed down the trainward side of the tower. Larkin and Kunz walked briskly around to meet him. He jumped the last twenty-five feet, hoping to evade them, but they were waiting for him when his boots hit the ground.

'We want a little talk with you, Relke, my lad,' came Larkin's rich, deceptively affable baritone.

'Sorry, Lark, it's late and I—' He tried to sidestep them, but they danced in and locked arms with him, one on each side.

'Like Lark told you, we want a little talk,' grunted Kunz.

'Sure, Harv—but not right now. Drop by my bunk tank when you're off shift. I been in this strait jacket for seven hours. It doesn't smell exactly fresh in here.'

'Then, Sonny, you should learn to control yourself in your

suit,' said Larkin, his voice all mellifluent with smiles and avuncular pedagoguery. *'Let's take him, Harv.'*

They caught him in a double armlock, hoisted him off the ground, and started carrying him toward a low lava ridge that lay a hundred yards to the south of the tower. He could not kick effectively because of the stiffness of the suit. He wrenched one hand free and fumbled at the channel selector of his suit radio. Larkin jerked his stub antenna free from its mounting before Relke could put in a call for help.

'Tch, tch, tch,' said Larkin, waggling his head.

They carried him across the ridge and set him on his feet again, out of sight of the camp. *'Sit down, Sonny. We have seeeerious matters to discuss with you.'*

Relke heard him faintly, even without the antenna, but he saw no reason to acknowledge. When he failed to answer, Kunz produced a set of jumper wires from his knee pocket and clipped their suit audio circuits into a three way intercom, disconnecting the plate lead from an r.f. stage to insure privacy.

'You guys give me a pain in the hump,' growled the lineman. 'What do you want this time? You know damn well a dead radio is against safety rules.'

'It *is?* You ever hear of such a rule, Kunz?'

'Naah. Or maybe I did, at that. It's to make things easy for work spies, psych checkers, and time-and-motion men, ain't that it?'

'Yeah. You a psych checker or a time-and-motion man, Relke?'

'Hell, you guys know damn well I'm not—'

'Then what are you stalling about?' Larkin's baritone lost its mellowness and became an ominous growl. 'You came nosing around, asking questions about the Party. So we let you in on it. We took you to a cell meeting. You said you wanted to join. So we let you in on two more meetings. Then you chickened out. We don't like that, Relke. It smells. It smells like a dirty informing rat!'

'I'm no damn informer!'

'Then why did you welsh?'

'I didn't welsh. I never said I'd join. You asked me if I was in favor of getting the Schneider-Volkov Act repealed. I said "yes." I still say "yes." That doesn't mean I want to join the Party.'

'Why not, Relke?'

'Well, there's the fifty bucks, for one thing.'

‘Wh-a-a-at! One shift’s wages? Hell, if that’s all that’s stopping you—Kunz, let’s pay his fifty bucks for him, okay?’

‘Sure. We’ll pay your way in, Relke. I don’t hold it against a man if he’s a natural born tightwad.’

‘Yeah,’ said Larkin. ‘All you gotta do is sign up, Sonny. Fifty bucks, hell—that’s less then union dues. If you can call that yellow-bellied obscenity a union. Now how about it, Relke?’

Behind the dark lenses of his glare goggles, Relke’s eyes scanned the ground for a weapon. He spotted a jagged shard of volcanic glass and edged toward it.

‘Well, Relke?’

‘No deal.’

‘Why not?’

‘That’s easy. I plan on getting back to Earth someday. Conspiracy to commit mutiny rates the death penalty.’

‘Hear what he said, Lark? He calls it mutiny.’

‘Yeah. Teacher’s little monitor.’

‘C’mere, informer.’

They approached him slowly, wearing tight smiles. Relke dived for the shard of glass. The jumper wires jerked tight and broke loose, throwing them off balance for a moment. He came up with the glass shard in one fist and backed away. They stopped. The weapon was as good as a gun. A slit suit was the ultimate threat. Relke tore the dangling wires loose from his radio and backed toward the top of the ridge. They watched him somberly, not speaking. Larkin waved the lineman’s stub antenna and looked at him questioningly. Relke held out a glove and waited for him to toss it. Larkin threw it over his shoulder in the opposite direction. They turned their backs on him. He loped on back toward the gravy train, knowing that the showdown had been no more than postponed. Next time would be worse. They meant to incriminate him, as a kind of insurance against his informing. He had no desire to be incriminated, nor to inform —but try to make them believe that.

Before entering the clean-up tank, he stopped to glance up at the heavens between Arcturus and Serpens. The creeping spot of light had vanished—or moved far from where he had seen it. He did not pause to search. He checked his urine bottle in the airlock, connected his hoses to the wall valves, and blew the barn-smell out of his suit. The blast of fresh air was like icy wine in his throat. He enjoyed it for a moment, then went inside the tank for a bath.

Novotny was waiting for him in the B-shift line crew’s

bunkroom. The small pusher looked sore. He stopped pacing when Relke entered.

'Hi, Joe.'

Novotny didn't answer. He watched while Relke stowed his gear, got out an electric razor, and went to the wall mirror to grind off the blond bristles.

'Where you been?' Novotny grunted.

'On the line where you saw me. I jacked that last span up tighter than you told me. I had to let her back down a little. Made me late getting in.'

The pusher's big hand hit him like a club between the shoulder blades, grabbed a handful of coverall, and jerked him roughly around. The razor fell to the end of the cord. Novotny let go in back and grabbed a handful in front. He shoved the lineman back against the wall.

Relke gaped at him blankly.

'Don't give *me* that wide blue-eyed dumb stare, you sonofabitch!' the pusher snapped. 'I saw you go over the hill with Kunz and Larkin.'

Relke's Adam's apple did a quick genuflection. 'If you saw me go, you musta seen *how* I went.'

Novotny shook him. 'What'd they want with you?' he barked.

'Nothing.'

Joe's eyes turned to dark slits. 'Relke, I told you, I told the rest of my men. I told you what I'd do to any sonofabitch on my team that got mixed up with the Party. Pappy don't allow that crap. Now shall I do it to you here, or do you want to go down to the dayroom?'

'Honest, Joe, I'm not mixed up in it. I got interested in what Larkin had to say—back maybe six months ago. But I never signed up. I never even meant to.'

'Six months? Was that about the time you got your Dear John letter from Fran?'

'Right after that, Joe.'

'Well, that figures. So what's Larkin after you about now?'

'I guess he wonders why I asked questions but never joined.'

'I don't want your guesses. What did he say out there, and what did you say to him?'

'He wanted to know why I didn't sign up, that's all.'

'And you told him what?'

'No deal.'

'So?'

'So, I came on back and took a shower.'

Novotny stared at him for a few seconds. 'You're lying,' he grunted, but released him anyway. 'OK, Relke, but you better listen to this. You're a good lineman. You've stayed out of trouble. You get along with the rest of the team. If you got out of line in some *other* way, I'd figure it was about time you let off some steam. I'd stick up for you. But get mixed up with the Party—and I'll stomp you. When I'm through stomping you, I'll report you off my team. Understand?'

'Sure, Joe.'

Novotny grunted and stepped away from him. 'No hard feelings, Relke.'

'Naah.' The lineman went back to the mirror and started shaving again. That his hand remained steady was a surprise to him. Novotny had never before laid a hand on him, and Relke hoped the first time would be the last. He had watched Joe mop up the dayroom with Benet for playing fast and loose with safety rules while working a hotstick job, and it put Benet in sick bay for three days. Novotny was small, but he was built like a bunker. He was a fair overseer, but he handled his men in the only way he knew how to handle them on such a job. He expected self-discipline and self-imposed obedience, and when he didn't get it, he took it as a personal insult and a challenge to a duel. Out on the lava, men were pressure-packed, hermetically sealed charges of high explosive blood and bone; one man's folly could mean the death of several others, and there was no recourse to higher authority or admonitions from the dean, with a team on the lava.

'What's your grudge against the Party, Joe?' Relke asked while he scraped under his neck.

'No grudge. Not as long as Benet, Braxton, Relke, Henderson, Beasley, Tremini, and Novotny stay out of it. No grudge at all. I'm for free love and nickel beer as much as the next guy. But I'm not for getting my ass shot off. I'm not for fouling up the whole Lunar project just to get the Schneider-Volkov Act repealed, when you can't get it repealed that way anyhow. I'm not for facing a General Space Court and getting sentenced to blowout. That's all. No grudge.'

'What makes you think a general strike couldn't force repeal, Joe?'

The pusher spat contemptuously at the disposal chute and missed. 'A general strike on the Lunar Project? Hell, Relke, use your head. It'd never work. A strike against the government is rough to pull off, even on Earth. Up here, it'd be suicide. The

Party's so busy yelling about who's right and who's wrong and who's getting a raw deal—and what they ought to do about it—that they forget the important point: who's in the driver's seat. So what if we shut down Copernicus and all the projects like this one? Copernicus has a closed ecology, its own plant-animal cycle, sure. We don't need much from Earth to keep it running—but there's the hitch: don't need *much*. The ecology slips out of balance now and then. Every month or two it has to get a transfusion from Earth. Compost bacteria, or a new strain of algae because our strain starts mutating—it's always something like that. If a general strike cut us off from Earth, the World Parliament could just sit passing solemn gas through their waffle-bottom chairs and wait. They could debate us to death in two months.'

'But world opinion—'

'Hell, *they* make world opinion, not *us*.'

Relke stopped shaving and looked around. 'Joe?'

'Yah.'

'Kunz and Larkin'd kill me for telling you. Promise not to say anything?'

The pusher glowered at him for a moment. 'Look, Relke, nobody brutalizes Joe Novotny's men, I'll handle Kunz and Larkin. You'd better spill. You think it's informing if you tell *me?*'

Relke shook his head. 'Guess not. OK, Joe. It's this: I've been to three cell meetings. I heard some stuff. I think the strike's supposed to start come sundown.'

'I heard that too. If it does, we'll all be—' He broke off. The cabin's intercom was suddenly blaring.

Attention, all personnel, attention. Unidentified bird at thirty degrees over horizon, south-southwest, braking fire for landing in our vicinity. All men on the line take cover. Safety team to the ready room on the double. Rescue team scramble, rescue team scramble.

Relke rolled the cord neatly around the razor and stared at it. 'I'll be damned,' he muttered. 'It *was* a ship I saw. What ship would be landing way the hell out here?' He glanced around at Novotny.

The pusher was already at the periscope viewer, his face buried in the sponge rubber eyepieces. He cranked it around in a search pattern toward the south-southwest.

'See anything?'

'Not yet . . . *yeah,* there she is. Braking in fast—now what the hell!'

'Give me a look.'

They traded turns at the viewer.

'She's a fusion furnace job. Cold fusion. Look at that blue tail.'

'Why land way out here?'

The hatch burst open and the rest of the men spilled in from the dayroom. A confused babble filled the cabin. 'I tole ya and I tole ya!' said Bama Braxton. 'That theah mine shaff at Tycho is the play-yun evvy-dance. Gennlemen, weah about to have stranjuhs in ouah midst.'

'Cut that superstitious bullspit, Brax,' Novotny grunted. 'There *aren't* any aliens. We got enough bogeys around here without you scaring the whoop out of yourself with that line of crap.'

'Theah ahn't no aliens!' Braxton howled. 'Theah ahn't no *aliens?* Joe, youah bline to the play-yun evvy-dance!'

'He right, Joe,' said Lije Henderson, the team's only Negro and Bama's chief crony. 'That mine shaff speak fo' itself.'

'That mine's a million years old,' Joe snorted, 'and they're not even sure it's a mine. I said drop it.'

'That *ship* speak fo' itself!'

'Drop it! This isn't the first time a ship overshot Crater City and had to set down someplace else. Ten to one it's full of Parliament waffle-bottoms, all complaining their heads off. Maybe they've got a meteor puncture and need help quick.'

The closed-circuit intercom suddenly buzzed, and Novotny turned to see the project engineer's face on the small viewer.

'Are all your men up and dressed, Joe?' he asked when Novotny had answered the call.

'EVERYBODY PIPE DOWN! Sorry, Suds. No—well, except for Beasley, they're up. Beasley's logging sack time.'

'The hell Beasley is!' complained Beasley from his bunk. 'With you verbing nouns of a noun all yapping like—'

'Shut up, Beez. Go on, Suds.'

'We got contact with that ship. They've got reactor troubles. I tried to get Crater City on the line, but there's an outage on the circuit somewhere. I need some men to take a tractor and backtrack toward Copernicus. Look for a break in the circuit.'

'Why call me?'

'The communication team is tied up, Joe.'

'Yeah, but I'm not a communic—'

'Hell!' Brodanovitch exploded. 'It doesn't take an electronics engineer to splice a broken wire, does it?'

'OK, Suds, we'll go. Take it easy. What about that ship?'

The engineer paused to mop his face. He looked rather bleak suddenly. 'I don't know if it's safe to tell you. But you'll find out anyhow. Watch out for a riot.'

'Not a runaway reactor—'

'Worse, Joe. Women.'

'WOMEN!' It was a high piping scream from Beasley. 'Did he say *women?*' Beasley was out of bed and into his boots.

'WOMEN!' They came crowding around the intercom screen.

'Back off!' Novotny barked. 'Go on, Suds.'

'It's a troupe of entertainers, Joe. Clearance out of Algiers. They say they're scheduled for a performance in Crater City, come nightfall. That's all I know, except they're mostly women.'

'Algiers! Jeez! Belly dancers . . . !'

The room was a confused babble.

'Wait a minute,' said Suds. His face slid off the screen as he talked to somebody in the boss tank. Moments later he was back. 'Their ship just put down, Joe. Looks like a safe landing. The rescue team is out there. You'll pass the ship on the way up the line. Get moving.'

'Sure, Suds.' Novotny switched off and looked around at the sudden scramble. 'I'll be damned if you do!' he yelled. 'You can't all go. Beasley, Henderson—'

'No, bigod you don't, Joe!' somebody howled. 'Draw straws!'

'OK. I can take three of you, no more.'

They drew. Chance favored Relke, Braxton, and Henderson. Minutes later they crowded into the electric runabout and headed southeast along the line of stately steel towers that filed back toward Copernicus. The ship was in sight. Taller than the towers, the nacelles of the downed bird rose into view beyond the broken crest of a distant lava butte. She was a freight shuttle, space-constructed and not built for landing on Earth. Relke eyed the emblem on the hull of her crew nacelle while the runabout nosed onto the strip of graded roadbed that paralleled the transmission line back to Crater City. The emblem was unfamiliar.

'That looks like the old *RS Voltaire,*' said the lineman. 'Somebody must have bought her, Joe. Converted her to passenger service.'

'Maybe. Now keep an eye on the telephone line.'

The pusher edged the runabout toward the trolley rods. The overhead power transmission line had been energized by sections during the construction of it, and the line was hot as far as the road had been extended. Transformer stations fed energy from the 200 kilovolt circuit into the 1,500 volt trolley bars that ran down the center of the roadbed. Novotny stopped the vehicle at the end of the finished construction and sidled it over until the feeler arms crackled against the electrified bus rods and locked in place. He switched the batteries to 'charge' and drove on again.

'Relke, you're supposed to be watching that talk circuit, not the ship.'

'OK, Joe, in a minute.'

'You horny bastard, you can't see their bloomers through that titanium hull. Put the glasses down and watch the line.'

'OK, just a minute. I'm trying to find out who owns her. The emblem's—'

'Now, dammit!'

'No marking on her except her serial number and a picture of a rooster—and something else that's been painted over.'

'RELKE!'

'Sure, Joe, OK.'

'Girls!' marveled Lije Henderson. 'Whenna lass time you touch a real girl, Brax?'

'Don' ass me, Lije, don' evum ass me. I sweah, if I evum touch a lady's li'l pink fingah right now, I could—'

'Hell, I could jus' sittin' heah lookin' at that ship. Girls. God! Lemme have those glasses, Relke.'

Novotny braked the runabout to a halt. 'All right, get your helmets on,' he snapped. 'Pressure your suits. I'm going to pump air out.'

'Whatthehell! *Why*, Joe?'

'So you can get out of this heap. You're walking back. I'll go on and find the break myself.'

Braxton squealed like a stuck pig; a moment later all three of them were on him. 'Please, Joe. . . . Fuh the love a heaven, Joe, have a haht. . . . Gawd, *women!*'

'Get off my lap, you sonofabitch!' he barked at Braxton, who sat on top of him, grabbing at the controls. 'Wait—I'll tell you what. Put the damn binoculars down and watch the line. Don't say another damn word about dames until we find the break and splice it. Swear to that, you bastards, and you can stay. I'll stop at their ship on our way back, and then you can stare all you want to. OK?'

'Joe, I sweah on a stack of—'

'All right, then watch the line.'

They drove on in silence. The ship had fired down on a flat stretch of ground about four miles from the construction train, a few hundred yards from the trolley road. They stared at it as the runabout crawled past, and Novotny let the vehicle glide to a halt.

'The ramp's out and the ladder's down,' said Relke. 'Somebody must have come out.'

'Unglue your eyes from that bird and look around,' Novotny grunted. 'You'll see why the ladder's down.' He jerked his thumb toward a row of vehicles parked near the massive ship.

'The rescue team's wagons. But wheah's the rescue team?'

No crewmen were visible in the vicinity of the ship or the parked runabouts. Novotny switched on the radio, punched the channel selector, and tried a call, reading the call code off the side of the safety runabout.

'Double Able Niner, this is One Four William. Talk back, please.'

They sat in silence. There was nothing but a hiss of solar interference from the radio and the sound of heavy breathing from the men.

'Those lucky ole bastahds!' Braxton moaned. 'You know wheah they gone, gennlemen? I taya weah they gone. They clambered right up the ladies' ladduh, thass wheah. You know wheah they gone? I taya, alright—'

'Knock it off. Let's get moving. Tell us on the way back.'

'Those lucky ole—'

The runabout moved ahead across the glaring land.

Relke: 'Joe?'

'Yeah?'

'Joe, on our way back, can we go over and see if they'll let us climb aboard?'

Novotny chuckled. 'I thought you were off dames, Relke. I thought when Fran sent you the Dear John, you said dames were all a bunch of—'

'Damn, Joe! You could have talked all day without saying "Fran."' The lineman's throat worked a brief spasm, and he stared out across the broken moonscape with dismal eyes.

'Sorry I mentioned it,' Novotny grunted. 'But sure, I guess

one of us could walk over and ask if they mind a little more company on board.'

Lije: *'One* of us! Who frinstance—*you?'*

Joe: 'No, you can draw for it—not now, you creep! Watch the line.'

They watched in silence. The communication circuit was loosely strung on temporary supports beside the roadbed. The circuit was the camp's only link with Crater City, for the horizon interposed a barrier to radio reception, such reception being possible only during the occasional overhead transits of the lunar satellite station which carried message-relaying equipment. The satellite's orbit had been shifted to cover a Russian survey crew near Clavius, however, and its passages over the Trolley Project were rare.

'I jus' *thought,'* Lije muttered suddenly, smacking his fist in his palm.

Relke: 'Isn't that getting a little drastic, Lije?'

'I jus' thought. If we fine that outage, less don' fix it!'

Joe: 'What kind of crazy talk is that?'

'Lissen, you know what ole Suds want to call Crater City *fo'? He* want to call 'em so's they'll senn a bunch of tank wagons down heah and tote those gals back to town. Thass what he want to call 'em fo'!'

Braxton slapped his forehead. 'Luvva God! He's right. Y'all heah that? Is he right, Joe, or is he right?'

'I guess that's about the size of it.'

'We mi'not evum get a look at 'em!' Braxton wailed.

'Less don' fix it, Joe!'

'I sweah, if I evum touch one of theah precious li'l fingahs, I'd—'

'Shut up and watch the line.'

Relke: 'Why didn't he use a bridge on the circuit and find out where the break was, Joe?'

'A bridge won't work too well on that line.'

'How fah we gonna keep on drivin', Joe?'

'Until we find the break. Relke, turn up that blower a little. It's beginning to stink in here.'

'Fresh ayah!' sighed Braxton as the breeze hit them from the fan.

Relke: 'I wonder if it's fresh. I keep wondering if it doesn't come out foul from the purifier, but we've been living in it too long to be able to tell. I even dream about it. I dream about going back to Earth and everybody runs away from me. Coughing and holding their noses. I can't get close to a girl even in a dream anymore.'

'Ah reckon a head-shrinker could kill hisself a-laughin' over that one.'

'Don't talk to me about head shrinkers.'

'Watch the damn line.'

Braxton: 'Talk about *dreams!* Listen, I had one lass sleep shift that I oughta tell y'all about. Gennlemen, if she wasn't the ohnriest li'l—'

Novotny cursed softly under his breath and tried to keep his eyes on both the road and the communications circuit.

Relke: 'Let 'em jabber, Joe. I'll watch it.'

Joe: 'It's bad enough listening to a bunch of jerks in a locker room bragging about the dames they've made. But Braxton! Braxton's got to brag about his dreams. Christ! Send me back to Earth. I'm fed up.'

'Aww, Joe, we got nothin' else to talk about up heah.'

They drove for nearly an hour and a half without locating the outage. Novotny pulled the runabout off the hot trolleys and coasted to a stop. 'I'm deflating the cab,' he told them. 'Helmets on, pressure up your suits.'

'Joe, weah not walkin' back from heah!' Bama said flatly.

'Oh, blow yourself out, Brax!' the pusher said irritably. 'I'm getting out for a minute. C'mon, get ready for vacuum.'

'Why?'

'Don't say *why* to me outside the sleep-tank, corn pone! Just do it.'

'Damn! Novotny's in a humah! Les say "yassah" to him, Bama.'

'You too, Lije!'

'Yassah.'

'Can it.' Novotny got the pressure pumped down to two pounds, and then let the rest of the air spew out slowly into vacuum. He climbed out of the runabout and loped over to the low-hanging spans of the communication circuit. He tapped into it with the suit audio and listened for a moment. Relke saw his lips moving as he tried a call, but nothing came through the lineman's suit radio. After about five minutes, he quit talking and beckoned the rest of them back to the runabout.

'That was Brodanovitch,' he said after they were inside and the pressure came up again. 'So the circuit break must be on up ahead.'

'Oh, hell, we'll *navah* get a look at those ladies!'

'Calm down. We're going back—' He paused a moment until the elated whooping died down. 'Suds says let them send a crew out of Copernicus to fix it. I guess there's no hurry about moving those people out of there.'

'The less hurry, the bettuh . . . *hot dawg!* C'mon, Joe, roll it!' Bama and Lije sat rubbing their hands. Only Relke seemed detached, his enthusiasm apparently cooled. He sat staring out at the meteor display on the dust-flats. He kept rubbing absently at the ring finger of his left hand. There was no ring there, nor even a mark on the skin. The pusher's eye fell on the slow nervous movement.

'Fran again?' Joe grunted.

The lineman nodded.

'I got my Dear John note three years ago, Relke.'

Relke looked around at him in surprise. 'I didn't know you were married, Joe.'

'I guess I wasn't as married as I thought I was.'

Relke stared outside again for awhile. 'How do you get over it?'

'You don't. Not up here on Luna. The necessary and sometimes sufficient condition for getting over a dame is the availability of other dames. So, you don't.'

'Hell, Joe!'

'Yeah.'

'The movement's not such a bad idea.'

'Can it!' the pusher snapped.

'It's true. Let women come to Crater City, or send us home. It makes sense.'

'You're only looking at the free love and nickel beer end of it, Relke. You can't raise kids in low gravity. There are five graves back in Crater City to prove it. Kids' graves. Six feet long. They grow themselves to death.'

'I know but . . .' He shrugged uncomfortably and watched the meteor display again.

'When do we draw?' said Lije. 'Come on Joe, less draw for who goes talk ouah way onto the ship.'

Relke: 'Say, Joe, how come they let dames in an entertainment troupe come to the moon, but they won't let our wives come? I thought the Schneider-Volkov Act was supposed to keep all women out of space, period.'

'No, they couldn't get away with putting it like that. Against the WP constitution. The law just says that all personnel on any member country's lunar project must be of a single sex.

Theoretically some country—Russia, maybe—could start an all-girl lunar mine project, say. Theoretically. But how many lady muckers do you know? Even in Russia.'

Lije: 'When do we draw? Come on, Joe, less draw.'

'Go ahead and draw. Deal me out.'

Chance favored Henderson. 'Fast-uh, Joe. Hell, less go fastuh, befo' the whole camp move over theah.'

Novotny upped the current to the redline and left it there. The long spans of transmission line, some of them a mile or more from tower to tower, swooped past in stately cadence.

'There she is! Man!'

'You guys are building up for a big kick in the rump. They'll never let us aboard.'

'Theah's two more cahs pahked over theah.'

'Yeah, and still nobody in sight on the ground.'

Novotny pulled the feelers off the trolleys again. 'OK, Lije, go play John Alden. Tell 'em we just want to look, not touch.'

Henderson was bounding off across the flats moments after the cabin had been depressurized to let him climb out. They watched him enviously while the pressure came up again. His black face flashed with sweat in the sunlight as he looked back to wave at them from the foot of the ladder.

Relke glanced down the road toward the rolling construction camp. 'You going to call in, Joe? Ought to be able to reach their antenna from here.'

'If I do, Brodanovitch is sure to say "haul-ass on back to camp." '

'Never mind, then! Forget I said it!'

The pusher chuckled. 'Getting interested, Relke?'

'I don't know. I guess I am.' He looked quickly toward the towering rocket.

'Mostly you want to know how close you are to being rid of her, maybe?'

'I guess—Hey, they're letting him in.'

'That lucky ole bastuhd!' Bama moaned.

The airlock opened as Lije scaled the ladder. A helmet containing a head of unidentifiable gender looked out and down, watching the man climb. Lije paused to wave. After a moment's hesitancy, the space-suited figure waved back.

'Hey, up theah, y'all mind a little company?'

The party who watched him made no answer. Lije shook his head and climbed on. When he reached the lock, he held out a glove for an assist, but the figure stepped back quickly. Lije stared inside. The figure was holding a gun. Lije stepped down a rung. The gun beckoned impatiently for him to get inside. Reluctantly Lije obeyed.

The hatch closed. A valve spat a jet of frost, and they watched the pressure dial slowly creep to ten psi. Lije watched the stranger unfasten his helmet, then undid his own. The stranger was male, and the white goggle marks about his eyes betrayed him as a spacer. His thin dark features suggested Semitic or Arabic origins.

'Parlez-vous français?'

'Naw,' said Lije. 'Sho' don't. Sorry.'

The man tossed his head and gave a knowing snort. 'Ah! Afrique-Américain. Yais. I had forgotten. I misthought you African. Apologeez?'

'Needn' bothuh,' said Lije. 'Coss, if you feelin' apologetic, you might put that pistola back in yo' boot.'

'Ho?' The man looked down at the gun in his hand as if he had forgotten it. 'Ho! It is first necessaire that we find out who you are,' he explained, and brandished the weapon under Lije's nose. He grinned a flash of white teeth. 'Who send you here?'

'Nobody send me. I come unduh my own steam. Some fellas in my moonjeep pulled cahds, and I—'

'Whup! You are—ah *tin Unteroffizier? Mais non,* wrong sprach—you *l'officiale?* Officer? Company man?'

'Who, me? Lahd, no. I'm juss a hot-stick man on B-shif'. You muss be lookin' fo' Suds Brodanovitch.'

'Why you come to this ship?'

'Well, the fellas and I heard tell theah was some gals, and we—'

The man waved the gun impatiently and pressed a button near the inner hatch. A red indicator light went on.

'Yes?' A woman's voice, rather hoarse. Lije's chest heaved with sudden emotion, and his sigh came out a bleat.

The man spoke in a flood of French. The woman did not reply at once. Lije noticed the movement of a viewing lens beside the hatch; it was scanning him from head to toe.

The woman's voice shifted to an intimate contralto. 'OK, dearie, you come right in here where it's nice and warm.'

The inner hatch slid open. It took Lije a few seconds to realize that she had been talking to him. She stood there smiling at him like a middle-aged schoolmarm.

'Why don't you come on in and meet the girls?'

Eyes popping, Lije Henderson stumbled inside.
He was gone a long time.

When he finally came out, the men in Novotny's runabout took turns cursing at him over the suit frequency. *'Fa chrissake, Henderson, we've been sitting here using up oxy for over an hour while you been horsing around . . .'* They waited for him with the runabout, cabin depressurized.

Lije was panting wildly as he ran toward them. *'Lissen to the bahstud giggle,'* Bama said disgustedly.

'Y'all juss don' know, y'all juss don' KNOW!' Lije was chanting between pants.

'Get in here, you damn traitor!'

'Hones', I couldn' help myself. I juss couldn'.'

'Well, do the rest of us get aboard her, or not?' Joe snapped.

'Hell, go ahead, man! It's wide open. Evahthing's wide open.'

'Girls?' Relke grunted.

'Girls. God yes! Girls.'

'You coming with us?' Joe asked. Lije shook his head and fell back on the seat, still panting. *'Lahd, no! I couldn't stand it. I juss want to lie heah and look up at old Mamma Earth and feel like a human again.'* He grinned beatifically. *'Y'all go on.'*

Braxton was staring at his crony with curious suspicion. *'Man, those must be some entuhtainuhs! Whass the mattah with you, Lije?'*

Henderson whooped and pounded his leg. *'Hoo hoo! Hooeee! Entuhtainuhs, he says. Hoo-hooeee! You mean y'all still don' know what that ship is?'*

They had already climbed out of the tractor. Novotny glared back in at Lije. *'We've been waiting to hear it from you, Henderson,'* he snapped.

Lije sat up grinning. *'That's no stage show troupe! That ship, so help me Hannah, is a—hoo hoo hooee—is a goddam flyin' HO-house.'* He rolled over on the seat and surrendered to laughter.

Novotny looked around for his men and found himself standing alone. Braxton was already on the ladder, and Relke was just starting up behind.

'Hey, you guys come back here!'

'Drop dead, Joe.'

Novotny stared after them until they disappeared through the lock. He glanced back at Lije. Henderson was in a grinning beatific trance. The pusher shrugged and left him lying there, still wearing his pressure suit in the open cabin. The pusher trotted after his men toward the ship.

Before he was halfway there, a voice broke into his headsets. *'Where the devil are you going, Novotny? I want a talk with you!'*

He stopped to glance back. The voice belonged to Brodanovitch, and it sounded sore. The engineer's runabout had nosed in beside Novotny's; Suds sat in the cab and beckoned at him angrily. Joe trudged on back and climbed in through the vehicle's coffin-sized airlock. Brodanovitch glared at him while the pusher removed his helmet.

'What the devil's going on over there?'

'At the ship?' Joe paused. Suds was livid. 'I don't know exactly.'

'I've been calling Safety and Rescue for an hour and a half. Where are they?'

'In the ship, I guess.'

'You *guess!*'

'Hell, chief, take it easy. We just got here. I don't know what's going on.'

'Where are your men?'

Novotny jerked his thumb at the other runabout. 'Henderson's in there. Relke and Brax went to the ship.'

'And that's where you were going just now, I take it,' Suds snarled.

'Take that tone of voice and shove it, Suds! You know where you told me to go. I went. Now I'm off. We're on our own time unless you tell us different.'

The engineer spent a few seconds swallowing his fury. 'All right,' he grunted. 'But every man on that rescue squad is going to face a Space Court, and if I have any say about it, they'll get decomped.'

Novotny's jaw dropped. 'Slow down, Suds. Explosive decompression is for mutiny or murder. What're you talking about?'

'Murder.'

'Wha-a-at?'

'That's what I call it. A demolition man—Hardin, it was—had a blowout. With only one man standing by on the rescue gear.'

'Meteor dust?'

'Yeah.'

'Would it have made any difference if Safety and Rescue had been on the job?'

Suds glowered. 'Maybe, maybe not. An inspector might have spotted the bulge in his suit before it blew.' He shook an angry finger toward the abandoned Safety & Rescue vehicles. 'Those men are going to stand trial for negligent homicide. It's the principle, damn it!'

'Sure, Suds. I guess you're right. I'll be right back.'

Henderson was sleeping in his pressure suit when Novotny climbed back into his own runabout. The cab was still a vacuum. He got the hatch closed, turned on the air pumps, then woke Henderson.

'Lije, you been with a woman?'

'Nnnnnngg-*nnnng!* I hope to tell!' He shot a quick glance toward the rocket as if to reassure himself as to its reality. 'And man, was she a little—'

Joe shook him again. 'Listen. Brodanovitch is in the next car. Bull mad. I'll ask you again. You been with a woman?'

'Woman? You muss of lost yoah mine, Joe. Lass time I saw a woman was up at Atlanta.' He rolled his eyes up toward the Earth crescent in the heavens. 'Sure been a long ole time. Atlanta . . . *man!*'

'That's better.'

Lije jerked his head toward Brodanovitch's jeep. 'What's ole wet blanket gonna do? Chase those gals out of here, I 'spect?'

'I don't know. That's not what he's frothing about, Lije. Hardin got killed while the S&R boys were shacking up over there. Suds doesn't even *know* what's in that ship. He acts like he's got about a dozen troubles running loose at once, and he doesn't know which way to grab.'

'He don't even *know?* How we evah gonna keep him from findin' out?' Lije shot another glance at the ship and jumped. 'Uh-oh! Looka theah! Yonder they come. Clamberin' down the ladies' ladduh. Theah's Joyce and Lander and Petzel—other one looks like Crump. Half the Safety team, Joe. Hoo-eee! They got that freshly bred look. You can evum tell it from heah. Uh-oh!'

Brodanovitch had climbed out of his runabout. Bellowing at his mic, he charged toward the ship. The S&R men took a few lopes toward their vehicles, saw Brodanovitch, and stopped. One man turned tail and bolted for the ladder again. Gesturing furiously, the engineer bore down on them.

'Leave the radio off, Joe. Sure glad we don' have to listen to that bull bellow.'

They sat watching the safety men, who managed somehow to look stark naked despite their bulgey pressure suits. Suds stalked toward them like an amok runner, beating a gloved fist into his palm and working his jaw at them.

'Suds don' know how to get along with men when he *want* to get along with 'em, and he don' know how to fuss at 'em when he don't want to get along. Man, look how he rave!'

'Yeah. Suds is a smart engineer, but he's a rotten overseer.'

The ship's airlock opened again and another man started out. He stopped with one foot on the top rung of the ladder. He looked down at Brodanovitch and the S&R men. He pulled his leg back inside and closed the hatch. Novotny chuckled.

'That was Relke, the damn fool.'

Lije smote his forehead. 'Look at Suds! They tole him! They went an *tole* him, Joe. We'll nevah get back in that ship now.'

The pusher watched the four figures on the plain. They were just standing there. Brodanovitch had stopped gesticulating. For a few seconds he seemed frozen. His head turned slowly as he looked up at the rocket. He took three steps toward it, then stopped.

'He gonna have apoplexy, thass what he gonna have.'

Brodanovitch turned slowly. He gave the S&R men a blank look, then broke into a run toward his tractor.

'I'd better climb out,' Joe said.

He met the engineer beside the command runabout. Sud's face was a livid mask behind the faceplate. *'Get in,'* he snapped at the pusher.

As soon as they were inside, he barked, 'Drive us to Crater City.'

'Slow down, Suds.'

'Joe. That ship. Damn brothel. Out to fleece the camp.'

'So what're you going to do in Crater City?'

'Tell Parkeson, what else?'

'And what's the camp going to be doing while you're gone?'

That one made him pause. Finally he shook his head. 'Drive, Joe.'

Novotny flipped the switch and glanced at the gauges. 'You haven't got enough oxygen in this bug to last out the trip.'

'Then we'll get another one.'

'Better take a minute to think it over, Suds. You're all revved up. What the hell can Parkeson do?'

'What can he *do?* What can—migawd, Joe!' Suds choked.

'Well?'

'He can get that ship out of here, he can have those women interned.'

'How? Suppose they refuse to budge. Who appointed Parkeson king of creation? Hell, he's only *our* boss, Suds. The moon's open to any nation that wants to send a ship, or to any corporation that can get a clearance. The W.P. decided that a long time ago.'

'But it's illegal—those women, I mean!'

'How do you know? Maybe their racket's legal in Algiers. That's where you told me they had clearance from, didn't you? And if you're thinking about the Schneider-Volkov Act, it just applies to the Integrated Projects, not wildcat teams.'

Brodanovitch sat silent for a few moments, his throat working. He passed a shaky hand over his eyes. 'Joe, we've got to keep discipline. Why can't I ever make the men understand that? On a moon project, it's discipline or die. You know that, Joe.'

'Sure I know it. You know it. Parkeson knows it. The First Minister of the Space Ministry knows it. But the men don't know it, and they never will. They don't know what the word "discipline" means, and it's no good trying to tell them. It's an overseer's word. It means your outfit's working for you like your own arms and legs. One brain and one body. When it cracks, you've just got a loose handful of stray men. No coordination. You can see it, but they can't see it. "Discipline" is just a dirty word in the ranks, Suds.'

'Joe, what'll I do?'

'It's your baby, not mine. Give it first aid. Then talk to Parkeson later, if you want to.'

Suds sat silent for half a minute, then: 'Drive back to the main wagon.'

Novotny started the motors. 'What are you going to do?'

'Announce Code Red, place the ship off limits, put an armed guard on it, and hope the Crater City crew gets that telephone circuit patched up quick. That's all I can do.'

'Then let me get a safe distance away from you before you do it.'

'You think it'll cause trouble?'

'Good Lord, Suds, use your head. You've got a campful of men who haven't been close to a dame in months and years, even to talk to. They're sick, they're scared, they're fed-up, they want to go home. The Party's got them bitter, agitated. I'd hate to be the guy who puts those women off limits.'

'What would you do?'

'I'd put the screws on the shift that's on duty. I'd work hell out of the crews that are supposed to be on the job. I'd make a horrible example out of the first man to goof off. But first I'd tell the off-duty team pushers they can take their crews over to that ship, one crew at a time, and in an orderly manner.'

'What? And be an accomplice? Hell, no!'

'Then do it your own way. Don't ask me.'

Novotny parked the runabout next to the boss-wagon. 'Mind if I use your buggy for awhile, Suds?' he asked. 'I left mine back there, and I've got to pick up my men.'

'Go ahead, but get them back here—fast.'

'Sure, Suds.'

He backed the runabout out again and drove down to B-shift's sleep-wagon. He parked again and used the airlock phone. 'Beasley, Benet, the rest of you—come on outside.'

Five minutes later they trooped out through the lock. 'What's the score, Joe?'

'The red belts are ahead, that's all I know.'

'Come on, you'll find out.'

'Sleep! I haven't had no sleep since—*Say!* You takin' us over to that ship, Joe?'

'That's the idea.'

'YAYHOO!' Beasley danced up and down. 'Joe, we love ya!'

'Cut it. This is once-and-once-only. You're going once, and you're not going again.'

'Who says?'

'Novotny says.'

'But *why?'* Benet wailed.

'What did you say?'

'I said "why!" '

'OK. I'll tell you why. Brodanovitch is going to put the ship off limits. If I get you guys in under the wire, you've got no gripe later on—when Suds hangs out the big No.'

'Joe, that's chicken.'

Novotny put on the brakes. 'Get out and walk back, Benet.'

'Joe—!'

'Benet.'

'Look, I didn't mean anything.'

Novotny paused. If Brodanovitch was going to try to do things the hard way, he'd lose control of his own men unless he gave them loose rein for a while first—keeping them reminded that he still *had* the reins. But Benet was getting out of hand lately. He had to decide. Now.

'Look at me, Benet.'

Benet looked up. Joe smacked him. Benet sat back, looking surprised. He wiped his nose on the back of a glove and looked at the red smear. He wiped it again. The smear was bigger.

'You can stay, Benet, but if you do, I'll bust your hump after we get back. You want it that way?'

Benet looked at the rocket; he looked at Joe; he looked at the rocket. 'Yeah. We'll see who does the busting. Let's go.'

'All right, but do you see any other guys taking their teams over?'

'No.'

'But you think you're getting a chicken deal.'

'Yeah.'

The pusher drove on, humming to himself. As long as he could keep them alternately loving him and hating him, everything was secure. Then he was Mother. Then they didn't stop to think or rationalize. They just reacted to Mother. It was easy to handle men reacting, but it wasn't so easy to handle men thinking. Novotny liked it the easy way, especially during a heavy meteor fall.

'It is of no importance to me,' said Madame d'Annecy, 'if you are the commandant of the whole of space, M'sieur. You wish entrance, I must ask you to contribute thees small fee. It is not in my nature to become unpleasant like thees, but you have bawl in my face, M'sieur.'

'Look,' said Brodanovitch, 'I didn't come over here for . . . for what you think I came over here for.' His ears reddened. 'I don't want a girl, that is.'

The madame's prim mouth made a small pink O of sudden understanding. 'Ah, M'sieur, I begin to see. You are one of those. But in that I cannot help you. I have only girls.'

The engineer choked. He started toward the hatch. A man with a gun slid into his path.

'Permit yourself to be restrained, M'sieur.'

'There are four men in there that are supposed to be on the job, and I intend to get them. And the others too, while I'm at it.'

'Is it that you have lost your boy friend, perhaps?'

Brodanovitch croaked incomprehensibly for a moment, then collapsed onto a seat beside the radar table that Madame d'Annecy was using for an accounting desk. 'I'm no fairy,' he said.

'I am pleased to hear it, M'sieur. I was beginning to pity you.

Now if you will please sign the sight draft, so that we may telecast it—'

'I am *not* paying twelve hundred dollars just to get my men out of there!'

'I do not haggle, M'sieur. The price is fixed.'

'Call them down here!'

'It cannot be done. They pay for two hours, for two hours they stay. Undisturbed.'

'All right, let's see the draft.'

Madame d'Annecy produced a set of forms from the map case and a small gold fountain pen from her ample bosom. 'Your next of kin, M'sieur?' She handed him a blank draft.

'Wait a minute! How did you know where my account—'

'Is it not the correct firm?'

'Yes, but how did you know?' He looked at the serial number on the form, then looked up accusingly. 'This is a telecopy form. You have a teletransmitter on board?'

'But of course! We could not risk having payment stopped after services rendered. The funds will be transferred to our account before you leave this ship. I assure you, we are well protected.'

'I assure you, you are all going to jail.'

Madame d'Annecy threw back her head and laughed heartily. She said something in French to the man at the door, then smiled at the unhappy engineer. 'What law prevails here, M'sieur?'

'UCOJE does. Uniform Code of Justice, Extraterrestrial. It's a semi-military—'

'U.N.-based, I believe?'

'Certainly.'

'Now I know little of thees matters, but my attorneys would be delighted, I am certain, if you can tell me: which articles of thees UCOJE is to be used for inducing us to be incarcerated?'

'Why . . . Uh . . .' Suds scratched nervously at one corner of his moustache. He glanced at the man with the gun. He gazed forlornly at the sight draft.

'Exactly!' Mme d'Annecy said brightly. 'There have been no women to speak of on the moon since the unfortunate predicament of *les enfants perdus*. The moon-born grotesque ones. How could they think to pass laws against thees—thees *ancien* establishment, thees *maison intime*— when there are no women, eh M'sieur?'

'But you falsified your papers to get clearance. You must have.'

'But no. Our clearance is "free nation," not "world federal." We are an entertainment troupe, and my government's officials are most lenient in defining "entertainment." *Chacun à son gout,* eh?'

Suds sat breathing heavily. 'I can place this ship off limits.'

'If you can do that, if the men do not come'—she shrugged eloquently and spread her hands—'then we will simply move on to another project. There are plenty of others. But do you think thees putting us off limits will make you very popular with your men?'

'I'm not trying to win a popularity contest,' Suds wheezed. 'I'm trying to finish the last twelve miles of this line before sundown. You've got to get out of here before there's a complete work stoppage.'

'Thees project. It is important? Of an urgent nature?'

'There's a new uranium mine in the crater we're building toward. There's a colony there without an independent ecology. It has to be supplied from Copernicus. Right now, they're shooting supplies to them by rocket missile. It's too far to run surface freight without trolley service—or reactor-powered vehicles the size of battleships and expensive. We don't have the facilities to run a fleet of self-powered wagons that far.'

'Can they not run on diesel, perhaps?'

'If they carry the oxygen to burn the diesel with, and if everybody in Copernicus agrees to stop breathing the stuff.'

'*Embarras de choix*. I see.'

'It's essential that the line be finished before nightfall. If it isn't, that mine colony will have to be shipped back to Copernicus. They can't keep on supplying it by bird. And they can't move out any ore until the trolley is ready to run.'

Mme d'Annecy nodded thoughtfully. 'We wish to make the cordial entente with the lunar workers,' she murmured. 'We do not wish to cause the *bouleversement*—the disruption. Let us then negotiate, M'sieur.'

'I'm not making any deals with you, lady.'

'Ah, but such a hard position you take! I was but intending to suggest that you furnish us a copy of your camp's duty roster. If you will do that, Henri will not permit anyone to visit us if he is —how you say?—goofing off. Is it not that simple?'

'I will not be a party to robbery!'

'How is it robbery?'

'Twelve hundred dollars! Pay for two day-hitches. Lunar

days. Nearly two months. And you're probably planning to fleece them more than once.'

'*A bon marché!* Our expenses are terrific. Believe me, we expect no profit from this first trip.'

'First trip and last trip,' Suds grumbled.

'And who has complained about the price? No one so far excepting M'sieur. Look at it *thus* it is an investment.' She slid one of the forms across the table. 'Please to read it, M'sieur.'

Suds studied the paper for a moment and began to frown. '*Les Folies Lunaires*, Incorporated . . . a North African corporation . . . in consideration of the sum of one hundred dollars in hand paid by—who?—Howard Beasley!—aforesaid corporation sells and grants to Howard Beasley . . . *one share of common stock!*'

'M'sieur! Compose yourself! It is no fraud. Everybody gets a share of stock. It comes out of the twelve hundred. Who knows? Perhaps after a few trips, there will even be dividends. M'sieur? But you look positively ill! Henri, bring brandy for the gentleman.'

'So!' he grated. 'That's the way it goes, is it? Implicate everybody—nobody squawks.'

'But certainly. It is for our own protection, to be sure, but it is really stock.'

'Blackmail.'

'But no, M'sieur. All is legal.'

Henri brought a plastic cup and handed it to him; Suds shook his head.

'Take it, M'sieur. It is real brandy. We could bring only a few bottles, but there is sufficient pure alcohol for the mixing of cocktails.'

The small compartment was filled with the delicate perfume of the liquor; Brodanovitch glanced longingly at the plastic cup.

'It is seventy-year-old Courvoisier, M'sieur. Very pleasant.'

Suds took it reluctantly, dipped it toward Mme d'Annecy in self-conscious toast, and drained it. He acquired a startled expression; he clucked his tongue experimentally and breathed slowly through his nose.

'Good Lord!' he murmured absently.

Mme d'Annecy chuckled. 'M'sieur has forgotten the little pleasures. It was a shame to gulp it so. *Encore, Henri*. And one for myself, I think. Take time to enjoy this one, M'sieur.' She studied him for a time while Henri was absent. She shook her head and began putting the forms away, leaving out the sight draft and stock agreement which she pushed toward him, raising one inquisitive brow. He gazed expressionlessly at them. Henri returned with the brandy; Madame questioned him in French. He seemed insistently negative for a time, but then seemed to give grudging assent. *'Bien!'* she said, and turned to Brodanovitch: 'M'sieur, it will be necessary only for you to purchase the share of stock. Forget the fee.'

'What?' Suds blinked in confusion.

'I said—' The opening of the hatch interrupted her thought. A dazzling brunette in a filmy yellow dress bounced into the compartment, bringing with her a breath of perfume. Suds looked at her and emitted a loud guttural cluck. A kind of glazed incredulity kneaded his face into a mask of shocked granite wearing a supercilious moustache. The girl ignored his presence and bent over the table to chat excitedly in French with Mme. d'Annecy. Suds's eyes seemed to find a mind and will of their own; involuntarily they contemplated the details of her architecture, and found manifest fascination in the way she relieved an itch at the back of one trim calf by rubbing it vigorously with the instep of her other foot while she leaned over the desk and bounced lightly on tiptoe as she spoke.

'M'sieur Brodanovitch, the young lady wishes to know —M'sieur Brodanovitch?—*M'sieur!'*

'What—? Oh.' Suds straightened and rubbed his eyes. 'Yes?'

'One of your young men has asked Giselle out for a walk. We have pressure suits, of course. But is it safe to promenade about this area?' She paused. 'M'sieur, *please!'*

'What?' Suds shook his head. He tore his eyes away from the yellow dress and glanced at a head suddenly thrust in through the hatch. The head belonged to Kelke. It saw Brodanovitch and withdrew in haste, but Suds made no sign of recognition. He blinked at Madame again.

'M'sieur, is it safe?'

'What? Oh. I suppose it is.' He gulped his brandy and poured another.

Mme. d'Annecy spoke briefly to the girl who, after a hasty *merci* and a nod at Suds, went off to join Relke outside. When they were gone, Madame smilingly offered her pen to the engineer. Suds stared at it briefly, shook his head, and helped himself to another brandy. He gulped it and reached for his helmet. La d'Annecy snapped her fingers suddenly and went to a locker near the bulkhead. She came back with a quart bottle.

'M'sieur will surely accept a small token?' She offered the

bottle for his inspection. 'It is Mumms 2064, a fine year. Take it, M'sieur. Or do you not care for champagne? It is our only bottle, and what is one bottle of wine for such a crowd? Take it—or would you prefer the brandy?'

Suds blinked at the gift while he fastened his helmet and clamped it. He seemed dazed. She held the bottle out to him and smiled hopefully. Suds accepted it absentmindedly, nodded at her, and stepped into the airlock. The hatch slid closed.

Mme. d'Annecy started back toward her counting table. The alarm bell burst into a sudden brazen clamor. She looked back. A red warning signal flashed balefully. Henri burst in from the corridor, eyed the bell and the light, then charged toward the airlock. The gauge by the hatch showed zero pressure. He pressed a starter button, and a meter hummed to life. The pressure needle crept upward. The bell and the light continued a frenetic complaint. The motor stopped. Henri glanced at the gauge, then swung open the hatch. *'Allons! Ma foi, quelle merde!'*

Mme. d'Annecy came to peer around him into the small cubicle. Her subsequent shriek penetrated to the farthest corridors. Suds Brodanovitch had missed his last chance to become a stockholder.

'It wasn't yo' fault, Ma'am,' said Lije Henderson a few minutes later as they half-led half-carried her to her compartment. 'He knew bettuh than to step outside with that bottle of booze. You didn't know. You couldn' be 'spected to know. But he been heah long enough to know—a man make one mistake, thass all. BLOOIE.'

Blooie was too graphic to suit Madame; she sagged and began retching.

'C'mon, Ma'am, less get you in yo hammock.' They carried her into her quarters, eased her into bed, and stepped back out on the catwalk.

Lije mopped his face, leaned against a tension member, and glanced at Joe. 'Now how come you s'pose he had that bottle of fizzling giggle water up close to his helmet that way, Joe?'

'I don't know. Reading the label, maybe.'

'He sho' muss have had something on his mine.'

'Well, it's gone now.'

'Yeah. BLOOIE. Man!'

Relke had led the girl out through the lock in the reactor nacelle in order to evade Brodanovitch and a possible command to return to camp. They sat in Novotny's runabout and giggled cozily together at the fuzzy map of Earth that floated in the darkness above them. On the ship's fuselage, the warning light over the airlock hatch began winking, indicating that the lock was in use. The girl noticed it and nudged him. She pointed at the light.

'Somebody coming out,' Relke muttered. 'Maybe Suds. We'd better get out of here.' He flipped the main switch and started the motor. He was backing onto the road when Giselle caught his arm.

'Beel! Look at the light!'

He glanced around. It was flashing red.

'Malfunction signal. Compressor trouble, probably. It's nothing. Let's take a ride. Joe won't care.' He started backing again.

'Poof!' she said suddenly.

'What?'

'Poof. It opened, and *poof*—' She puckered her lips and blew a little puff of steam in the cold air to show him. 'So. Like smoke.'

He turned the car around in the road and looked back again. The hatch had closed. There was no one on the ladder. 'Nobody came out.'

'Non. Just poof.'

He edged the car against the trolley rails, switched to autosteering, and let it gather speed.

'Beel?'

'Yeah, kid?'

'Where you taking me?'

He caught the note of alarm in her voice and slowed down again. She had come on a dare after several drinks, and the drinks were wearing off. The landscape was frighteningly alien, and the sense of falling into bottomlessness was ever-present.

'You want to go back?' he asked gloomily.

'I don't know. I don't like it out here.'

'You said you wanted some ground under your feet.'

'But it doesn't feel like ground when you walk on it.'

'Rather be inside a building?'

She nodded eagerly.

'That's where we're going.'

'To your camp?'

'God, no! I'm planning to keep you to myself.'

She laughed and snuggled closer to him. 'You can't. Madame d'Annecy will not permit—'

'Let's talk about something else,' he grunted quickly.

'OK. Let's talk about Monday.'

'Which Monday?'

'Next Monday. It's my birthday. When is it going to be Monday, Bill?'

'You said *Bill.*'

'Beel? That's your name, isn't eet? Weeliam Q. Relke, who weel not tell me what ees the *Q?*'

'But you said *Bill.*'

She was silent for a moment. 'OK, I'm a phony,' she muttered. 'Does the inquisition start now?'

He could feel her tighten up, and he said nothing. She waited stiffly for a time. Gradually she relaxed against him again. 'When's it going to be Monday?' she murmured.

'When's it going to be Monday where?'

'Here, anywhere, silly!'

He laughed. 'When will it be Monday all over the universe?'

She thought for a moment. 'Oh. Like time zones. OK, when will it be Monday here?'

'It won't. We just have periods, hitches, and shifts. Fifty shifts make a hitch, two hitches make a period. A period's from sunrise to sunrise. Twenty-nine and a half days. But we don't count days. So I don't know when it'll be Monday.'

It seemed to alarm her. She sat up. 'Don't you even have *hours?'* She looked at her watch and jiggled it, listened to it.

'Sure. Seven hours in a shift. *We* call them hours, anyhow. Forty-five seconds longer than an Earth hour.'

She looked up through the canopy at the orb of Earth. 'When it's Monday on Earth, it'll be Monday here too,' she announced flatly.

Relke laughed. 'OK, we'll call it that.'

'So when will it start being Monday on Earth?'

'Well, it'll start at twenty-four different times, depending on where you are. Maybe more than twenty-four. It's August. Some places, they set the clocks ahead an hour in Summer.'

She looked really worried.

'You take birthdays pretty seriously?' he asked.

'Only this one. I'll be—' She broke off and closed her mouth.

'Pick a time zone,' Relke offered, 'and I'll try to figure out how long until Monday starts. Which zone? Where you'd be now, maybe?'

She shook her head.

'Where you were born?'

'That would be—' She stopped again. 'Never mind. Forget it.' She sat brooding and watching the moonscape.

Relke turned off the road at the transformer station. He pulled up beside a flat-roofed cubicle the size of a sentrybox. Giselle looked at it in astonishment.

'That's a building?' she asked.

'That's an entrance. The "building's" underground. Come on, let's seal up.'

'What's down there?'

'Just a transformer vault and living quarters for a substation man.'

'Somebody *lives* down there?'

'Not yet. The line's still being built. They'll move somebody in when the trolley traffic starts moving.'

'What do we want to go down there for?'

He looked at her forlornly. 'You'd rather go back to the ship?'

She seemed to pull herself together professionally. She laughed and put her arms around him and whispered something in French against his ear. She kissed him hard, pressed her forehead against his, and grinned. 'C'mon, babee! Let's go downstairs.'

Relke felt suddenly cold inside. He had wanted to see what it felt like to be alone with a woman again in a quiet place, away from the shouting howling revelry that had been going on aboard the ship. Now he knew what it was going to feel like. It was going to feel counterfeit. 'Christ!' he grunted angrily. 'Let's go back!' He reached roughly around her and cut on the switch again. She recoiled suddenly and gaped at him as he started the motor and turned the bug around.

'Hey!' She was staring at him oddly, as if seeing him for the first time.

Relke kept his face averted and his knuckles were white on the steering bar. She got up on her knees on the seat and put her hands on his shoulders. 'Bill. Good Lord, you're *crying!*'

He choked out a curse as the bug hit the side of the cut and careened around on the approach to the road. He lost control, and the runabout went off the approach and slid slowly sideways down a gentle slope of crushed-lava fill. A sharp clanking sound came from the floor plates.

'Get your suit sealed!' he yelled. 'Get it sealed!'

The runabout lurched to a sudden stop. The cabin pressure stayed up. He sat panting for a moment, then started the motor. He let it inch ahead and tugged at the steering bar. It was locked.

The bug crept in an arc, and the clanking resumed. He cut off the motor and sat cursing softly.

'What's wrong?'

'Broke a link and the tread's fouled. We'll have to get out.'

She glanced at him out of the corner of her eye. He was glowering. She looked back toward the sentrybox entrance to the substation and smiled thoughtfully.

It was chilly in the vault, and the only light came from the indicator lamps on the control board. The pressure gauge inside the airlock indicated only eight pounds of air. The construction crew had pumped it up to keep some convection currents going around the big transformers, but they hadn't planned on anyone breathing it soon. He changed the mixture controls, turned the barostat up to twelve pounds, and listened to the compressors start up. When he turned around, Giselle was taking off her suit and beginning to pant.

'*Hey*, stay in that thing!' he shouted.

His helmet muffled his voice, and she looked at him blankly. '*What?*' she called. She was gasping and looking around in alarm.

Relke sprinted a few steps to the emergency rack and grabbed a low pressure walk-around bottle. When he got back, she was getting blue and shaking her head drunkenly. He cracked the valve on the bottle and got the hose connection against her mouth. She nodded quickly and sucked on it. He went back to watch the gauges. He found the overhead lighting controls and turned them on. Giselle held her nose and anxiously sipped air from the bottle. He nodded reassuringly at her. The construction crews had left the substation filled with nitrogen-helium mixture, seeing no reason to add rust-producing moisture and oxygen until someone moved into the place; she had been breathing inert gases, nothing more.

When the partial oxygen pressure was up to normal, he left the control panel and went to look for the communicator. He found the equipment, but it was not yet tied into the line. He went back to tell the girl. Still sipping at the bottle, she watched him with attentive brown eyes. It was the gaze of a child, and he wondered about her age. Aboard ship, she and the others had seemed impersonal automata of Eros; painted ornaments and sleekly functional decoys designed to perform stereotyped rituals of enticement and excarnation of desire, swiftly, lest a customer be kept waiting. But here in stronger light, against a neutral background, he noticed suddenly that she was a distinct individual. Her lipstick had smeared. Her dark hair kept spilling out in tangled wisps from beneath a leather cap with fleece ear flaps. She wore a pair of coveralls, several sizes too large and rolled up about the ankles. With too much rouge on her solemnly mischievous face, she looked ready for a role in a girls' school version of *Chanticler.*

'You can stop breathing out of the can,' he told her. 'The oxygen pressure's okay now.'

She took the hose from her mouth and sniffed warily. 'What was the matter? I was seeing spots.'

'It's all right now.'

'It's cold in this place. Are we stuck here?'

'I tried to call Joe, but the set's not hooked up. He'll come looking for us.'

'Isn't there any heat in here? Can't you start a fire?'

He glanced down at the big 5,000 kva transformers in the pit beyond the safety rail. The noise of corona discharge was very faint, and the purr of thirty-two cycle hum was scarcely audible. With no trucks drawing power from the trolley, the big pots were cold. Normally, eddy current and hysteresis losses in the transformers would keep the station toast-warm. He glanced at a thermometer. It read slightly under freezing: the ambient temperature of the subsurface rock in that region.

'Let's try the stationman's living quarters,' he grunted. 'They usually furnish them fancy, as bunk tanks go. Man has to stay by himself out here, they want to keep him sane.'

A door marked PRIVATE flipped open as they approached it. A cheery voice called out: *'Hi, Bo. Rugged deal, ain't it?'*

Giselle started back in alarm. 'Who's there?'

Relke chuckled. 'Just a recorded voice. Back up, I'll show you.'

They moved a few paces away. The door fell closed. They approached it again. This time a raucous female squawked at them: '*Whaddaya mean coming home at this hour? Lemme smell your breath.'*

Giselle caught on and grinned. 'So he won't get lonesome?'

'Partly, and partly to keep him a little sore. The stationmen hate it, but that's part of the idea. It gives them something to talk back to and throw things at.'

They entered the apartment. The door closed itself, the lights went on. Someone belched, then announced: *'I get just as sick of looking at you as you do looking at me, button head. Go take a bath.'*

Relke flushed. 'It can get pretty rough sometimes. The tapes weren't edited for mixed company. Better plug your ears if you go in the bathroom.'

Giselle giggled. 'I think it's cute.'

He went into the kitchenette and turned on all the burners of the electric range to help warm the place. 'Come stand next to the oven,' he called, 'until I see if the heat pumps are working.' He opened the oven door. A libidinous purr came from within.

'Dah-ling, now why bother with breakfast when you can have meee?'

He glanced up at Giselle.

'I didn't say it,' she giggled, but posed invitingly.

Relke grinned and accepted the invitation.

'You're not crying now,' she purred as he released her.

He felt a surge of unaccountable fury, grunted, 'Excuse me,' and stalked out to the transformer vault. He looked around for the heat pumps, failed to find them, and went to lean on the handrail over-looking the pit. He stood there with his fists in his pockets, vaguely anguished and enraged, for no reason he understood. For a moment he had been too close to feeling at home, and that brought up the wrath somehow. After a couple of minutes he shook it off and went back inside.

'Hey, I wasn't teasing you,' Giselle told him.

'What?'

'About crying.'

'Listen,' he said irritably, 'did you ever see a looney or a spacer without leaky eyes? It's the glare, that's all.'

'Is that it? Huh—want to know something? I can't cry. That's funny. You're a man and you can cry, but I can't.'

Relke watched her grumpily while she warmed her behind at the oven. *She's not more than fifteen*, he decided suddenly. It made him a little queasy. *Come on, Joe, hurry.*

'You know,' she went on absently, 'when I was a little girl, I got mad at . . . at somebody, and I decided I was never going to cry anymore. I never did, either. And you know what?—now I can't. Sometimes I try and I try, but I just *can't.*' She spread her hands to the oven, tilted them back and forth, and watched the way the tendons worked as she stiffened her fingers. She seemed to be talking to her hands. 'Once I used an onion. To cry, I mean. I cut an onion and rubbed some of it on a handkerchief and laid the handkerchief over my eyes. I cried that time, all right. That time I couldn't stop crying, and nobody could make me stop. They were petting me and scolding me and shaking me and trying to give me smelling salts, but I just couldn't quit. I blubbered for two days. Finally Mother Bernarde had to call the doctor to give me a sedative. Some of the sisters were taking cold towels and—'

'Sisters?' Relke grunted.

Giselle clapped a hand to her mouth and shook her head five or six times, very rapidly. She looked around at him. He shrugged.

'So you were in a convent.'

She shook her head again.

'So what if you were?' He sat down with his back to her and pretended to ignore her. She was dangerously close to that state of mind which precedes the telling of a life history. He didn't want to hear it; he already knew it. So she was in a nunnery; Relke was not surprised. Some people had to polarize themselves. If they broke free from one pole, they had to seek its opposite. People with no middle ground. Black, or if not black, then white, never gray. Law, or criminality. God, or Satan. The cloister, or a whorehouse. Eternally a choice of all or nothing-at-all, and they couldn't see that they made things that way for themselves. They set fire to every bridge they ever crossed—so that even a cow creek became a Rubicon, and every crossing was on a tightrope.

You understand that too well, don't you, Relke? he asked himself bitterly. There was Fran and the baby, and there wasn't enough money, and so you had to go and burn a bridge—a 240,000-mile bridge, with Fran on the other side. And so, after six years on Luna, there would be enough money; but there wouldn't be Fran and the baby. And so, he had signed another extended contract, and the moon was going to be home for a long long time. *Yeh, you know about burned bridges, all right, Relke.*

He glanced at Giselle. She was glaring at him.

'If you're waiting for me to say something,' she snapped, 'you can stop waiting. I don't have to tell you anything.'

'I didn't ask you anything.'

'I was just a novice. I didn't take permanent vows.'

'All *right*.'

'They wouldn't let me. They said I was—unstable. They didn't think I had a calling.'

'Well, you've got one now. Stop crawling all over me like I said anything. I didn't ask you any questions.'

'You gave me that pious look.'

'Oh, garbage!' He rolled out of the chair and loped off to the other room. The stationman's quarters boasted its own music system and television (permanently tuned to the single channel that broadcast a fairly narrow beam aimed at the lunar stations). He tried the television first, but solar interference was heavy.

'Maybe it'll tell us when it's going to be Monday,' she said, coming to watch him from the doorway.

He gave her a sharp look, then softened it. The stove had warmed the kitchen, and she had stepped out of the baggy coveralls. She was still wearing the yellow dress, and she had taken a moment to comb her hair. She leaned against the side of the doorway, looking very young but excessively female. She had that lost pixie look and a tropical climate tan too.

'Why are you looking at me that way?' she asked. 'Is this all we're going to do? I mean, just wait around until somebody comes? Can't we dance or something?' She did a couple of skippity steps away from the door jamb and rolled her hips experimentally. One hip was made of India rubber. 'Say! Dancing ought to be fun in this crazy gravity.' She smirked at him and posed alluringly.

Relke swallowed, reddened, and turned to open the selector cabinet. *She's only a kid, Relke.* He paused, then dialed three selections suitable for dancing. *She's only a kid, damn it!* He paused again, then dialed a violin concerto. *A kid—back home they'd call her 'jail bait.'* He dialed ten minutes' worth of torrid Spanish guitar. *You'll hate yourself for it, Relke.* He shuddered involuntarily, dialed one called *The Satyricon of Lily Brown, an orgy in New African Jazz (for adults only).*

He glanced up guiltily. She was already whirling around the room with an imaginary partner, dancing to the first selection.

Relke dialed a tape of Palestrina and some plainchant, but left it for last. Maybe it would neutralize the rest.

She snuggled close and they tried to keep time to the music —not an easy task, with the slow motion imposed by low gravity mismatched to the livelier rhythms of dancing on Earth. Two attempts were enough. Giselle flopped down on the bunk.

'What's that playing now, Bill?'

'Sibelius. Concerto for Something and Violin. I dunno.'

'Bill?'

'Yeah.'

'Did I make you mad or something?'

'No, but I don't think—' He turned to look at her and stopped talking. She was lying on her back with her hands behind her head and her legs cocked up, balancing her calf on her other knee and watching her foot wiggle. She was lithe and brown and . . . ripe.

'Damn,' he muttered.

'Bill?'

'Uh?'

She wrinkled her nose at him and smiled. 'Don't you even know what you wanted to come over here for?'

Relke got up slowly and walked to the light switch. He snapped it.

'Oh, dahling!' said a new voice in the darkness. *'What if my husband comes home!'*

After Sibelius came the Spanish guitar. The African jazz was wasted.

Relke sat erect with a start. Giselle still slept, but noises came from the other room. There were voices, and a door slammed closed. Shuffling footsteps, a muffled curse. 'Who's there?' he yelled 'Joe?'

The noises stopped, but he heard the hiss of someone whispering. He nudged the girl awake with one elbow. The record changer clicked, and the soft chant of an *Agnus Dei* came from the music system.

'Oh, God! It's Monday!' Giselle muttered sleepily.

'A dame,' grunted a voice in the next room.

'Who's there?' Relke called again.

'We brought you some company.' The voice sounded familiar. A light went on in the other room. 'Set him down over here, Harv.'

Relke heard rattling sounds and a chair scraped back. They dumped something into the chair. Then the bulky silhouette of a man filled the doorway. 'Who's in here, anyhow?' He switched on the lights. The man was Larkin. Giselle pulled a blanket around herself and blinked sleepily.

'Is it Monday?' she asked.

A slow grin spread across Larkin's face. 'Hey, Harv!' he called over his shoulder. 'Look what we pulled out of the grab bag! Come look at lover boy. . . . Now, Harv—is that sweet? Is that romantic?'

Kunz looked over Larkin's shoulder. 'Yuh. Real homey, ain't

it. Hiyah, Rat. Lookit that cheese he's got with him. Some cheese. Round like a provolone, huh? Hiyah, cheesecake, know you're in bed with a rat?'

Giselle glanced questioningly at Relke. Relke was surveying the tactical situation. It looked unpromising. Larkin laughed.

'Look at him, Harv—wondering where he left his shiv. What's the matter, Relke? We make you nervous?' He stepped inside, Kunz followed.

Relke stood up in bed and backed against the wall. 'Get out of the way,' he grunted at Giselle.

'Look at him!' Larkin gloated. 'Getting ready to kick. You planning to kick somebody, sonny?'

'Stay back!' he snapped. 'Get out of here, Giselle!'

'A l'abri? Oui—' She slid off the bed and darted for the door. Kunz grabbed at her, but she slipped past. She stopped in the doorway and backed up a step. She stared into the next room. She put her hand to her mouth. 'Oh! *Oh!*' she yelped. Larkin and Kunz glanced back at her. Relke lunged off the bed. He smashed against Larkin, sent him sprawling into Kunz. He dodged Giselle and sprinted for the kitchen and the cutlery rack. He made it a few steps past the door before he saw what Giselle had seen. Something was sitting at the table, facing the door. Relke stopped in his tracks and began backing away. The something at the table was a blistered caricature of a man, an icy frost-figure in a deflated pressure suit. Its mouth was open, and the stomach had been forced up through . . . He closed his eyes. Relke had seen men blown out, but it hadn't gotten any pleasanter to look at since the last time.

'Get him, Harv!'

They pinned his arms from behind. 'Heading for a butcher knife, Relke?' He heard a dull crack and felt his head explode. The room went pink and hazy.

'That's for grabbing glass on us the other day, Sonny.'

'Don't mess him up too much, Lark. The dame's here.'

'I won't mess him up. I'll be real clean about it.'

The crack came again, and the pink haze quivered with black flashes.

'That's for ratting on the Party, Relke.'

Dimly he heard Giselle screaming at them to stop it.

'Take that little bitch in the other room and play house with her, Harv. I'll work on Sonny awhile, and then we'll trade around. Don't wear her out.'

'Let go,' she yelled. 'Take your hands off—listen, I'll go in there with you if you'll quit beating him. Now stop—'

Another crack. The pink haze flew apart, and blackness engulfed him. Time moved ahead in jerks for awhile. First he was sitting at the table across from the corpse. Larkin was there too, dealing himself a hand of solitaire. Loud popular music blared from the music system, but he could hear Kunz laughing in the next room. Once Giselle's voice cried out in protest. Relke moved and groaned. Larkin looked his way.

'Hey, Harv—he's awake. It's your turn.'

'I'm busy,' Kunz yelled.

'Well, hurry up. Brodanovitch is beginning to thaw.'

Relke blinked at the dead man. 'Who? Him? Brodan—' His lips were swollen, and it was painful to talk.

'Yeah, that's Suds. Pretty, isn't he? You're going to look like that one of these days, kid.'

'You—killed—Suds?'

Larkin threw back his head and laughed. 'Hey, Harv, hear that? He thinks we killed Suds.'

'What happened to him, then?'

Larkin shrugged. 'He walked into an airlock with a bottle of champagne. The pressure went down quick, the booze blew up in his face, and there sits Suds. A victim of imprudence, like you. Sad looking schlemazel, isn't he?'

'Wha'd you bring him here for?'

'You know the rules, Sonny. A man gets blown out, they got to look him over inch by inch, make sure it wasn't murder.'

Giselle cried out again in protest. Relke started to his feet, staggering dizzily. Larkin grabbed him and pushed him down.

'Hey, Harv! He's getting frisky. Come take over. The gang'll be rolling in pretty quick.'

Kunz came out of the bunkroom. Larkin sprinted for the door as Giselle tried to make a run for it. He caught her and dragged her back. He pushed her into the bunkroom, went in after her, and closed the door. Relke lunged at Kunz, but a judo cut knocked numbness into the side of his neck and sent him crashing against the wall.

'Relke, get wise,' Harv growled. 'This'll happen every now and then if you don't join up.'

The lineman started to his feet. Kunz kicked him disinterestedly. Relke groaned and grabbed his side.

'We got no hard feelings, Relke. . . .' He chopped his boot

down against the back of Relke's neck. 'You can join the Party any time.'

Time moved ahead in jerks again.

Once he woke up. Brodanovitch was beginning to melt, and the smell of brandy filled the room. There were voices and chair scrapings and after a while somebody carried Brodanovitch out. Relke lay with his head against the wall and kept his eyes closed. He assumed that if the apartment contained a friend, he would not still be lying here on the floor; so he remained motionless and waited to gather strength.

'So that's about the size of it,' Larkin was telling someone. 'Those dames are apt to be dynamite if they let them into Crater City. We've got enough steam whipped up to pull off the strike, but what if that canful of cat meat walks in on Copernicus about sundown? Who's going to have their mind on politics?'

'Hell, Lark,' grunted a strange voice. 'Parkeson'll never let them get in town.'

'No? Don't be too damn sure. Parkeson's no idiot. He knows trouble's coming. Hell, he could *invite* them to Crater City, pretend he's innocent as a lamb, just didn't know what they are, but take credit for them being there.'

'Well, what can we do about it?'

'Cripple that ship.'

'Wha-a-at?'

'Cripple the ship. Look, there's nothing else we can do on our own. We've got no orders from the Party. Right before we break camp, at sundown, we cripple the ship. Something they can't fix without help from the base.'

'Leave them *stuck* out here?'

'Only for a day or two. Till the Party takes over the base. Then *we* send a few wagons out here after dark and pick up the wenches. Who gets credit for dames showing up? The Party. Besides, it's the only thing we dare do without orders. We can't be sure what'd happen if Parkeson walked in with a bunch of Algerian whores about the time the show's supposed to start. And says, "Here, boys, look what Daddy brought." '

'Parkeson hasn't got the guts.'

'The hell he hasn't. He'd say *that* out of one side of his mouth. Out of the other side, he'd be dictating a vigorous protest to the WP for allowing such things to get clearance for blasting off, making it sound like they're at fault. That's just a guess. We've got to keep those women out of Crater City until we're sure, though. And there's only one way; cripple the ship.'

There were five or six voices in the discussion, and Relke recognized enough of them to understand dimly that a cell meeting was in progress. His mind refused to function clearly, and at times the voices seemed to be speaking in senseless jargon, although the words were plain enough. His head throbbed and he had bitten a piece out of the end of his tongue. He felt as if he were lying stretched out on a bed of jagged rocks, although there was only the smooth floor under his battered person.

Giselle cried out from the next room and beat angrily on the door.

Quite mindlessly, and as if his body were being directed by some whimsical puppet master, Relke's corpse suddenly clambered to its feet and addressed itself to the startled conspirators.

'Goddam it, gentlemen, can't you let the lady out to use the crapper?'

They hit him over the head with a jack handle.

He woke up again. This time he was in the bunkroom. A faint choking sound made him look up. Giselle sat on the foot of the bed, legs tightly crossed, face screwed up. She was trying to cry.

'Use an onion,' he told her thickly, and sat up. 'What's the matter?'

'It's Monday now.'

'Where are they?'

'They left. We're locked in.'

He fell back with a groan. A stitch in his side felt like a broken rib. He turned his face to the wall. 'What's so great about Monday?' he muttered.

'Today the others are taking their vows.'

When he woke up again, Novotny was watching him from the foot of the bed. The girl was gone. He sat up and fell back with a groan.

'Fran,' he said.

'It wasn't Fran, it was a hustler,' said Joe. 'I had Beasley take her back. Who busted you?'

'Larkin and Kunz.'

'It's a good thing.'

'What?'

'They saved me the trouble. You ran off with the jeep.'

'Sorry.'

'You don't have to be sorry. Just watch yourself, that's all.'

'I wanted to see what it was like, Joe.'

'What? Playing house with a wench?'

He nodded.

'What was it like?'

'I don't know.'

'You woke up calling her Fran.'

'I did?'

'Yah. Before you start feeling that way, you better ask Beasley what they did together on the rug while you were asleep, Romeo.'

'What?'

'She really knows some tricks. Mme. d'Annecy really educates her girls. You been kissing and cooing with her, Relke?'

'I'm sick, Joe. Don't.'

'By the way, you better not go back. The Madame's pretty sore at you.'

'Why?'

'For keeping the wench gone so long. There was going to be a show. You know, a circus. Giselle was supposed to be in it. You might say she had the lead role.'

'Who?'

'Giselle. Still feel like calling her Fran?—Hey! if you're going to vomit, get out of bed.'

Relke staggered into the latrine. He was gone a long time.

'Better hurry up,' Novotny called. 'Our shift goes on in half an hour.'

'I can't go on, Joe.'

'The hell you can't. Unless you want to be sent up N.L.D. You know what they do to N.L.D. cases.'

'You wouldn't report me N.L.D.'

'The hell I wouldn't, but I don't have to.'

'What do you mean?'

'Parkeson's coming, with a team of inspectors. They're probably already here, and plenty sore.'

'About the ship? The women?'

'I don't know. If the Commission hear about those bats, there'll be hell to pay. But who'll pay it is something else.'

Relke buried his face in his hands and tried to think. 'Joe, listen. I only half remember, but . . . there was a cell meeting here.'

'When?'

'After Larkin and Kunz worked me over. Some guys came in, and . . .'

'Well?'

'It's foggy. Something about Parkeson taking the women back to Crater City.'

'Hell, that's a screwy ideá. Who thinks that?'

Relke shook his head and tried to think. He came out of the latrine mopping his face on a towel. 'I'm trying to remember.'

Joe got up. 'All right. Better get your suit. Let's go pull cable.'

The lineman breathed deeply a few times and winced at the effect. He went to get his suit out of the hangar, started the routine safety check, and stopped halfway through. 'Joe, my suit's been cut.'

Novotny came to look. He pinched the thick corded plastic until the incision opened like a mouth. 'Knife,' he grunted.

'Those sons of—'

'Yah.' He fingered the cut. 'They meant for you to find it, though. It's too conspicious. It's a threat.'

'Well, I'm fed up with their threats. I'm going to—'

'You're not going to do anything, Relke. *I'm* going to do it. Larkin and Kunz have messed around with my men one time too often.'

'What have you got in mind, Joe?'

'Henderson and I will handle it. We'll go over and have a little conference with them, that's all.'

'Why Henderson? Look, Joe, if you're going to stomp them, it's *my* grudge, not Lije's.'

'That's just it. If I take you, it's a grudge. If Lije and I do it, it's just politics. I've told you guys before—leave the politics to me. Come on, we'll get you a suit from the emergency locker.'

They went out into the transformer vault. Two men wearing blue armbands were bending over Brodanovitch's corpse. One of them was fluently cursing unknown parties who had brought the body to a warm place and allowed it to thaw.

'Investigating team,' Novotny muttered. 'Means Parkeson is already here.' He hiked off toward the emergency lockers.

'Hey, are you the guy that left this stiff near a stove?' one of the investigators called out to Relke.

'No, but I'll be glad to rat on the guys that did, if it'll get them in trouble,' the lineman told him.

'Never mind. You can't hang them for being stupid.'

'What are you going to do with *him?*' Relke asked, nodding at the corpse.

'Promote him to supervisory engineer and give him a raise.'

'Christ but they hire smart boys for the snooper team, don't they? What's your I.Q., friend? I bet they had to breed you to get you smart.'

The checker grinned. 'You looking for an argument, Slim?'

Relke shook his head. 'No, I just asked a question.'

'We're going to take him back to Copernicus and bury him, friend. It takes a lot of imagination to figure that out, doesn't it?'

'If he was a class three laborer, you wouldn't take him back to Copernicus. You wouldn't even bury him. You'd just chuck him in a fissure and dynamite the lip.'

The man smiled. Patient cynicism was in his tone. 'But he's *not* a class three laborer, Slim. He's Mister S. K. Brodanovitch. Does that make everything nice and clear?'

'Sure. Is Parkeson around?'

The checker glanced up and snickered. 'You're a chum of his, I guess? Hear that, Clyde? We're talking to a wheel.'

Relke reddened. 'Shove it, chum. I just wondered if he's here.'

'Sure, he's out here. He went over to see that flying bordello you guys have been hiding out here.'

'What's he going to do about it?'

'Couldn't say, friend.'

Novotny came back with an extra suit.

'Joe, I just remembered something.'

'Tell me about it on the way back.'

They suited up and went out to the runabout. Relke told what he could remember about the cell meeting.

'It sounds crazy in a way,' Novotny said thoughtfully. 'Or maybe it doesn't. It *could* mess up the Party's strike plans if Parkeson brought those women back before sundown. The men want women back on the moon project. If they can get women bootlegged in, they won't be quite so ready to start a riot on the No Work Without a Wife theme.'

'But Parkeson'd get fired in a flash if—'

'If Parliament got wind of it, sure. Unless he raised the squawk later himself. UCOJE doesn't mention prostitution. Parkeson could point out that some national codes on Earth tolerate it. Nations with delegates in the Parliament, and with work teams on the moon. Take the African team at Tycho. And the Japanese team. Parkeson himself is an Aussie. Whose law is he supposed to enforce?'

'You mean maybe they can't keep ships like that from visiting us?'

'Don't kid yourself. It won't last long. But maybe long

enough. If it goes on long enough, and builds up, the general public will find out. You think that wouldn't cause some screaming back home?'

'Yeah. That'll be the end.'

'I'm wondering. If there turns out to be a profit in it for whoever's backing d'Annecy, well—anything that brings a profit is pretty hard to put a stop to. There's only one sure way to stop it. Kill the demand.'

'For women? Are you crazy, Joe?'

'They could bring in decent women. Women to marry. That'll stop it.'

'But the kids. They can't have kids.'

'Yeah, I know. That's the problem, and they've got to start solving it sometime. Hell, up to now, they haven't been trying to solve it. When the problem came up, and the kids were dying, everybody got hysterical and jerked the women back to Earth. That wasn't a solution, it was an evasion. The problem is growth-control—in low gravity. It ought to have a medical answer. If this d'Annecy dame gets a chance to keep peddling her wares under the counter, well—she'll force them to start looking for a solution.'

'I don't know, Joe. Everybody said homosexuality would force them to start looking for it—after Doc Reiber made his survey. The statistics looked pretty black, but they didn't do anything about it except send us a shipful of ministers. The fairies just tried to make the ministers.'

'Yeah, but this is different.'

'I don't see how.'

'Half the voters are women.'

'So? They didn't do anything about homosex—'

'Relke, wise up. Listen, did you ever see a couple of Lesbians necking in a bar?'

Relke snickered. 'Sure, once or twice.'

'How did you feel about it?'

'Well, this once was kind of funny. You see, this one babe had on—'

'Never mind. You thought it was funny. Do you think it's funny the way MacMillian and Wickers bill and coo?'

'That gets pretty damn nauseating, Joe.'

'Uh-huh, but the Lesbians just gave you a giggle. Why?'

'Well, I don't know, Joe it's—'

'I'll tell you why. You like dames. You can understand other guys liking dames. You like dames so much that you can even understand two dames liking each other. You can see what they see in each other. But it's incongruous, so it's funny. But you *can't* see what two fairies see in each other, so that just gives you a bellyache. Isn't that it?'

'Maybe, but what's that got to do with the voters?'

'Ever think that maybe a woman would feel the same way in reverse? A dame could see what MacMillian and Wickers see in each other. The dame might morally disapprove, but at the same time she could sympathize. What's more, she'd be plenty sure that she could handle that kind of competition if she ever needed to. She's a woman, and wotthehell, Wickers is only a substitute woman. It wouldn't worry her too much. Worry her morally, but not as a personal threat. Relke, Mme d'Annecy's racket is a personal threat to the home girl and the womenfolk.'

'I see what you mean.'

'Half the voters are women.'

Relke chuckled. 'Migod, Joe, if Ellen heard about that ship . . .'

'Ellen?'

'My older sister. Old maid. Grim.'

'You've got the idea. If Parkeson thinks of all this . . .' His voice trailed off. 'When is Larkin talking about crippling that ship?'

'About sundown, why?'

'Somebody better warn the d'Annecy dame.'

The cosmic gunfire had diminished. The Perseid shrapnel still pelted the dusty face of the plain, but the gram-impact-per-acre-second had dropped by a significant fraction, and with it fell the statisticians's estimate of dead men per square mile. There was an ion storm during the first half of B-shift, and the energized spans of high voltage cable danced with fluttering demon light as the trace-pressure of the lunar 'atmosphere' increased enough to start a glow discharge between conductors. High current surges sucked at the line, causing the breakers to hiccup. The breakers tried the line three times, then left the circuit dead and waited for the storm to pass. The storm meant nothing to the construction crews except an increase in headset noise.

Parkeson's voice came drawling on the general call frequency, wading waist-deep through the interference caused by the storm. Relke leaned back against his safety strap atop the trusswork of the last tower and tried to listen. Parkeson was reading the Articles of Discipline, and listening was compulsory. All teams on the job had stopped work to hear him. Relke gazed across the plain toward the slender nacelles of the bird from Algiers in the distance. He had gotten used to the ache in his side where Kunz had kicked him, but it was good to rest for a time and watch the rocket and remember brown legs and a yellow dress. Properties of Earth. Properties belonging to the communion of humanity, from which fellowship a Looney was somehow cut off by 238,000 miles of physical separation.

'We've got a job to finish here,' Parkeson was telling the men.

Why? What was in space that was worth the wanting? What followed from its conquest? What came of finishing the job?

Nothing.

Nothing.

Nothing. Nothing anybody ever dreamed of or hoped for.

Parkeson scolded on. *'I know the question that's foremost in your minds,'* his voice continued, *'but you'd better forget it. Let me tell you what happens if this line isn't finished by sundown.* (But by God, it *will* be finished!) *Listen, you wanted women. All right, now you've all been over to visit the uh—"affectionate institution"—and you got what you wanted; and now the work is behind schedule. Who gives a damn about the project, eh! I know what you're thinking. "That's Parkeson's worry." OK, so let's talk about what you're going to breathe for the next couple of periods. Let's talk about how many men will wind up in the psycho-respiratory ward, about the overload on the algae tanks. That's not your responsibility either, is it? You don't* have *to breathe and eat. Hell, let Nature take care of air and water, eh? Sure. Now look around. Take a good look. All that's between you and that hungry vacuum out there is ten pounds of man-made air and a little reinforced plastic. All that keeps you eating and drinking and breathing is that precarious life-cycle of ours at Copernicus. That plant-animal feedback loop is so delicately balanced that the biology team gets the cold shakes every time somebody sneezes or passes gas. It has to be constantly nursed. It has to be planned and kept on schedule. On Earth, Nature's a plenum. You can chop down her forests, kill off her deer and buffalo and fill her air with smog and hot isotopes; the worst you can do is cause a few new deserts and dust bowls, and make things a little unpleasant for a while.*

'Up here, we've got a little bit of Nature cooped up in a bottle, and we're in the bottle too. We're cultured like mold on agar. The biology team has to chart the ecology for months in advance. It has to know the construction and survey teams are

going to deliver exactly what they promise to deliver, and do it on schedule. If you don't deliver, the ecology gets sick. If the ecology gets sick, you get sick.

'Do you want another epidemic of the chokers like we had three years back? That's what'll happen if there's a work slowdown while everybody goes off on a sex binge at that ship. If the line isn't finished before sundown, the ecology gets bled for another two weeks to keep that mine colony going, and the colony can't return wastes to our cycle. Think it over, but think fast. There's not much time. "We all breathe the same air"—on Earth, that's just a political slogan. Here, we all breathe it or we all choke in it. How do you want it, men?'

Relke shifted restlessly on the tower. He glanced down at Novotny and the others who lounged around the foot of the steel skeleton listening to Parkeson. Lije caught his eye. He waved at Relke to haul up the hoist-bucket. Relke shook his head and gave him a thumbs-down. Henderson gestured insistently for him to haul it up. Relke reeled the bucket in. It was empty, but chalked on the sides and bottom was a note from Lije: 'They toll me what L and K did to you and yr girl. I and Joe will take care of it, right after this sermon. You can spit on my fist first if you want. Lije.'

Relke gave him a half-hearted screw-twist signal and let the bucket go. Revenge was no good, and vicarious revenge was worse than no good; it was hollow. He thought of asking Joe to forget it, but he knew Joe wouldn't listen. The pusher felt his own integrity was involved, and a matter of jurisdictional ethics: nobody can push my men around but me. It was gang ethics, but it seemed inevitable somehow. Where there was fear, men huddled in small groups and counted their friends on their fingers, and all else was Foe. In the absence of the family, there had to be the gang, and fear made it quarrelsome, jealous, and proud.

Relke leaned back against his strap and glanced up toward Earth. The planet was between quarter and half phase, for the sun was lower in the west. He watched it and tried to feel something more than a vague envy. Sometimes the heartsick nostalgia reached the proportions of idolatrous adoration of Gaea's orb overhead, only to subside into a grudging resentment of the gulf between worlds. Earth—it was a place where you could stop being afraid, a place where fear of suffocation was not, where fear of blowout was not, where nobody went berserk with the chokers or dreamed of poisoned air or worried about shorthorn cancer or burn blindness or meteoric dust or low-gravity muscular atrophy. A place where there was wind to blow your sweat away.

Watching her crescent, he felt again that vague anger of separation, that resentment against those who stayed at home, who had no cause for constant fear, who could live without the tense expectancy of sudden death haunting every moment. One of them was Fran, and another was the one who had taken her from him. He looked away quickly and tried to listen to the coordinator.

'This is no threat,' Parkeson was saying. *'If the line isn't finished on time, then the consequences will just happen, that's all. Nobody's going to punish you, but there are a few thousand men back at the Crater who have to breathe air with you. If they have to breathe stink next period—because you guys were out having one helluva party with Madame d'Annecy's girls—you can figure how popular you'll be. That's all I've got to say. There's still time to get the work back on schedule. Let's use it.'*

Parkeson signed off. The new engineer who was replacing Brodanovitch gave them a brief pep-talk, implying that Parkeson was a skunk and would be forced to eat his own words before sundown. It was the old hard-guy-soft-guy routine: first a bawling-out and then a buttering-up. The new boss offered half of his salary to the first team to forge ahead of its own work schedule. It was not stated nor even implied that Parkeson was paying him back.

The work was resumed. After half an hour, the safety beeper sounded on all frequencies, and men switched back to general call. Parkeson and his party were already heading back toward Copernicus.

'Blasting operation at the next tower site will occur in ten minutes,' came the announcement. *'Demol team requests safety clearance over all of zones two and three, from four forty to five hundred hours. There will be scatter-glass in both zones. Zone two is to be evacuated immediately, and all personnel in zone three take line-of-sight cover from the red marker. I repeat: there will be scatter-glass . . .'*

'That's us,' said Novotny when it was over. 'Everybody come on. Brax, Relke, climb down.'

Braxton swore softly in a honey-suckle drawl. It never sounded like cursing, which it wasn't, but like a man marveling at the variety of vicissitudes invented by an ingenious universe for the bedevilment of men. 'I sweah, when the angels ahn't shootin' at us from up in Perseus, it's the demol boys. Demol says froggie, and ev'body jumps. It gives 'em that suhtain feelin' of impohtance. Y'all know what I think? I got a thee-orry. I think weah all really dead, and they don't tell us it's hell weah in, because not tellin' us is paht of the tohture.'

'Get off the damn frequency, Brax, and stay off!' Novotny snapped when the Alabaman released his mic button. 'I've told you and Henderson before—either learn to talk fast, or don't talk on the job. If somebody had a slow leak, he'd be boiling blood before he could scream—with you using the frequency for five minutes to say "yeah." '

'*Mistuh* Novotny! My mothuh always taught me to speak slowly and de-stinct-ly. If you think that yo' Yankee upbringin' . . .'

Joe rapped on his helmet until he shut up, then beckoned to Henderson. 'Lije, we got twenty minutes.'

'Yeah, Joe, want to go see a couple of guys now?' He flashed white teeth and stared back toward the barrack train.

'Think we can handle it in twenty minutes?'

'I don't know. It seem like a short time to do a real good job of it, but maybe if we don't waste any on preliminary fisticuffin' . . .'

'Hell, they didn't waste any ceremony on Relke.'

'Less go, then!' He grinned at Relke and held out his fist. 'Spit on it?'

Relke shook his head. Henderson laughed. 'Wanted to see if you'd go ptooey in your helmet.'

'Come on, Lije. The rest of you guys find cover.'

Relke watched the two of them lope off toward the rolling barracks. 'Hey, Joe,' he called after a few seconds.

The lopers stopped to look back. 'Relke?'

'Yeah. Don't lose.'

'What?'

'They'll say I sicced you. Don't lose.'

'Don't worry.' They loped again. The longer Relke watched them, the less he liked the idea. If they didn't do a pretty thorough job on Kunz and Larkin, things would be worse for Relke than if they did nothing at all. Then there was the movement to think about; he didn't know to what extent *they* looked out for their own.

Relke walked out of the danger zone and hiked across the hill where he could get a clear view of the rocket. He stopped for a while on the slope and watched four distant figures moving around on the ground beneath the towering ship. For a moment, he thought they were women, but then he saw that one of them was coiling mooring cable, and he knew they were ship's crew. What sort of men had the d'Annecy women been able to hire for such a job? he wondered.

He saw that they were getting ready to lift ship. *Lift ship!*

Relke was suddenly running toward them without knowing why. Whenever he topped a rise of ground and could see them, he tried calling them, but they were not using the project's suit frequency. Finally he found their voices on the seldom used private charter band, but they were speaking French.

One of the men looped a coil of cable over his shoulder and started up the ladder toward the lock. Relke stopped atop an outcropping. He was still two or three miles from the ship. The 'isobar' valve system for the left knee of his suit had jammed, and it refused to take up the increased pressure caused by flexure. It was like trying to bend a fully inflated rubber tire, and he hobbled about for a moment with one leg stiff as a crutch.

'Listen!' he called on the p.c. frequency. 'You guys at the ship. Can you hear me?' He was panting, and he felt a little panicky. The man on the ladder stopped climbing and looked around.

There was a staccato exchange in French.

'No, no! Over here. On the rock.' He waved at them and jumped a few times. 'Look toward the camp. On the rock.'

They conversed heatedly among themselves for a time.

'Don't any of you speak English?' he begged.

They were silent for a moment. 'Whoevair ees?' one of them ventured. 'You conversation with wrong radio, M'sieur. Switch a button.'

'No, no. I'm trying to call you . . .'

A carrier drowned him out.

'We close for business,' the man said. 'We go now.' He started climbing again.

'Listen!' Relke yelled. 'Ten thousand dollars. Everything.'

'You crazy man.'

'Look, it won't get you in any trouble. I've got plenty in the bank. I'll pay—'

The carrier cut him off again.

'You crazy. Get off the air. We do not go to Earth now.'

'Wait! Listen! Tell Giselle . . . No, let me talk to her. Get her to use the radio. It's important.'

'I tell you, we close for business now.' The man climbed in the airlock. The others climbed up behind. They were jeering at him. This time it sounded like Arabic. He watched until they were all inside.

White fury lanced the ground and spread in a white sheet beneath the ship and roiled up in a tumult of dust and expanding gasses. It climbed on a white fan, gathering velocity. Relke could still make it out as a ship when its course began arcing away from the vertical. It was beginning a trajectory in the direction of Copernicus. When it was out of sight, he began trudging back toward the work site. He was nearly an hour overdue.

'Where you been?' Novotny asked him quietly after watching him hobble the last quarter of a mile in stony silence. He was squinting at the lineman with that faintly puzzled look that Relke recognized as a most ominous omen. The squint was lopsided because of a cut under one eye, and it looked like a chip was missing from a tooth.

Relke showed his stiff leg and bounced the heel against the ground a couple of times. 'I walked too far, and the c.p. valves got jammed. Sorry, Joe.'

'You don't have to be sorry. Let's see.'

The pusher satisfied himself that the suit was malfunctioning. He waved the lineman toward the barrack train. 'Go to supply and get it fixed. Get back on the double. You've slowed us down.'

Relke paused. 'You sore, Joe?'

'We're on duty. I don't get sore on duty. I save it up. Now—haul ass!'

Relke hobbled off. 'What about . . . what you went for, Joe?' he called back. 'What happened?'

'I told you to keep your nose out of politics!' the pusher snapped. 'Never mind what happened.'

Joe, Relke decided, was plenty sore. About something. Maybe about a beating that backfired. Maybe about Relke taking an hour awol. Either way, he was in trouble. He thought it over and decided that paying a bootleg ship ten thousand to take him back to Earth with them hadn't been such a hysterical whim after all.

But then he met Larkin in the supply wagon. Larkin was stretched out flat on his back, and a medic kept saying, 'Who did it to you? Who did it to you?' and Larkin kept telling him to go to hell out of a mouth that looked like a piece of singed stew meat. Kunz was curled up on a blanket and looked even worse. He spat in his sleep and a bit of tooth rattled across the deck.

'Meanest bunch of bastards I ever saw,' the clerk told Relke while he checked in the suit. 'They don't even give you a chance. Here were these two guys sleeping in their bunks and not bothering anybody, and what do you think?'

'I quit thinking. What?'

'Somebody starts working them over. Wham. Don't even wake them up first. Just wham. You ever see anything like it? Mean, John, just mean. You can't even get a shift's sleep anymore. You better go to bed with a knife in your boot, John.'

'It's Bill.'

'Oh. What do you suppose makes a guy that mean anyway?'

'I don't know. Everybody's jumpy, I guess.'

The clerk looked at him wisely. 'There you have put your finger on it, John. Looney nerves. The jitters. Everybody's suit-happy.' He leaned closer and lowered his voice. 'You know how I tell when the camp's getting jittery?'

'Listen, check me out a suit. I've got to get back to the line.'

'Now wait, this'll surprise you. I can tell better than the psych checkers when everybody's going on a slow panic. It's the sleeping bag liners.'

'What?'

'The bed wetters, John. You'd be surprised how many grown men turn bed wetters about the middle of a hitch. At first, nobody. Then somebody gets killed on the line. The bag liners start coming in for cleaning. By the end of the hitch, the wash tank smells like a public lavatory, John. Not just the men, either. Some of the engineers. You know what I'm doing?'

'Look, Mack, the suit . . .'

'Not Mack. Frank. Look, I'll show you the chart.' He got out a sheet of paper with a crudely drawn graph on it. 'See how it goes? The peak? I've done ten of them.'

'Why?'

The clerk looked at him blankly. 'For the idea box, John. Didn't you know about the prizes? Doctor Esterhall ought to be glad to get information like this.'

'Christ, they'll give you a medal, Charley. Now give me my damn suit before I get it myself. I'm due on the line.'

'OK, OK. You got the jitters yourself, haven't you?' He went to get the suit. 'I just happened to think,' he called back. 'If you've been turning in liners yourself, don't worry about me. I don't keep names, and I don't remember faces.'

'You blab plenty, though,' Relke grumbled to himself.

The clerk heard him. 'No call to get sore, John.'

'I'm not sore, I'm just in a hurry. If you want to beg for a stomping, it's nothing to me.'

The clerk came back bristling. 'Who's going to stomp?'

'The bed wetters, I guess.' He started getting into the suit.

'Why? It's for science, isn't it?'

'Nobody likes to be watched.'

'There you put your finger on it, John. It's the watching part that's worst. If they'd only quit watching us, or come out where we could see them? You know what I think? I think there's some of them among us. In disguise.' The clerk smirked mysteriously at what-he-knew-but-wouldn't-tell.

Relke paused with a zipper half-way up. 'Who do you mean—watching? Checkers?'

The clerk snorted and resumed what he had been doing when Relke entered: he was carefully taping his share of stock in Mme. d'Annecy's venture up on the wall among a display of pin-ups. 'You know who I mean,' he muttered.

'No, I don't.'

'The ones that dug that mine, that's who.'

'Aliens? Oh, bullspit.'

'Yeah? You'll see. They're keeping an eye on us, all right. There's a guy on the African team that even talked to some of them.'

'Nuts. He's not the first guy that ever talked to spooks. Or demons. Or saucer pilots. You don't have to be a Looney to be a lunatic.'

That made the clerk sore, and he stomped off to his sanctum to brood. Relke finished getting into the suit and stepped into the airlock. Some guys had to personify their fear. If there was no danger, somebody must be responsible. They had to have an Enemy. Maybe it helped, believing in gremlins from beyond Pluto. It gave you something to hate when your luck was bad.

He met Joe just outside the lock. The pusher was waiting to get in.

'Hey, Pappy, I own up. I was goofing off awhile ago. If you want to be sore—' Relke stopped. Something was wrong. Joe was breathing hard, and he looked sick.

'Christ, I'm not sore! *Not now!*'

'What's wrong, Joe?'

The pusher paused in the hatchway. 'Run on back to the line. Keep an eye on Braxton. I'm getting a jeep. Back in a minute.' He went on inside and closed the hatch.

Relke trotted toward the last tower. After a while he could

hear Braxton talking in spasms on the frequency. It sounded like sobbing. He decided it *was* sobbing.

'Theah just isn't any God,' Bama was moaning. 'Thea just couldn't be a God and be so mean. He was the bes' friend a man evah had, and he nevah did nothin' to deserve it. Oh, God, oh, God, why did it have to be *him?* I've done penance fo' what my gran'pa did to his, an' I been as color blind as any Yankee evah bohn, an' I love him like my own brother. Theah jus' can't be any God in Heaven, to treat a man that way, when he been so . . .' Braxton's voice broke down into incoherent sobbing.

There was a man lying on the ground beside the tower. Relke could see Benet bending over him. Benet was clutching a fistful of the man's suit. He crossed himself slowly and stood up. A safety team runabout skidded to a halt beside the tower, and three men piled out. Benet spread his hands at them in a wide shrug and turned his back.

'What happened?' Relke asked as he loped up to Beasley.

'Bama was welding. Lije walked over to ask him for a wrench or something. Bama turned around to get it, and Lije sat down on the strut with the hot weld.'

'Blow out?'

'He wasn't that lucky. Call it a fast slowout.'

Novotny drove up, saw the safety jeep, and started bellowing furiously at them.

'Take it easy, chum. We got here as quick as we could.'

'Theah jus' can't be any God in Heaven . . .'

They got Henderson in the safety runabout. Novotny manufactured a hasty excuse to send Braxton off with them, for grief had obviously finished his usefulness for awhile. Everybody stood around in sickly silence and stared after the jeep.

'Benet, you know how to pray,' Novotny muttered. 'Say something, altar boy.'

'Aw, Joe, that was fifteen years ago. I haven't lived right.'

'Hell, who has? Go ahead.'

Benet muttered for a moment and turned his back. *'In nomine Patris et Filii et Spiritus Sancti . . .'* He paused.

'Can't you pray in English?' Joe asked.

'We always said it in Latin. I only served at a few masses.'

'Go ahead.'

Benet prayed solemnly while they stood around with bowed heads and shuffled their boots in the dust. Nobody understood the words, not even Benet, but somehow it seemed important to listen.

'Requiem aeternam dona ei, Domine. Et lux perpetua luceat . . .'

Relke looked up slowly and let his eyes wander slowly across the horizon. There were still some meteorites coming in, making bright little winks of fire where they bit into the plain. Deadly stingers out of nowhere, heading nowhere, impartially orbiting, random as rain, random as death. The debris of creation. Relke decided Braxton was wrong. There was a God, all right, maybe personal, maybe not, but there was a God, and He wasn't mean. His universe was a deadly contraption, but maybe there wasn't any way to build a universe that wasn't a deadly contraption —like a square circle. He made the contraption and He put Man in it, and Man was a fairly deadly contraption himself. But the funny part of it was, there wasn't a damn thing the universe could do to a man that a man wasn't built to endure. He could even endure it when it killed him. And gradually he could get the better of it. It was the consistency of matched qualities—random mercilessness and human endurance—and it wasn't mean, it was a fair match.

'Poor Lije. God help him.'

'All right,' Novotny called. 'Let's pull cable, men.'

'Yeah, you know what?' said Beasley. 'Those dames went to Crater City. The quicker we get the line finished, the quicker we get back. Damn Parkeson anyhow!'

'Hell, why do you think he let them go there, Beeze?' Tremini jeered. 'So we'd work our butts off to finish quick, that's why. Parkeson's no idiot. If he'd sent them packing for somewhere else, maybe we'd finish, maybe we wouldn't.'

'Cut the jawing. Somebody run down and get the twist out of that span before she kinks. Relke, start taking up slack.'

Atop the steel truss that supported the pendulous insulators, the lineman began jacking up the slack line. He glanced toward the landing site where the ship had been, and it was hard to believe it had ever been there at all. A sudden improbable dream that had come and gone and left nothing behind. Nothing? Well, there was a share of stock . . .

'Hey, we're all capitalists!' Relke called.

Benet hooted. 'Take your dividends out in trade.'

'Listen, someday they'll let dames come here again and get married. That's one piece of community property you better burn first.'

'That d'Annecy dame thought of everything.'

'Listen, that d'Annecy dame is going to force an issue. She'll clean up, and a lot of guys will throw away small fortunes, but before it's over, they'll let women in space again. Now quit jawing, and let's get to work.'

Relke glanced at the transformer station where he had taken the girl. He tried to remember what she looked like, but he got Fran's face instead. He tried to transmute the image into Giselle's, but it stayed Fran. Maybe he hadn't really seen Giselle at all. Maybe he had looked at her and seen Fran all along, but it had been a poor substitution. It had accomplished one thing, though. He felt sorry for Fran now. He no longer hated her. She had stuck it out a long time before there had been another guy. And it was harder for a wife on Earth than it was for a husband on Luna. She had to starve in the midst of plenty. He had only to deny himself what he couldn't get anyhow, or even see. She was the little girl with her nose against the bakery window. He was only fasting in the desert. It was easy; it put one beyond temptation. To fast in a banquet hall, one had to be holy. Fran wasn't holy. Relke doubted he'd want a wife who was holy. It could get damnably dull.

A quick glance at Earth told him it was still in the skyless vault. Maybe she'll come, if they ever let them come, he thought wistfully. Maybe the guy'll be a poor substitute, and she'll figure out who she's really married to, legal instruments notwithstanding. Maybe . . . O God, let her come! . . . women had no business on Luna, but if they didn't then neither did men, nor Man, who had to be a twosome in order to be recognizably human.

'Damn it, Relke, work that jack!' Joe yelled. 'We got to build that line!'

Relke started cranking again, rocking his body to the rhythm of the jack, to the rhythm of echoes of thought. Got to build the line. Damn it, build the line. Got to build the line. Build the damn it line. The line was part of a living thing that had to grow. The line was yet another creeping of life across a barrier, a lungfish flopping from pool to pool, an ape trying to walk erect across still another treeless space. Got to build the line. Even when it kills you, got to build the line, the bloody endless line. The lineman labored on in silence. The men were rather quiet that shift.

BIG JOE AND THE NTH GENERATION

A thief, he was about to die like a thief.

He hung from the post by his wrists. The wan sunlight glistened faintly on his naked back as he waited, eyes tightly closed, lips moving slowly as he pressed his face against the rough wood and stood on tiptoe to relieve the growing ache in his shoulders. When his ankles ached, he hung by the nails that pierced his forearms just above the wrists.

He was young, perhaps in his tenth Marsyear, and his crisp black hair was close-cropped in the fashion of the bachelor who had not yet sired a pup, or not yet admitted that he had. Lithe and sleek, with the quick knotty muscles and slender rawhide limbs of a wild thing, half-fed and hungry with a quick furious hunger that crouched in ambush. His face, though twisted with pain and fright, remained that of a cocky pup.

When he opened his eyes he could see the low hills of Mars, sun-washed and gray-green with trees, trees brought down from the heavens by the Ancient Fathers. But he could also see the executioner in the foreground, sitting spraddlelegged and calm while he chewed a blade of grass and waited. A squat man with a thick face, he occasionally peered at the thief with empty blue eyes—while he casually played mumblety-peg with the bleeding-blade. His stare was blank.

'Ready for me yet, Asir?' he grumbled, not unpleasantly.

The knifeman sat beyond spitting range, but Asir spat, and tried to wipe his chin on the post. 'Your dirty mother!' he mumbled.

The executioner chuckled and played mumblety-peg.

After three hours of dangling from the spikes that pierced his arms, Asir was weakening, and the blood throbbed hard in his temples, with each jolt of his heart a separate pulse of pain. The red stickiness had stopped oozing down his arms; they knew how to drive the spike just right. But the heartbeats labored in his head like a hammer beating at red-hot iron.

How many heartbeats in a lifetime—and how many left to him now?

He whimpered and writhed, beginning to lose all hope. Mara had gone to see the Chief Commoner, to plead with him for the pilferer's life—but Mara was about as trustworthy as a wild hüffen, and he had visions of them chuckling together in Tokra's villa over a glass of amber wine, while life drained slowly from a young thief.

Asir regretted nothing. His father had been a renegade before him, had squandered his last ritual formula to buy a wife, then impoverished, had taken her away to the hills. Asir was born in the hills, but he came back to the village of his ancestors to work as a servant and steal the rituals of his masters. No thief could last for long. A ritual-thief caused havoc in the community. The owner of a holy phrase, not knowing that it had been stolen, tried to spend it—and eventually counter-claims would come to light, and a general accounting had to be called. The thief was always found out.

Asir had stolen more than wealth, he had stolen the strength of their souls. For this they hung him by his wrists and waited for him to beg for the bleeding-blade.

Woman thirsts for husband,
Man thirsts for wife,
Baby thirsts for breast-milk
Thief thirsts for knife . . .

A rhyme from his childhood, a childish chant, an eenie-menie-miney for determining who should drink first from a nectar-cactus. He groaned and tried to shift his weight more comfortably. Where was Mara?

'Ready for me yet, Asir?' the squat man asked.

Asir hated him with narrowed eyes. The executioner was bound by law to wait until his victim requested his fate. But Asir remained ignorant of what the fate would be. The Council of Senior Kinsmen judged him in secret, and passed sentence as to what the executioner would do with the knife. But Asir was not informed of their judgment. He knew only that when he asked for it, the executioner would advance with the bleeding-blade and exact the punishment—his life, or an amputation, depending on the judgment. He might lose only an eye or an ear or a finger.

But on the other hand, he might lose his life, both arms, or his masculinity.

There was no way to find out until he asked for the punishment. If he refused to ask, they would leave him hanging there. In theory, a thief could escape by hanging four days, after which the executioner would pull out the nails. Sometimes a culprit managed it, but when the nails were pulled, the thing that toppled was already a corpse.

The sun was sinking in the west, and it blinded him. Asir knew about the sun—knew things the stupid council failed to know. A thief, if successful, frequently became endowed with wisdom, for he memorized more wealth than a score of honest men. Quotations from the ancient gods—Fermi, Einstein, Elgermann, Hanser and the rest—most men owned scattered phrases, and scattered phrases remained meaningless. But a thief memorized all transactions that he overheard, and the countless phrases could be fitted together into meaningful ideas.

He knew now that Mars, once dead, was dying again, its air leaking away once more into space. And Man would die with it, unless something were done, and done quickly. The Blaze of the Great Wind needed to be rekindled under the earth, but it would not be done. The tribes had fallen into ignorance, even as the holy books had warned:

It is realized that the colonists will be unable to maintain a technology without basic tools, and that a rebuilding will require several generations of intelligently directed effort. Given the knowledge, the colonists may be able to restore a machine culture if the knowledge continues to be bolstered by desire. But if the third, fourth, and Nth generations fail to further the gradual retooling process, the knowledge will become worthless.

The quotation was from the god Roggins, *Progress of the Mars-Culture*, and he had stolen bits of it from various sources. The books themselves were no longer in existence, remembered only in memorized ritual chants, the possession of which meant wealth.

Asir was sick. Pain and slow loss of blood made him weak, and his vision blurred. He failed to see her coming until he heard her feet rustling in the dry grass.

'Mara—'

She smirked and spat contemptuously at the foot of the post. The daughter of a Senior Kinsman, she was a tall, slender girl with an arrogant strut and mocking eyes. She stood for a moment with folded arms, eyeing him with amusement. Then, slowly, one eye closed in a solemn wink. She turned her back on him and spoke to the executioner.

'May I taunt the prisoner, Slubil?' she asked.

'It is forbidden to speak to the thief,' growled the knifeman.

'Is he ready to beg for justice, Slubil?'

The knifeman grinned and looked at Asir. 'Are you ready for me yet, thief?'

Asir hissed an insult. The girl had betrayed him.

'Evidently a coward,' she said. 'Perhaps he means to hang four days.'

'Let him then.'

'No—I think that I should *like* to see him beg.'

She gave Asir a long searching glance, then turned to walk away. The thief cursed her quietly and followed her with his eyes. A dozen steps away she stopped again, looked back over her shoulder, and repeated the slow wink. Then she marched on toward her father's house. The wink made his scalp crawl for a moment, but then . . .

Suppose she hasn't betrayed me? Suppose she had wheedled the sentence out of Tokra, and knew what his punishment would be. *I think that I should like to see him beg.*

But on the other hand, the fickle she-devil might be tricking him into asking for a sentence that she *knew* would be death or dismemberment—just to amuse herself.

He cursed inwardly and trembled as he peered at the bored executioner. He licked his lips and fought against dizzyness as he groped for words. Slubil heard him muttering and looked up.

'Are you ready for me yet?'

Asir closed his eyes and gritted his teeth. 'Give it to me!' he yelped suddenly, and braced himself against the post.

Why not? The short time gained couldn't be classed as living. Have it done with. Eternity would be sweet in comparison to this ignominy. A knife could be a blessing.

He heard the executioner chuckle and stand up. He heard the man's footsteps approaching slowly, and the singing hiss of the knife as Slubil swung it in quick arcs. The executioner moved about him slowly, teasing him with the whistle of steel fanning the air about him. He was expected to beg. Slubil occasionally laid the knife against his skin and took it away again. Then Asir heard the rustle of the executioner's cloak as his arm went back. Asir opened his eyes.

The executioner grinned as he held the blade high—aimed at

Asir's head! The girl had tricked him. He groaned and closed his eyes again, muttering a half-forgotten prayer.

The stroke fell—and the blade chopped into the post above his head. Asir fainted.

When he awoke he lay in a crumpled heap on the ground. The executioner rolled him over with his foot.

'In view of your extreme youth, thief,' the knifeman growled, 'the council has ordered you perpetually banished. The sun is setting. Let dawn find you in the hills. If you return to the plains, you will be chained to a wild hüffen and dragged to death.'

Panting weakly, Asir groped at his forehead, and found a fresh wound, raw and rubbed with rust to make a scar. Slubil had marked him as an outcast. But except for the nail-holes through his forearms, he was still in one piece. His hands were numb, and he could scarcely move his fingers. Slubil had bound the spike-wounds, but the bandages were bloody and leaking.

When the knifeman had gone, Asir climbed weakly to his feet. Several of the townspeople stood nearby, snickering at him. He ignored their catcalls and staggered toward the outskirts of the village, ten minutes away. He had to speak to Mara, and to her father if the crusty oldster would listen. His thief's knowledge weighed upon him and brought desperate fear.

Darkness had fallen by the time he came to Welkir's house. The people spat at him in the streets, and some of them flung handfuls of loose dirt after him as he passed. A light flickered feebly through Welkir's door. Asir rattled it and waited.

Welkir came with a lamp. He set the lamp on the floor and stood with feet spread apart, arms folded, glaring haughtily at the thief. His face was stiff as weathered stone. He said nothing, but only stared contemptuously.

Asir bowed his head. 'I have come to plead with you, Senior Kinsman.'

Welkir snorted disgust. 'Against the mercy we have shown you?'

He looked up quickly, shaking his head. 'No! For that I am grateful.'

'What then?'

'As a thief, I acquired much wisdom. I know that the world is dying, and the air is boiling out of it into the sky. I wish to be heard by the council. We must study the words of the ancients and perform their magic, lest our children's children be born to strangle in a dead world.'

Welkir snorted again. He picked up the lamp. 'He who listens to a thief's wisdom is cursed. He who acts upon it is doubly cursed and a party to the crime.'

'The vaults,' Asir insisted. 'The key to the Blaze of the Winds is in the vaults. The god Roggins tells us in the words—'

'Stop! I will not hear!'

'Very well, but the blaze can be rekindled, and the air renewed. The vaults—' He stammered and shook his head. 'The council must hear me.'

'The council will hear nothing, and you shall be gone before dawn. And the vaults are guarded by the sleeper called Big Joe. To enter is to die. Now go away.'

Welkir stepped back and slammed the door. Asir sagged in defeat. He sank down on the doorstep to rest a moment. The night was black, except for lamp-flickers from an occasional window.

'Ssssst!'

A sound from the shadows. He looked around quickly, searching for the source.

'Ssssst! Asir!'

It was the girl Mara, Welkir's daughter. She had slipped out the back of the house and was peering at him around the corner. He arose quietly and went to her.

'What did Slubil do to you?' she whispered.

Asir gasped and caught her shoulders angrily. 'Don't you *know?*'

'No! Stop! You're hurting me. Tokra wouldn't tell me. I made love to him, but he wouldn't tell.'

He released her with an angry curse.

'You *had* to take it sometime,' she hissed. 'I knew if you waited you would be too weak from hanging to even run away.'

He called her a foul name.

'Ingrate!' she snapped. 'And I bought you a hüffen!'

'You *what?*'

'Tokra gave me a ritual phrase and I bought you a hüffen with it. You can't *walk* to the hills, you know.'

Asir burned with full rage. 'You slept with Tokra!' he snapped.

'You're jealous!' she tittered.

'How can I be jealous! I hate the sight of you!'

'Very well then, I'll keep the hüffen.'

'Do!' he growled. 'I won't need it, since I'm not going to the hills!'

She gasped. 'You've got to go, you fool! They'll kill you!'

He turned away, feeling sick. She caught at his arm and tried to pull him back. 'Asir! Take the hüffen and *go!*'

'I'll go,' he growled. 'But not to the hills. I'm going out to the vaults.'

He stalked away, but she trotted along beside him, trying to tug him back. 'Fool! The vaults are sacred! The priests guard the entrance, and the Sleeper guards the inner door. They'll kill you if you try it, and if you linger, the council will kill you tomorrow.'

'Let them!' he snarled. 'I am no sniveling townsman! I am of the hills, and my father was a renegade. Your council had no right to judge me. Now *I* shall judge *them!*'

The words were spoken hotly, and he realized their folly. He expected a scornful rebuke from Mara, but she hung onto his arm and pleaded with him. He had dragged her a dozen doorways from the house of her father. Her voice had lost its arrogance and became pleading.

'Please, Asir! Go away. Listen! I will even go with you—if you want me.'

He laughed harshly. 'Tokra's leavings.'

She slapped him hard across the mouth. 'Tokra is an impotent old dodderer. He can scarcely move for arthritis. You're an idiot! I sat on his lap and kissed his bald pate for you.'

'Then why did he give you a ritual phrase?' he asked stiffly.

'Because he likes me.'

'You lie.' He stalked angrily on.

'Very well! Go to the vaults. I'll tell my father, and they'll hunt you down before you get there.'

She released his arm and stopped. Asir hesitated. She meant it. He came back to her slowly, then slipped his swollen hands to her throat. She did not back away.

'Why don't I just choke you and leave you lying here?' he hissed.

Her face was only a shadow in darkness, but he could see her cool smirk.

'Because you love me, Asir of Franic.'

He dropped his hands and grunted a low curse. She laughed low and took his arm.

'Come on. We'll go get the hüffen,' she said.

Why not? he thought. *Take her hüffen, and take her too*. He could dump her a few miles from the village, then circle back to the vaults. She leaned against him as they moved back toward her father's house, then skirted it and stole back to the field behind the row of dwellings. Phobos hung low in the west, its tiny disk lending only a faint glow to the darkness.

He heard the hüffen's breathing as they approached a hulking shadow in the gloom. Its great wings snaked out slowly as it sensed their approach, and it made a low piping sound. A native Martian species, it bore no resemblance to the beasts that the ancients had brought with them from the sky. Its back was covered with a thin shell like a beetle's, but its belly was porous and soft. It digested food by sitting on it, and absorbing it. The wings were bony—parchment stretched across a fragile frame. It was headless, and lacked a centralized brain, the nervous functions being distributed.

The great creature made no protest as they climbed up the broad flat back and strapped themselves down with the belts that had been threaded through holes cut in the hüffen's thin, tough shell. Its lungs slowly gathered a tremendous breath of air, causing the riders to rise up as the huge air-sacs became distended. The girth of an inflated hüffen was nearly four times as great as when deflated. When the air was gathered, the creature began to shrink again as its muscles tightened, compressing the breath until a faint leakage-hiss came from behind. It waited, wings taut.

The girl tugged at a ring set through the flesh of its flank. There was a blast of sound and a jerk. Nature's experiment in jet propulsion soared ahead and turned into the wind. Its first breath exhausted, it gathered another and blew itself ahead again. The ride was jerky. Each tailward belch was a rough lurch. They let the hüffen choose its own heading as it gained altitude. Then Mara tugged at the wing-straps, and the creature wheeled to soar toward the dark hills in the distance.

Asir sat behind her, a sardonic smirk on his face, as the wind whipped about them. He waited until they had flown beyond screaming distance of the village. Then he took her shoulders lightly in his hands. Mistaking it for affection, she leaned back against him easily and rested her dark head on his shoulder. He kissed her—while his hand felt gingerly for the knife at her belt. His fingers were numb, but he managed to clutch it, and press the blade lightly against her throat. She gasped. With his other hand, he caught her hair.

'Now guide the hüffen down!' he ordered.

'Asir!'

'Quickly!' he barked.

'What are you going to do?'

'Leave you here and circle back to the vaults.'

'No! Not out here at night!'

He hesitated. There were slinking prowlers on the Cimerian plain, beasts who would regard the marooned daughter of Welkir a delicious bit of good fortune, a gustatory delight of a sort they seldom were able to enjoy. Even above the moan of the wind, he would hear an occasional howl-cry from the fanged welcoming committee that waited for its dinner beneath them.

'Very well,' he growled reluctantly. 'Turn toward the vaults. But one scream and I'll slice you.' He took the blade from her throat but kept the point touching her back.

'Please, Asir, *no!*' she pleaded. 'Let me go on to the hills. Why do you want to go to the vaults? Because of Tokra?'

He gouged her with the point until she yelped. 'Tokra be damned, and you with him!' he snarled. 'Turn back.'

'Why?'

'I'm going down to kindle the Blaze of the Winds.'

'You're *mad! The spirits of the ancients live in the vaults.'*

'I am going to kindle the Blaze of the Winds,' he insisted stubbornly. 'Now either turn back, or go down and I'll turn back alone.'

After a hesitant moment, she tugged at a wing rein and the hüffen banked majestically. They flew a mile to the south of the village, then beyond it toward the cloister where the priests of Big Joe guarded the entrance to the vaults. The cloister was marked by a patch of faint light on the ground ahead.

'Circle around it once,' he ordered.

'You can't get in. They'll kill you.'

He doubted it. No one ever tried to enter, except the priests who carried small animals down as sacrifices to the great Sleeper. Since no outsider ever dared go near the shaft, the guards expected no one. He doubted that they would be alert.

The cloister was a hollow square with a small stone tower rising in the center of the courtyard. The tower contained the entrance to the shaft. In the dim light of Phobos, assisted by yellow flickers from the cloister windows, he peered at the courtyard as they circled closer. It seemed to be empty.

'Land beside the tower!' he ordered.

'Asir—please—'

'Do it!'

The hüffen plunged rapidly, soared across the outer walls, and burst into the courtyard. It landed with a rough jolt and began squeaking plaintively.

'Hurry!' he hissed. 'Get your straps off and let's go.'

'I'm not going.'

A prick of the knife point changed her mind. They slid quickly to the ground, and Asir kicked the hüffen in the flanks. The beast sucked in air and burst aloft.

Startled faces were trying to peer through the lighted cloister windows into the courtyard. Someone cried a challenge. Asir darted to the door of the tower and dragged it open. Now forced to share the danger, the girl came with him without urging. They stepped into a stair-landing. A candle flickered from a wall bracket. A guard, sitting on the floor beneath the candle, glanced up in complete surprise. Then he reached for a short barbed pike. Asir kicked him hard in the temple, then rolled his limp form outside. Men with torches were running across the courtyard. He slammed the heavy metal door and bolted it.

Fists began beating on the door. They paused for a moment to rest, and Mara stared at him in fright. He expected her to burst into angry speech, but she only leaned against the wall and panted. The dark mouth of the stairway yawned at them—a stone throat that led into the bowels of Mars and the realm of the monster, Big Joe. He glanced at Mara thoughtfully, and felt sorry for her.

'I can leave you here,' he offered, 'but I'll have to tie you.'

She moistened her lips, glanced first at the stairs, then at the door where the guards were raising a frantic howl. She shook her head.

'I'll go with you.'

'The priests won't bother you, if they see that you were a prisoner.'

'I'll go with you.'

He was pleased, but angry with himself for the pleasure. An arrogant, spiteful, conniving wench, he told himself. She'd lied about Tokra. He grunted gruffly, seized the candle, and started down the stairs. When she started after him, he stiffened and glanced back, remembering the barbed pike.

As he had suspected, she had picked it up. The point was a foot from the small of his back. They stared at each other, and she wore her self-assured smirk.

'Here,' she said, and handed it casually. 'You might need this.'

They stared at each other again, but it was different this time.

Bewildered, he shook his head and resumed the descent toward the vaults. The guards were battering at the doors behind them.

The stairwell was damp and cold. Blackness folded about them like a shroud. They moved in silence, and after five thousand steps, Asir stopped counting.

Somewhere in the depths, Big Joe slept his restless sleep. Asir wondered grimly how long it would take the guards to tear down the metal door. Somehow they had to get past Big Joe before the guards came thundering after them. There was a way to get around the monster: of that he was certain. A series of twenty-four numbers was involved, and he had memorized them with a stolen bit of ritual. How to use them was a different matter. He imagined vaguely that one must call them out in a loud voice before the inner entrance.

The girl walked beside him now, and he could feel her shivering. His eyes were quick and nervous as he scanned each pool of darkness, each nook and cranny along the stairway wall. The well was silent except for the mutter of their footsteps, and the gloom was full of musty odors. The candle afforded little light.

'I told you the truth about Tokra,' she blurted suddenly.

Asir glowered straight ahead and said nothing, embarrassed by his previous jealousy. They moved on in silence.

Suddenly she stopped. 'Look,' she hissed, pointing down ahead.

He shielded the candle with his hand and peered downward toward a small square of dim light. 'The bottom of the stairs,' he muttered.

The light seemed faint and diffuse—with a slight greenish cast. Asir blew out the candle, and the girl quickly protested.

'How will we see to climb again?'

He laughed humorlessly. 'What makes you think we will?'

She moaned and clutched at his arm, but came with him as he descended slowly toward the light. The stairway opened into a long corridor whose ceiling was faintly luminous. White-faced and frightened, they paused on the bottom step and looked down the corridor. Mara gasped and covered her eyes.

'Big Joe!' she whispered in awe.

He stared through the stairwell door and down the corridor through another door into a large room. Big Joe sat in the center of the room, sleeping his sleep of ages amid a heap of broken and whitening bones. A creature of metal, twice the height of Asir, he had obviously been designed to kill. Tri-fingered hands with gleaming talons, and a monstrous head shaped like a Marswolf, with long silver fangs. Why should a metal-creature have fangs, unless he had been built to kill?

The behemoth slept in a crouch, waiting for the intruders.

He tugged the girl through the stairwell door. A voice droned out of nowhere: *'If you have come to plunder, go back!'*

He stiffened, looking around. The girl whimpered.

'Stay here by the stairs,' he told her, and pushed her firmly back through the door.

Asir started slowly toward the room where Big Joe waited. Beyond the room he could see another door, and the monster's job was apparently to keep intruders back from the inner vaults where, according to the ritual chants, the Blaze of the Winds could be kindled.

Halfway along the corridor, the voice called out again, beginning a kind of sing-song chant: *'Big Joe will kill you, Big Joe will kill you, Big Joe will kill you—'*

He turned slowly, searching for the speaker. But the voice seemed to come from a black disk on the wall. The talking-machines perhaps, as mentioned somewhere in the ritual.

A few paces from the entrance to the room, the voice fell silent. He stopped at the door, staring in at the monster. Then he took a deep breath and began chanting the twenty-four numbers in a loud but quavering voice. Big Joe remained in his motionless crouch. Nothing happened. He stepped through the doorway.

Big Joe emitted a deafening roar, straightened with a metallic groan, and lumbered toward him, taloned hands extended and eyes blazing furiously. Asir shrieked and ran for his life.

Then he saw Mara lying sprawled in the stairway entrance. She had fainted. Blocking an impulse to leap over her and flee alone, he stopped to lift her.

But suddenly he realized that there was no pursuit. He looked back. Big Joe had returned to his former position, and he appeared to be asleep again. Puzzled, Asir stepped back into the corridor.

'If you have come to plunder, go back!'

He moved gingerly ahead again.

'Big Joe will kill you, Big Joe will kill you, Big Joe will kill—'

He recovered the barbed pike from the floor and stole into the zone of silence. This time he stopped to look around. Slowly he reached the pike-staff through the doorway. Nothing happened.

He stepped closer and waved it around inside. Big Joe remained motionless.

Then he dropped the point of the pike to the floor. The monster bellowed and started to rise. Asir leaped back, scalp crawling. But Big Joe settled back in his crouch.

Fighting a desire to flee, Asir reached the pike through the door and rapped it on the floor again. This time nothing happened. He glanced down. The pike's point rested in the center of a gray floor-tile, just to the left of the entrance. The floor was a checkerboard pattern of gray and white. He tapped another gray square, and this time the monster started out of his drowse again.

After a moment's thought, he began touching each tile within reach of the door. Most of them brought a response from Big Joe. He found four that did not. He knelt down before the door to peer at them closely. The first was unmarked. The second bore a dot in the center. The third bore two, and the fourth three—in order of their distance from the door.

He stood up and stepped inside again, standing on the first tile. Big Joe remained motionless. He stepped diagonally left to the second—straight ahead to the third—then diagonally right to the fourth. He stood there for a moment, trembling and staring at the Sleeper. He was four feet past the door!

Having assured himself that the monster was still asleep, he crouched to peer at the next tiles. He stared for a long time, but found no similar markings. Were the dots coincidence?

He reached out with the pike, then drew it back. He was too close to the Sleeper to risk a mistake. He stood up and looked around carefully, noting each detail of the room—and of the floor in particular. He counted the rows and columns of tiles—twenty-four each way.

Twenty-four—and there were twenty-four numbers in the series that was somehow connected with safe passage through the room. He frowned and muttered through the series to himself——0,1,2,3,3,3,2,2,1 . . .

The first four numbers—0,1,2,3. And the tiles—the first with no dots, the second with one, the third with two, the fourth with three. But the four tiles were not in a straight line, and there were no marked ones beyond the fourth. He backed out of the room and studied them from the end of the corridor again.

Mara had come dizzily awake and was calling for him weakly. He replied reassuringly and turned to his task again. 'First tile, then diagonally left, then straight, then diagonally right—'

0,1,2,3,3.

A hunch came. He advanced as far as the second tile, then reached as far ahead as he could and touched the square diagonally right from the fourth one. Big Joe remained motionless but began to speak. His scalp bristled at the growling voice.

'If the intruder makes an error, Big Joe will kill.'

Standing tense, ready to leap back to the corridor, he touched the square again. The motionless behemoth repeated the grim warning.

Asir tried to reach the square diagonally right from the fifth, but could not without stepping up to the third. Taking a deep breath, he stepped up and extended the pike cautiously, keeping his eyes on Big Joe. The pike rapped the floor.

'If the intruder makes an error, Big Joe will kill.'

But the huge figure remained in his place.

Starting from the first square, the path went left, straight, right, right, right. And after zero, the numbers went 1, 2, 3, 3, 3. Apparently he had found the key. One meant a square to the southeast; two meant south; and three southwest. Shivering, he moved up to the fifth square upon which the monster growled his first warning. He looked back at the door, then at Big Joe. The taloned hands could grab him before he could dive back into the corridor.

He hesitated. He could either turn back now, or gamble his life on the accuracy of the tentative belief. The girl was calling to him again.

'Come to the end of the corridor!' he replied.

She came hurriedly, to his surprise.

'No!' he bellowed. 'Stay back of the entrance! Not on the tile! *No!'*

Slowly she withdrew the foot that hung poised over a trigger-tile.

'You can't come in unless you know how,' he gasped.

She blinked at him and glanced nervously back over her shoulder. 'But I hear them. They're coming down the stairs.'

Asir cursed softly. Now he *had* to go ahead.

'Wait just a minute,' he said. 'Then I'll show you how to come through.'

He advanced to the last tile that he had tested and stopped. The next two numbers were two—for straight ahead. And they would take him within easy reach of the long taloned arms of the murderous sentinel. He glanced around in fright at the crushed bones scattered across the floor. Some were human. Others were animal-sacrifices tossed in by the priests.

He had tested only one two—back near the door. If he made a mistake, he would never escape; no need bothering with the pike.

He stepped to the next tile and closed his eyes.

'If the intruder makes an error, Big Joe will kill.'

He opened his eyes again and heaved a breath of relief.

'Asir! They're getting closer! I can hear them!'

He listened for a moment. A faint murmur of angry voices in the distance. 'All right,' he said calmly. 'Step only on the tiles I tell you. See the gray one at the left of the door?'

She pointed. 'This one?'

'Yes, step on it.'

The girl moved up and stared fearfully at the monstrous sentinel. He guided her up toward him. 'Diagonally left—one ahead—diagonally right. Now don't be frightened when he speaks—'

The girl came on until she stood one square behind him. Her quick frightened breathing blended with the growing sounds of shouting from the stairway. He glanced up at Big Joe, noticing for the first time that the steel jaws were stained with a red-brown crust. He shuddered.

The grim chess-game continued a cautious step at a time, with the girl following one square behind him. What if she fainted again? And fell across a triggered tile? They passed within a foot of Big Joe's arm.

Looking up, he saw the monster's eyes move—following them, scrutinizing them as they passed. He froze.

'We want no plunder,' he said to the machine.

The gaze was steady and unwinking.

'The air is leaking away from the world.'

The monster remained silent.

'Hurry!' whimpered the girl. Their pursuers were gaining rapidly and they had crossed only half the distance to the opposing doorway. Progress was slower now, for Asir needed occasionally to repeat through the whole series of numbers, looking back to count squares and make certain that the next step was not a fatal one.

'They won't dare to come in after us,' he said hopefully.

'And if they do?'

'If the intruder makes an error, Big Joe will kill,' announced the machine as Asir took another step.

'Eight squares to go!' he muttered, and stopped to count again.

'Asir! They're in the corridor!'

Hearing the tumble of voices, he looked back to see blue-robed men spilling out of the stairway and milling down the corridor toward the room. But halfway down the hall, the priests paused—seeing the unbelievable: two intruders walking safely past their devil-god. They growled excitedly among themselves. Asir took another step. Again the machine voiced the monotonous warning.

'If the intruder makes an error . . .'

Hearing their deity speak, the priests of Big Joe babbled wildly and withdrew a little. But one, more impulsive than the rest, began shrieking.

'Kill the intruders! Cut them down with your spears!'

Asir glanced back to see two of them racing toward the room, lances cocked for the throw. If a spear struck a trigger-tile—

'Stop!' he bellowed, facing around.

The two priests paused. Wondering if it would result in his sudden death, he rested a hand lightly against the huge steel arm of the robot, then leaned against it. The huge eyes were staring down at him, but Big Joe did not move.

The spearmen stood frozen, gaping at the thief's familiarity with the horrendous hulk. Then, slowly they backed away.

Continuing his bluff, he looked up at Big Joe and spoke in a loud voice. 'If they throw their spears or try to enter, kill them.'

He turned his back on the throng in the hall and continued the cautious advance. Five to go, four, three, two—

He paused to stare into the room beyond. Gleaming machinery—all silent—and great panels, covered with a multitude of white circles and dials. His heart sank. If here lay the magic that controlled the Blaze of the Great Wind, he could never hope to re-kindle it.

He stepped through the doorway, and the girl followed. Immediately the robot spoke like low thunder.

'The identity of the two technologists is recognized. Hereafter they may pass with impunity. Big Joe is charged to ask the following: why do the technologists come, when it is not yet time?'

Staring back, Asir saw that the robot's head had turned so that he was looking directly back at the thief and the girl. Asir also saw that someone had approached the door again. Not priests, but townspeople.

He stared, recognizing the Chief Commoner, and the girl's father Welkir, three other Senior Kinsmen, and—Slubil, the executioner who had nailed him to the post.

'Father! Stay back.'

Welkir remained silent, glaring at them. He turned and whispered to the Chief Commoner. The Chief Commoner whispered to Slubil. The executioner nodded grimly and took a short-axe from his belt thong. He stepped through the entrance, his left foot striking the zero-tile. He peered at Big Joe and saw that the monster remained motionless. He grinned at the ones behind him, then snarled in Asir's direction.

'Your sentence has been changed, thief.'

'Don't try to cross, Slubil!' Asir barked.

Slubil spat, brandished the axe, and stalked forward. Big Joe came up like a resurrection of fury, and his elbow was explosive in the vaults. Slubil froze, then stupidly drew back his axe.

Asir gasped as the talons closed. He turned away quickly. Slubil's scream was cut off abruptly by a ripping sound, then a series of dull cracks and snaps. The girl shrieked and closed her eyes. There were two distinct thuds as Big Joe tossed Slubil aside.

The priests and the townspeople—all except Welkir—had fled from the corridor and up the stairway. Welkir was on his knees, his hands covering his face.

'Mara!' he moaned. 'My daughter.'

'Go back, Father,' she called.

Dazed, the old man picked himself up weakly and staggered down the corridor toward the stairway. When he passed the place of the first warning voice, the robot moved again—arose slowly and turned toward Asir and Mara who backed quickly away, deeper into the room of strange machines. Big Joe came lumbering slowly after them.

Asir looked around for a place to flee, but the monster stopped in the doorway. He spoke again, a mechanical drone like memorized ritual.

Big Joe is charged with announcing his function for the intelligence of the technologists. His primary function is to prevent the entrance of possibly destructive organisms into the vaults containing the control equipment for the fusion reaction which must periodically renew atmospheric oxygen. His secondary function is to direct the technologists to records containing such information as they may need. His tertiary function is to carry out simple directions given by the technologists if such directions are possible to his limited design.

Asir stared at the lumbering creature and realized for the first time that it was not alive, but only a machine built by the ancients to perform specific tasks. Despite the fresh redness about his hands and jaws, Big Joe was no more guilty of Slubil's death than a grinding mill would be if the squat sadist had climbed into it while the Marsoxen were yoked to the crushing roller.

Perhaps the ancients had been unnecessarily brutal in building such a guard—but at least they had built him to *look* like a destroyer, and to give ample warning to the intruder. Glancing around at the machinery, he vaguely understood the reason for Big Joe. Such metals as these would mean riches for swordmakers and smiths and plunderers of all kinds.

Asir straightened his shoulders and addressed the machine. 'Teach us how to kindle the Blaze of the Great Wind.'

'Teaching is not within the designed functions of Big Joe. I am charged to say: the renewal reaction should not be begun before the Marsyear 6,000, as the builders reckoned time.'

Asir frowned. The years were no longer numbered, but only named in honor of the Chief Commoners who ruled the villages. 'How long until the year 6,000?' he asked.

Big Joe clucked like an adding machine. 'Twelve Marsyears, technologist.'

Asir stared at the complicated machinery. Could they learn to operate it in twelve years? It seemed impossible.

'How can we begin to learn?' he asked the robot.

'This is an instruction room, where you may examine records. The control mechanisms are installed in the deepest vault.'

Asir frowned and walked to the far end of the hall where another door opened into—*another anteroom with another Big Joe!* As he approached the second robot spoke:

'If the intruder has not acquired the proper knowledge, Big Oswald will kill.'

Thunderstruck, he leaped back from the entrance and swayed heavily against an instrument panel. The panel lit up and a polite recorded voice began reading something about 'President Snell's role in the Eighth World War.' He lurched away from the panel and stumbled back toward Mara who sat glumly on the foundation slab of a weighty machine.

'What are you laughing about?' she muttered.

'We're still in the first grade!' he groaned, envisioning a sequence of rooms. 'We'll have to learn the magic of the ancients before we pass to the next.'

'The ancients weren't so great,' she grumbled. 'Look at the mural on the wall.'

Asir looked, and saw only a strange design of circles about a bright splash of yellow that might have been the sun. 'What about it?' he asked.

'My father taught me about the planets,' she said. 'That is supposed to be the way they go around the sun.'

'What's wrong with it?'

'One planet too many,' she said. 'Everyone knows that there is only an asteroid belt between Mars and Venus. The picture shows a planet there.'

Asir shrugged indifferently, being interested only in the machinery. 'Can't you allow them one small mistake?'

'I suppose.' She paused, gazing miserably in the direction in which her father had gone. 'What do we do now?'

Asir considered it for a long time. Then he spoke to Big Joe. 'You will come with us to the village.'

The machine was silent for a moment, then: *'There is an apparent contradiction between primary and tertiary functions. Request priority decision by technologist.'*

Asir failed to understand. He repeated his request. The robot turned slowly and stepped through the doorway. He waited.

Asir grinned. 'Let's go back up,' he said to the girl.

She arose eagerly. They crossed the anteroom to the corridor and began the long climb toward the surface, with Big Joe lumbering along behind.

'What about your banishment, Asir?' she asked gravely.

'Wait and see.' He envisioned the pandemonium that would reign when girl, man, and robot marched through the village to the council house, and he chuckled. 'I think that I shall be the next Chief Commoner,' he said. 'And my councilmen will all be thieves.'

'Thieves!' she gasped. 'Why?'

'Thieves who are not afraid to steal the knowledge of the gods—and become technologists, to kindle the Blaze of the Winds.'

'What is a "technologist", Asir?' she asked worshipfully.

Asir glowered at himself for blundering with words he did not understand, but could not admit ignorance to Mara who clung tightly to his arm. 'I think,' he said, 'that a technologist is a thief who tells the gods what to do.'

'Kiss me, Technologist,' she told him in a small voice.

Big Joe clanked to a stop to wait for them to move on. He waited a long time.

YOU TRIFLIN' SKUNK!

The rain sang light in the sodden palmettos and the wind moaned through the pines about the unpainted shack, whipping the sea of grass that billowed about the islands of scrub. The land lay bathed in rain-haze beneath the pines. Rain trickled from the roof of the shack and made a rattling spray in the rivulets under the eaves. Rain blew from the roof in foggy cloudlets. Rain played marimba-sounds on the wooden steps. A droopy chicken huddled in the drenched grass, too sick to stir or seek a shelter.

No road led across the scrublands to the distant highway, but only a sandy footpath that was now a gushing torrent that ran down to an overflowing creek of brackish water. A possum hurried across the inundated footpath at the edge of the clearing, drenched and miserable, seeking the higher ground.

The cabin was without a chimney, but a length of stovepipe projected from a side window, and bent skyward at a clumsy angle. A thin trail of brown smoke leaked from beneath the rain-hood, and wound away on the gusty breeze. In the cabin, there was life, and an aura of song lingered about the rain-washed walls, song as mournful as the sodden land, low as the wail of a distant train.

Whose hands was drivin' the nails O Lord?
Whose hands was drivin' the nails?
Lord O Lord!
My hands was drivin' the nails O Lord!
My hands was drivin' the nails
And I did crucify my God!

The song was low and vibrant in the cabin, and Lucey rocked to it, rolling her head as she sang over the stove, where a smoked possum simmered in pot-likker with sweet-taters, while corn bread toasted in the oven. The cabin was full of food-smells and sweat-smells, and smoky light through dusty panes.

From a rickety iron bed near the window came a sudden choking sob, an animal sound of almost unendurable torment and despair. Lucey stopped singing, and turned to blink toward the cry, sudden concern melting her pudgy face into a mountain woman cherub's face, full of compassion.

'Awwwwwww . . .' The sound welled unbidden from her throat, a rich low outpouring of love and sympathy for the sallow twitching youth who lay on the yellowish sheets, his eyes wild, his hands tensing into claws.

'Awwwww, Doodie—you ain't gonna have another spell?' she said.

Only a small hurt this time, my son. It can't be helped. It's like tuning a guitar. You can't do it without sounding the strings, or pulsing the neural fibers. But only a small hurt this time. . . .

The youth writhed and shuddered, stiffening into a puppet strained by steel springs. His back arched, and his muscles quivered. He flung himself suddenly into reflexive gymnastics, sobbing in small shrieks.

Lucey murmured softly. An immense mass of love, she waddled toward the bed in bounces of rubbery flesh. She bent over him to purr low in her throat.

'Poor Doodie . . . poor li'l Doodie. Mama's lamb.'

The boy sobbed and thrashed. The paroxysm brought froth to his lips and jerked his limbs into cramped spasms. He jerked and writhed and tumbled on the bed.

'You jus' try to lay calm, Doodie. You jus' try. You gonna be all right. It ain't gonna last long, Doodie. It's gonna go away.'

'No!' he whimpered. 'No! Don't touch me, Mama! *Don't!'*

'Now, Doodie . . .'

She sat on the edge of the bed to gather him up in her massive arms. The spasms grew more frantic, less reflexive. He fought her, shrieking terror. She lay beside him, moaning low with pity. She enveloped him with her arms, enfolding him so that he could no longer kick. She pulled his face into the hollow of her huge bosom and squeezed him. With his tense body pressed tightly against the bulky mass of her, she melted again with love, and began chanting a rhythmic lullaby while he twitched and slavered against her, fighting away, pretending to suffocate.

Gradually, as exhaustion overcame him, the spasm passed. He lay wheezing quietly in her arms.

The strings are tuned, my son, and it was only a small hurt. Has the hurt stopped, my son?

Yes, father, if only this monstress would let me be.

Accept my knowledge, and be content. The time will come.

'Who you whisperin' to, Doodie? Why are you mumblin' so?' She looked down at his tousled head, pressed tightly between her breasts.

His muttering ceased, and he lay quietly as if in a trance. It was always so. The boy had fits, and when the paroxysm had passed, he went into a rigid sleep. But it was more like a frozen moment of awareness, and old Ma Kutter said the boy was 'witched.' Lucey had never believed in 'witchin'.'

When he was tensely quiet, she tenderly disengaged herself and slid off the bed. He lay on his side, face toward the window, eyes slitted and mouth agape. Humming softly, Lucey returned to the stove and took a stick of oak out of the bucket. She paused to glance back at him—and he seemed to be rigidly listening to something. The rain?

'Doodie . . . ?'

'When are you coming for us, father?' came in a ghost whisper from the bed. 'When, *when?*'

'What are you talking about, Doodie?' The cast-iron stove-lid clattered on the hot metal as she lifted it nervously aside. She glanced down briefly at the red coals in the stove, then back at Doodie.

'Very soon . . . very soon!' he whispered.

Lucey chucked the stick of wood in atop the coals, then stood staring at the bed until the flames licked up about the lid-hole to glisten orange on her sweat-glazed face.

'Who are you talkin' to, Doodie?'

She expected no answer, but after several seconds, his breathing grew deeper. Then it came: 'My *father*.'

Lucey's plump mouth went slowly shut and her hand quivered as she fumbled for the stove lid.

'Your pa is dead, Doodie. You know that.'

The emaciated youth stirred on the bed, picked himself up slowly on one arm, and turned to look at her, his eyes blazing. 'You lie!' he cried. 'Mama, you lie!'

'Doodie!'

'I hate you, Mama. I hate all of you, and I'll make you pay. I'll be like *him*.'

The stove-lid clattered back in place. She wiped her hands

nervously on her dress. 'You're sick, Doodie! You're not right in the mind. You never even *seed* your pa.'

'I talk to him,' the boy said. 'He tells me things. He told me why you're my mother. He told me how. And he told me who *I* am.'

'You're my son!' Lucey's voice had gone up an octave, and she edged defensively away.

'Only half of me, Mama,' the boy said, then laughed defiantly. 'Only half of me is even human. You knew that when he came here, and paid you to have his baby.'

'Doodie!'

'You can't lie to me, Mama. *He* tells me. *He* knows.'

'He was just a man, Doodie. Now he's gone. He never came back, do you hear?'

The boy stared out the window at the rain-shroud. When he spoke again, it was in a small slow voice of contempt.

'It doesn't matter. He doesn't want you to believe—any of you.' He paused to snicker. 'He doesn't want to warn you what we're going to do.'

Lucey shook her head slowly. 'Lord, have mercy on me,' she breathed. 'I know I done wrong. But please, punish old Lucey and not my boy.'

'I ain't crazy, Mama.'

'If you ain't crazy, you're "witched," and talkin' to the dead.'

'He ain't dead. He's Outside.'

Lucey's eyes flickered quickly to the door.

'And he's comin' back—soon.' The boy chuckled. 'Then he'll make me like him, and it won't hurt to listen.'

'You talk like he wasn't a man. I seed him, and you didn't. Your pa was just a man, Doodie.'

'No, Mama. He showed you a man because he wanted you to see a man. Next time, he'll come the way he *really* is.'

'Why would your pa come back?' she snorted, summoning courage to stir the pot. 'What would he want here? If you was right in the head, you wouldn't get fits, and you'd know you never seed him. What's his name? You don't even know his name.'

'His name is a purple bitter with black velvet, Mama. Only there isn't any word.'

'Fits,' she moaned. 'A child with fits.'

'The crawlers, you mean? That's when he talks to me. It hurts at first.'

She advanced on him with a big tin spoon, and shook it at

him. 'You're sick, Doodie. And don't you carry on so. A doctor's what you need . . . if only Mama had some money.'

'I won't fuss with you, Mama.'

'Huh!' She stood there for a moment, shaking her head. Then she went back to stir the pot. Odorous steam arose to perfume the shack.

The boy turned his head to watch her with luminous eyes. 'The fits are when he talks, Mama. Honest they are. It's like electricity inside me. I wish I could tell you how.'

'Sick!' She shook her head vigorously. 'Sick, that's all.'

'If I was all like him, it wouldn't hurt. It only hurts because I'm half like you.'

'Doodie, you're gonna drive your old mother to her grave. Why do you torment me so?'

He turned back to the window and fell silent . . . determinedly, hostilely silent. Lucey's noises at the stove only served to punctuate it.

'Where does your father stay, Doodie?' she asked at last, in cautious desperation.

'Outside . . .'

'Gitalong! Wheah outside, in a palmetto scrub? In the cypress swamp?'

'*Way* Outside. Outside the world.'

'Who taught you such silliness? Spirits an' such! I ought to tan you good, Doodie!'

'From another world,' the boy went on.

'An' he talks to you from the other world?'

Doodie nodded solemnly.

Lucey stirred vigorously at the pot, her face creased in a dark frown. Lots of folks believed in spirits, and lots of folks believed in mediums. But Lucey had got herself straight with the Lord.

'I'm gonna call the parson,' she grunted flatly.

'Why?'

'Christian folks don't truck with spirits.'

'He's no spirit, Mama. He's like a man, only he's not. He comes from a star.'

She set her jaw and fell grimly silent. She didn't like to remember Doodie's father. He'd come seeking shelter from a storm, and he was big and taciturn, and he made love like a machine. Lucey had been younger then—younger and wilder, and not afraid of shame. He'd vanished as quickly as he'd come.

When he had gone, it almost felt like he'd been there to

accomplish an errand, some piece of business that had to be handled hastily and efficiently.

'Why'd he want a son?' she scoffed. 'If what you say is true —which it ain't.'

The boy stirred restlessly. 'Maybe I shouldn't tell.'

'You tell Mama.'

'You won't believe it anyway,' he said listlessly. 'He fixed it so I'd *look* human. He fixed it so he could talk to me. I tell him things. Things he could find out himself if he wanted to.'

'What does he want to know?'

'How humans work inside.'

'Livers and lungs and such? Ssssst! Silliest I ever—'

'And brains. Now they know.'

'*They?*'

'Pa's people. *You'll see*. Now they know, and they're coming to run things. Things will be different, lots different.'

'When?'

'Soon. Only pa's coming sooner. He's their . . . their . . .' The boy groped for a word. 'He's like a detective.'

Lucey took the corn bread out of the oven and sank despairingly into a chair. 'Doodie, Doodie . . .'

'What, Mama?'

'Oh, Sweet Jesus! What did I do, what did I do? He's a child of the devil. Fits an' lies and puny ways. Lord, have mercy on me.'

With an effort, the boy sat up to stare at her weakly. 'He's no devil, Mama. He's no man, but he's better than a man. You'll see.'

'You're not right in the mind, Doodie.'

'It's all right. He wouldn't want you to believe. Then you'd be warned. They'd be warned too.'

'They?'

'Humans—white and black and yellow. He picked poor people to have his sons, so nobody would believe.'

'Sons? You mean you ain't the only one?'

Doodie shook his head. 'I got brothers, Mama—half-brothers. I talk to them sometimes too.'

She was silent a long time. 'Doodie, you better go to sleep,' she said wearily at last.

'Nobody'll believe . . . until he comes, and the rest of them come after him.'

'He ain't comin', Doodie. You ain't seed him—never.'

'Not with my eyes,' he said.

She shook her head slowly, peering at him with brimming eyes. 'Poor little boy. Cain't I do somethin' to make you see?'

Doodie sighed. He was tired, and didn't answer. He fell back on the pillow and lay motionless. The water that crawled down the pane rippled the rain-light over his sallow face. He might have been a pretty child, if it had not been for the tightness in his face, and the tumor-shape on his forehead.

He said it was the tumor-shape that let him talk to his father. After a few moments, Lucey arose, and took their supper off the stove. Doodie sat propped up on pillows, but he only nibbled at his food.

'Take it away,' he told her suddenly. 'I can feel it starting again.'

There was nothing she could do. While he shrieked and tossed again on the bed, she went out on the rain-swept porch to pray. She prayed softly that her sin be upon herself, not upon her boy. She prayed for understanding, and when she was done she cried until Doodie was silent again inside.

When she went back into the house, he was watching her with cold, hard eyes.

'It's tonight,' he said. 'He's coming *tonight*, Mama.'

The rain ceased at twilight, but the wind stiffened, hurling drops of water from the pines and scattering them like shot across the sagging roof. Running water gurgled in the ditch, and a rabbit ran toward higher ground. In the west, the clouds lifted a dark bandage from a bloody slash of sky, and somewhere a dog howled in the dusk. Rain-pelted, the sick hen lay dying in the yard.

Lucey stood in the doorway, nervously peering out into the pines and the scrub, while she listened to the croak of the tree frogs at sunset, and the conch-shell sounds of wind in the pines.

'Ain't no night for strangers to be out wanderin',' she said. 'There won't be no moon till nearly midnight.'

'He'll come,' promised the small voice behind her. 'He's coming from the Outside.'

'Shush, child. He's nothing of the sort.'

'He'll come, all right.'

'What if I won't let him in the door?'

Doodie laughed. 'You can't stop him, Mama. I'm only *half* like you, and it hurts when he talks-inside.'

'Yes, child?'

'If he talks-inside to a human, the human dies. He told me.'

'Sounds like witch-woman talk,' Lucey said scornfully and

stared back at him from the doorway. 'I don't want no more of it. There's nobody can kill somebody by just a-talkin'.'

'*He* can. And it ain't just talking. It's talking *inside*.'

'Ain't nobody can talk inside your mother but your mother.'

'That's what I been saying.' Doodie laughed. 'If he did, you'd die. That's why he needed *me*.'

Lucey's eyes kept flickering toward the rain-soaked scrub, and she hugged her huge arms, and shivered. 'Silliest I ever!' she snorted. 'He was just a man, and you never even seed him.'

She went inside and got the shotgun, and sat down at the table to clean it, after lighting a smoky oil lamp on the wall.

'Why are you cleaning that gun, Mama?'

'Wildcat around the chicken yard last night!' she muttered. 'Tonight I'm gonna watch.'

Doodie stared at her with narrowed eyes, and the look on his face started her shivering again. Sometimes he did seem not-quite-human, a shape witched or haunted wherein a silent cat prowled by itself and watched, through human eyes.

How could she believe the wild words of a child subject to fits, a child whose story was like those told by witching women and herb healers? A thing that came from the stars, a thing that could come in the guise of a man and talk, make love, eat, and laugh, a thing that wanted a half-human son to which it could speak from afar.

How could she believe in a thing that was like a spy sent into the city before the army came, a thing that could make her conceive when it wasn't even human? It was wilder than any of the stories they told in the deep swamps, and Lucey was a good Christian now.

Still, when Doodie fell asleep, she took the gun and went out to wait for the wildcat that had been disturbing the chickens. It wasn't unchristian to believe in wildcats, not even tonight.

Doodie's father had been just a man, a triflin' man. True, she couldn't remember him very clearly, because she had been drinking corn squeezin's with Jacob Fleeter before the stranger came. She had been all giggly, and he had been all shimmery, and she couldn't remember a word he'd said.

'Lord forgive me,' she breathed as she left the house.

The wet grass dragged about her legs as she crossed the yard and traversed a clearing toward an island of palmetto scrub from which she could cover both the house and the chicken-yard.

The clouds had broken, and stars shone brightly, but there was no moon. Lucey moved by instinct, knowing each inch of land for half a mile around the shack.

She sat on a wet and rotting log in the edge of the palmetto thicket, laid the shotgun across her lap, stuffed a corncob pipe with tobacco from Deevey's field, and sat smoking in the blackness while whippoorwills mourned over the land, and an occasional owl hooted from the swamp. The air was cool and clean after the rain, and only a few nightbirds flitted in the brush while crickets chirped in the distance and tree frogs spoke mysteriously.

'*AAAaaaAAaaarrrwww . . . Na!*'

The cry was low and piercing. Was it Doodie, having another spasm—or only a dream? She half-arose, then paused, listening. There were a few more whimpers, then silence. A dream, she decided, and settled back to wait. There was nothing she could do for Doodie, not until the State Healthmobile came through again, and examined him for 'catchin' ' ailments. If they found he wasn't right in the mind, they might take him away.

The glowing ember in the pipe was hypnotic—the only thing to be clearly seen except the stars. She stared at the stars, wondering about their names, until they began to crawl before her eyes. Then she looked at the ember in the pipe again, brightening and dimming with each breath, acquiring a lacy crust of ashes, growing sleepy in the bowl and sinking deeper, deeper, while the whippoorwills pierced the night with melancholy.

'. . . Na na naaaAAAAhhhaaa. . . . !'

When the cries woke her, she knew she had slept for some time. Faint moonlight seeped through the pine branches from the east, and there was a light mist over the land. The air had chilled, and she shivered as she arose to stretch, propping the gun across the rotten log. She waited for Doodie's cries to cease.

The cries continued, unabated.

Stiffening with sudden apprehension, she started back toward the shack. Then she saw it—a faint violet glow through the trees to the north, just past the corner of the hen house! She stopped again, tense with fright. Doodie's cries were becoming meaningful.

'Pa! I can't stand it any closer! Naa, naaa! I can't think, I can't think at all. No, *please*. . . .'

Reflexively, Lucey started to bolt for the house, but checked herself in time. No lamp burned in the window. She picked up the shotgun and a pebble. After a nervous pause, she tossed the pebble at the porch.

It bounced from the wall with a loud crack, and she slunk low into the shadows. Doodie's cries continued without pause. A minute passed, and no one emerged from the house.

A sudden metallic sound, like the opening of a metal door, came from the direction of the violet light. Quickly she stepped over the log and pressed back into the scrub thicket. Shaking with fear, she waited in the palmettos, crouching in the moonlight among the spiny fronds, and lifting her head occasionally to peer toward the violet light.

She saw nothing for a time, and then, gradually the moonlight seemed to dim. She glanced upward. A tenuous shadow, like smoke, had begun to obscure the face of the moon, a translucent blur like the thinnest cloud.

At first, she dismissed it as a cloud. But it writhed within itself, curled and crawled, not dispersing, but seeming to swim. Smoke from the violet light? She watched it with wide, upturned eyes.

Despite its volatile shape, it clung together as a single entity as smoke would never have done. She could still see it faintly after it had cleared the lunar disk, scintillating in the moon-glow.

It swam like an airborne jellyfish. A cluster of silver threads it seemed, tangled in a cloud of filaments—or a giant mass of dandelion fluff. It leaked out misty pseudopods, then drew them back as it pulled itself through the air. Weightless as chick-down, huge as a barn, it flew—and drifted from the direction of the sphere in a semi-circle, as if inspecting the land, at times moving against the wind.

It was coming closer to the house.

It moved with purpose, and therefore was alive. This Lucey knew. It moved with its millions of spun threads, finer than a spider's web, the patterns as ordered as a neural array.

It contracted suddenly and began to settle toward the house. Glittering opaquely, blotting out half the cabin, it kept contracting and drawing itself in, becoming denser until it fell in the yard with a blinding flash of incandescent light.

Lucey's flesh crawled. Her hands trembled on the gun, her breath came in shallow gasps.

Before her eyes it was changing into a manlike thing.

Frozen, she waited, thinking swiftly. Could it be that Doodie was right?

Could it be—

Doodie was still whimpering in the house, weary now, as he always was when the spasm had spent itself. But the words still came, words addressed to his father.

The thing in the yard was assuming the shape of a man—and Lucey knew who the man would be.

She reared up quickly in the palmettos, like an enraged, hulking river animal breaking to the surface. She came up shotgun-in-hand and bellowed across the clearing. 'Hey theah! You triflin' skunk! *Look at me!'*

Still groping for human shape, the creature froze.

'Run off an' leave me with child!' Lucey shouted. 'And no way to pay his keep!'

The creature kept coming toward her, and the pulsing grew stronger.

'Don't come any nearer, you hear?'

When it kept coming, Lucey grunted in a gathering rage and charged out of the palmettos to meet it, shotgun raised, screaming insults. The thing wobbled to a stop, its face a shapeless blob with black shadows for eyes.

She brought the gun to her shoulder and fired both barrels at once.

The thing tumbled to the ground. Crackling arcs danced about it, and a smell of ozone came on the breeze. For one hideous moment it was lighted by a glow from within. Then the glow died, and it began to expand. It grew erratically, and the moonlight danced in silvery filaments about it. A blob of its substance broke loose from the rest, and wind-borne, sailed across the clearing and dashed itself to dust in the palmettos.

A sudden gust took the rest of it, rolling it away in the grass, gauzy shreds tearing loose from the mass. The gust blew it against the trunk of a pine. It lodged there briefly, quivering in the breeze and shimmering palely under the moon. Then it broke into dust that scattered eastward across the land.

'Praised be the Lord,' breathed Lucey, beginning to cry.

A high whining sound pierced the night, from the direction of the violet light. She whirled to stare. The light grew brighter. Then the whine abruptly ceased. A luminescent sphere, glowing with violet haze, moved upward from the pines. It paused, then in stately majesty continued the ascent, gathering speed until it became a ghostly chariot that dwindled. Up, up, up toward the gleaming stars. She watched it until it vanished from sight.

Then she straightened her shoulders, and glowered toward the dust traces that blew eastward over the scrub.

'Ain't nothing worse than a triflin' man,' she philosophized. 'If he's human, or if he's not.'

Wearily she returned to the cabin. Doodie was sleeping peacefully. Smiling, she tucked him in, and went to bed. There was corn to hoe, come dawn.

Report: Servopilot recon six, to fleet. Missionman caught in transition phase by native organism, and devastated, thus destroying liaison with native analog. Suggest delay of invasion plans. Unpredictability factors associated with mothers of genetic analogs. Withdraw contacts. Servo Six.

END